THEY HAD
EVEN ENSLAVED
THE SYNDICATE...

and almost got Saul Goodman, New York's savviest cop. Soberly he feared Illuminatus now, this ancient core of concentrated evil, this black-magical band poising the planet for World War III.

Was Drake the high priest, Goodman asked himself, or only another Mafioso mechanic?

Who was the brilliant Robert Putney Drake, who had gone to Vienna a savage young psychopath—and returned a suave banker with money in his voice? What witchcraft had he learned in Europe?

If he could solve the enigma of Drake, Goodman felt, he could break the power of Illuminatus to turn the light out on the world . . .

The triumphant finale of ILLUMINATUS, a trilogy you will never forget for its sinister satire—and its artfully distorted vision of a society standing on the brink of madness.

ILLUMINATUS, PART III

LEVIATHAN

Robert Shea
and
Robert Anton Wilson

A DELL BOOK

Published by
Dell Publishing Co., Inc.
1 Dag Hammarskjold Plaza
New York, New York 10017
Dell ® TM 681510, Dell Publishing Co., Inc.
Printed in the United States of America
First printing—November 1975

The mutation from terrestrial to interstellar life
must be made, because the womb planet itself is going
to blow up within a few billion years . . . Planet Earth
is a stepping stone on our time-trip through the galaxy.
Life has to get its seed-self off the planet
to survive . . .
There are also some among us who are bored with the
amniotic level of mentation on this planet and look
up in hopes of finding someone entertaining to talk to.
                    —TIMOTHY LEARY, Ph.D., and
                    L. WAYNE BRENNER, *Terra II*

PROLOGUE*

Long shot of a gigantic shadow falling across a map of the United States. A tiny hand rises and pins a flag on Chicago. Camera pans back, and we see Markoff Chaney, a midget with an incredibly malignant smile. He chuckles.

Mr. Chaney, in fact, is carrying on a one-man war against the standardization (he is very substandard) and mechanization (he is very alive) of modern society. It is he who has rewired the traffic signals in all large cities so that the WALK sign flashes on red and DON'T WALK on green; he who, infiltrating printing plants, set the instructions on tax forms; he who decorates business places with idiotic instructions, signed THE MGT. (i.e., the Midget—but most people think the abbreviation means The Management, and dutifully obey). "The Midget versus the Digits" is his *mahamantrum*—"I'll get them before they get me!" he cackles.

(On the side, Markoff is writing a book proving that all culture and science was created by men under five feet tall. *Little Men with Big Balls*, he calls it; but you can be sure that when it is finally published the publisher will have changed the title to *Little Men with Big Ideas*. If you ever see the graffito STAMP OUT SIZEISM, you can be sure Chaney has been there before you.)

Alas, unknown to himself the very small Chaney has become a very large monkey wrench in the plans of the Illuminati, a secret society seemingly dedicated to rationality, science, law'n'order, and Total Control of Everybody. Not being able to trace the activities of the elusive midget, however, the Illuminati attribute his surrealist insurrectionary activities to ELF (the Erisian Liberation Front), another vast conspiracy, headed by the Dealy Lama, an old mystic

*If you'd go out and buy Volumes I and II, you wouldn't have to read this synopsis.

who lives in the sewers below Dealy Plaza, Dallas, and
seemingly plots irrationality, mysticism, anarchy, and Total
Liberation of Everybody.

Cut. Tight closeup of Joe Malik as he tells us about his
own involvement. "Uh . . . I put out *Confrontation* magazine—you know, the last of the red-hot liberals." He shrugs
ambiguously, Arab-American intellectual out of his depth,
feeling as archaic as the Underground Railroad. "It . . .
uh . . . all began at the Democratic Convention of 1968,
when I . . . uh . . . lost faith in liberalism and joined
the JAMs. Simon Moon recruited me."

Simon enters the frame, all wild hair and curly black
beard, eyes aglow with LSD visions. "Tim Moon was my
father, and he taught me to sing 'Joe Hill' and 'Union
Maid' before I knew the alphabet. I knew Wobbly headquarters in Chicago before I saw a classroom. When I got
my Master's in math from Antioch I could have gone to
work for any corporation in the country, but ten thousand
dead Wobs rose from their graves singing 'Which Side Are
You On?' and I decided it was more honorable to make my
living selling weed . . ."

Simon, in fact, is a marijuana dealer only by profession;
by avocation he is a fanatic member of the JAMs—Justified
Ancients of Mummu, a secret society which has endured
since Babylon and worships Mummu, goddess of chaos.
The JAMs are now in the fifty-ninth century of their war
against the Illuminati.

"Before joining the JAMs," Joe Malik says, "the only
people I ever heard talk about the Illuminati conspiracy
were right-wing cranks. I was sure Simon was putting me
on at first. But then I met the leader of the JAMs . . ."
(Thunder on the sound track; eerie shadows cross Joe's
face.)

We are standing outside a bungalow in Los Angeles; Simon knocks, and Joe looks nervous. The door opens, and a
feisty old man says, "So you're the new recruit. Come in
and tell me how a goddamn intellectual can help us beat
the shit out of the cocksucking Illuminati motherfuckers."
This little old gentlemen has a peculiarly mocking and
stony glitter in his eyes, and why not? He is John Dillinger,
now living under the name Frank Sullivan, and president of
Laughing Phallus Productions, king of the rock-music industry.

Flashback to 1923: Dillinger unsteadily holds a gun on grocer B. F. Morgan, who is giving the Masonic Signal of Distress. John makes a deal with the D.A. but lands in prison for nine years anyway. Sure that the Masons are behind this betrayal (although older cons tell him, *"Never* trust a D.A.'s deal or an automatic pistol"), John joins the JAMs and subsequently uses their motto—"Lie down on the floor and keep calm"—during each of his bank heists. This is his way of taunting J. Edgar Hoover, a thirty-third-degree Mason and high Illuminatus Primus. Hoover, in turn, recognizes John as a JAM revolutionary and gives shoot-on-sight orders that result in the massacre of three businessmen who are mistaken for the Dillinger gang at Little Bohemia lodge in Wisconsin. Smarting from criticism after this embarrassing incident, the FBI subsequently keeps quiet when the man they shoot at the Biograph Theatre, July 22, 1934, also turns out to be an innocent bystander. Dillinger is promoted to higher rank in the JAMs and abandons such "crude tactics" as knocking over banks.

Now, in the mid-1970s, an old man, Dillinger has decided to amalgamate the JAMs with still another secret society, the Legion of Dynamic Discord, headed by enigmatic Hagbard Celine: engineer, lawyer, mystic, and owner/designer of FUCKUP (First Universal Cybernetic Kinetic Uni-Programmer, the world's smartest computer).

SIMON MOON: "Hagbard's a right-wing crank."

JOE MALIK: "I don't know. Hagbard's a genius, that's for sure. Unfortunately, his IQ is mostly devoted to keeping the world confused about his real motives. I just don't know . . ."

Hagbard, in fact, fancies himself a sociologist, and has created the Snafu Principle, which holds that *Communication is possible only between equals.* All hierarchical organizations in which people function as non-equals are therefore in perpetual communication jam, he asserts; the paradigm is the Army, where the phrase SNAFU (Situation Normal: All Fucked Up) indeed originated. But every hierarchy has the same jam-up, Hagbard holds, and this includes corporations, governments, and every other variety of unequal social construct. According to this theory, Hagbard cheerfully announces, the Illuminati plot to create law'n'order must always lead to greater and greater chaos.

Where the JAMs worship Mummu, Babylonian goddess

of chaos, Hagbard's Legion of Dynamic Discord honors Eris, Greek goddess of confusion. Unbeknown to the JAMs, Hagbard is also allied with the Erisian Liberation Front (ELF), in its program of Operation Mindfuck (OM), a project to overthrow authority by spreading confusion and uncertainty everywhere. Even Hagbard, however, does not realize that the tiny Markoff Chaney is serving that cause better than all these conspiracies . . .

Closeup of FUCKUP, Hagbard's genius computer, as it throws an internal *I Ching* reading (scanning open circuits as yin lines, closed circuits as yang.) These are correlated with current astronomical-astrological parameters, CBS news, *Facts on File,* and reports from Hagbard's agents in world capitals. FUCKUP summarizes: "World War III is imminent. Prognosis: many megadeaths. No blame."

"My ass, no blame!" Hagbard rages; he now realizes the true importance of the Fernando Poo incident.

Fernando Poo is a tiny island in the Bay of Biafra, off the coast of Africa, where Captain Ernesto Tequila y Mota has arranged his own promotion to Generalissimo by staging a *coup d'état.* Crack CIA agents quickly report to Washington that the new regime is under the control of Russia *and* China; top Soviet agents report to Moscow that it is controlled by China; Chinese Intelligence pronounces it under Moscow domination. As the three gigantic empires quarrel with one another under this mutual misapprehension, Hagbard, recognizing the fine hand of the Illuminati, reprograms FUCKUP to locate the source of the *real* threat. (Fernando Poo is, of course, only a smokescreen.) The computer warns that Las Vegas needs watching.

Sherri Brandi gives us her version: "In this hardass town, the only way to make the scratch is to sell your snatch, sister. So I work for Carmel, who isn't bad as pimps go, if you don't mind getting beat all black-and-blue every so often. But now Carmel thinks we can get rich . . ."

Carmel is convinced that Sherri's new john, Charlie Mocenigo, who obviously works at a secret government installation in the desert, has discovered the Ultimate Secret Weapon. Oddly, Carmel is right: The weapon is Anthrax Leprosy Pi (ALP), a virus of omnivorous appetite. Carmel's plan to steal the formula and sell it to the first communist he can find in Las Vegas backfires, and Sherri and Mocenigo are both killed by an accidental infection. Carmel, also unknowingly infected, becomes a kind of Typhoid Mary.

Meanwhile, acting on a tip from Hagbard, Joe Malik sends *Confrontation*'s ace reporter, George Dorn, to Mad Dog, Texas, to investigate right-wing groups there rumored to be behind the assassinations of John and Robert Kennedy, Martin Luther King, George Lincoln Rockwell, and Spiro Agnew.

In Mad Dog George is busted for possession of marijuana and locked in jail by Sheriff Jim Cartwright. George's cellmate, a snaky-looking individual named Harry Coin, first boasts about killing various famous people, then attempts to rape George. The jail is then invaded by a mysterious group led by Mavis, a young lady with a Tommy gun, and they remove George by way of a secret temple with a pyramid-shaped altar bearing the slogan EWIGE BLUMEN-KRAFT! Mavis tells George that Mad Dog Jail is the secret chapel of the Illuminati.

George is driven to the Gulf of Mexico, where he and Mavis quarrel about politics and enjoy some oral sex until the *Leif Erikson* appears. This is a gigantic golden submarine owned by Hagbard Celine. George is whisked off with Hagbard to the ruins of Atlantis.

Back in New York, Saul Goodman, inspector on the Homicide Squad, investigates the bombing of *Confrontation*, the mysterious disappearance of editor Joe Malik, and the even more mysterious disappearance of all of Malik's dogs. Danny Pricefixer, a young detective, finds a series of memos to Joe Malik from a researcher, and Saul reads them. They allege that:

1. According to French sociologist Jacques Ellul, the Illuminati were founded in the 11th century and were a Christian-Communist heresy dedicated to redistributing the wealth.
2. According to Daraul's *History of Secret Societies*, the Illuminati were based on two medieval Arabian secret societies, the Roshinaya and the Assassins.
3. According to the *Encyclopedia Britannica*, the Illuminati were founded by professor Adam Weishaupt in Ingolstadt, Bavaria, in 1776, and destroyed by the government in 1786.
4. According to a letter in *Playboy*, the Illuminati still exist, and masterminded the assassinations of recent years.
5. According to *Teenset* magazine, the Illuminati control the rock-music business.
6. According to *American Opinion* magazine, the Council on Foreign

Relations (which has included virtually all recent Presidents and
Secretaries of State in its membership) is an Illuminati front.

7. According to the *Spark*, a Chicago newspaper, Mayor Richard
Daley used the Illuminati slogan *"Ewige Blumenkraft!"* during his
diatribe at the 1968 Democratic convention. Furthermore, George
Washington was actually Adam Weishaupt in disguise.

8. According to CBS-radio news release, portraits of Washington
appear to depict several different men.

9. According to the *East Village Other* (New York), the known
leaders of the Illuminati in 1969 were Malaclypse the Younger,
Mao Tse-tung, Mordecai the Foul, Richard Nixon, the Aga Khan,
Saint Yossarian, Nelson Rockefeller, Saint McMurphy, Lord
Omar, and Mark Lane. ("This one," Saul decides thoughtfully,
"must be a hoax . . .")

10. According to *Flying Saucers in the Bible*, the eye-on-pyramid
Illuminati symbol was given to Jefferson by a man in a black
cloak.

11. According to the *Planet* (San Francisco), the eye-on-pyramid
was the symbol of Dr. Timothy Leary during his campaign for
governor.

12. According to *Proofs of a Conspiracy*, by 19th-century freemason
John Robison, the Illuminati controlled European masonic lodges
but not the English lodges.

13. According to *World Revolution*, by Nesta Webster, the Illuminati
inspire and finance all socialist and communist revolutions.

14. According to *History of Magic*, by Eliphas Levi, the Illuminati
are black magicians.

15. According to *High IQ Bulletin*, the Illuminati are invaders from
Venus.

16. According to *Libertarian American*, the Illuminati taught black
magic and psycho-politics to Adolph Hitler and J. Edgar Hoover.

17. According to the *Los Angeles Free Press*, the Illuminati are
thought to control the Theosophical Society through California
right-wingers.

Barney Muldoon, of the Bomb Squad, meanwhile uncov-
ers evidence that the Illuminati are actually Jesuits.

Comparing notes, Goodman and Muldoon emerge with
the tentative theory that the Illuminati are Satanists and
have infiltrated virtually every organization from the Catholic Church to freemasonry. Unfortunately, Saul next finds
himself in a mental hospital, where the staff assures him he
is Barney Muldoon, suffering from the hallucination that he
is Saul Goodman.

Hagbard Celine, meanwhile, is rushing toward sunken
Atlantis to seize some long-buried art works before the Illuminati spider-ships get them. (On the way, George Dorn is
initiated into the Legion of Dynamic Discord by Stella, a
lovely black lady. "When can I be initiated again?" he asks
immediately. "Soon," Stella says lewdly . . .)

In the battle between the *Leif Erikson* and the spider-ships, Hagbard is aided by a dolphin named Howard, leader of the AA (Atlantean Adepts), a delphine secret society. ("Lot of conspiracies on this planet," George decides.)

George is next sent to the Blue Point, Long Island, home of Boston banker Robert Putney Drake, richest man in the world and secret governor of the Mafia and other crime syndicates. In exchange for the Atlantean statues, Drake switches his allegiance from the Illuminati to the Legion of Dynamic Discord.

Flashback: Drake in 1918, Château-Thierry, the last, wounded survivor of a dead platoon, weeping among the corpses: "Dear Jesus, let me live, let me live . . ."

Drake in 1936, Zurich, mescaline-tripping with the Eastern Brotherhood, investigating Aleister Crowley's Ordo Templi Orientis, seeking the Illuminati.

Carl Jung musing on Drake, 1936: "He doesn't want to murder his father and possess his mother. He wants to murder God and possess the universe."

Arthur Flengenheimer (Dutch Schultz) dying in a Newark hospital, October 23, 1934, raving in delirium: "A boy has never wept nor dashed a thousand kim. . . French Canadian bean soup . . . The bears are in trouble and the sidewalks are in trouble . . ."

Drake studying Schultz's last words under hashish, gradually reading the secret of the Illuminati control over organized crime.

Present time again: George Dorn, after the deal with Drake, is being entertained in his bedroom by Tarantella Serpentine, the lady who taught Linda Lovelace everything. George is very entertained indeed; but later, waking suddenly, he finds the house under attack by a gigantic sea monster. With Drake's help, George escapes in a Silver Wraith Rolls-Royce.

Drake, with a strange grin: "We deserve to die." (He is quoting the last scene of *Bride of Frankenstein,* but George doesn't know that.)

THE NINTH TRIP, OR YESOD
(WALPURGISNACHT ROCK)

SINK is played by Discordians and people of much ilk.
PURPOSE: To sink object or an object or a thing . . . in
water or mud or anything you can sink something in.
RULES: Sinking is allowed in any manner. To date, ten-
pound chunks of mud have been used to sink a tobacco can.
It is preferable to have a pit of water or a hole to drop things
into. But rivers—bays—gulfs—I dare say even oceans—can
be used.
TURNS are taken thusly: whosoever gets the junk up and in
the air first.
DUTY: It shall be the duty of all persons playing SINK to help
find more objects to sink, once one object is sunk.
UPON SINKING: The sinker shall yell, "I sank it!" or something equally as thoughtful.
NAMING OF OBJECTS is sometimes desirable. The object is
named by the finder of such object, and whoever sinks it can
say (for instance), "I sank Columbus, Ohio."

> —ALA HERA, E.L., N.S., Rayville Apple Panthers,
> quoted in *Principia Discordia,* by Malaclypse the
> Younger, K.S.C.

For over a week the musicians had been boarding planes
and heading for Ingolstadt. As early as April 23, while Simon and Mary Lou listened to Clark Kent and His Supermen and George Dorn wrote about the sound of one eye
opening, the Fillet of Soul, finding bookings sparse in London, drove into Ingolstadt in a Volvo painted seventeen
Day-Glo colors and flaunting Ken Kesey's old slogan,
"Furthur!" On April 24 a real trickle began, and while Harry Coin looked into Hagbard Celine's eyes and saw no mercy there (Buckminster Fuller, just then, was explaining
"omnidirectional halo" to his seatmate on a TWA Whisper-

jet in mid-Pacific), the Wrathful Visions, the Cockroaches, and the Senate and the People of Rome all drove down Rathausplatz in bizarre vehicles, while the Ultra-Violet Hippopotamus and the Thing on the Doorstep both navigated Friedrich-Ebert-Strasse in even more amazing buses. On April 25, while Carmel looted Maldonado's safe and George Dorn repeated "I Am the Robot," the trickle turned to a stream and in came Science and Health with Key to the Scriptures, the Glue Sniffers, King Kong and His Skull Island Dinosaurs, the Howard Johnson Hamburger, the Riot in Cell Block Ten, the House of Frankenstein, the Signifying Monkey, the Damned Thing, the Orange Moose, the Indigo Banana, and the Pink Elephant. On April 26 the stream became a flood, and while Saul and Barney Muldoon tried to reason with Markoff Chaney and he struggled in their grip, Ingolstadters found themselves inundated by Frodo Baggins and His Ring, the Mouse That Roars, the Crew of the Flying Saucer, the Magnificent Ambersons, the House I Live In, the Sound of One Hand, the Territorial Imperative, the Druids of Stonehenge, the Heads of Easter Island, the Lost Continent of Mu, Bugs Bunny and His Fourteen Carrots, the Gospel According to Marx, the Card-Carrying Members, the Sands of Mars, the Erection, the Association, the Amalgamation, the St. Valentine's Day Massacre, the Climax, the Broad Jumpers, the Pubic Heirs, the Freeks, and the Windows. Mick Jagger and his new group, the Trashers, arrived on April 27, while the FBI was interviewing every whore in Las Vegas, and there quickly followed the Roofs, Moses and Monotheism, Steppenwolf, Civilization and Its Discontents, Poor Richard and His Rosicrucian Secrets, the Wrist Watch, the Nova Express, the Father of Waters, the Human Beings, the Washington Monument, the Thalidomide Babies, the Strangers in a Strange Land, Dr. John the Night Tripper, Joan Baez, the Dead Man's Hand, Joker and the One-Eyed Jacks, Peyote Woman, the Heavenly Blues, the Golems, the Supreme Awakening, the Seven Types of Ambiguity, the Cold War, the Street Fighters, the Bank Burners, the Slaves of Satan, the Domino Theory, and Maxwell and His Demons. On April 28, while Dillinger loaded his gun and the kachinas of Orabi began the drum-beating, the Acapulco Gold-Diggers arrived, followed by the Epic of Gilgamesh, the Second Law of Thermodynamics, Dracula and His Brides, the

Iron Curtain, the Noisy Minority, the International Debt, Three Contributions to the Theory of Sex, the Cloud of Unknowing, the Birth of a Nation, the Zombies, Attila and His Huns, Nihilism, the Catatonics, the Thorndale Jag Offs, the Haymarket Bomb, the Head of a Dead Cat, the Shadow Out of Time, the Sirens of Titan, the Player Piano, the Streets of Laredo, the Space Odyssey, the Blue Moonies, the Crabs, the Dose, the Grassy Knoll, the Latent Image, the Wheel of Karma, the Communion of Saints, the City of God, General Indefinite Wobble, the Left-Handed Monkey Wrench, the Thorn in the Flesh, the Rising Podge, SHA-ZAM, the Miniature Sled, the 23rd Appendix, the Other Cheek, the Occidental Ox, Ms. and the Chairperson, Cohen Cohen Cohen and Kahn, and the Joint Phenomenon.

On April 29, while Danny Pricefixer listened raptly to Mama Sutra, the deluge descended upon Igolstadt: Buses, trucks, station wagons, special trains, and every manner of transport except dog sleds, brought in the Wonders of the Invisible World, Maule's Curse, the Jesus Head Trip, Ahab and His Amputation, the Horseless Headsmen, the Leaves of Grass, the Gettysburg Address, the Rosy-Fingered Dawn, the Wine-Dark Sea, Nirvana, the Net of Jewels, Here Comes Everybody, the Pisan Cantos, the Snows of Yesteryear, the Pink Dimension, the Goose in the Bottle, the Incredible Hulk, the Third Bardo, Aversion Therapy, the Irresistible Force, MC Squared, the Enclosure Acts, Perpetual Emotion, the 99-Year Lease, the Immovable Object, Spaceship Earth, the Radiocarbon Method, the Rebel Yell, the Clenched Fist, the Doomsday Machine, the Rand Scenario, the United States Commitment, the Entwives, the Players of Null-A, the Prelude to Space, Thunder and Roses, Armageddon, the Time Machine, the Mason Word, the Monkey Business, the Works, the Eight of Swords, Gorilla Warfare, the Box Lunch, the Primate Kingdom, the New Aeon, the Enola Gay, the Octet Truss, the Stochastic Process, the Fluxions, the Burning House, the Phantom Captain, the Decline of the West, the Duelists, the Call of the Wild, Consciousness III, the Reorganized Church of the Latter-Day Saints, Standard Oil of Ohio, the Zig-Zag Men, the Rubble Risers, the Children of Ra, TNT, Acceptable Radiation, the Pollution Level, the Great Beast, the Whores of Babylon, the Waste Land, the Ugly Truth, the Final Diagnosis, Solution Unsatisfactory, the Heat Death of the Universe, Mere Noise, I Opening, the Nine Unknown Men, the Horse of Another Color, the Falling Rock Zone, the Ascent of the Serpent, Reddy Willing and Unable, the Civic Monster, Hercules and the Tortoise, the Middle Pillar, the Deleted Expletive, Deep Quote, LuCiFeR, the Dog Star, Nuthin' Sirius, and Preparation H.

(But, on April 23, while Joe Malik and Tobias Knight were setting the bomb in *Confrontation*'s office, the Dealy Lama broadcast a telepathic message to Haghard Celine saying *It's not too late to turn back* and Joe hesitated a moment, blurting finally, "Can we be sure? Can we be really sure?" Tobias Knight raised weary eyes. "We can't be sure of anything," he said simply. "Celine has popped up at banquets and other social occasions where Drake was present five times now, and each conversation eventually got around to the puppet metaphor and Celine's favorite bit about the unconscious saboteur in everybody. What else can we assume?" He set the timer for 2:30 A.M. and then met Joe's eyes again. "I wish I could have given George a few more hints," Joe said lamely. "You gave him too damned many hints as it is," Knight replied, closing the bomb casing.)

On April 1, while God's lightning paraded about UN Plaza and Captain Tequila y Mota was led before a firing squad, John Dillinger arose from his cramped lotus position and stopped broadcasting the mathematics of magic. He stretched, shook all over like a dog, and proceeded down the tunnel under the UN building to Alligator Control. OTO yoga was always a strain, and he was glad to abandon it and return to more mundane matters.

A guard stopped him at the AC door, and John handed over his plastic eye-and-pyramid card. The guard, a surly-looking woman whose picture John had seen in the newspapers as a leader of the Radical Lesbians, fed the card into a wall slot; it came out again almost at once, and a green light flashed.

"Pass," she said. *"Heute die Welt."*

"Morgens das Sonnensystem," John replied. He entered the beige plastic underworld of Alligator Control, and walked through geodesic corridors until he came to the door marked MONOTONY MONITOR. After he inserted his card in the appropriate slot, another green light blinked and the door opened.

Taffy Rheingold, wearing a mini-skirt and still pert and attractive despite her years and gray hair, looked up from her typing. She sat behind a beige plastic desk that matched the beige plastic of the entire Alligator Control headquarters. A broad smile spread across her face when she recognized him.

"John," she said happily. "What brings you here?"

"Gotta see your boss," he answered, "but before you buzz him, do you know you're in another book?"

"The new Edison Yerby novel?" She shrugged philosophically. "Not quite as bad as what Atlanta Hope did to me in *Telemachus Sneezed.*"

"Yeah, I suppose, but how did this guy find out so much? Some of those scenes are *absolutely true.* Is he in the Order?" John demanded.

"A mind leak," Taffy said. "You know how it is with writers. One of the Illuminati Magi scanned Yerby and he thought he had invented all of it. Not a clue. The same kind of leak we had when Condon wrote *The Manchurian Candidate.*" She shrugged. "It just happens sometimes."

"I suppose," John said absently. "Well, tell your boss I'm here."

In a minute he was in the inner office, being effusively greeted by the old man in the wheelchair. "John, John, it's so *good* to see you again," said the crooning voice that had hypnotized millions; otherwise, it was hard, in this aged figure, to recognize the once handsome and dynamic Franklin Delano Roosevelt.

"How did you get stuck with a job like this?" Dillinger asked finally, after the amenities had been exchanged.

"You know how it is with the new gang in Agharti," Roosevelt murmured. " 'New blood, new blood'—that's their battle cry. All of us old and faithful servants are being pushed into minor bureaucratic positions."

"I remember your funeral," John said wistfully. "I was envious, thinking of you going to Agharti and working directly with the Five. And now it's come to this . . . Monotony Monitor in Alligator Control. Sometimes I get pissed with the Order."

"Careful," Roosevelt said. "They might be scanning. And a double agent, such as you are, John, is always under special surveillance. Besides, this isn't really so bad, considering how they reacted in Agharti when the Pearl Harbor revelations started coming out in the late forties. I did not handle that matter too elegantly, you know, and they had a right to demote me. And Alligator Control is interesting."

"Maybe," John said dubiously. "I never have understood this project."

"It's very significant work," Roosevelt said seriously. "New York and Chicago are our major experiments in testing the *mehum* tolerance level. In Chicago we concentrate on mere ugliness and brutality, but in New York we're simultaneously carrying on a long-range boredom study. That's where Alligator Control comes in. We've got to keep the alligators in the sewers down to a minimum so the Bureau of Sanitation doesn't reactivate their own Alligator Control Project, which would be an opportunity for adventure and a certain natural *mehum* hunting-band mystique among some of the young males. It's the same reason we took out the trolley cars: Riding them was more fun than buses. Believe me, Monotony Monitoring is a very important part of the New York project."

"I've seen the mental-health figures," John said, nodding. "About seventy percent of the people in the most congested part of Manhattan are already prepsychotic."

"We'll have it up to eighty percent by 1980!" Roosevelt cried, with some of his old steely-eyed determination. But then he fixed a joint in his ivory holder and, clenching it at his famous jaunty angle, added, "And *we're* immune, thanks to Sabbah's Elixir." He quoted cheerfully: " 'Grass does more than Miltown can/ To justify God's ways to man.' But what *does* bring you here, John?"

"A 'small job,' " Dillinger said. "There's a man in my organization named Malik who is getting a little too close to the secret of the whole game. I need some help here in New York to set him off on a snark hunt until after May first. I'd like to know who you've got on your staff closest to him."

"Malik," Roosevelt said thoughtfully. "That would be the Malik of *Confrontation* magazine?" John nodded, and Roosevelt sat back in his wheelchair, smiling. "This is a lead-pipe cinch. We've got an agent in his office."

(But neither of them realized that ten days later a dolphin swimming through the ruins of Atlantis would discover that no Dragon Star had ever fallen. Nor could they have guessed how Hagbard Celine would reevaluate Illumi-

nati history when that revelation was reported to him, and
they had no clue of the decision he would then make,
which would change everybody's conspiracies shockingly
and unexpectedly.)

"Here are the five alternate histories," Gruad said, his
wise old eyes crinkling humorously. "Each of you will be
responsible for planting the evidence to make one of these
histories seem fairly credible. Wo Topod, you get the Car-
cosa story. Evoe, you get the lost continent of Mu." He
handed out two bulky envelopes. "Gao Twone, you get this
charming snake story—I want variations of it scattered
throughout Africa and the Near East." He handed out another envelope. "Unica, you get the Urantia story, but that
one isn't to be released until fairly late in the Game." He
picked up the fifth envelope and smiled again. "Kajeci, my
love, you get the Atlantis story, with certain changes that
make us out to be the most double-dyed bastards in all history. Let me explain the purpose behind that . . ."

And in 1974 the four members of the American Medical Association gazed somberly down at Joe Malik from his
office wall. It looked to be a long day, and there was nothing to anticipate as exciting as last night had been. There
was a thick manuscript in a manila envelope in the IN box;
he noticed that the stamps had been removed. That was
doubtless Pat Walsh's work; her kid brother was a stamp
collector. Joe smiled, remembering the diary he'd kept
when he was a teen-ager. In case his parents found it, he always referred to masturbation as stamp collecting. "Collected five stamps today—a new record." "After five days of no
stamps, collected a beauty in several colors. Enormous, but
the negotiations were tiring." Doubtless today's kids, if they
kept diaries (they probably used casette tape recorders), either talked openly about it or considered it too incidental to
mention. Joe shook his head. The Catholic teen-ager he had
been in 1946 was no more remote than the crumbling liberal he'd been in 1968. And yet, in spite of all he'd been
through, much of the time he felt that all of the knowledge
didn't make a difference. People like Pat and Peter still
treated him as if he were the same man, and he still did the
same job in the same way.

He took the heavy manuscript out and shook the envelope. Damn it, there was no return envelope. Well, working
at a magazine like *Confrontation,* whose contributors were

mostly radicals and the kind of kooks who were willing to write for no bread, you didn't really expect them to enclose stamped self-addressed envelopes. There was a covering letter. Joe sucked in his breath when he saw the golden apple embossed in the upper left-hand corner.

Hail Eris and Hi, Joe,

Here is a brilliant, original interpretation of international finance called "Vampirism, the Heliocentric Theory and the Gold Standard." It's by Jorge Lobengula, a really far-out young Discordian thinker. JAMs don't go in much for writing, but Discordians, fortunately, do. If you find it worth printing, you may have it at your usual rates. Make the check payable to the Fernando Poo Secessionist Movement and sent it to Jorge at 15 Rue Hassan, Algiers 8.

Incidentally, Jorge will not be involved in the Fernando Poo coup. He is turning toward a synergistic economics, which will gradually lead him to see the folly of Fernando Poo going it alone. And the coup itself, of course, will not be any of our doing. But Jorge will be a key figure in Equatorial Guinea's subsequent economic recovery—assuming the world pulls through that particular mess. If you can't use this paper, burn it. Jorge has plenty of copies.

Five tons of flax,

Mal

P.S. The Fernando Poo rebellion may still be one or two years in the future, so don't jump to the conclusion that the pot is coming to a boil already. Remember what I told you about the goose in the bottle.

M.

(Down the hall in the lady's room, bolting the door for privacy, Pat Walsh takes her transistorized transmitter from her pantyhose and broadcasts to the receiver at the Council on Foreign Relations headquarters half a block east. "I'm still writing lots of Illuminati research papers, and they'll give him plenty of false leads. The big news today is an article on Erisian economics by a Fernando Poo national. It came with a covering letter signed 'Mal,' and from the context, I feel fairly certain it's the original—Malaclypse the Elder himself. If not, at last we've got a lead on that damned elusive Malaclypse the Younger. The envelope was postmarked Mad Dog, Texas . . .")

Joe put down Mal's letter, trying to remember the obscure references to Fernando Poo before the movie last night. Someone had said something was going to happen there. Maybe he should get a stringer on the island, or even send somebody over. A malicious grin crossed his face: It might be interesting to send Peter. First some AUM, then a trip to Fernando Poo. That might fix Peter up.

Joe flipped through the Lobengula manuscript quickly, scanning. There were no fnords. That was a relief. He had become painfully conscious of them since Hagbard had removed the aversion reflex, and each fnord had sent a pang through him that was a ghost of the low-grade emergency in which he had previously lived. He turned back to the first page and began to read in earnest:

VAMPIRISM, THE HELIOCENTRIC THEORY AND THE GOLD
STANDARD
by Jorge Lobengula
Do What Thou Wilt Shall Be The Whole Of The Law

Joe stopped. That sentence had been used in the Black Mass in Chicago and further back, he knew, it was the code of the Abbey of Theleme in Rabelais; but there was something else about it that chewed at his consciousness, something that suggested a hidden meaning. This was not just a first axiom of anarchism—there was something else there, something more hermetic. He looked back at Mal's letter: "Remember what I told you about the goose in the bottle."

That was a simple riddle used by Zen Masters in the training of monks, Joe remembered. You take a newborn gosling and slip it through the neck of a bottle. Month after month you keep it in there and feed it, until it is a full-grown goose and can no longer be passed through the bottle's neck. The question is: Without breaking the bottle, how do you get the goose out?

Neither riddle seemed to shed much light on the other.
Do what thou wilt shall be the whole of the law.
How do you get the goose out of the bottle?

"Holy God." Joe laughed. "Do what *thou* wilt shall be the whole of the law."

The goose gets out of the bottle the same way John Dillinger got out of the "escape-proof" Crown Point jail.

"Jesus motherfucking Christ," Joe gasped. *"It's alive!"*
JUST LIKE A TREE THAT'S STANDING BY THE WAAATER
WE SHALL NOT   WE SHALL NOT BE MOVED

The only place where all five Illuminati Primi met was the Great Hall of Gruad in Agharti, the thirty-thousand-year-old Illuminati center on the peaks of the Tibetan Himalayas, with a lower-level water front harbor on the vast underground Sea of Valusia.

"We will report in the usual order," said Brother Gracchus Gruad, pressing a button in the table before him so his words would automatically be recorded on impervium wire for the Illuminati archives. "First of all, Fernando Poo. Jorge Lobengula, having decided that the combined resources of Fernando Poo and Rio Muni can be reallocated so as to increase the per-capita wealth of citizens of both provinces, has accordingly broken with the Fernando Poo separatists and returned to Rio Muni, where he hopes to persuade Fang leaders to go along with his schemes for economic redevelopment. Our plans now center on a Captain Ernesto Tequila y Mota, one of the few Caucasians left on Fernando Poo. He has good contacts among the wealthier Bubi, the ones who favor separatism, and he is inordinately ambitious. I don't think we need contemplate a change in timetable."

"I should hope not," said Brother Marcus Marconi. "It would be such a shame not to immanentize the Eschaton on May first."

"Well, we can't count on May first," said Brother Gracchus Gruad. "But with three distinct plans pointing in that direction, one of them is bound to hit. Let's hear from you, Brother Marcus."

"Charles Mocenigo has now reached Anthrax Leprosy Mu. A few more nightmares at the right moment and he'll be home."

Sister Theda Theodora spoke next. "Atlanta Hope and God's Lighting are becoming more powerful all the time. The President will be scared shitless of her when the time comes, and he'll be ready to be even more totalitarian than her, just to keep her from taking over."

"I don't trust Drake," said Brother Marcus Marconi.

"Of course," said Brother Gracchus Gruad. "But he has builded his house by the sea."

"And he who builds by the sea builds on sand," said Brother Otto Ogatai. "My turn. Our record, *Give, Sympathize, Control,* is an international hit. Our next tour of Europe should be an extraordinary success. Then we can begin, very slowly and tentatively, negotiations for the *Walpurgisnacht* festival. Anyone who tries to develop the idea prematurely, of course, will have to be deflected."

"Or liquidated," said Brother Gracchus Gruad. He looked down the long table at the man who sat by himself at the far end. "Now you. You've been silent all this time. What do you have to say?"

The man laughed. "A few words from the skeleton at the feast, eh?" This was the fifth and most formidable Illuminatus Primus, Brother Henry Hastur, the only one who would have the gall to name himself after a lloigor. "It is written," he said, "that the universe is a practical joke by the general at the expense of the particular. Do not be too quick to laugh or weep, if you believe this saying. All I can say is, there is a serious threat in being to all your plans. I warn you. You have been warned. You may all die. Are you afraid of death? You need not answer—I see that you are. That in itself may be a mistake. I have tried to explain to you about not fearing death, but you will not listen. All your other problems follow from that."

The other four Illuminati Primi listened in cold, disdainful silence and did not reply.

"If all are One," the fifth Illuminatus added significantly, "all violence is masochism."

"If all are One," Brother Otto replied nastily, "all sex is masturbation. Let's have no more *mehum* metaphysics here."

HARE KRISHNA HARE HARE

"George!"

Then George was here, with Celine, in Ingolstadt. This was going to be tricky. George's head was bent over an earthenware stein, doubtless full of the local brew.

"George!" Joe called again. George looked up, and Joe was astonished. He had never seen George like this before. George shook his shoulder-length blond hair to clear it away from his face, and Joe looked deep into his eyes.

They were strange eyes, eyes without fear or pity or guilt, eyes that acknowledged that the natural state of man was one of perpetual surprise, and therefore could not be greatly surprised by any one thing, even the unexpected appearance of Joe Malik. What has Celine done to him in the past seven days? Joe wondered. Has he destroyed his mind or has he—illuminated him?

Actually, it was George's tenth stein of beer that day, and he was very, very drunk.

HARRY ROBOT HARRY HARRY

(Civil liberties were suspended and a state of national emergency declared during a special presidential broadcast on all channels between noon and 12:30 on April 30. Fifteen minutes later the first rioting started in New York, at the Port Authority on Forty-first Street, where a mob attempted to overrun the police and steal buses in which to escape to Canada. It was 6:45 P.M. just then in Ingolstadt, and Count Dracula and His Brides were giving forth a raga-rock version of an old Walt Disney cartoon song . . . And in Los Angeles, where it was 9:45 A.M., a five-person Morituri group, hurriedly convened, decided to use up all its bombs against police stations immediately. "Cripple the motherfucker before it's *heavy*," said their leader, a sixteen-year-old girl with braces on her teeth . . . Her idiom, in standard English, meant: "Paralyze the fascist state before it's entrenched" . . . and Saul, trusting the pole-vaulter in the unconscious, was leading Barney and Markoff Chaney into the mouth of Lehman Cavern . . . Carmel, nearly a kilometer south of them, and several hundred feet closer to the center of the earth, still clutched his briefcase and its five million green gods, but he did not move . . . Near him were the bones of a dozen bats he had eaten . . .)

TO BE A BAT'S A BUM THING
A SILLY AND A DUMB THING
BUT AT LEAST A BAT IS SOMETHING
AND YOU'RE NOT A THING AT ALL

Joe Malik, hit by the raga rock as if by an avalanche of separate notes which were each boulders, felt his body dissolve. Count Dracula wailed it again (YOU'RE NOT A THING AT ALL), and Joe felt mind crumble along with body and could find no center, no still point in the waves of sound and energy; the fucking acid was Hagbard's ally and had turned against him, he was dying; even the words "Hey

that cat's on a bummer" came from far away, and his effort
to determine if they really meant him collapsed into an effort to remember what the words were, which imploded into
an uncertainty about what effort he was trying to make,
mental or physical, and why. "Because," he cried out, "because, because—" . . . but "because" meant nothing.

YOU'RE NOTHING BUT A NOTHING
NOTHING BUT A NOTHING

"But I can't take acid now," George had protested. "I'm
so damned drunk on this Bavarian beer, it's sure to be a
down trip."

"Everybody takes acid," Hagbard said coldly. "Those are
Miss Portinari's orders, and she's right. We can only face
this thing if our minds are completely open to the Outside."

"Hey, dig," Clark Kent said. "That French cat eating the
popsicle."

"Yeah?" said one of the Supermen.

"It's Jean-Paul Sartre. Who'd ever expect to see *him*
here?" Kent shook his head. "Hope to hell he stays long
enough to hear our gig. Sheee-it, the influence that *man* has
had on me! He should hear it come back at him in music."

"That's your trip, baby," a second Superman said. "I
don't give a fuck what *any* motherfuckin' honky thinks
about our music."

YOU'RE NOTHING BUT A NOTHING

"Mick Jagger hasn't even played 'Sympathy for the Devil' yet and already the trouble has started," an English voice
drawled . . . Attila and His Huns were trying to do acute
bodily damage to the Senate and the People of Rome . . .
Both groups were speeding, and they had gotten into a very
intellectual discussion of the meaning of one of Dylan's
lyrics . . . A Hun bopped a Roman with a beer stein as
another voice mumbled something about Tyl Eulenspiegel's
merry pranks.

· YOU'RE NOT A THING AT ALL

Joe had always had the policy at *Confrontation* that real
screwballs should be sent to him for interviewing, but the
little fat man who came in didn't seem particularly crazy.
He just had the bland, regular, somewhat smallish features
of a typical WASP.

"The name is James Cash Cartwright," the fat man said,
holding out his hand, "and the subject is consciousness energy."

"The subject of what?"

"Oh—this here article I have written for you." Cartwright reached into his alligator briefcase and pulled out a thick sheaf of typewritten paper. It was an odd size, possibly eight by ten. He handed the manuscript to Joe.

"What kind of paper is this?" said Joe.

"It's the standard size in England," said Cartwright. "When I was over there in 1963 visiting the tombs of my ancestors, I bought ten reams of it. I took the plane from Dallas on November 22, the day Kennedy was shot. Synchronicity. Also, I sneezed the moment the gunman squeezed. More synchronicity. But about this paper, I've never used anything else for my writing since then. Kind of gives a man a nice feeling to know that all the trees that went into my paper were chopped down over ten years ago, and no trees have died since then to support the proliferation of Jim Cartwright's philosophical foliage."

"That certainly is a wonderful thing," said Joe, thinking how much he loathed ecological moralists. During the height of the ecology fad, back in 1970 and '71, several people actually had had the nerve to write Joe saying that ecologically responsible journals like *Confrontation* had a duty to cease publication in order to save trees. "Just what fruit have your philosophical researches borne, Mr. Cartwright?" he asked.

"Golden apples of the sun, silver apples of the moon," said Cartwright with a smile. Joe saw Lilith Velkor defying Gruad atop the Pyramid of the Eye.

"Well, sir," said Cartwright, "my basic finding is that life energy pervades the entire universe, just as light and gravity do. Therefore, all life is one, just as all light is one. All energies, you see, are broadcast from a central source, yet to be found. If four amino acids—adenine, cytosine, guanine, and thymine—suddenly become life when you throw them together, then all chemicals are potentially alive. You and me and the fish and bugs are that kind of life made from adenine, cytosine, guanine, and thymine: DNA life. What we call dead matter is another kind of life: non-DNA life. Okay so far? If awareness is life and if life is one, then the awareness of the individual is just one of the universe's sensory organs. The universe produces beings like us in order to perceive itself. You might think of it as a giant, self-contained eye."

Joe remained impassive.

Cartwright went on. "Consciousness is therefore also manifested as telepathy, clairvoyance, and telekinesis. Those phenomena are simply non-localized versions of consciousness. I'm very interested in telepathy, and I've had a lot of success with telepathic research. These cases of communication are just further evidence that consciousness is a seamless web throughout the universe."

"Now wait a minute," said Joe. "Automobiles run on mechanical energy, heat energy, and electrical energy, but that doesn't mean that all the automobiles in the world are in contact with each other."

"What burns?" said Cartwright, smiling.

"You mean in a car? Well, the gas ignites explosively in the cylinder—"

"Only organic matter burns," said Cartwright smugly. "And all organic matter is descended from a single cell. All fire is one. And all automobiles do communicate with each other. You can't tell me anything about gas or oil. Or cars. I'm a Texan. Did I tell you that?"

Joe shook his head. "Just what part of Texas are you from?"

"Little place called Mad Dog."

"Had a notion you might be. Tell me, Mr. Cartwright, do you know anything about a conspiratorial organization called the Ancient Illuminated Seers of Bavaria?"

"Well, I know three organizations that have similar names: the Ancient Bavarian Conspiracy, the New Bavarian Conspiracy, and the Conservative Bavarian Seers."

Joe nodded. Cartwright didn't seem to have the facts straight—as Joe knew them. Perhaps the fat man had other pieces of the puzzle, perhaps fewer pieces than Joe had. Still, if they were different, they might be useful.

"Each of these organizations controls one of the major TV networks in the U.S.," said Cartwright. "The initials of each network have been intentionally chosen to refer back to the name of the group that runs it. They also control all the big magazines and newspapers. That's why I came to you. Judging by the stuff you've been getting away with printing lately, not only do the Illuminati not control your magazine, but you seem to have the benefit of some pretty powerful protection."

"So, there are three separate Illuminati groups, and

among them they dominate all the communications media —is that correct?" said Joe.

"That's right," said Cartwright, his face as cheerful as if he were explaining how his wife made ice cream with a hand freezer. "They dominate the motion-picture industry too. They took a hand in the making of hundreds of movies, the best known of which are *Gunga Din* and *Citizen Kane*. Those two movies are especially full of Illuminati references, symbols, code messages, and subliminal propaganda. 'Rosebud,' for instance, is their code name for the oldest Illuminati symbol, the so-called Rosy Cross. You know what that means." He snickered lewdly.

Joe nodded. "So—you know about 'flowery combat.'"

Cartwright shrugged. "Who doesn't? Dr. Horace Naismith, a learned friend of mine, and head of the John Dillinger Died for You Society, has written an analysis of *Gunga Din*, pointing out the real meaning of the thuggee, the evil goddess Kali, the pit full of serpents, the elephant medicine, the blowing of the bugle from the top of the temple, and so forth. *Gunga Din* celebrates the imposition of law and order in an area terrorized by the criminal followers of a goddess who breeds evil and chaos. The thuggee are a caricature of the Discordians, and the English represent the Illuminati's view of themselves. The Illuminati love that movie."

"Sometimes I wonder if we're not all working for them, one way or another," said Joe, trying deliberately to be ambivalent to see which way Cartwright would move.

"Well, sure we are," said Cartwright. "Everything we do that contributes to a lack of harmony in the human race helps them. They are forever shaking up society with experiments involving suffering and death for large numbers of people. For instance, consider the *General Slocum* disaster on June 15, 1904. Note that 19 plus 04 equals 23, by the way."

Him too? Joe groaned mentally. He's got to be either one of us or one of them, and if he's one of them, why is he telling me so much?

"You tell me," Cartwright said, "if all consciousness is not *one*, just how did Joyce happen to pick the very next day for *Ulysses*, so the *General Slocum* disaster would be in the newspaper his characters read? You see, Joyce knew he was a genius, but he never did understand the nature of genius, which is to be in better touch with the universal consciousness than the average man is. Anyway, the Illuminati were trying, with the *General Slocum* disaster, a new, more economical technique for achieving transcendental illumination—one that would require only a few hundred sudden deaths instead of thousands. Not that they care about saving lives, you understand, though the desire might result from the return of the repressed original purpose of the Illuminati, which was benign."

"Really?" said Joe. "What was the benign purpose?"

"The preservation of human knowledge after the natural catastrophe that destroyed the continent of Atlantis and the first human civilization, thirty thousand years ago," said Cartwright.

"Natural catastrophe?"

"Yes. A solar flare that erupted just when Atlantis was turned toward the sun. The original Illuminati were scientists who predicted the solar flare but were scoffed at by their fellows, so they fled by themselves. The benevolence of those early Illuminati was replaced by elitist attitudes in their successors, but the benign purpose keeps coming back in the form of factions which arise among the Illuminati and split off. The factions preserve traditional Illuminati secrecy, but they aim to thwart the destructiveness of the parent body. The Justified Ancients of Mummu were expelled from the Illuminati back in 1888. But the oldest anti-Illuminati conspiracy is the Erisian Liberation Front, which splintered off before the beginnings of the current civilization. Then there's the Discordian Movement—another splinter faction, but they're almost as bad as the Illuminati. They're sort of like a cross between followers of Ayn Rand and Scientologists. They've got this guy named Hagbard Celine, their head honcho. You didn't read about it because the governments of the world were too scared shitless to do anything about it, but five years ago this Celine character infiltrated the nuclear-submarine service of the U.S. Navy for the Illuminati—and stole a sub. He's a supersalesman, Celine is—he could talk old H. L. Hunt right out of half his oil wells. He was a Chief Petty Officer. First he converted about half the crew with the most incredible line of bullshit you've heard since Tim Leary was in his prime. Then he put some kind of drug in the ship's air supply, and while they were under the influence he converted most of the others. The ones that were stubborn he just blew out through the torpedo tubes. Nice guy. Now, mind you, this sub was armed with Polaris missiles. So the next thing Celine does is get himself off to someplace in the ocean where they can't find him and blackmail the fucking governments of the U.S., the U.S.S.R., and Red China to each give him ten million dollars in gold, and after he gets the thirty million he will scuttle his missiles. Otherwise he will dump 'em on a city of one of those three countries."

"Was Celine still working for the Illuminati at that point?"

"Hell, no!" Cartwright snorted. "That's not how they play the game. They like to operate stealthily, behind the throne-room curtains. They work with poison and daggers and things, not H-bombs. No, Celine told the Illuminati to go fuck themselves, and there was nothing they could do but grind their teeth. He's been operating like a pirate ever since. And I'll tell you something else. There's more than one world leader, including the Illuminati leaders, that hasn't been able to sleep at night because of what else Hagbard Celine has on that submarine."

"What's that, Mr. Cartwright?"

"Well, see, the U.S. Government did a very dumb thing. They weren't satisfied to have just nuclear weapons aboard their Polaris submarines for a while. They also thought the subs should be armed with the other kind of weapon—bugs."

Joe felt himself go cold, and the back of his neck prickled. Let others worry about the nuclear devastation all they want. Disease—the extinction of the human race through the spread of some manmade plague for which man would have no remedy—was his particular nightmare. Maybe because at the age of seven he'd very nearly died of polio; though he'd been healthy ever since, the fear of fatal illness had been impossible to shake.

"This Hagbard Celine—these Discordians—have a bacteriological weapon aboard the submarine?"

"Yeah. Something called Anthrax Tau. All Celine has to do is release it in the water and within a week the whole human race would be dead. It spreads faster'n a two-dollar whore on Saturday night. Any living thing can carry it. But one nice thing about it—it's fatal only to man. If Celine ever gets crazy enough to use it—and he's pretty crazy these days, and getting worse all the time—it'll give the planet a fresh start, so to speak. Some other life form could evolve into sentience. Now, if we have a nuclear war, or if we pollute the planet to death, there won't be *any* life left worth talking about. Might be the best thing that ever happened if Hagbard Celine shot that Anthrax Tau down the tube. It would sure prevent worse things from happening."

"If there were no one left alive," said Joe, "from whose point of view would it be the best thing that ever happened?"

"Life's," said Cartwright. "I told you, all life is one. Which gets me back to my manuscript. I'll just leave it with you. I realize it's much longer than what you usually publish, so feel free to excerpt from it as you please, and to pay me at your usual rates for whatever you publish."

That evening Joe stayed till nine at his office. He was, as usual, a day late getting copy to the typesetter on his editorial column and the letters column. These were two parts of the magazine that he felt only he could do right, and he refused to delegate either job to Peter or anyone else on the staff. First he ran the letters through his typewriter, shortening and pointing them up, then adding brief editorial answers where called for. After that he put aside his notes and research for the editorial he'd planned for this August issue, and instead he wrote an impassioned plea that each reader make himself personally responsible for doing something about the menace of bacteriological warfare. Even if what Cartwright had told him was a crock, it reminded him of his long-held conviction that germ warfare was far more likely to put the quietus to the human race than nuclear weapons. It was just too easy to unleash. He envisioned Hagbard in his submarine spewing the microbes of all-destroying plague out into the seas, and he shuddered.

His briefcase weighed down by Cartwright's manuscript, which he'd decided to take home with him, he stood in the lobby of his office building, gazing gloomily at the tanks full of tropical fish in the window of the pet store. One tank had, as an ornament, a china model of a sunken pirate ship. It made Joe think again of Hagbard Celine. Did he trust Hagbard or didn't he? Was it possible to really believe in a Hagbard with the Captain Nemo psychosis, brooding over tubes and jars full of bacteria cultures, one hairy finger hovering tentatively over a button that would send a torpedo full of Anthrax Tau germs out into the inky waters of the Atlantic? Within a week all humans would die, Cartwright had said. And it was hard to think that Cartwright was lying, since he knew so much about so many other things.

When Joe got home he put on his favorite Museum of National History record, *The Language and Music of the Wolves,* and lit up a joint. He liked listening to the wolves when he was high, and trying to understand their language. Then he took Cartwright's manuscript out of his briefcase and looked at the title page. It didn't say a word about consciousness energy, indeed, it referred to a subject Joe found much more interesting:

HOW THE ANCIENT BAVARIAN CONSPIRACY
   PLOTTED AND CARRIED OUT
THE ASSASSINATIONS OF MALCOLM X, JOHN F. KENNEDY,
MARTIN LUTHER KING, JR., GEORGE LINCOLN ROCKWELL,
ROBERT KENNEDY, RICHARD M. NIXON, GEORGE WALLACE,
JANE FONDA, GABRIEL CONRAD, AND HANK BRUMMER

"Well," said Joe, "I'll be fucked."

"It was quite a trip," said Hagbard Celine.

"You're quite a tripper," Miss Portinari replied. "You really did Harry Coin very well. Probably just the way he'll do it, when he gets up the nerve to come see me."

"It was simpler than doing my own trip," Hagbard said wearily. "My guilt is much deeper, because I know more. It was easier to take his guilt trip than to take my own."

"And it's over? Your fur no longer bristles?"

"I know who I am and why I'm here. Adenine, cytosine, guanine, thymine."

"How did you ever forget?"

Hagbard grinned. "It's easy to forget. You know that."

She smiled back. "Blessed be, Captain."

"Blessed be," he said.

Returning to his stateroom, he was still subdued. The vision of the self-begotten and the serpent eating its own tail had broken the lines of word, image, and emotional energy that were steering him toward the Dark Night of the Soul again—but resolving his personal problem did not rescue the Demonstration or help him cope with the oncoming disaster. It merely freed him to begin anew. It merely reminded him that the end is the beginning and humility is endless.

It merely, merrily, turned the Wheel another Tarot-towery connection . . .

He realized he was still tripping a little. That was readily fixed: Harry Coin was tripping, and he wasn't Harry Coin right now.

Hagbard, remembering again who he was and why he was there, opened his stateroom door. Joe Malik sat in a chair, under an octopus mural, and regarded him with a level glance.

"Who killed John Kennedy?" Joe asked calmly. "I want a straight answer this time, H.C."

Hagbard relaxed into another chair, smiling gently. "That one finally registered, eh? I told John, all those years ago, to emphasize that you should never trust anyone with the initials H.C., and yet you've gone on trusting me and never noticing."

"I noticed. But it seemed too wild to take seriously."

"John Kennedy was killed by a man named Harold Canvera who lived on Fullerton Avenue in Chicago, near the Seminary Restaurant, where you and Simon first discussed his theories of numerology. Dillinger had moved back to that neighborhood for a while in the late fifties, because he liked to go to the Biograph Theatre for old times' sake, and Canvera was his landlord. A very sane, ordinary, rather dull individual. Then, in Dallas in 1963, John saw him blow the President's head off before Oswald or Harry Coin or the Mafia gun could fire." Hagbard paused to light a cigar. "We investigated Canvera afterward, like scientists investigating the first extraterrestrial life form. You can imagine how thorough we were. He had no politics at all at the time, which puzzled the hell out of us. It turned out that Canvera had put a lot of money into Blue Sky, Inc., a firm that made devices for landing on low-gravity planets. That was back in the very early fifties. Finally, Eisenhower's hostility to the space program drove Blue Sky to the bottom of the board, and Canvera sold out at a terrible loss. Then Kennedy came in and announced that the U.S. was going to put a man on the moon. The stocks he'd sold were suddenly worth millions. Canvera's brain snapped—that was all. Killing Kennedy and getting away with it turned him schizzy finally. He went in for spiritualism for a while, and then later joined White Heroes Opposing Red Extremism, one of the really paranoid anti-Illuminati groups, and ran a telephone message service giving WHORE propaganda."

"And nobody else ever suspected?" Joe asked. "Canvera is still there in Chicago, going about his business, just another face on the street?"

"Not quite. He was shot a few years ago. Due to you."

"Due to *me*?"

"Yes. He was one of the subjects in the first AUM test. He subsequently made the mistake of knocking up the daughter of a local politician. It appears that the AUM made him susceptible to libertine ideas."

WE'RE GONNA ROCK ROCK ROCK TILL BROAD DAYLIGHT

"You sound very convincing, and I almost believe you," Joe said slowly. "Why, all of a sudden? Why no more put-ons and runarounds?"

"We're getting to the chimes at midnight," Hagbard replied simply, with a Latin shrug. "The spell is ending. Soon the coach turns back to a pumpkin, Cinderella goes back to the kitchen, everybody takes their masks off, and the carnival is over. I mean it," he added, his face full of sincerity. "Ask me anything and you get the truth."

"Why are you keeping George and me apart? Why do I have to skulk around the sub like a wanted fugitive and eat with Calley and Eichmann? Why don't you want George and me to compare notes?"

Hagbard sighed. "The real explanation for that would take a day. You'd have to understand the whole Celine System first. In the baby talk of conventional psychology, I'm taking away George's father figures. You're one: his first and only boss, an older man he trusts and respects. I became another very quickly, and that's one of the thousand and one reasons I turned the guru-hood over to Miss Portinari. He had to confront Drake, the bad father, and lose you and me, the good fathers, before he could really learn to ball a woman. The next step, if you're curious, is to take the woman away from him. Temporarily," Hagbard added quickly. "Don't be so jumpy. You've been through a large part of the Celine System, and it hasn't killed you. You're stronger because of it, aren't you?"

Joe nodded, accepting this, but shot the next question immediately. "Do you know who bombed *Confrontation*?"

"Yes, Joe. And I know *why* you did it."

YOU'RE NOT A   THING   AT ALL

"Okay, then, here's the payoff, and your answer better be good. Why are you helping the Illuminati to immanentize the Eschaton, Hagbard?"

"It steam-engines when it comes steam-engine time, as a very wise man once said."

"Jesus," Joe said wearily. "I thought I had crossed that *pons asinorum.* When I figured out how you get the goose out of the bottle in the Zen riddle—you do nothing and wait for the goose to peck its way out, just like a chick pecks its way out of an egg—I realized 'Do what thou wilt' becomes 'the whole of the law' by a mathematical process. The equation balances when you realize who the 'thou' is, as distinguished from the ordinary 'you.' The whole fucking works, the universe—all of it alive in the same way we're alive, and mechanical in the same way we're mechanical. The Robot. The one more trustworthy than all the Buddhas and sages. Oh, Christ, yes, I thought I understood it all. But this, this . . . this stone fatalism—*what the hell are we going to Ingolstadt for, if we can't do anything?*"

"The coin has two sides. It's the only coin that comes up at this time, but it still has two sides." Hagbard leaned forward intensely. "It's mechanical *and* alive. Let me give you a sexual metaphor, since you usually hang out with New York intellectuals. You look at a woman across a room and you know you're going to bed with her before the night is over. That's mechanical: Something has happened when your eyes met. But the orgasm is organic; what it will be like, neither of you can predict. And I know, just as the Illuminati know, that immanentization is going to happen on May first because of a mechanical process Adam Weishaupt started on another May first two centuries ago, and because of other processes other people started before then and since then. But neither I nor the Illuminati know what form immanentization will take. It doesn't have to be hell on earth. It can be heaven on earth. And that's why we're going to Ingolstadt."

THREE O'CLOCK   TWO O'CLOCK   ONE O'CLOCK
ROCK

I became a cop because of Billie Freshette. Well, I don't want to jive you—that wasn't the whole reason. But she sure as hell was one bodacious big part of the reason, and that's the curious thing about what finally happened, and how Milo Flanagan assigned me to infiltrate the Lincoln

Park anarchist group, getting me in right up to my black ass in all that international intrigue and yoga-style balling with Simon Moon. But maybe I should start over from the beginning again, from Billie Freshette. I was a little kid and she was an old woman—it was in the early 1950s, you see (Hassan i Sabbah X was operating in the open then, going around the South Side preaching that the greatest of the White Magicians had just died recently in England and now the age of the Black Magicians was beginning; everybody thought he was one stone-crazy stud), and my father was a cook in a restaurant on Halsted. He pointed her out to me on the street once (it must have been just a while before she went back to the reservation in Wisconsin to die). "See that old woman, child? She was John Dillinger's girl friend."

Well, I looked, and I saw she was really heavy and together and that whatever the law had done to her never broke her, but I also saw that sorrow hung around her like a dark halo. Daddy went on and told me a lot more about her, and about Dillinger, but it was the sorrow that got printed all over every cell in my little baby brain. It took years for me to figure it out, but what it really meant, as an omen or conjure, was that she was basically just like the women of the black gang leaders on the South Side, even if she was an Indian. There's just one way for a black in Chicago, and that's to join a gang—Solidarity Forever, as Simon would say—but I dug that there was only one gang that was really safe, the biggest gang of all, Mister Charlie's boys, the motherfucking establishment.

I guess every black cop has that in the back of his head, before he finds out that we never really can join that gang, not as full members anyway. I found out quicker, being not just black but female. So I was in the gang, the baddest and heaviest gang, but I was always looking for something better, the impossible, the boss gimmick that would get me off the Man's black-and-white chessboard entirely into some place where I was myself and not just a pawn being moved around at Charlie's whim.

Otto Waterhouse never had that feeling, at least not until near the end of the game. I never did get inside his head enough to know what was going on there (he was a real cop and got into my head almost as soon as we met, and I could always feel him watching me, waiting for the time when I would round on Charlie and go over to the other side), so the best I can do in making him is to say that he was no Tom in the ordinary sense: He didn't screw blacks for the Man, he screwed blacks for himself; it was strictly his own trip.

Otto was my drop after I got assigned to underground work. We met in a place that I could always have an excuse to visit, a rundown law firm called Washington, Weishaupt, Budweiser and Kief, on 23 North Clark. Later, for some reason I was never told, they changed the name to Ruly, Kempt, Sheveled and Couth, and then to Weery, Stale, Flatt and Profitable, and to keep up the front they actually did hire a couple of lawyers and did some real law work for a corporation called Blue Sky, Inc.

On April 29, still harboring a cargo of doubt about Hagbard, Joe Malik decided to try the simplest method of Tarot divination. Concentrating all his energy on the question, he cut the deck and picked out one card that would reveal Hagbard Celine's true nature, if the divination worked. With a sinking heart, he saw that he had come up with the Hierophant. Running the mnemonics Simon had taught him, Joe quickly identified this figure with the number five, the Hebrew letter *Vau* (meaning "nail"), and the traditional interpretation of a false show: a hypocrisy or a trick. Five was the number of *Grummet,* the destructive and chaotic end of a cycle. *Vau* was the letter associated with quarrels, and the meaning "nail" was often related to the implement of Christ's death. The card was telling him that Hagbard was a hypocritical trickster aiming at destruction, a murderer of the Dreamer-Redeemer aspect of humanity. Or, taking a more mystical reading, as was usually advisable with the Tarot, Hagbard only seemed to be these things, and was actually an agent of Resurrection and Rebirth—as Christ had to die before he could become the Father, as (in Vedanta) the false "self" must be obliterated to join the great Self. Joe swore. The card was only reflecting his own uncertainty. He rummaged in the bookshelf Hagbard had provided for his stateroom and found three books on the Tarot. The first, a popular manual, was absolutely useless: It identified the Hierophant with the letter of religion in contrast to the spirit, with conformity, and with all the plastic middle-class values Hagbard conspicuously lacked. The second (by a true adept of the Tarot) just led him back to his own confused reading of the card, remarking that the Hierophant is "mysterious, even sinister. He seems to be enjoying a very secret joke at somebody's expense." The third work raised more doubts: It was *Liber 555*, by somebody named Mordecai Malignatus, which vaguely reminded Joe that the old *East Village Other* chart of the Illuminati conspiracy showed a "Mordecai the Foul" in charge of the Sphere of Chaos—and "Mordecai Malignatus" was a fair Latinization of "Mordecai the Foul." Mordecai, Joe remembered, was, according to that half-accurate and half-deceptive chart, in dual control (along with Richard Nixon, then living) of the Elders of Zion, the House of Rothschild, the Politburo, the Federal Reserve System, the U.S. Communist Party, and Students for a Democratic Society. Joe flipped the pages to see what the semimythical Mord had to say about the Hierophant. The chapter was brief; it was in "The Book of Republicans and Sinners," and said:

| 5 | *Vau*
(nail) | THE HIEROPHANT | They nailed Love to a Cross Symbolic of their Might But Love was undefeated It simply didn't fight. |

Five stoned men were in a courtyard when an elephant entered.

The first man was stoned on sleep, and he saw not the elephant but dreamed instead of things unreal to those awake.

The second man was stoned on nicotine, caffeine, DDT, carbohydrate excess, protein deficiency, and the other chemicals in the diet which the Illuminati have enforced upon the half-awake to keep them from fully waking. "Hey," he said, "there's a big, smelly beast in our courtyard."

The third stoned man was on grass, and he said, "No, dads, that's the Ghostly Old Party in its true nature, the Dark Nix on the Soul," and he giggled in a silly way.

The fourth stoned man was tripping on peyote, and

he said, "You see not the mystery, for the elephant is a
poem written in tons instead of words," and his eyes
danced.

The fifth stoned man was on acid, and he said nothing, merely worshipping the elephant in silence as the
Father of Buddha.

And then the Hierophant entered and drove a nail
of mystery into all their hearts, saying, "You are all el-
ephants!"

Nobody understood him.

(At eight o'clock in Ingolstadt an unscheduled group
called the Cargo Cult managed to get the mike and began
blasting out their own outer-space arrangement of an old
children's song:

SHE'LL BE COMING 'ROUND THE MOUNTAIN WHEN SHE
COMES
SHE'LL BE COMING 'ROUND THE MOUNTAIN WHEN SHE
COMES

And, in Washington, where it was still only two in the afternoon, the White House was in flames, while the National
Guard machine-gunned an armed mob crossing the Mall in
front of the Washington Monument, a single finger pointing
upward in an eloquent and vulgar gesture which only the
Illuminati knew meant "Fuck you!" . . . In Los Angeles,
where it was eleven in the morning, the bombs started to go
off in police stations . . . And in Lehman Cavern, Markoff
Chaney disgustedly pointed out a graffito to Saul and Barney: HELP STAMP OUT SIZEISM: TAKE A MIDGET TO LUNCH.
"You see?" he demanded. "That's supposed to be funny.
It's not funny at all. Not one damned bit.")

SHE'LL BE DRIVING SIX WHITE HORSES
SHE'LL BE DRIVING SIX WHITE HORSES
SHE'LL BE DRIVING SIX WHITE HORSES WHEN SHE COMES

On April 29 Hagbard invited George to join him on the
bridge of the *Leif Erikson*. They had been sailing through a
smooth-walled tubular passage that was completely filled
with water and was both underground and below sea level.
It had been built by the Atlanteans and not only had survived the catastrophe but had been maintained in good condition for the next thirty thousand years by the Illuminati.
There was even a salt lock, located, roughly, under Lyon,

France, which served to keep the salt water of the Atlantic out of the further reaches of the passage and the underground freshwater Sea of Valusia. The underground waterways were connected with many lakes in Switzerland, Bavaria, and eastern Europe, Hagbard explained, and if salt water were found in all of those lakes the existence of the weird subsurface world of the Illuminati would be suspected. As the submarine approached a huge circular hatchway barring the passage, Hagbard turned off the devices that rendered the craft indetectable. Immediately the enormous round metal door swung toward them.

"Won't the Illuminati know we've activated this machinery?" said George.

"No. This works automatically," said Hagbard. "It's never occurred to them that anyone else might use this passageway."

"But they know *you* could. And you guessed wrong about their spider-ships being able to detect you."

Hagbard whirled on George, a hairy arm lifted to punch him in the chest. "Shut up about the fucking spider-ships! I don't want to hear any more about the spider-ships! Portinari's running the show now. And she says it's safe. Okay?"

"Commander, you're out of your fucking mind," George said firmly.

Hagbard laughed, his shoulders slumping slightly in relaxation. "All right. You can get off the sub any time you want to. We'll just open the hatch and let you swim out."

"You're out of your fucking mind, but I'm stuck with you," said George, clapping Hagbard on the shoulder.

"You're either on the sub or off the sub," said Hagbard. "Watch this."

The *Leif Erikson* had sailed through the round metal gateway, which closed behind it. Here the ceiling of the underwater passage was about fifty feet higher than it had been in the section they just left, and the tunnel was only partially filling with water. The air seemed to be coming from vents in the ceiling. There was another metal hatchway in the distance down the tunnel.

"This lock is pretty big," George said. "The Illuminati must have sailed some enormous submarines through here."

"And animals," said Hagbard.

The hatchway ahead of them opened, and fresh water

came pouring in. The water level in the lock rose until it reached the ceiling, and the *Leif Erikson*'s engines turned over and began to propel it forward once more.

Now George is writing in his diary again:

April 29

And what the hell does it mean to say that life shouldn't change too rapidly? How fast is evolution? Do you measure it in terms of lifetime? A year is more than a lifetime to many kinds of animals, while seventy years is an hour in the lifetime of a sequoia. And the universe is only ten billion years old. How fast do ten billion years go? To a god they might go very fast indeed. They might all happen at once. Suppose the lifetime of your typical basic god was a hundred quintillion years. The whole lifetime of this universe would be to him no more than the amount of time it takes us to watch a movie.

So, from the point of view of a god or of the universe, things evolve very quickly. It's like one of those Walt Disney films where you watch a plant growing before your eyes and the whole cycle from bud to fruit takes about two minutes. To a god, life is a single organism proliferating in all directions all over the earth, and now on the moon and Mars, and the whole process from the first of the protobionts to George Dorn and fellow humans takes no longer than

Hagbard's voice over the intercom jolted him out of his reverie. "Come on back up, George. There's more to see."

This time Mavis was on the bridge with Hagbard. As George entered, Hagbard withdrew his hand from her left breast in an unhurried movement. George wanted to kill Hagbard, but he was thankful that he hadn't seen Mavis touching Hagbard in any sexual way. That would have been past bearing. He might have tested his new-found courage by taking a poke at Hagbard, and Goddess only knows what karate or yoga or magic would be the response. Besides, Mavis and Hagbard must be balling all the time. Who else but Hagbard would a woman like Mavis take for her regular lover? Who else but Hagbard could satisfy her?

Mavis greeted George with a comradely hug that made the entire front of his body ache. Hagbard pointed to an inscription carved into the wall of the cave. There was a row of symbols that George didn't recognize, but above them was something quite familiar: a circle with a downward-pointing trident carved inside it.

"The peace symbol," said George. "I didn't know it was that old."

"In the days when it was put up there," said Hagbard, "it was called the Cross of Lilith Velkor, and its meaning is simply that anyone who attempts to thwart the Illuminati will suffer from the most horrible torture the Illuminati can devise. Lilith Velkor was one of the first of their victims. They crucified her on a revolving cross that looked very much like that."

"You told me it wasn't really a peace symbol," said George, looking wistfully back at the carving, "but I didn't know what you meant."

"There was a Dirigens-grade Illuminatus in Bertrand Russell's circle who put it in somebody's mind that the circle and trident would be a good symbol for the Aldermaston marchers to carry. It was very cleverly and subtly done. If the Committee for Nuclear Disarmament had thought about it, what did they need any kind of a symbol for? But Russell and his people fell for it. What they didn't know was that the circle-and-trident had been a traditional symbol of evil among left-hand-path Satanists for thousands of years. So many right-wingers are secret left-hand-path magicians and Satanists that of course they spotted the symbol for what it was right away. That made them think the Illuminati were behind the peace movement, which threw them off the track, and they accused the peaceniks of using a Satanist symbol, which to a small extent discredited the peace movement. A cute gambit."

"Why is it there on the wall?" said George.

"The inscription warns the passer-by to purify his heart because he is about to enter the Sea of Valusia, which belongs exclusively to the Illuminati. Traveling across the Sea of Valusia, you come eventually to the underground port of Agharti, which was the first Illuminati refuge after the Atlantean catastrophe. We are emerging into the Sea of Valusia right now. Watch."

Hagbard gestured, and George watched, open-mouthed, as the walls of the cave that closed around them fell away. They were sailing out of the tunnel, but what they seemed to be entering was an infinite fog. The television cameras and their laser wave-guides penetrated just as far into this lightless ocean that they were about to navigate as they had into the Atlantic, but this ocean was neither blue nor green, but gray. It was a gray that seemed to extend infinitely in all directions, like an overcast sky. It was impossible to gauge distance. The farthest depth of the gray around them might be hundreds of miles away, or it might be right outside the submarine.

"Where's the bottom?" he asked.

"Too far below us to see," said Mavis. "The top of this ocean is just a little above the level of the bottom of the Atlantic."

"You're so smart," said Hagbard, pinching her buttock and causing George to flinch.

"Don't pay any attention to him, George," said Mavis. "He's a little bit nervous, and it's making him silly."

"Shut the fuck up," said Hagbard.

Beginning to feel anxious himself, wondering if the noble mind of Hagbard Celine was being overthrown by the weight of responsibility, George turned to look out at the empty ocean. Now he saw that it wasn't quite empty. Fish swam by, some large, some small, many of them grotesque. All were totally eyeless. An octopoidal monster with extremely long, slender tentacles drifted past the submarine, feeling for its prey. There was a covering of fine hairs on the tips of the tentacles. A small fish, also blind, swam close enough to one tentacle to set up a current that disturbed the hairs. Instantly the octopus's whole body moved in that direction, the disturbed tentacle wrapped itself around the hapless fish, and several others joined in to help scoop it up. The octopus devoured the fish in three bites. George was glad to see that at least the blood of these creatures was red.

The door behind them opened, and Harry Coin stepped out onto the bridge. "Morning, everybody. I was just wondering if I might find Miss Mao up here."

"She's doing her stint in Navigation right now," said Hagbard. "But stay here and have a look at the Sea of Valusia, Harry."

Harry looked all around, slowly and thoughtfully, then shook his head. "You know, there's times when I start to think you're doing this."

"What do you mean, Harry?" asked Mavis.

"You know"—Harry waved a long, snakelike hand—"doing this, like a science-fiction movie. You've just got us in an abandoned hotel somewheres, and you've got a big engine in the basement that shakes the whole place, and here you've got some movie cameras, only they point at the screen instead of away from you, if you know what I mean."

"Rear projection," said Hagbard. "Tell me, Harry, what difference would it make if it wasn't real?"

Harry thought a moment, his chinless face sour. "We wouldn't have to do what we think we have to do. But even if we don't have to do what we think we have to do, it won't make any difference if we do it. Which means we should just go ahead."

Mavis sighed. "Just go ahead."

"Just go ahead," said Hagbard. "A powerful mantra."

"And if we don't go ahead," said George, "it doesn't matter either. Which means that we just do go ahead."

"Another powerful mantra," said Hagbard. "Just do go ahead."

George noticed a small speck in the distance. As it got closer, he reccognized it. He shook his head. Was there no end to the surrealism he'd been subjected to in the last six days? A dolphin wearing scuba gear!

"Hi, man-friends," said Howard's voice over the loud-speaker on the bridge. George cast a glance at Harry Coin. The former assassin was standing open-mouthed and limp with astonishment.

"Greetings, Howard," said Hagbard. "How goes it with the Nazis?"

"Dead, sleeping, whatever it is they are. I have a whole porpoise horde—most of the Atlantean Adepts—watching them."

"And ready to perform other tasks as needed, I hope," said Hagbard.

"Ready indeed," said Howard. He turned a somersault.

"All right," said Harry Coin softly. "All *right*," he said more firmly. "It's a talking fish. But why the hell is it wearing an oxygen tank and breathing through a fucking mask?"

"I see we have a new friend on the bridge," said Howard. "I got the mask from Hagbard's on-shore representative at

Fernando Poo. After all, a porpoise has to breathe air. And there is no surface in most of this underground ocean. It's water all the way to the top of the cavernous chambers that contain it. The only place I can get air near here is by swimming up to the top of Lake Totenkopf."

"The Lake Totenkopf monster," said George with a laugh.

"We'll moor the submarine in Lake Totenkopf later today," said Hagbard. "Howard, I'd like you and your people to stand by tonight and tomorrow night. Tomorrow night be ready to do a lot of hard physical work. Meanwhile, stay out of the way of the Nazis—the protection they're under is particularly aimed at sea animals, since that was the presumed greatest danger to them. We'll have oxygen equipment as needed for any of your people who want it. Tell them to try to avoid surfacing on the lake unless absolutely necessary. We don't want to attract more attention than we have to."

"I salute you in the name of the porpoise horde," said Howard. "Hail and farewell." He swam away.

A little later, sailing on, they saw in the distance an enormous reptile with four paddles for swimming and a neck twice the length of its body. It was in hot pursuit of a school of blind fish.

"The Loch Ness monster," said Hagbard, and George remembered his little joke about Howard's surfacing in Lake Totenkopf. "One of Gruad's genetic experiments with reptiles," Hagbard went on. "He was really queer for reptiles. He filled the Sea of Valusia with these plesiosaurlike things. Blind, of course, so they could navigate in darkness. Think about that—eyes are a liability under certain conditions. Graud figured monsters like that would be another protection against anybody finding Agharti. But the *Leif Erikson* is too big for Nessie to tangle with, and she knows it."

At last there was a column of yellow light ahead. This was the light let into the Sea of Valusia by Lake Totenkopf. Hagbard explained that the lake was simply a place where the ceiling of rock over the Sea of Valusia had been soft and unstable enough to collapse. The resulting hole, being at sea level, filled with water. Debris falling down through the bottom of the lake had formed a mountain below the place where the roof of the Sea of Valusia was punctured.

"The Jesuits, of course, always knew that Lake Toten-

kopf connected with the Sea of Valusia and thus made possible easy contact with Agharti," Hagbard said. "That's
why, when they gave Weishaupt the assignment of founding
an overt branch of the Illuminati, they sent him to Ingolstadt, which is right by Lake Totenkopf. And there's the
mountain under the lake."

It loomed ahead of them, dark and forbidding. As the
submarine sailed over it, George saw a cloud of dolphins
circling in the distance. The mountain top had been sheared
off in a fashion that seemed too precise to be natural; it
formed a plateau about two miles long and one mile wide.
There were what appeared to be dark squares on this gray
plateau. The submarine swooped down, and George saw
that the squares were huge formations of men. In a moment they were hovering over the army, like a helicopter
observing troops on parade. George could clearly see the
black uniforms, the green tanks with black-and-white
crosses painted on them, the long, dark, upjutting snouts of
big guns. They stood there silent and immobile, thousands
of feet below the surface of the lake.

"That's the weapon the Illuminati plan to use to immanentize the Eschaton?" asked George. "Why don't we destroy them now?"

"Because they're under a protective biomystic field," said
Hagbard, "and we can't. I did want you to see them,
though. When the electrical, Astral, and orgonomic vibra-
tions of the American Medical Association, amplified by the
synergetic clusters of sound, image, and emotional energy
of all these young people responding to the beat, bring that
Nazi legion back to life, it will call for nothing less than the
appearance on the field of battle of the goddess Eris Herself
to save the day."

"Hagbard," George protested disgustedly. "Are you telling me Eris is real? *Really real* and not just an allegory or
symbol? I can't buy that any more than I can believe Jehovah or Osiris is really real."

But Hagbard answered very solemnly, "When you're
dealing with these forces or powers in a philosophic and
scientific way, contemplating them from an armchair, that
rationalistic approach is useful. It is quite profitable then to
regard the gods and goddesses and demons as projections of
the human mind or as unconscious aspects of ourselves. But
every truth is a truth only for one place and one time, and

that's a truth, as I said, for the armchair. When you're actually dealing with these figures, the only safe, pragmatic, and operational approach is to treat them as having a being, a will, and a purpose entirely apart from the humans who evoke them. If the Sorcerer's Apprentice had understood that, he wouldn't have gotten into so much trouble."

SHE'LL BE WEARING RED PAJAMAS
SHE'LL BE WEARING RED PAJAMAS
SHE'LL BE WEARING RED PAJAMAS WHEN SHE COMES

Approaching the outskirts of the crowd, Fission Chips saw a group of musicians who were obviously English, from their dress and hair style. Their name, he saw on the biggest drum, was Calculated Tedium, and the guitar player had a canteen strapped to his hip. It reminded 00005 of how thirsty he was, and he asked, "Pardon me, do you know where I could get some water or a soft drink?"

"Take a snort from my canteen," the guitarist said affably, passing it over. He pointed to the west. "See that geodesic plywood dome there? It's a bleeding giant Kool-Aid station set up by the Kabouters and guaranteed to hold out even if the crowd doubles in size before this is over. I just filled the canteen from there, so it's fresh. You can get more over there any time you need it."

"Thanks," 00005 said warmly, taking a long, cold, delightful swallow.

He had a very low threshhold for LSD. The world began to seem brighter, stranger, and more colorful within only a few minutes.

(The joker was actually Rhoda Chief, the vocalist who sang with the Heads of Easter Island, and who had inspired much admiration in the younger generation—and much horror in the older—when she named her out-of-wedlock baby Jesus Jehovah Lucifer Satan Chief. A former Processene and Scientologist, currently going the Wicca route, the buxom Rhoda was renowned through show biz for "giving head like no chick alive," a reputation which often provoked certain Satanists on the Linda Lovelace for President Committee to send very deadly vibes in her direction, all of which bounced off due to her Wicca shield. She was also possibly the greatest singer of her generation, and firmly believed that most human problems would be solved if the whole world could be turned on to acid. She had been preparing for the Ingolstadt festival for several months, buying only the top-quality tabs from the most reliable dealers, and she had crept into the geodesic Kool-Aid station only a few moments earlier, dumping enough pure lysergic acid diethylamide to blow the minds of the population of a small country. Actually, the idea had been subtly planted in her consciousness by the leader of her Wiccan, an astonishingly beautiful woman with flaming red hair and smoldering green eyes who had once played a starring role in a Black Mass celebrated by Padre Pederastia at 2323 Lake Shore Drive. This woman called herself Lady Velkor, and often made jokes about her memories of 18th-century Bavaria, which Rhoda assumed were references to reincarnation.)

On April 10, while Howard made his discovery in the ruins of Atlantis and Tlaloc grinned in Mexico D.F., Tobias Knight, in his room at the Hotel Pan Kreston in Santa Isobel, concluded a broadcast to the American submarine in the Bight of Biafra. "The Russkies and Chinks have completed their withdrawal, and Generalissimo Puta is definitely friendly to our side, besides being popular with both the Bubi and the Fang. My work is definitely finished, and I'll await orders to return to Washington."

"Roger. Over and out."

(Frank Sullivan, capitalizing on his only real asset, was operating in Havana as a Cuban Superman, using the name Papa Piaba, when the Brotherhood spotted his resemblance to John Dillinger. "Gosh," he said when they made their offer, "five thousand dollars just to take two ladies to a movie one night? And it's only a practical joke, you say?" "It'll be a very funny joke," Jaicapo Mocenigo promised him. And the Smithsonian acquired Mr. Sullivan's asset as one of their most interesting relics.)

WE'LL KILL THE OLD RED ROOSTER

(Hagbard was accompanied by Joe Malik when he returned to the stateroom. "You go to the beer hall in Munich," he was saying, "and steal any item, anything at all, as long as it's obviously old enough to have been there the night he tried the *Putsch*. Then you rejoin the rest of us in Ingolstadt. Understood?"

WE'LL KILL THE OLD RED ROOSTER

Lady Velkor, wearing a green peasant blouse and green hotpants, looked around the geodesic Kool-Aid dome. A man in a green turtleneck sweater and green slacks caught her eye, and she walked over to him, asking, "Are you a turtle?"

"You bet your sweet ass I am," he answered eagerly and so she had failed to make contact—and owed this oaf a free drink also. But she smiled pleasantly and concealed her annoyance.

WE'LL KILL THE OLD RED ROOSTER WHEN SHE COMES

Robinson and Lehrman of the Homicide Department actually started the last phase of the operation. I was in New York to see Hassan i Sabbah X about a new phase of Laotian opium operation (I had just come from Chicago, after staging that conversation with Waterhouse for Miss Servix's benefit), and I decided to check with them for those little nuances that can't go into an official report. We met in Washington Square and found a bench far enough from the chess nuts to give us some privacy.

"Muldoon is on to us," Robinson told me right off. He was wearing a beard; I figured that meant he was currently in a Weather Underground group, since he was too old to pass for under twenty-one and get into Morituri.

"Are you sure?" I asked.

He made the usual reply: "Who's ever sure of anything in this business? But Barney is pure cop through and through," he added, "and his instincts are like dowsing rods. Everybody on the force knows we've infiltrated them by now, anyway. They even make jokes about it. 'Who's the CIA man in your department?'—that kind of thing."

"Muldoon is on to us, all right," Lehrman agreed. "But he's not the one I worry about."

"Who is?" I brushed my walrus mustache nervously; being the first pentuple agent in the history of espionage was starting to grind me down. I really wasn't sure which of my bosses should hear about this, although the CIA certainly had to be told, since for all I know Robinson and Lehrman might be reporting to them twice, having another contact as a fail-safe check on my own integrity.

"The head of Homicide North," Lehrman said. "An old geezer named Goodman. He's so damned smart, I sometimes wonder if *he's* a double agent for the Eye themselves. His mind jumps ahead of facts just like an Adeptus Exemptus in the Order."

I looked up at the statue of Garibaldi, remembering the old NYU myth that he would pull his sword the rest of the way out of the scabbard if a virgin ever walked through Washington Park. "Tell me more about this Goodman," I said.

("Check out the pair on that chick," a Superman said enthusiastically.

("Watermelons," a second Superman agreed enthusiastically. "And you know how us *cullud folk* dig watermelons," he added, licking his lips.

("Skin!" the first cried.

("Skin!" the second agreed.

(They slapped palms, and Clark Kent came out of his reverie. Having sampled the Kool-Aid a while earlier, he was beginning to float a little, although not yet aware of what was happening—he just felt a rather unusual tug of memory from his days as an anthropologist, and was deeply concerned with a new insight about the relationship between the black Virgin of Guadalupe, the Greek goddess Persephone, and his own sexual proclivities—and he came out of it with a start, looking at the woman whose breasts had inspired such reverence.

("Son of a *bitch*," he said piously, his mouth spreading in a grin.)

Rebecca Goodman left the house at 3 P.M., hauling a shopping cart and walking past the garage. The nearest supermarket was a good ten minutes on foot, and big enough to keep her busy for a half-hour finding what she wanted and getting through one of those checkout lines. I slipped out of the car and walked right to the back of the house, perfectly secure from neighboring eyes in my Bell Telephone overalls.

The kitchen door had an easy slip-lock, and I didn't even need my keys. A playing card did the job, and I was in.

My first thought was to head for the bedroom—the old man from Vienna was right, and that's where you'll find the real clues to a man's character—but one chair in the kitchen stopped me. The vibes were so strong that I closed my eyes and psychometered it according to the difficult Third Alko of the A∴ A∴.. It was Rebecca herself: She had sat there and thought about shooting heroin. It faded fast, before I could read what had stopped her.

The bedroom almost knocked me over when I found it. "Who would have thought the old man had so much hot blood in him?" I paraphrased, backing out. It was a profan-

ation to read too much in there, and what I did scan was
enough. As Miss Mao would say, this man was Tao-Yin
(Beta prime in the terminology of the I). No wonder Robinson kept talking about his "intuition."

The living room had a statue of the Mermaid of Copen-
hagen that stopped me. I read it and chuckled; Lord, the
hangups we all have.

One wall was a built-in bookcase, but Rebecca seemed to
be the reader in the family. I started scanning experimental-
ly and found Saul's vibes on a shelf of detective stories and
a *Scientific American* anthology of mathematical and logical
puzzles. The man had no concept of his own latent powers,
and thought only in terms of solving riddles. Sherlock
Holmes, without even the violin and the dope for relief
from all that cortical activity. Everything else went into his
marriage, that hothouse bedroom upstairs.

No; there was a sketchpad on the coffee table. His, according to the aura.

I flipped pages rapidly: all detailed, precise, perfectly na-
turalistic. Mostly faces: criminals he had dealt with pro-
fessionally, all touched with a perception and compassion
that he kept out of his work hours. Trees in Central Park.
Nudes of Rebecca, adoration in every line of the pencil. A
surprising face of a black kid, with some Harem slum
building in the background—another touch of unexpected
compassion. Then a switch—the first abstract. It was a Star
of David, basically, but he had started adding energetic
waves coming out of it, and the descending triangle was
shaded—somewhere, in the back of his head, he had been
working out the symbolism, and coming amazingly close to
the truth. More faces of obvious criminal types. A scene in
the Catskills, with Rebecca reading a book under a tree—
something wrong, gloom and fear in the shading. I closed
my eyes and concentrated: The picture came in with a
second woman . . . I opened my eyes, sweating. It was
his first wife, and she had died of cancer. He was afraid of
losing Rebecca too, but she was young and healthy. Another
man. He thought she might leave him for a younger man.
Well, that was the key, then. I flipped a few more pages and
saw a unicorn—some more of the unconscious work that
went into that erotic Star of David.

A quick scan of Rebecca's books then. Mostly anthropology, mostly African. I took one off the shelf and held it.

Eros again, thinly sublimated. The other part of the key. As Hassan i Sabbah X once remarked to me, "Breathes there a white woman with soul so dead, she never yearned for a black in her bed?"

I returned everything to its place carefully and headed for the back door. I stopped in the kitchen to read the chair again, since relapse is as much a part of the syndrome in heroin addiction as in black-lung disease. This time I found what stopped her. If I say love, I'll sound sentimental, and if I say sex, I'll sound cynical. I'll call it pair bonding and sound scientific.

Slipping back into my car, I checked the time elapsed: seventeen minutes. It would have taken several hours to unearth as many facts by ordinary detection methods, and they would have been different, less significant, facts. A∴ A∴ training has certainly made all my other jobs easier.

There was only one remaining problem: I didn't want to kill anybody at this point, and a bombing would only get Muldoon in. Even having Malik disappear might only bring in Missing Persons.

Then I remembered the dummies used by the clothier on the eighteenth floor, right above the *Confrontation* office. Burn the dummy just right before setting the bomb and it might work . . . I drove back toward Manhattan whistling "Ho-Ho-Ho, Who's Got the Last Laugh Now?"

(The bomb went off at 2:30 A.M. one week later. Simon, leaving O'Hare Airport, where it was 1:30 A.M., decided he still had time to get to the Friendly Stranger and meet that cute lady cop who had so cleverly infiltrated the Nameless Anarchist Horde. He could get her into bed easily enough, since female spies always expect men to reveal secrets when they're in the dreamy afterglow with their guard down; he would teach her some sexual yoga, he decided, and see what secrets she might slip. But he remembered the midnight conference at the UN building after the bomb was set, and Malik's grim words: "If we're right about this, we might all be dead before Woodstock Europa opens next week.")

"Are you a turtle?" Lady Velkor asks again, approaching another man in green. "No," he says, "I have no armor." She smiles as she murmurs, "Blessed be," and he replies, "Blessed be" . . . Doris Horus heard the voice behind her say "And how's the Miskatonic Messalina?" and her heart leaped, not believing it, but when she turned it was him, Stack . . . "Jesus," one Superman said to another, "does he personally know all the good-looking white chicks in the world?" . . . The Senate and the People of Rome were still tussling with Attila and His Huns, but Hermie "Speed King" Trismegistos, drummer with the Credibility Gap, watched placidly from only a few feet away, seeing them as a very complicated, almost mathematical ballet; he was concerned only with determining whether they illustrated the eternal warfare of Set and Osiris or the joining of atoms to make molecules. He knew he was on acid, but, what the hell, that must have been the Kool-Aid, another of Tyl Eulenspiegel's merry pranks . . .

The submarine rose above the plateau, lifting into the waters of Lake Totenkopf. Mooring it well below the surface on the shore opposite Ingolstadt, Hagbard and about thirty of his crew entered scuba launches and buzzed to the surface. Parked on a road beside the lake was a line of cars, led by a magnificent Bugatti Royale. Hagbard grandly ushered George, Stella, and Harry Coin into the enormous car. George was shocked to see that the chauffeur was a man whose face was covered with gray fur.

It was a long drive around the lake to the town of Ingolstadt. It was very much as George had imagined it, all turrets and spires and Gothic towers mixed with modern-Martian edifices straight from Mad Avenue, but most of the buildings looking like they had been put up in the days of Prince Henry the Fowler.

"This place is full of beautiful buildings," said Hagbard. "The big Gothic cathedral in the center of town is called the Liebfrauenminister. There's another rococo church called the Maria Victoria—I've always wanted to get stoned on acid and go look at the carvings, they're so intricate."

"Have you been here before, Hagbard?" Harry asked.

"On scouting missions. I know where all the good places are. Tonight you're all going to be my guests at the Schlosskeller in Ingolstadt Castle."

"We have to be your guests," said George. "None of us have any money."

"If you have flax," said Hagbard, "you can pay in flax at the Schlosskeller."

They went first to the Donau-Hotel, which Hagbard said

was the most modern and comfortable in Ingolstadt, where Hagbard had reserved almost all the rooms for his people. With every hotel in Ingolstadt bursting at the seams, it had taken a huge advance payment to bring this off. The hotel's staff jumped to attention when they saw the line of cars with Hagbard's splendid Bugatti in the vanguard. Even in a town crowded with celebrities, overrun with wealthy rock musicians and affluent rock fans from all over the world, a machine like Hagbard's commanded respect.

George, following Hagbard into the lobby, suddenly found himself face to face with two ancient, bent German men. One, with a long white mustache and a lock of white hair that fell over his forehead, said, in heavily accented English, "Get out of my way, degenerate Jewish Communist homosexual." The other old man winced and said something placating to his colleague in a soft voice. The first man waved his hand in dismissal, and they tottered toward the elevators together. Several more old men joined them as George watched, too surprised to be angry. Here, though, in the fatherland of that kind of mentality, the old man's hatred seemed historical curiosity to him more than anything else. Doubtless such men as that had actually seen Hitler in the flesh.

Hagbard grandly took a handful of room keys from the desk clerk. "For simplicity's sake, I've assigned a man and a woman to each room," he said as he passed them out. "Choose your roommates and switch around as you like. When you get up to your rooms you'll find suitable Bavarian peasant costumes laid out on the bed. Please put them on."

Stella and George went upstairs together. George unlocked the door and surveyed the large room with its two double beds. On top of one lay a man's outfit of lederhosen with silk shirt and knee socks, while on the other bed was a woman's peasant skirt, blouse, and vest.

"Costumes," Stella said. "Hagbard's really crazy." She shut the door and tugged at the zipper of her one-piece gold knit pantsuit. She had nothing on underneath. She smiled as George regarded her with admiration.

When the group was assembled in the lobby, only Stella looked good in costume. Of the men, Hagbard looked most natural and happy in lederhosen—which was, perhaps, why he'd had the notion of dressing that way. Long, skinny Har-

ry looked ridiculous and uncomfortable, but his buck-
toothed grin showed he was trying to be a good sport.

George looked around. "Where's Mavis?" he asked Hagbard.

"She didn't come with us. She's back minding the store."
Hagbard raised his arm imperiously. "On to the Schlosskeller."

The Ingolstadt Castle, a battlemented medieval building
built on a hill, had a magnificent restaurant in what had
formerly been either a dungeon or a wine cellar or both.
Hagbard had reserved the entire cellar for the evening.

"Here," he said, "we'll rally our forces around us, have
some fun, and prepare for the morrow." He seemed in an
agitated, almost giddy mood. He took his place at the center of a big table in a blackened carved chair that looked
like a bishop's throne. On the wall behind him was a famous painting. It depicted the Holy Roman Emperor Henry IV barefoot in the snow at Canossa, but with one foot on
the neck of Pope Gregory the Great, who lay prone, his
tiara knocked off, his face ignominiously buried in a snow-
drift.

"The story goes that this was commissioned by the noto-
rious Bavarian jester Tyl Eulenspiegel when he was at the
height of his fortunes," Hagbard said. "Later, when he was
old and penniless, he was hanged for his anarchistic attitudes and his low Bavarian sense of humor. So it goes."

SHE'LL BE WEARING RED PAJAMAS

("There he is!" Markoff Chaney whispers tensely. Saul
and Barney lean forward, peering at the figure ahead of
them. About five-seven, Saul estimates, and Carmel was
five-two, according to the R&I packet they had lifted from
Las Vegas police headquarters . . . But who else would be
down here, so far from the route of the guided
tours? . . . Saul's hand moves toward his gun, but the other figure whirls on them, flashing a pistol, and shouts,
"Hold it right there, all of you!")

SHE'LL BE WEARING RED PAJAMAS

"Oh Christ," Saul says disgustedly. "Hail Eris, friend—
we're on the same side." He holds up his hands, empty.
"I'm Saul Goodman and this is Barney Muldoon, both formerly of the New York Police Force. This is our friend
Markoff Chaney, a man of great imagination and a true

servant of Goddess. All hail Discordia, Twenty-three Ski-doo, Kallisti, and do you need any more passwords, Mr. Sullivan?"

"Gosh," Markoff Chaney says. "You mean that's really John Dillinger?"

SHE'LL BE WEARING RED PAJAMAS WHEN SHE COMES

(Rhoda Chief, vocalist and apprentice witch, sampled some of her own Kool-Aid early in the evening. She swore until the day she died that what happened in Ingolstadt that *Walpurgisnacht* was nothing less than the appearance of a giant sea serpent in Lake Totenkopf. The beast, she insisted, turned, took its own tail in its mouth, and gradually dwindled to a dot, giving off good vibes and flashes of Astral Light as it diminished.)

There were many empty places at the big table when the Discordians sat down. Hagbard seemed in no hurry to order dinner. Instead he called for round after round of the local beer, of which enormous stocks had been laid in to prepare for the great rock festival. George, Stella, and Harry Coin sat together near Hagbard, and George and Harry discussed sodomy objectively, between long, thoughtful pauses and deep drinking. Hagbard sent the beer around so fast that George frequently had to swill down a whole stein in a minute or two, just to keep up. Various people came in and sat down at empty places at the table. George shook hands with a man around thirty who introduced himself as Simon Moon. He had a lovely black woman with him named Mary Lou Servix. Simon immediately began telling everybody about a fantastic novel he had been reading on the plane coming over. George was interested until he found out that the book was *Telemachus Sneezed*, by Atlanta Hope. He didn't see how anyone could take trash like that seriously.

Just around the time George was finishing his tenth stein of Ingolstadt's fabled beer and feeling quite woozy, a man who looked very familiar floated into his line of vision. The man wore a brown suit and horn-rimmed glasses, and his gray hair was crew-cut.

"George!" the man shouted.

"Yes, it's me, Joe," said George. "Of course it's me. That's you, Joe, isn't it?" He turned to Harry Coin. "That's the guy who sent me down to Mad Dog to investigate." Harry laughed.

"My God," said Joe. "What's happened to you, George?" He looked vaguely frightened.

"A lot of things," said George. "How many years has it been since I've seen you, Joe?"

"Years? It's been seven days, George. I saw you just before you caught the plane to Texas. What have you been doing?"

George shook his finger. "You were holding out on me, Joe. You wouldn't be here now if you didn't know a lot more than you claimed to when you sent me to Mad Dog. Maybe good old Hagbard can tell you what I've been doing. There's good old Hagbard looking over at us from his end of the table right now. What do you say, Hagbard? Do you know good old Joe Malik?"

Hagbard lifted a huge, ornamented stein of beer, which the management of the Schlosskeller had provided him as an honored guest. It was adorned with elaborate bas-reliefs of pagan woodland scenes, including tumescent satyrs pursuing chubby nymphs.

"How you doing, Malik?" called Hagbard.

"Great, Hagbard, just great," said Joe.

"We're gonna save the earth, aren't we, Joe?" Hagbard yelled. "Gonna save the earth, that right?"

"Jesus saves," said George. He began to sing:

> I've got the peace that passeth understanding
> Down in my heart,
> Down in my heart,
> Down in my heart.
> I've got the peace that passeth understanding
> Down in my heart—
> Down in my heart—to—stay!

Hagbard and Stella laughed and applauded. Harry Coin shook his head and muttered, "Takes me back. Sure does take me back."

Joe took a few steps away from George, moving so he could face Hagbard across the table. "What do you mean, save the earth?"

Hagbard looked at him stupidly, his mouth hanging open. "If you don't know that, why are you here?"

"I just want to know—we're going to save the earth, but are we going to save the people?"

"What people?"

"The people that live on the earth."

"Oh—those people," said Hagbard. "Sure, sure, we're gonna save *everybody.*"

Stella frowned. "This is the silliest conversation I've ever heard."

Hagbard shrugged. "Stella, honey, why don't you go on back to the *Leif Erikson?*"

"Well, fuck you, Charley." Stella stood up and flounced off, her peasant skirt swinging.

At that moment a little wall-eyed man tapped Joe on the shoulder. "Sit down, Joe. Have a drink. Sit down with George and me."

"I've seen you before," said Joe.

"Perhaps. Come, sit down. Let's have some of this good Bavarian beer. It has great integrity. Have you ever tried it? Waitress!" The newcomer snapped his fingers impatiently, all the while staring owlishly at Joe through lenses as thick as the bottoms of beer glasses. Joe let himself be led to a chair.

"You look exactly like Jean-Paul Sartre," said Joe as he sat down. "I've always wanted to meet Jean-Paul Sartre."

"Sorry to disappoint you, then, Joe," said the man. "Put your hand into my side."

"Mal, baby!" Joe cried, attempting to embrace the apparition and ending up hugging himself while George, bleary-eyed, stared and shook his head. "Am I glad to see you here," Joe went on. "But how come you're doing Jean-Paul Sartre instead of your hairy taxi driver?"

"This is a good cover," said Malaclypse. "People would expect Jean-Paul Sartre to be here, covering the world's biggest rock festival from an existentialist point of view. On the other hand, this is Lon Chaney, Jr., country, and if I started showing up as Sylvan Martiset, with a face covered with fur, I'd have a mob of peasants carrying torches looking for me all over town."

"I saw a hairy chauffeur today," said George. "Do you suppose it was Lon Chaney, Jr.?"

"Don't worry, George," said Malaclypse with a smile. "The hairy people are on our side."

"Really?" said Joe. He looked around. Hagbard Celine was the hairiest person at the table. His fingers, hands, and bare forearms were black with hair. The stubble of his beard came high up on his cheekbones, just below his eyes. On the back of his neck the hair didn't stop growing, but continued down into his collar. Stripped, Joe thought, the man must look like a bear rug. Many of the other people at the table had long hair or Afro haircuts, and the men had beards and mustaches. Joe remembered Miss Mao's hairy armpits. The peasant blouses on the women in this room hid their armpits from examination. George, of course, had that shoulder-length blond hair that made him look like a Giotto angel. But, Joe thought, what about me? I'm not hairy at all. I keep my hair in a crew cut because I prefer it that way. Where does that leave me?

"What difference does hair make?" he asked Malaclypse.

"Hair is the most important thing in this society," said George. "I've tried repeatedly to explain that to you, Joe, and you've always never listened. Hair is the whole thing."

"Hair in this society at this moment is a symbol," said Malaclypse. "However, there is a real aspect to hair which enables me, for instance, to look around this room and surmise that many of these people are enemies of the Illuminati. You see, all humans were once fur-bearing."

Joe nodded. "I saw that in the movie."

"Oh, yes, you saw *When Atlantis Ruled the Earth*, didn't you?" said Malaclypse. "Well, hairlessness, you'll recall, was Gruad's peculiarity. Most of the people whom the Illuminati permitted to live—and to eventually become recivilized, Illuminati-style—were mated with or raped by descendants of Gruad. But the fur-bearing gene, found in all humans before the catastrophe, has not disappeared. It is quite common in enemies of the Illuminati. My suspicion is that if we knew the histories of ELF and the Discordians and the JAMs, we'd find that they go back to Atlantean origins and preserve to some extent the genes of Gruad's foes. I'm inclined to believe that hairy people, in whom the genes of Atlanteans other than Gruad predominate, are inherently predisposed to anti-Illuminati activities. Conversely, people who work against the Illuminati are also likely to favor lots of hair. These factors have given rise to legends about werewolves, vampires, beast-men of all kinds, abominable snowmen, and furry demons. Note the general success of the Illuminati propaganda campaign to portray all such hirsute beings as fearsome and evil. The propensity for hairiness among anti-Illuminati types also explains why lots of hair is a common characteristic of bohemians, beatniks, leftists generally, scientists, artists, and hippies. All such people tend to make good recruits for the anti-Illuminati organizations."

"Sometimes we make it sound as if the Illuminati were the only menace on earth," said Joe. "Isn't it equally possible that people who are opposed to the Illuminati may be dangerous?"

"Oh, yes indeed," said Malaclypse. "Good and evil are two ends of the same street. But the street was built by the Illuminati. They had excellent reasons, from their viewpoint, to preach the Christian ethic to the masses, you know. What is John Guilt?"

Joe remembered what he'd said to Jim Cartwright several years ago: *Sometimes I wonder if we're not all working for them, one way or another.* He hadn't meant it at the time, but now he realized it was probably true. He might be doing the Illuminati's work right now, when he thought he was saving the human race. Just as Celine might be doing the will of the Illuminati while thinking that he was preserving the earth.

George, bleary-eyed and smiling, said, "Where'd you meet Sheriff Jim, Joe?"

Joe stared at him. "What?"

"Hairlessness is the reason why Gruad and his successors were partial to reptiles," said Malaclypse, adjusting his thick glasses. "They had a real feeling of kinship. One of their symbols was a serpent with its tail in its mouth, which was intended to refer both to Gruad's Ophidian assassins and to his other experiments with reptilian lifeforms."

Joe, still shaken by George's question, yet not wanting to probe further in that direction, said, "All kinds of myths involving serpents crop up in all parts of the world."

"All of them go back to Gruad," said Malaclypse. "The serpent symbol and the Atlantean catastrophe gave rise to the myth that Adam and Eve, tempted by the serpent, fell into misery when they acquired the knowledge of good and evil. Just as Atlantis fell through the moralistic ideology of Gruad the serpent-scientist. Then there's the old Norse myth of the World Serpent with its tail in its mouth that holds the universe together. The Illuminati serpent symbol was also the origin of the brazen serpent of Moses, the plumed serpent of the Aztecs, and their legend of the eagle devouring the snake, the caduceus of Mercury, St. Patrick casting the snakes out of Ireland, various Baltic tales of the serpent king, legends of dragons, the monster guarding the fabulous treasure at the bottom of the Rhine, the Loch Ness monster, and a whole raft of other stories connecting serpents with the supernatural. In fact, the name 'Gruad' comes from an Atlantean word that translates variously as 'worm,' 'serpent,' or 'dragon,' depending on context."

"I'd say he was all three," said Joe. "From what I know."

George said, "I saw the Loch Ness monster today. Hagbard called it a she, which surprised me. But this is the first I've heard about this serpent business. I thought the Illuminati symbol was an eye in a pyramid."

"The Big Eye is their most important symbol," said Malaclypse, "but it isn't the only one. The Rosy Cross is another. But most widely copied is the serpent symbol. The eye in the pyramid and the serpent are often seen in combination. Together they represent the sea monster Leviathan, whose tentacles are depicted as serpents and whose central body is shown as an eye in a pyramid. Since each of Leviathan's tentacles is said to have an independent brain, that's not half bad. The swastika, which was a pretty important symbol around these parts some decades ago, was originally a stylized drawing of Leviathan and his many tentacles. Early versions of it have more than four hooks, and they often include a triangle, sometimes even an eye-and-triangle, in the center. A common transitional form is a triangle with the sides extended and then hooked to form tentacle shapes. There are two tentacles for each of the three angles, which yields a twenty-three. Polish archeologists found a swastika painted in a cave. The drawing dated back to Cro-Magnon times, not long after the fall of Atlantis, and there were twenty-three swirling tentacles around a beautifully executed pyramid with an ocher eye in its center."

George held his breath. Mavis had come into the room. Instead of the peasant-skirt outfit Hagbard had decreed, she was wearing what might have been called hot lederhosen, a very short, very tight pair of leather breeches that made her legs look fantastically long and underlined the round curves of her ass.

"Wow—that's some attractive woman," said Joe.

"Don't you know her?" asked George. "Well, that puts me one up on you. You're going to meet her."

Mavis came over, and George said, "Mavis, this is Joe Malik, the guy who put me in the cell you got me out of."

"That's a little unfair," Joe said, taking Mavis's hands with a smile, "but I did send him down to Mad Dog."

"Excuse me," said Mavis. "I want to talk with Hagbard." She disengaged her hand and walked away. Both Joe and George looked stricken. Malaclypse merely smiled.

Just then a tall, stern-looking black man came into the room. He too was wearing Bavarian peasant costume. He went up to Hagbard and shook hands.

"Hey, it's Otto Waterhouse, the infamous killer cop and cop killer!" roared Hagbard, swilling down beer from his huge stein. Waterhouse looked pained for a moment, then sat down and surveyed the room through narrowed eyes.

"Where's my Stella?" he demanded gruffly. George felt his hackles rise. He knew he had no right of possession where Stella was concerned. But then, neither did this guy. Exclusive possession seemed the one type of sexual relationship not practiced among the Discordians and their allies. There was a kind of tribal, general love among them which didn't prevent anybody from sleeping with anybody else. An unsympathetic observer might call it "promiscuity," but that word, as George understood it, meant using another's body for sex without feeling anything for the person you were physically involved with. The Discordians were all too close, too concerned about each other as people, for the word "promiscuity" to fit their sex lives. And George loved them all: Hagbard, Mavis, Stella, the other Discordians, Joe, even Harry Coin, maybe even Otto Waterhouse, who had just appeared.

Mavis said, "Stella's gone down to the submarine, Otto. She'll join us at the proper time."

Hagbard suddenly lurched to his feet. "*Quiet!*" he roared. A silence fell around the smoky room. People stared at Hagbard curiously.

"We're all here now," he said. "So, I got an announcement to make. I want you to all join me in drinking to an engagement announcement."

"*Engagement?*" somebody called incredulously.

"Shut the fuck up," Hagbard snarled. "I'm talking, and if anybody interrupts me again I'll throw them out. Yes, I'm talking about an engagement. To be married. Day after to-morrow, when the Eschaton has been immanentized and all of this is over—lift your steins—Mavis and I will be married aboard the *Leif Erikson* by Miss Portinari."

George sat there still for a moment, absorbing it, looking at Hagbard. He looked from Hagbard to Mavis, and tears started to well up in his eyes. He stood and lifted his stein.

"Here's to ya, Hagbard!" he said, and he drew his arm back in a sidearm motion so as not to spill any of the beer and then let the whole stein fly at Hagbard's head. Laughing, Hagbard swayed to one side, a movement so casual it didn't appear that he was ducking. The stein struck the painted head of Emperor Henry IV. The painting apparently had been done on a heavy board, because the stein smashed to bits without marking it. A waiter rushed forward to wipe the beer away, looking reproachfully at George.

"Sorry," said George. "Hate to damage a work of art. You should have kept your head in place, Hagbard. It would have been less of a loss." He took a deep breath and roared, "Sinners! Sinners in the hands of an angry God! You are all spiders in the hand of the Lord!" He held out his hand, palm upward. "And he holds you over a fiery pit!" George turned his palm over. He noticed suddenly that everyone in the room was silent and looking at him. Then he passed out, falling into the arms of Joe Malik.

"Beautiful," said Hagbard. "Exquisite."

"Is that what you meant by taking the woman away from him?" said Joe angrily as he eased George into a chair. "You're a sadistic prick."

"That's only the first step," said Hagbard. "And I said it was *temporary*. Did you see the way he threw that stein? His aim was perfect. He would have brained me if I hadn't known it was coming."

"He should have," said Joe. "You mean you were lying about you and Mavis getting married? You were just saying that to bug George?"

"He certainly was not," said Mavis. "Hagbard and I have both had it with this catch-as-catch-can single life. And I'll never find another man who more perfectly fits my value system than Hagbard. I don't need anybody else." As if to prove that she meant what she said, she knelt abruptly and kissed Hagbard's hairy left instep.

"A new mysticism," Simon cried. "The Left-Foot Path."

Joe looked away, embarrassed by the gesture; then another thought crossed his mind, and he looked back. There was something about the scene that stirred a memory in him—but was it a memory of the past or of the future?

"What can I say?" Hagbard asked, grinning. "I love her."

More food arrived, and Harry Coin leaned over to ask, "Hagbard, are you dead sure that this goddess, Eris, is real and is going to be here tonight, just as solid as you and me?"

"You still have doubts?" Hagbard asked loftily. "If you have seen me, you have seen Our Lady." And he made a campy gesture.

The man really is going ape, Joe thought. "I can't eat any more," he said, motioning the waiter away and feeling dizzy.

Hagbard heard him and shouted, "Eat! Eat, drink, and be merry. You may never see me again, Joe. Somebody at this table is going to betray me, didn't you know that?"

Two thoughts collided in Joe's brain: *He knows; he is a Magician* and *He thinks he's Jesus; he's nuts.* But just then George Dorn woke up and said, "Oh, Jesus, Hagbard, I can't take acid."

Hagbard laughed. "The *Morgenheutegesternwelt.* You're ahead of the script, George. I hadn't started to hand the acid out yet." He took a bottle from his pocket and dumped a pile of caps on the table.

Just then, Joe distinctly heard a rooster crow.

Cars, except for official cars and the vehicles of the performers, their assistants, and the festival staff, were banned within ten miles of the festival stage. Hagbard, George, Harry Coin, Otto Waterhouse, and Joe pushed their way through shuffling crowds of young people. A VW camper carrying Clark Kent and His Supermen rolled past. Next a huge, black, 1930s-vintage Mercedes slowly made its way past cheering kids. It was surrounded by a square of motorcyclists in white overalls to keep eager fans away. Joe shook his head in admiration at the gleaming supercharger pipes, the glistening hand-rubbed black lacquer, and the wire-spoked wheels. The landau top of the car was up, but, by peering inside, Joe could see several crew-cut blond heads. A blond girl suddenly put her face to the window and stared out expressionlessly.

"That's the American Medical Association in that Mercedes," George said.

"Hey," said Harry Coin, "we could pitch a bomb into their car and get all of them right now."

"You'd kill a lot of other people, too, and leave a lot of unfinished business hanging fire," said Hagbard, looking after the Mercedes, which slowly disappeared down the road ahead of them. "That's a nice machine. It belonged to Field Marshal Gerd von Rundstedt, one of Hitler's ablest generals."

An elephantine black bus carrying the AMA's equipment followed close behind the Mercedes. Silently it trundled past.

WE'LL KILL THE OLD RED ROOSTER
WE'LL KILL THE OLD RED ROOSTER

The Closed Corporation was generally recognized to be the most esoteric and experimental of all rock groups; this was why their following, although fanatical, was relatively small. "It's *heavy*, all right," most of the youth culture said, *"but is it really rock?"* The same question, more politely worded, had often been asked by interviewers, and their leader, Peter "Pall" Mall, had a standard answer: "It's rock," he would say somberly, "and on this rock I will build a new church." Then he would giggle, because he was usually stoned during interviews. (Reporters made him nervous.) In fact, the religious tone was rather prominent when the Closed Corporation appeared in concert, and the chief complaint was that nobody could understand the chants that accompanied some of the more interplanetary chords they employed. These chants derived from the Enochian Keys which Dr. John Dee had deciphered from the acrostics in the *Necronomicon,* and in modern times had been most notably employed by the well-known poet Aleister Crowley and the Reverend Anton Lavey of the First Church of Satan in San Francisco. On the night of April 30 the Closed Corporation ritually sacrificed a rooster within a pentagram (it gave one last despairing crow before they slit its throat), called upon the Barbarous Names, dropped a tab of mescaline each, and departed for the concert grounds prepared to unleash vibes that would make even the American Medical Association turn pale with awe.

WE'LL KILL THE OLD RED ROOSTER WHEN SHE COMES

"I just saw Hagbard Celine," said Winifred Saure.

"Naturally he'd be here with all his minions and catam-ites," said Wilhelm Saure. "We've got to expect to go right down to the wire on this."

"I wonder what he's planning," said Werner Saure.

"Nothing," said Wolfgang Saure. "In my opinion he's planning nothing at all. I know how his mind works—head full of Oriental mystical mush. He's going to rely on his in-tuition to tell him what to do. He hopes to make it more difficult for us to anticipate his actions, since he himself doesn't know what they will be. But he's wrong. His field of action is drastically limited, and there's nothing he can do to stop us."

First the towers appeared over the black-green tops of the pines. They looked like penitentiary guard towers, though in fact the men in them were unarmed and their primary purpose was to house spotlights and loudspeakers. Then the road turned and they were walking next to a twenty-foot-high wire fence. Running parallel to this was an inner fence thirty feet away and about the same height. Be-yond that were bright green hillsides. The promoters of the fesival had chopped down and sold all the trees on the hills within the fenced-off area, bulldozed the stumps, and cov-ered the raw earth with fresh sod. Already the green was partically covered by crowds of people. Tents had popped up like mushrooms, and banners waved in the air. Portable outhouses, painted Day-glo orange to make them easy to spot, were set at regular intervals. A vast hum of talking, shouting, singing, and music rose over the hills. Beyond the hills, beyond the central hill where the stage stood, the blue-black waters of Lake Totenkopf heaved and tossed. Even that side of the festival area had its fences and towers.

Joe said, "You'd think they were really worried about someone sneaking in for free."

"These people really know how to build this kind of place," said Otto Waterhouse.

Hagbard laughed. "Come on, Otto, are you a racist about Germans?"

"I was talking about whites. They've got good big ones in the U.S., too. I've seen a couple."

"I never saw one with a geodesic dome, though," said George. "Look at how big that thing is. Wonder what's in it."

"I read that the Kabouters were going to set up a dome,"

said Joe. "As a first-aid or bad-trip station, or something like that."

"Maybe it's a place where you can go hear the music," said Harry Coin. "Hell, size of this thing, you can barely see people on the stage, much less hear them."

"You haven't heard the loudspeakers they've got," said Hagbard. "When the music starts they'll be able to hear it all the way to Munich."

They came to a gate. Arching over it was a sign that declared, in red-painted Gothic letters: EWIGE BLUMENKRAFT UND EWIGE SCHLANGEKRAFT.

"See?" said Hagbard. "Right out in the open. For anyone who understands to read and know that the hour is at hand. They won't be hiding much longer."

"Well," said Joe, "at least it doesn't say 'Arbeit macht frei.'"

Hagbard handed in the orange week-long tickets for his group, and a black-uniformed usher punched them neatly and returned them. They were inside the Ingolstadt Festival. As the sun sank over the far side of Lake Totenkopf, Hagbard and his contingent mounted a hill. A huge sign over the stage announced that the Oklahoma Home Demonstration Club was playing, and the loudspeakers thundered out an old favorite of that group: "Custer Stomp."

Behind the stage the four members of the American Medical Association stood apart and gazed out at the sunset. They were wearing iridescent black tunics and trousers. Members of other bands stood together and talked, many of the groups happy to be meeting each other for the first time. They even fraternized with a few intrepid kids who managed to infiltrate past the guards and make it to the back side of the stage hill. But white-suited attendants kept the public and fellow performers away from the American Medical Association. This was generally accepted as the AMA's privilege. They were, after all, universally acclaimed as the greatest rock group in the world. Their records sold the most. Their tours drew audiences that dwarfed even those of the Beatles. Their sound was everywhere. As the Beatles had, for a time, expressed the new freedom of the '60s, so the AMA seemed to epitomize the repressive spirit of the '70s. The secret of their popularity was that they were so appalling. They reminded their fans of all the evils that were being daily visited upon them, and thus hearing and seeing them was like scratching a very bad itch. They suggested that perhaps youth had captured its oppressors or identified with them, and they momentarily turned the pain of the whole scene into pleasure. To learn how to enjoy suffering, since suffering was their lot, kids by the millions flocked to hear the AMA.

"Like a radiant heater," said Wolfgang. "We at the center. Our message projected into a bowl of vibrant young human consciousnesses. Massively reflected by them back across the lake—into the lake to the depth of a mile. There, reaching the sunken army. Raising them, in a sense, from the dead."

"We are so close to realizing the dream of thirty thousand years," said Winifred. "Will we be able to do it? Will we be the ones who complete the work begun by great Gruad? And, if not, what will become of us?"

"Doubtless we will scream in hell for all eternity," said Werner matter-of-factly. "What would you do to us if we failed?"

"We need fear eternity only if the Eater of Souls is on the scene," said Wilhelm. "And they've still got him imprisoned inside the Pentagon."

"Let no one speak of failure," said Wolfgang. "It is absolutely impossible for us to fail. The plan is foolproof."

Winifred shook her head. "Fools are precisely what it is not proof against. And you, Wolfgang, know that best of all."

It was dark now. The large tent made of cloth-of-gold was sheltered between the fence and a relatively secluded grassy knoll. There was greatest privacy here, because this corner of the festival area was farthest from the stage, and because the area was full of Discordians. Hagbard went into the tent and stayed there awhile. Joe and George stood outside, talking. George was thinking that Hagbard was probably in there with Mavis and he wished he could dash in there and kill the son of a bitch. Joe, agonizingly nervous, suspected that Hagbard was in the tent with a woman, probably Mavis, and he wondered if he should rush in and kill Hagbard while the Discordian leader was occupied. He kept his hand in his pocket, fingers curled around the small pistol.

I circle around, I circle around . . .

After about half an hour Hagbard emerged from the

tent, smiling. "Go on in," he said to Joe. "You're needed in there."

George grabbed Hagbard's arm, trying to sink his fingers in. But the muscle felt like iron, and Hagbard didn't seem to notice. "Who's in there?" he demanded.

"Stella," said Hagbard, looking down at the stage, where the Plastic Canoe was playing.

"And you were fucking her?" Joe asked. "To release the energies? And now I'm supposed to fuck her too? And George after me? And then everybody else? That's left-hand magic, and it's creepy."

"Just go in," Hagbard said. "You'll be surprised. I wasn't fucking Stella. Stella wasn't in there when I was."

"Who was?" George asked, thoroughly confused.

"My mother," said Hagbard happily.

Joe turned toward the tent. He would make one more effort to trust Celine, but then . . . Suddenly the hawk face leaned close to him and Hagbard whispered, "I know what you're planning for afterwards. Do it quickly."

SHE'LL BE WEARING RED PAJAMAS WHEN SHE COMES

On February 2 Robert Putney Drake received a book in the mail. The return address, he noted, was Gold & Appel Transfers on Canal Street, one of the corporations owned by that intriguing Celine fellow who had kept appearing at the best parties for the last year or so. It was titled *Never Whistle While You're Pissing,* and the flyleaf had a bold scrawl saying, "Best regards from the author," followed by a gigantic C like a crescent moon. The publisher was Green and Pleasant Publications, P.O. Box 359, Glencoe, Illinois 60022.

Drake opened it and read a few pages. To his astonishment, several Illuminati secrets were spelled out rather clearly, although in a hostile and sarcastic tone. He flipped the pages, looking for other interesting tidbits. Toward the middle of the book he found:

DEFINITIONS AND DISTINCTIONS

FREE MARKET: That condition of society in which all economic transactions result from voluntary choice without coercion.

THE STATE: That institution which interferes with the Free Market through the direct exercise of coercion or the granting of privileges (backed by coercion).

TAX: That form of coercion or interference with the Free Market in which the State collects tribute (the tax), allowing it to hire armed forces to practice coercion in defense of privilege, and also to engage in such wars, adventures, experiments, "reforms," etc., as it pleases, not at its own cost, but at the cost of "its" subjects.

PRIVILEGE: From the Latin *privi*, private, and *lege*, law. An advantage granted by the State and protected by its powers of coercion. A law for private benefit.

USURY: That form of privilege or interference with the Free Market in which one State-supported group monopolizes the coinage and thereby takes tribute (interest), direct or indirect, on all or most economic transactions.

LANDLORDISM: That form of privilege or interference with the Free Market in which one State-supported group "owns" the land and thereby takes tribute (rent) from those who live, work, or produce on the land.

TARIFF: That form of privilege or interference with the Free Market in which commodities produced outside the State are not allowed to compete equally with those produced inside the State.

CAPITALISM: That organization of society, incorporating elements of tax, usury, landlordism, and tariff, which thus denies the Free Market while pretending to exemplify it.

CONSERVATISM: That school of capitalist philosophy which claims allegiance to the Free Market while actually supporting usury, landlordism, tariff, and sometimes taxation.

LIBERALISM: That school of capitalist philosophy which attempts to correct the injustices of capitalism by adding new laws to the existing laws. Each time conservatives pass a law creating privilege, liberals pass another law modifying privilege, leading conservatives to pass a more subtle law recreating privilege, etc., until "everything not forbidden is compulsory" and "everything not compulsory is forbidden."

SOCIALISM: The attempted abolition of all privilege

by restoring power entirely to the coercive agent behind privilege, the State, thereby converting capitalist oligarchy into Statist monopoly. Whitewashing a wall by painting it black.

ANARCHISM: That organization of society in which the Free Market operates freely, without taxes, usury, landlordism, tariffs, or other forms of coercion or privilege. RIGHT ANARCHISTS predict that in the Free Market people would voluntarily choose to compete more often than to cooperate. LEFT ANARCHISTS predict that in the Free Market people would voluntarily choose to cooperate more often than to compete.

Drake, now totally absorbed, turned the page. What he found seemed to be an anthropological report on an obscure tribe he had never heard of; he quickly recognized it as a satire and a parable. Putting it aside for a moment, he buzzed his secretary and asked to be connected with Gold and Appel Transfers.

In a moment a voice said, "G and A T. Miss Maris."

"Mr. Drake calling Mr. Celine," Drake's secretary said.

"Mr. Celine is on an extended voyage," Miss Maris replied, "but he left a message in case Mr. Drake called."

"I'll take it," Drake said quickly. There was a click as his secretary went off the line.

"Mr. Celine will send an emissary to you at the appropriate time," Miss Maris said. "He says that you will recognize the emissary because he will bring with him certain artworks of the Gruad era. I'm afraid that is all, sir."

"Thank you," Drake said hollowly, hanging up. He knew the technique: he had used it himself in moving in on the Syndicate back in 1936.

"You were fucking Stella?"

"Who says I was fucking anybody?"

Joe went in. The tent was as richly hung as that of any Moorish chieftain. At one end was a diaphanous veil, behind it a figure on a pile of cushions. The figure was light-skinned, so Hagbard had been lying about being in here with Stella. Joe went over and pulled the veil aside.

It was Mavis, all right, just as Joe had guessed. She was wearing harem pajamas, red but translucent, through which he could see her dark nipples and the full bush of hair between her legs. At the expectation of making love to her,

Joe could feel his cock begin to swell. But he was determined to impose his head trip on this scene.

"Why am I here?" he said, still holding the curtain back with one hand, trying to assume a casual pose. Mavis smiled faintly and motioned him to sit down on the cushions beside her. He did so, and found himself automatically sliding to a half-reclining position. There was a faint suggestion of perfume from Mavis, and he felt the tension in his loins build up a little more.

"I need all the energies we can set in motion to defeat the Illuminati," said Mavis. "Help me, Joe." She held out her arms.

"Were you fucking Hagbard? I never did like sloppy seconds."

Mavis gave a little snarl and threw herself on him. She slathered her drooling lips over his and plunged her tongue deep into his mouth, at the same time pressing her thigh between his legs. Joe fell back and gave up struggling against her. She was just too goddamned attractive. In a minute she had his pants open and his stiff hot prick throbbing in her hand. She lowered her head over it and began sucking it rhythmically.

"Wait," said Joe. "I'm going to go off in your mouth. It's been a week since I got laid, and I'm on a hair trigger."

She looked up at him with a smile. "Eat me, then. I hear you're good at that."

"Who'd you hear that from?" asked Joe.

"A gay priest friend of mine," she said with a laugh as she undid the drawstring of her red trousers.

Joe explored the lips of her vulva with his tongue, reveling in the acrid, musky odor of her bush. He began a businesslike up-and-down, up-and-down motion with his tongue over her clitoris. After a moment he felt her body tensing. It grew more and more rigid. Her pelvis began to buck, and he clamped both hands on her hips and lapped away inexorably. At last she gave a small shriek and tried to drive her whole mons veneris into his mouth.

"Now fuck me, quickly, quickly," she said, and Joe, his pants pulled down and his shirttail flapping, mounted her. He came in a series of exquisite spasms and dropped his head to the pillow, beside hers. She let him rest that way for a few minutes, then gently nudged him to pull out and rolled to her side to face him.

"Am I dismissed?" Joe said. "Have I done my job? Released the energies, or whatever?"

"You sound bitter," said Mavis, "and sad. I'd like you to stay with me a while longer. What's bothering you?"

"A lot of things. I feel like I did the wrong thing. George is obviously in love with you, and you and Hagbard treat it as a joke. And Hagbard treats me as a joke. And both of you are quite obviously using me. You're using me sexually, and I'm beginning to think Hagbard is using me in other ways. And I think you know about it."

"You didn't take the acid, did you?" she said, looking at him sadly.

"No. I knew what Hagbard was doing. This is too serious a moment to play games about the Passion of Christ."

Mavis smiled. She pressed her body closer to him and began playing with his limp penis, rubbing the head gently into her bush. "Joe, you were raised as a Catholic. Catholics have a finer appreciation of blasphemy than anybody. That's why Hagbard chose you. How's your passion, Joe? Is it mounting?" Pressing her naked body against his, she whispered, "How'd you like to fuck the Virgin Mary?"

Joe saw his mother's face, and he felt the blood throbbing in his penis. Now he thought perhaps he knew what Hagbard meant when he said his mother was in the tent.

A little later, when he was in her, she said, "I am a perpetual virgin, Joe. And every woman is, if only you have eyes to see. We wanted to give you eyes tonight. But you refused the Sacrament. You've chosen the hardest way of all, Joe. If you're going to make it through this night you're going to have to find a way to see for yourself. By other means than the one Hagbard provided. You'll have to find your own Sacrament."

And after she came, and he came, she whispered, "Was that the Sacrament?"

He pushed himself up and looked down at the triangular red tattoo between her breasts. "No. You're not the Virgin Mary. You're still Mavis."

"And you still have to make the decision," she said. "Good-bye, Joe. Send George to me."

As Joe was dressing, feeling the weight of the pistol in his trouser pocket, Mavis rolled over so that she was lying on her stomach, not looking at him. Her naked buttocks seemed utterly defenseless. He looked at the pillow on which her bottom had been resting during their lovemaking. It was a cloth-of-gold pillow, and embroidered on it in swirling letters was the word KALLISTI. Joe shook his head and left the tent.

As he emerged, Hagbard was saying in a low voice to Otto Waterhouse, ". . . would have been up your alley if we hadn't had other work for you. Anthrax Leprosy Pi can wipe out the whole population of the earth in a matter of days."

Suddenly, the white of Hagbard's shirt, the gold of the tent cloth, the blazing spotlights of the festival, all were coming in super-bright. That was adrenalin. My mouth was dry—dehydration. All the classic flight-fight symptoms. The activation syndrome, Skinner calls it. I was so keyed up that it was a trip.

"Hello, Joe," said Hagbard softly. Joe suddenly realized that his hand was clenched around the pistol. Hagbard smiled at him, and Joe felt like a little boy caught playing with himself, with his hand in his pocket. He took his hand out quickly.

"She wants George," Joe said weakly. He turned his back on Hagbard to look down at the stage, where the sign, glowing in the darkness, said LOAF AND THE FISHES. They were singing, "I circle around, I circle around, the borders of the earth . . ."

On a pile of cushions behind a diaphanous veil at one end of the tent lay Stella, wearing nothing but a red chiffon pajama top.

"Were you letting Joe fuck you?" George said.

"Joe has never fucked *me*," Stella replied. "You'll be the first person to do that tonight. Look, George, we've got to get every bit of available energy flowing to combat the Illuminati. Come over here and get the energies going with me."

"This is Danny Pricefixer," Doris Horus said. "I met him on the plane coming over."

("Holy Jesus," said Maria Imbrium, vocalist with the Sicilian Dragon Defense, "there are angels coming out of the lake. Angels in golden robes. Look!"

("You're tripping on that Kabouter Kool-Aid, baby," a much-bandaged Hun told her. "There's nothing coming out of the lake."

("*Something* is coming out of the lake," the drummer

with the Sicilian Dragons said, "and you're so stoned you don't see it."

("And what is it, if it isn't angels?" Maria demanded.

("Christ, I don't know. But whoever they are, they're walking on the water.")

Wearing my long green feathers, as I fly,
I circle around, I circle around . . .

("Jesus. Walking on the water. You people are zonked out of your skulls."

("It's just a bunch of surfers, wearing green capes for some crazy reason."

("Surfers? My ass! That's some kind of gang of Bavarian demons. They all look like the Frankenstein monster wrapped up in seaweed.")

"Pricefixer?" said Kent. "Didn't I meet you five or six years ago in Arkham? Aren't you a cop?"

("It's a gigantic green egg . . . and it *loves* me . . .")

John Dillinger muttered to Hagbard, "That red-headed guy over there—the one with the black musician and the girl with the fantastic boobs. He's a cop on the New York Bomb Squad. Wanta bet he's here investigating the *Confrontation* bombing?"

"He must have been talking to Mama Sutra," Hagbard said thoughtfully.

SHE'LL BE WEARING RED PAJAMAS SHE'LL BE WEARING RED PAJAMAS

WHEN SHE   COMES

When Otto Waterhouse entered the tent, it was Miss Mao who was waiting for him. "I never fucked a Chinese broad," said Otto, stripping off his clothing. "I don't think Stella is going to like this."

"It will be okay with Stella," said Miss Mao. "We need to get all the energies moving to combat the Illuminati. And we need your help." She held out her arms.

"You don't have to ask twice," said Otto, crouching over her.

At 5:45 in Washington, D.C., the switchboard at the Pentagon was warned that bombs planted somewhere in the building would go off in ten minutes. "You killed hundreds of us today in the streets of Washington," said the woman's voice. "But we are still giving you a chance to evacuate the building. You do not have time to find the bombs. Leave the Pentagon now, and let history be the judge of which side truly fought for life and against death."

The highest-ranking personnel in the Pentagon (and, with revolution breaking out in the nation's capital, *everybody* was there) were immediately moved to underground bombproof shelters. The Secretary of Defense, after consulting with the Joint Chiefs of Staff, declared that there was a 95 percent probability that the threat was a hoax, intended to disrupt the job of coordinating the suppression of revolution across the nation. A search would be instituted, but meanwhile work would go on as usual. "Besides," the Secretary of Defense joked to the Chief of Staff, Army, "one of those little radical bombs would do as much damage to *this* building as a firecracker would to an elephant."

Somehow the fact that the caller had said bombs (plural) had not gotten through. And the actual explosions were far more powerful than the caller had implied. Since a proper investigation was never subsequently undertaken, no one knows precisely what type of explosive was used, how many bombs there were, how they were introduced into the Pentagon, where they were placed, and how they were set off. Nor was the most interesting question of all ever satisfactorily answered: Who done it? In any case, at 5:55 P.M., Washington time, a series of explosions destroyed one-third of the river side of the Pentagon, ripping through all four rings from the innermost courtyard to the outermost wall.

There was great loss of life. Hundreds of people who had been working on that side of the building were killed. Although the explosion had not visibly touched their bombproof shelter, the Secretary of Defense, the Joint Chiefs of Staff, and numerous other high-ranking military persons were found dead; it was assumed that the concussion had killed them, and in the ensuing chaos nobody bothered to examine the bodies carefully. After the explosions the Pentagon was belatedly evacuated, in the expectation that there might be more of the same. There was no more, but the U.S. military establishment was temporarily without a head.

Another casualty was Mr. H. C. Winifred of the U.S. Department of Justice. A civil servant with a long and honorable career behind him, Winifred, apparently deranged by the terrible events of that day of infamy, took the wheel of a Justice Department limousine and drove wildly, running twenty-three red lights, to the Pentagon. He raced to the scene of the explosion brandishing a large piece of chalk, and was trying to draw a chalk line from one side of the gap in the Pentagon wall to the other when he collapsed and died, apparently of a heart attack.

At 11:45 Ingolstadt time the loudspeakers and the sign over the stage announced the American Medical Association. After a ten-minute ovation, the four strange-eyed, ash-blond young people began to play their most popular song, "Age of Bavaria." (In Los Angeles the Mercalli scale on the UCLA seismograph jumped abruptly to grade 1. "Gonna be a little disturbance," Dr. Vulcan Troll said calmly, noting the rise. Grade 1 wasn't serious.) *What made you think we'd find him down here?* Saul asked.

"Common sense and psychology," Dillinger said. "I know pimps. He'd shit purple before he'd get the guts to try to cross a border. They're strictly mama's boys. The first place I looked was his own cellar, because he might have a hidden room there."

Barney laughed. "That's the first place Saul looked, too."

"We seem to think alike, Mr. Dillinger," Saul said drily.

"There isn't much difference between a cop and a crook, psychologically speaking," Dillinger mused.

"One of my own observations," Hagbard agreed. "What conclusion do you draw from it?"

"Well," Dillinger said. "Pricefixer didn't just pick up that girl because he wanted a lay. She has to fit somehow."

"The musician doesn't know that," Hagbard commented. "Watch his hands. He's repressing a fight impulse; in a few minutes he'll start a quarrel. He and the lady were lovers once—see the way her pelvis tilts when she talks to him?— and he wants Whitey to go away. But Whitey won't go away. He has her linked with the case he's working on."

"I *used to be* a cop," Danny said with an engaging imitation of frankness. "But that was years ago, and the work really didn't appeal to me. I'm a salesman for *Britannica* now. Better hours, and people only slam doors in my face —they don't shoot at me through them."

"Listen," Doris said excitedly. "The AMA is playing 'Age of Bavaria.'" It was the song that, more than any other, both expressed and mocked the aspirations of youth around the world, and the accuracy with which it expressed their yearnings and the savagery with which it denied them had won them over.

It started almost the instant the music began. A mile below the surface of the lake, near the opposite shore, an army began to rise from the dead. The black-uniformed corpses broke loose from their moorings, rose to the surface, and began to drift toward shore. As more and more of the semblance of life returned, the drifting became swimming motions, then wading. They fell into ranks on the shore. Under the steel helmets their complexions were greenish, their eyes heavily lidded, their black lips drawn back in wide grimaces. The mouths of the officers and noncoms moved, forming words of command, though no sound came forth. No sound was needed, it seemed, for the orders were instantly obeyed. Once again the power that had been granted to Adolf Hitler by the Illuminated Lodge in 1923 ("Because you are so preposterous," they told him at the time)—the power that had manifested itself in steel-helmed armies that had won Hitler an empire stretching from Stalingrad to the Atlantic, from the Arctic Circle to the Sahara Desert—once again that power was visible on the earth.

"They are coming. I can feel it," Werner whispered to his twin, Wilhelm, as Wolfgang thundered on the drums and Winifred belted out:

> This is the dawning of the Age of Bavaria—
> Age of Bavaria—
> Bavaria—Bavaria!

The tanks and artillery were rolling into position. The caterpillar treads of the troop carriers were churning. Motorcycle couriers sped up and down the beach. A squadron of partially dismantled Stukas was lined up in the road. After the festivalgoers had been massacred and Ingolstadt had been overrun, the planes would be trucked to the nearby Ingolstadt Aerodrome, where they would be assembled and ready to fly by morning.

The dead men removed black rubber sheaths from rolled up red-white-and-black banners and unfurled them. Many of them were the familiar swastika flags and banners of the Third Reich, with one addition: a red eye-and-pyramid device superimposed on the center of each swastika. Other banners carried Gothic-lettered mottos such as DRANG NACH

OESTEN and HEUTE DIE WELT, MORGENS DAS SONNENSYS-
TEM.

At last all was in readiness. The blue-black lips of General-of-the-SS Rudolf Hanfgeist, thirty years dead, shaped the
command to march, which was relayed in similar fashion
from the higher-ranking officers to the lower-ranking
officers to the men. The lights and music on the opposite
shore beckoned across the dark, bottomless waters. Moonlight glinting on the death's heads on their caps and runic
SS insignia on their collars, the soldiers moved out, company by company. The only sound was the growl of the diesel
engines of troop carriers and the clank of weapons.

"They're coming," said the woman under Hagbard, who
was neither Mavis nor Stella nor Mao, but a woman with
straight black hair, olive skin, fierce black eyebrows, and a
bony face.

"Coming, Mother," said Hagbard, giving himself up to
the irresistible onward sweep of sensation to the brink of
orgasm and over.

"I'm not your mother," said the woman. "Your mother
was a blond, blue-eyed Norweigian. And I look Greek now,
I think."

"You're the mother of all of us," said Hagbard, kissing
her sweat-damp neck.

"Ah," said the woman. "Is that who I am? Then we're
getting somewhere."

Then I started to flip, Malik eclipsed by Malaclypse and
Celine hardly serene, Mary Lou I Worship You, the Red
Eye is my own Mooning, what is the meaning of moaning?
and suchlike seminal semantic antics (my head is a Quick-
tran quicksand where *The Territorial Imperative* always
triggers *Stay Off My Turf*, the Latin and the Saxon at war
in poor Simon's synapses, dead men fighting for use of my
tongue, turning Population Explosion into We're Fucking
Overcrowded and backward also, so it might emerge Copu-
lation Explosion, and besides Hag barred straights from this
Black-and-White Mass, the acid was in me, I was tripping,
flipping, skipping, ripping, on my Way with Maotsey Taot-
sey for the number of Our Lady is an hundred and fifty
and six—there is Wiccadom!), but I never expected it this
way.

"What do you see?" I asked Mary Lou.

"Some people who were swimming, coming out of the lake. What do you see?"

"Not what I'm supposed to see."

For the front line, clear as *claritas*, was Mescalito from my peyote visions and Osiris with enormous female breasts and Spider Man and the Tarot Magus and Good Old Charlie Brown and Bugs Bunny with a Tommy gun and Jughead and Archie and Captain America and Hermes Thrice-Blessed and Zeus and Athene and Zagreus with his lynxes and panthers and Micky Mouse and Superman and Santa Claus and Laughing Buddha Jesus and a million million birds, canaries and budgies and gaunt herons and holy crows and crowly hose and eagles and hawks and mourning doves (for mourning never ends), and they'd all been stoned since the late Devonian period, when they first started eating hemp seeds, no wonder Huxley found birds "the most emotional class of life," singing all the time, stoned out of their bird-brained skulls, all singing "I circle around, I circle around," except the mynah Birds squawking "Here, kitty-kitty-kitty!" and I remembered again that existence isn't sensible any more than it's hot or red or high or sour, only parts of existence have those qualities, and then there was the Zig-Zag man and my God my god my father leading them in singing
SOLIDARITY FOREVER
    SOLIDARITY FOREV   ERRRR
       THE UNION MAKES US STRONG

"I say," said an Englishman, "I thought he was a monster, and he's only Toad of Toad Hall . . . with Rat . . . and Tinker Bell . . . and Wendy . . . and Bottom . . ."

"That's who *you* are," said Hagbard, "if you can call that any kind of a fucking identity."

"I think it's time you went up on stage and made our little announcement," said the woman. "I think everyone is ready for that."

"I'll send Dillinger in to you."

"Goody!"

"It's not true, you know. That was the other guy, Sullivan."

"I wasn't thinking about that. I don't care if it's no bigger than my little finger. It's just the idea of fucking with *John Dillinger*. If that doesn't put me over, nothing will."

Hagbard stood up and laughed. "You're starting to look

and sound like Mavis again. I think you're slipping, Super-bitch."

The American Medical Association had left the stage, and Clark Kent and His Supermen were playing as Hagbard, accompanied by George, Harry, Otto, and Mala-clypse, made his way down their own hill and up to the crest of the hill where the stage was erected. The journey took a half-hour as they picked their way through groups of people engaged in Mongolian clusterfuck, sitting Za-Zen, or just listening to the music. At the stage Hagbard took out a gold card, which he showed to a group of marshals guard-ing the area from intrusion. "I have an announcement to make," he said firmly. The marshals allowed him to climb on stage, and told him to wait till the Supermen had fin-ished their set.

As soon as Pearson saw Hagbard he motioned his men to stop playing. A murmur arose from the audience. "Well, all right, Hagbard," said Robert Pearson, "I was wondering if you were ever going to show up." He walked over to the side of the stage where Hagbard and his group were stand-ing.

"Good evening, Waterhouse," said Pearson. "How's my gal, Stella?"

"Where the fuck do you get off calling her your girl?" said Waterhouse, his tone containing nothing but menace.

"The acid only opens your eyes, George. It doesn't work miracles."

And it shall come to pass, that whosoever call on the name of the Lord shall be saved.

"Wonder what the hell is in that suitcase," Dillinger mur-mured.

"I'll open it," Saul said. "We'll all have to take the anti-dote anyway, after this. I have a supply out in the car." And he leaned forward, parted Carmel's stiff blue hands, and tugged the suitcase free. Barney, Dillinger, and Mar-koff Chaney crowded close to look as he snapped the lock and lifted the top.

"I'll be damned and double damned," Barney Muldoon said in a small, hollow voice.

"Hagbard has been putting us on all along," Simon says dreamily. (It doesn't matter in the First Bardo.) "Those Nazis have been dead for thirty years, period. He just brought us here to put us on a Trip. Nothing is coming out of the lake. I'm hallucinating everything."

"Something is happening," Mary Lou insisted vehemently. "It's got nothing to do with the lake—that's a red herring to distract us from the real battle between your Hagbard and those crazy musicians up there. If I wasn't tripping my head would work better, damn it. It's got something to do with sound waves. The sound waves are turning solid in the air. Whatever it is, the rest of us aren't supposed to understand it. This lake thing is just to give us something we can understand, or almost understand." Her black face was intense with intelligence battling against the ocean of undigestible information pouring in through all of her senses.

"Dad!" Simon cried, weeping happily. "Tell me the Word. You must know now. What is the Word?"

"Kether," said Tim Moon blissfully.

"Kether? That's all? Just Cabalism?" Simon shook his head. "It can't be that simple."

"Kether," Tim Moon repeats firmly. "Right here in the middle of Malkuth. As above, so below."

I see the throne of the world. One single chair twenty-three feet off the ground, studded with seventeen rubies, and brooding over it the serpent swallowing its tail, the Rosy Cross, and the Eye.

"Who was that nice man?" Mary Lou asked.

"My father," Simon said, really weeping now. "And I may never see him again. Mourning never ends."

And then I understood why Hagbard had given us the acid—why the Weather Underground and Morituri used it constantly—because I started to die, I literally felt myself dwindling to a point and approaching absolute zero. I was so shit-scared I grabbed Simon's hand and said "help" in a weak voice, and if he had said "Admit you're a cop first, then I'll help," I sure as hell would have told him everything, blurted it all out, but he just smiled, squeezed my hand gently, and murmured, *"It's alive!"*—and it was, the point was giving off light and energy, my light and my energy but God's also, and it wasn't frightening because it was alive and growing. The word "omnidirectional halo" came to me from somewhere (was it Hagbard talking to Dillinger?), and I looked, holy Key-rizt, Dillinger split in two as I watched. That was the answer to one question: There were two Dillingers, twins, in addition to the fake Dillinger who got shot at the Biograph, $0 = 2$, I thought, feeling some abstract eternal answer there, along with the answer to some of the questions that had bugged so many writers about Dillinger's criminal career (like why some witnesses claimed he was in Miami on that day in 1934 when other witnesses claimed he was robbing a bank and killing a bank guard in East Chicago, and why Hagbard had said something about him being in Las Vegas when I could see him right here in Ingolstadt), but it was all moving, moving, a single point, but everything coming out of it was moving, a star with swords and wands projecting outward as rays, a crown that was also a cup and a whirling disc, a pure white brilliance that said "I am Ptah, come to take you from Memphis to heaven," but I only remembered the cops who beat Daddy up in Memphis and made him swear when he got back that he'd never go south again (and how did that tie in with why I became a cop?), and Ptah became Zeus, Iacchus, Wotan, and it didn't matter, all were distant and indifferent and cold, not gods of humanity but gods above humanity, gods of the void, brilliant as the diamond but cold as the diamond, the three whirling in the point until they became a turning swastika, then the face of the doctor who gave me the abortion that time I got knocked up by Hassan i Sabbah X, saying, "You have killed the Son of God in your womb, black woman," and I started to weep again, Simon holding my hand and repeating, *"It's alive,"* but I felt that it was dying and I had somehow killed it. I was Otto Waterhouse in reverse: I wanted to castrate Simon, to castrate all white men, but I wouldn't; I would go on castrating black men—the Nightmare Life-in-Death am I.

"It's alive, baby," Simon repeated, "it's alive. And I love you, baby, even if you are a cop."

("The whole lake is *alive,*" the vibe man with the Fillet of Soul was trying to explain to the rest of that group, "one big spiral rising and turning, like the DNA molecule, but with a hawk's head at the top . . .")

"Good evening, Waterhouse," said Pearson. "How's my gal, Stella?"

"Where the fuck do you get off calling her *your* girl?" said Waterhouse, his tone containing nothing but menace.

"Cool it brother," said Pearson reasonably.

"Don't hand me that brother shit. I asked you a question."

"You and your question come out of a weak, limp bag," said Pearson.

Hagbard said, "Robert only fucks white women, Otto. I'm sure he's never laid Stella Maris."

"Don't be *too* sure," said Pearson.

"Don't play with Otto, Robert," said Hagbard. "He specializes in killing black men. In fact, he's only just killed his first white man, and he's not at all sure he enjoyed it."

"I never knew what killing was before," said Waterhouse. "I was crazy all those years, and I enjoyed what I did because I didn't know what I was doing. After I killed Flanagan I understood what I'd been doing all along, and it was like I killed all the others all over again." His cheeks were wet, and he turned away.

Pearson stood looking at him for a moment, then said softly, "Wow. Come on, Hagbard. Let's get you on stage." They walked out to the microphone together. A few people in the audience had begun clapping rhythmically for more music. Most, though, had been waiting silently, happily, for whatever might happen next.

What happened was that Robert Pearson said to them, "Brothers and sisters, this is Freeman Hagbard Celine, my ace, and the heaviest dude on the planet Earth. Listen while he runs it down to you what's happening."

He stepped aside and deferentially ushered Hagbard to the microphone.

Into the silence Hagbard said, "My name, as Clark Kent just told you, is Hagbard Celine . . ."

(In Mad Dog, Texas, John Dillinger and Jim Cartwright looked up from the chess board as the radio music stopped and an announcer's voice said, "We interrupt this show to bring you a special message from Washington." John moved a knight and said softly, "Checkmate. That'll be the President, I bet. I hope to hell my brother finds that missing pimp before things get much worse." Cartwright surveyed the board dismally. "Checkmate," he agreed finally. "I hope your other brother, and Hagbard, are handling things right in Ingolstadt," he added, as they both turned, with a reflex acquired from TV watching, and looked at the radio . . .)

Being a woman is bad enough, but being a black woman is even worse. I always feel split in two, a divided lion (I'm thinking like Simon) with a hole in the middle (and that's all men are interested in, the hole in the middle), but the acid was making the split into a conscious agony and then was healing it, I was a whole Lion, ready to devour my enemies: I understood my father and why he felt he finally had to stand up to the whites even if it killed him. A knight moved across a wasteland, the desert around Las Vegas, but it was laid out in squares like a chess board; he raised a fiery wand, crying "Black Power," and it was Hassan i Sabbah, my lover, my enemy, a Black Christ and yet also a baboon with a crazy grin, all blue pearl gray like semen, inside every woman there's an angry man trying to get out, a man-woman with the eyes of an owl, and the joy came over me as my clit got hot and grew into a penis; I was my father; I was afraid of nothing; I could destroy the world without caring, with one angry flash of my eye, like Shiva. MY PENIS IS THE INVISIBLE STAR RUBY AND MEN CONSPIRE TO MAKE ME HIDE IT; THAT'S WHY I MUST TAKE THEIRS. I am two-faced, always deceiving, like all women; deception is our only defense, I understand it more clearly as the wisdom of my insanity increases, and the musky smell of hashish coming from the Plastic Canoe trailer is like me, a female plant with male strength, they are nailing me to the cross (literally) but the cross is inside a spinning wheel of flame, oh Holy Moses, I'm finding Buddha not Eris in my pineal gland, the third eye is opening, I am the earth beneath your feet, I am Billie Freshette, I am legion, there are millions of me, a plague of locusts to devour your White Male Technology, "My name is Hagbard Celine" he is saying, they sold heroin in my grammar school (that's the way a Chicago black gets educated), Simon is still trying to bring me through it saying now "Death shall have no dominion," and I try to believe Love shall have the dominion but first I must spend my hate to the last penny, they made me kill my baby, I really am going to go crazy because I have the hots again and want Simon's lance in my cup but I also know the real God is beyond God and the real Illuminati is beyond the Illuminati, there's a secret society behind the secret society: The Illuminati we're fighting are puppets of another Illuminati and so are we.

MY NAME IS HAGBARD CELINE, AND THE CARNIVAL IS OVER. REMOVE YOUR MASKS ALL PLAYERS.

"That's a funny thing for Toad of Toad Hall to say," muttered Fission Chips to nobody in particular. But the voice came booming back MY NAME IS HAGBARD CE-LINE. PLEASE DON'T PANIC WHEN YOU HEAR WHAT I'VE GOT TO SAY TO YOU and Chips saw that it wasn't Toad of Toad Hall or even the sinister Saint Toad but just a well-dressed wop with two faces, one smiling and one frowning in wrath. "You know," 00005 said aloud, "I do believe there was a fucking *drug* in that water."

MY NAME IS HAGBARD CELINE. PLEASE DON'T PANIC WHEN YOU HEAR WHAT I HAVE TO SAY TO YOU. PAY CLOSE ATTENTION. I HAVE COME TO TELL YOU THAT YOUR LIVES ARE IN GRAVE DANGER. AT THIS MOMENT AN ARMY IS MARCH-ING AROUND THE SHORE OF LAKE TOTENKOPF FOR THE PURPOSE OF MASSACRING ALL THE PEOPLE ATTENDING THIS FESTIVAL.

"Jesus," said George, "this is never going to work. He's putting it so badly. They'll never believe him. They'll laugh at him. Three-quarters of them don't even understand Eng-lish."

"Is that how it sounds to you?" said Malaclypse. "As if he's speaking in English? It also sounds to me as if he's say-ing everything in a flat, direct way. But I hear him speaking in the Greek dialect of Athens in the fifth century B.C.E."

"What do you mean?"

"He's actually talking in Norwegian or Italian, whichever language he knows best. He's using what I call the Pente-cost Gimmick. It's described in the Acts of the Apostles as the gift of tongues. After the death of Jesus the Apostles were sitting together on the feast of Pentecost, when tongues of fire appeared over their heads. Then they went out and preached to a crowd of people from many different countries, and each person heard the sermons in his own language and in the form most likely to persuade him. They made tens of thousands of converts to Christianity that way. I was the one who laid the trick on them, though they never knew that."

"Speaking in tongues!" said George in wonderment. "They used to preach about it in Bible class: 'And it shall come to pass in the last days, saith God, I will pour out of my Spirit upon all flesh: and your sons and your daughters shall prophesy, and your young men shall see visions and your old men shall dream dreams.' "

("Don't play games with yourself, George. You know perfectly well that a moment ago I *was* Mavis.")

"It's a giant black woman . . . it's Goethe's Mother Night," somebody was saying, but I was thinking of 69ing with Simon oh the tricks that cat knows to please a woman to make you feel like a queen on a throne and I don't care if he knows I'm a cop there's always a sorrow after a joy on this plane yes I will always be split in two the void will always be there at the center God yes the mask of night is on my face like I read in Shakespeare in school I am the river yellow with sewage and cocksucker is a dirty word but what else is the sign of cancer or that yin-yang all about Christ I loved doing it women who claim they don't are just liars I hate him and I love him the ambiguity is always there that detective who wanted to praise me that time said "You've got balls for a woman" but how would it sound if I said to him "You've got tits for a man" throne after throne cast down into the void and yet I have the power all they're worshipping in their trinities and pyramids are symbols of the cunt and it's hot again but I just want him to hold me I can't ball now I can't speak I see my father's face but it's silver instead of black and all of a sudden I knew Joe Malik had a gun and even that he had a silver bullet in it Mother of God does he think Hagbard is something inhuman and I smelled opium mixed with the hash those are heavy cats in the Plastic Canoe I could feel the energy surging through me I'm in the tent and I'm being fucked by all the men I'm Mavis and Stella and I'm the mother of all of them I am Demeter and Frigga and Cybelle as well as Eris and I am Napthys the Black Sister of Isis of whom none dare speak and I can even see why Joe Malik blew up his own office it was a trap and Hagbard fell into it Joe knows his secret now

"They used to preach about it in Bible class: 'And it shall come to pass in the last days, saith God, I will pour out of my Spirit upon all flesh: and your sons and your daughters shall prophesy and your young men shall see visions and your old men shall dream dreams.' And 'All flesh will see it in one instant.' "

Malaclypse smiled. " 'To conceive of pentecostal training it is necessary to die. These are the words of the first, last, and between, Kallisti.' You must have won the prize for memorizing verse in that Bible class, George."

"I would have, only the teacher didn't like my attitude."

"Good," said Malaclypse. "I also taught the Pentecost Gimmick to Hagbard. What he's saying sounds flat to you, because you don't need to be persuaded. Everybody else is hearing as much emotion and rhetoric as is needed to motivate them. It's a good gimmick, the Pentecost Gimmick."

It all came in solid and three-dimensional and I felt mercy flowing from me like some psychological monthly with water instead of blood I even forgave the American Medical Association all four of them separately and distinctly I was Isis all purple and blue and veiled and even if Poseidon was rising in that lake I could forgive him too He was covered with olives and shamrocks a green water god glistening like amethyst with one huge unicorn horn and then he was Indra the rainmaker whose voice of thunder was only a disguised blessing I obeyed him and put the doll in the tetrahedron there was nothing to fear for all that would happen were blessings and good things as the Brilliant Ones descended bringing their white fire to the red earth the work would be perfected in pleasure not pain for I even knew that Joe found out Pat Walsh's memos were misleading because Hagbard wanted him to find out and wanted him to plant the bomb and even wanted him to come here tonight with the gun so it all makes sense if you had a model of the globe with a black light flashing for every death and a white light for everytime somebody comes it would seem to be glowing all the time that's what's so good about being a woman I can come and come and come oh God as many times as I want and men even Simon hardly ever come more than once in a night that mean Miss Forbes in first grade she needed a good lay but I can even forgive her

LADIES AND GENTLEMEN, THE PRESIDENT OF THE UNITED STATES

"Everyone must leave the festival area," Hagbard was saying. "The resurrected Nazis intend to slaughter all of you. Fortunately, we have had time to build you a pathway to safety. Behold!" He stretched out his arm and the spotlight moved beyond him to the lake, illuminating a great pontoon bridge stretching from the festival area on the eastern shore diagonally to the lake's northwest corner. It had been silently erected by Hagbard's crew, with the indispensable help of Howard and the dolphins, during the last hour.

"Wow," George said to Malaclypse. "I suppose you'd call that the Red Sea Gimmick."

Hagbard lifted his hands. "I name that the Adam Weishaupt Bridge. Everyone will now rise and proceed in an orderly fashion to walk across the lake."

MY FELLOW AMERICANS, IT IS WITH A HEAVY HEART THAT I COME BEFORE YOU FOR THE SECOND TIME TODAY. MANY IRRESPONSIBLE ELEMENTS HAVE REACTED TO THE NATIONAL EMERGENCY WITH MAD, ANIMAL PANIC, AND THEY ARE ENDANGERING ALL THE REST OF US. I ASSURE YOU AGAIN, IN THE WORDS OF A GREAT FORMER LEADER, THAT WE HAVE NOTHING TO FEAR BUT FEAR ITSELF.

The face on the TV screen expressed absolute confidence, and many citizens felt a slight upsurge in hope; actually, he was totally around the bend on Demerol, and when the White House had burned earlier in the day his most constructive suggestion had been "Let's toast some marshmallows before we leave."

EVEN AS I SPEAK TO YOU THE DIRECTOR OF THE FBI HAS ASSURED ME THAT HIS MEN ARE CLOSING IN ON THE ONE SINGLE PLAGUE-CARRIER WHO HAS CAUSED ALL THIS HYSTERIA. IF YOU STAY IN YOUR HOMES, YOU WILL BE SAFE, AND THE EMERGENCY WILL SOON BE OVER.

"We can send the army to the west side of the lake to intercept them," said Wilhelm.

("Rosebuds," cried John Dillinger. "Why the hell would he bring a suitcase full of rosebuds down here?")

Suddenly everybody was aroused and moving Simon was leading me gently along I was back in Time again there was a real fight going on between Hagbard and the American Medical Association and a fight means that somebody is going to lose the Gates of Hell were opening and I could hardly move my feet Daddy's head on the floor of that Memphis police station and those cops stomping him and stomping him why didn't they put a spear through his side while they were at it and how can I really forgive that's just the drug and underneath I'll always hate white men even Simon if this is the Last Judgment I know what Christ will do with every blue-eyed bastard among them they own all the power and make all the wars they've fucked the planet their only god is Death they destroy everything living a giant blond god Thor swinging his hammer and smashing all the colored races red scarlet red blood on that hammer black blood especially but Hagbard is Horus this is the way it will always be fighting and killing to the end of time and women and children the chief victims only the flesh is holy and men are killers of the flesh cannibals.

"How many do you think there are?" the leader of the Closed Corporation asked dreamily.

"Six hundred and sixty-six," one of his group answered. "When you sacrifice a rooster in a pentagram on Walpurgis Night, you always get six sixty-six."

"And they're coming right toward us," the leader went on in his dreamy voice. "To bow down and serve us."

The Closed Corporation sat perfectly still, in silent ecstasy, awaiting the arrival of the 666 horned-and-tailed demons they saw approaching them . . . Outside Lehman Cave, Saul loads the antidote needle. "I'll go first," says John Herbert Dillinger, rolling up his sleeve . . . AT THIS HOUR WHEN YOUR GOVERNMENT NEEDS YOUR FAITH . . . In a fusilade of bullets, the President sank beneath the podium, leaving only the Seal of the Chief Executive on the TV screens. The viewers saw the same confident expression on his face as he floated in Demerol tranquility toward death. *"Oh my God!"* said an announcer's voice off screen . . . In Mad Dog, John Hoover Dillinger looks at Jim Cartwright quizzically. "Whose conspiracy was behind that?" he asks as the announcer gibbers hysterically. "There seem to have been five people shooting from five different parts of the press corps, but the President may not be dead—" "They blew his fucking head to pulp," another voice near the microphone said, distinctly and hopelessly . . . In New York, August Personage, one of the few people neither rioting nor listening to TV, reads *Atlas Shrugged* with total absorption, getting Religion . . .

"Are you a turtle?" Lady Velkor asks.

"Huh?" Danny Pricefixer responds.

"Never mind," she says hurriedly. He hears her asking the next man on the right, "Are you a turtle?"

"We can send the army to the west side of the lake to intercept them," said Wilhelm.

"Nein," said Wolfgang, who was standing in the rear of the slowly moving command car, studying the situation through field glasses. "That *verdammte* bridge goes toward the northern shore of the lake. They can go straight, while

our men go around. They'd all be across before we could reach them."

"We could shell the bridge from here," said Werner.

"We daren't use the artillery," said Wolfgang. "We'd have the whole West German army blundering down here, getting in the way of our drive to the east. If the West Germans start fighting us, the East Germans will not make the mistake we want them to make. They won't think we are an invading West German army. The Russians, in turn, will have plenty of warning. The whole plan will fall through."

"Let's skip this phase, then," said Winifred. "It's too much of a hassle. Let's head immediately eastward, and the hell with these kids."

"*Nein* again, dear sister, my love," said Wolfgang. "We have twenty-three candidates for transcendental illumination, including Hitler himself, waiting up there in the old Fuehrer Suite of the Donau-Hotel. The speedy mass termination of all those lives is to translate them to eternal life on the energy plane. And I will not let that *Scheisskopf* Hagbard Celine thwart us at this juncture. I mean to show him once and for all which of us is master. And all the rest of those *Schweinen*—Dillinger, the Dealy Lama, Malaclypse, the old Lady herself, if she's here. If all of them *are* here, it's our chance to make a clean sweep and annihilate the opposition once and for all, at the beginning of the immanentizing of the Eschaton, rather than in the final stage."

"But we can't catch the kids," said Wilhelm.

"We can. We shall. It will take a long, long time to move them all across that pontoon bridge, and they are all on foot. We have vehicles and can catch up with them before half of them are even on the bridge. They'll all be bunched together, and those on the bridge will be a perfect target for machine guns. We shall simply sweep in on them, harvesting their lives as we go. We spent years building up our identity as the American Medical Association just so we could organize the Ingolstadt festival and trap masses of human beings on the shore of Lake Totenkopf, that our sacred lake might run red with their blood. Would you throw all that away?"

"I agree. A brilliant analysis," said Wilhelm.

"We must move on at full speed, then," said Wolfgang. He turned to the car behind him and shouted. "*Vorwarts* at maximum speed!" General-of-the-SS Hanfgeist stood up, turned toward his subordinates, and moved his blackened lips to form the same words. Immediately the tanks, half-tracks, motorcycles, and armored cars began to rev up their engines and the troops started to trot down the road on the double.

A lookout in one of the festival light-and-sound towers spotted them and relayed a warning to the stage, where Robert Pearson spoke into a microphone. "It is my sad duty to inform you that the pigs are intensifying their approach. Now, don't run. But *do* quicken your pace with all deliberate speed."

Hagbard called in through the doorway of the gold tent, "John, you've had enough, for Discordia's sake. Come on out and let Malaclypse go in."

"I thought you were noncorporeal," said George.

"If you'd known me any length of time you would have noticed that I frequently pick my nose," said the Sartrelike apparition.

"Whew," said John-John Dillinger, emerging from the tent, "who would have thought the old man'd have so much come in him? She says she wants George in there after Mal."

The woman behind the veil was glowing. There was no light in the tent, save for the deep golden radiance that came from her body.

"Come closer, George," she said. "I don't want you to make love to me now—I only want you to learn the truth. Stand here before me."

The woman behind the veil was Mavis. "Mavis, I love you," said George. "I've loved you ever since you took me out of that jail in Mad Dog."

"Look again, George," said Stella.

"Stella! What happened to Mavis?"

I circle around, I circle around . . .

"Don't play games with yourself, George. You know perfectly well that a moment ago I *was* Mavis."

"It's the acid," said George.

"The acid only opens your eyes, George. It doesn't work miracles," said Miss Mao.

I circle around, I circle around . . .

"Oh, my God!" said George. And he thought: *And it*

*shall come to pass, that whosoever shall call on the name of
the Lord shall be saved.*

Mavis was there again. "Do you understand, George? Do
you understand why you never saw all of us together at
once? Do you understand why, all the time you wanted to
fuck me, that when you were fucking Stella you *were* fucking me? And do you understand that I am not one woman
or three women but an infinite number of women?" Before
his eyes she turned red, yellow, black, brown, young, mid-
dle-aged, a child, an old woman, a Norwegian blonde, a Sicilian brunette, a wild-eyed Greek woman, a tall Ashanti, a
slant-eyed Masai, a Japanese, a Chinese, a Vietnamese, and
on and on and on.

The paleface kept turning colors, the way people do
when you're on peyote. Now he looked almost like an Indian. That made it easier to talk to him. Why shouldn't people turn colors? All the trouble in the world came from the
fact that they usually stayed the same color. James nodded
profoundly. As usual, peyote had brought him a big Truth.
If whites and blacks and Indians were turning colors all the
time, there wouldn't be any hate in the world, because nobody would know which people to hate.

Who the hell's mind was that? George wondered. The
tent was dark. He looked around for the woman. He rushed
out of the tent. No one was looking at him. They were all,
Hagbard and the rest of them, staring in awe at a colossal
figure that grew ever taller as it strode away from them. It
was a golden woman in golden robes with wild gold, red,
black hair flowing free. She stepped over the fence that
guarded the festival grounds as casually as if it were the
threshold of a door. She towered over the Bavarian pines.
In her left hand she carried an enormous golden orb.

Hagbard put his hand on George's shoulder. "It is possible," he said, "to achieve transcendental illumination
though a multiplicity of orgasms as well as through a multiplicity of deaths."

There were lights advancing down the road. The woman,
now ninety-three feet tall, strode toward those lights. She
laughed, and the laughter echoed across Lake Totenkopf.

"Great Gruad! What's that?" cried Werner.

"It's the Old Woman!" shouted Wolfgang, his lips falling
away from his teeth in a snarl.

The sudden cry *"Kallisti!"* reverberated through the Bavarian hills louder than the music of the Ingolstadt festival had been. Trailing a cometlike cloud of sparks, the golden apple fell into the center of the advancing army.

The Supernazis might have been the living dead, but they were still human. What each man saw in the apple was his heart's desire. Private Heinrich Krause saw the family he had left behind thirty years ago—not knowing that his living grandchildren were at this moment on the pontoon bridge across Lake Totenkopf, fleeing his advance. Corporal Gottfried Kuntz saw his mistress (who in reality had been raped and then disemboweled by Russian soldiers when Berlin fell in 1945). Oberlieutenant Sigmund Voegel saw a ticket to the Wagner festival at Bayreuth. Colonel-SS Konrad Schein saw a hundred Jews lined up before a machine gun that awaited his hand on the trigger. Obergruppenfuehrer Ernst Bickler saw a blue china soup tureen standing in an empty fireplace at his grandmother's house in Kassel. It was brimful of steaming brown dogshit into which was plunged a silver spoon. General Hanfgeist saw Adolf Hitler, his face blackened, his eyes and tongue bulging out, his neck broken, spinning at the end of a hangman's rope.

All of the men who saw the apple, in whatever form, began to fight and kill one another for possession. Tanks smashed into one another head-on. Artillerymen lowered the barrels of their guns and fired point-blank into the center of the melee.

"What is it, Wolfgang?" said Winifred imploringly, her arms thrown in panic around his waist.

"Look into the center of the battle," said Wolfgang grimly. "What do you see?"

"I see the throne of the world. One single chair twenty-three feet off the ground, studded with seventeen rubies, and brooding over it the serpent swallowing its tail, the Rosy Cross, and the Eye. I see that throne and know that I alone am to ascend it and occupy it forever. What do you see?"

"I see Hagbard Celine's *teufelscheiss* head on a silver platter," Wolfgang snarled, thrusting her from him with trembling hands. "Eris has thrown the Apple of Discord, and our Supernazis will fight and kill each other until we destroy it."

"Where did she go?" asked Werner.

"She's lurking about somewhere in some other form, no doubt," said Wolfgang. "As a toadstool or an owl or some such thing, cackling over the chaos she's caused."

Suddenly Wilhelm stood up, his fingers clawing at empty air. In a frightfully clumsy fashion, as if he were deaf, dumb, and blind, he clawed and clamored his way over the side of the Mercedes that had belonged to von Rundstedt. Once out of the car, he took a position about ten feet away from his brothers and sister, turned, and faced them. His eyes stared—every muscle in his body was rigid—the crotch of his trousers bulged.

The voice that came out of his mouth was deep, rich, oleaginous, and horrid: "There are long accounts to settle, children of Gruad."

Wolfgang forgot the sounds of battle that raged around him. "You! Here! How did you escape?"

The voice was like crude petroleum seeping through gravel, and, like petroleum, it was a fossil thing, the voice of a creature that had arisen on the planet when the South Pole was in the Sahara and the great cephalopods were the highest form of life.

"I took no notice. The geometries ceased to bind me. I came forth. I ate souls. Fresh souls, not the miserable plasma you have fed me all these years."

"Great Gruad! Is that your gratitude?" Wolfgang stormed. In a lower voice he said to Werner, "Find the talisman. I think it's in the black case sealed with the Seal of Solomon and the Eye of Newt." To the being that occupied Wilhelm's body he said, "You come at an opportune time. There will be much killing here, and many souls to eat."

"These around us have no souls. They have only pseudo-life. It sickens me to sense them."

Wolfgang laughed. "Even the Iloigor can feel disgust, then."

"I have been sick for many hundreds of years, while you kept me sealed in one pentagon after another, feeding me not fresh souls but those wretched stored essences."

"We gave you much!" cried Werner. "Every year, just for you, thirty thousand—forty thousand—fifty thousand deaths in traffic accidents alone."

"But not fresh. Not fresh! Perhaps, though, you can settle your debt to me tonight. I sense many lives nearby— lives you have somehow lured here. They can be mine."

Werner handed Wolfgang a stick with a silver pentagon at the tip. Wolfgang pointed it at the possessed Wilhelm, who shrieked and fell to his knees. For a moment there was silence, broken only by the sound of Winifred's terrified sobbing and the crack of rifles and the chatter of machine guns in the background.

"You shall not have those lives, Yog Sothoth. They are for the transcendental illumination of our servants. Wait, though, and there shall be lives in plenty for all of us."

Werner said, "While we parley our army is destroying itself, and there will be no lives for anyone."

"Really?" said the thick voice. "How has your plan gone astray? Let me read you and learn." Wolfgang felt goose pimples break out all over his body. He shuddered as coarse, boneless fingers dripping with slime turned the pages of his mind.

"Mmm—I see. *She* is here, then. My ancient enemy. It would be good to meet her in battle once again."

"Are your powers equal to hers?" said Wolfgang eagerly.

"I yield to none" came the proud reply.

"Ask him why he's always getting trapped in pentagons, then," said Werner in a low voice.

"Shut up!" Wolfgang whispered savagely. To the lloigor he said, "Destroy her golden apple and release my army to move ahead, and I will withhold the power of this pentagon and give you all the lives you seek."

"Done!" said the voice. Wilhelm suddenly threw his head back, mouth wide open. A choking sound came from his throat. He collapsed on his back, spread-eagled. A strange, greenish, glowing gas rose from his throat.

Werner jumped from the car and rushed over to Wilhelm. "He's alive."

"Of course he's alive," said Wolfgang. "The Eater of Souls simply took possession of his body to communicate with us."

Winifred screamed, "Look!"

The same phosphorescent gas, a huge cloud of it, now obscured the heart of the battle. It seemed to take a shape like a spider with an uncountable number of legs, arms, antennae, and tentacles. Gradually the shape changed, glowing brighter and brighter. A nearby tower on the festival grounds was as visible in the reflected light as if it were day. Then the glow faded, and the tower was silhouetted in moonlight. A great silence fell over the hills around Lake Totenkopf, broken only by the glad cries of the last contingent of festivalgoers as they made it safely to the opposite shore.

"There's no time to lose," Wolfgang said to Werner and Wilhelm. "Round up some officers. See if you can find Hanfgeist."

Hanfgeist had disappeared. The highest-ranking officer surviving was Obergruppenfuehrer Bickler, visions of dog turds sadly fading in a mind that possessed only a horrid semblance of life. A quick survey showed the four Illuminati Primi that the Apple of Discord had cost them half their army.

"Onward!" roared Wolfgang, and, tanks in the van, they smashed through the festival fence, raced over the hills, troops trotting double-time, and unhesitatingly charged out onto the bridge. Wolfgang stood in the back seat of the von Rundstedt Mercedes, his black-gloved hands gripping the back of the front seat, the wind blowing through his crew cut like a field of wheat. Suddenly, beside him, Wilhelm screamed.

"What is it now?" yelled Wolfgang over the roar of his advancing army.

"The lives we are about to take," the voice of the lloigor grated. "They are mine, yes? All mine?"

"Listen to me, you energy vampire. We have other debts to discharge, and other projects to complete. There are twenty-three of our faithful servants waiting in the Donau-Hotel to be transcendentally illuminated. They come first. You'll get yours. Wait your turn."

"Farewell," said the lloigor. "I shall see you at the hour of your death."

"I will never die!"

"Fool!" the voice shrieked with Wilhelm's mouth. Suddenly Wilhelm stood up, threw open the door of the car, and hurled himself out into the lake. He struck with a huge splash, then sank like a stone. A greenish glow spread in the black water where he had gone down.

And then there were four.

Hagbard stood atop a hill, watching the tanks roll across the bridge, followed by the black Mercedes, followed by troop carriers and artillery, followed by trotting foot soldiers. He knelt beside a detonator and shoved down the handle.

From end to end the bridge and those upon it disappeared in geysers of white water. The thunder of the explosions—demolition charges placed by the porpoise horde under the direction of Howard—re-echoed through the hills around the lake.

The tanks went under first. As the front end of the command car sank under water, Werner Saure screamed, "My foot's caught!" He went down with the car, while Wolfgang and Winifred, their tears mingling with the water of Lake Totenkopf, splashed about in the water with the few remaining Supernazis.

And then there were three.

Hagbard shouted, "I sank it! I sank the George Washington Bridge!"

"Is anything changed?" said George.

"Of course," said Hagbard. "We've got them on the run. We'll be able to finish them off in a few more minutes. Then there'll be no more evil in the world. Everything will be *ginger-peachy*." His tone seemed sarcastic rather than victorious, George noted apprehensively.

"Now I'll admit," Fission Chips said reasonably, "that I'm under the influence of some bloody drug from the Kool-Aid. But this simply cannot all be hallucination. Very definitely, thirteen people took their clothes off and started dancing. I quite certainly heard them singing 'Blessed be, blessed be,' over and over. Then a simply gigantic woman rose up from somewhere and all the sirens and undines and mermaids went back into the water. If this was Armageddon, it was not precisely the way the Bible described it. Is that a fair summary of the situation?"

The tree he was talking to didn't answer.

"Blessed be, blessed be," Lady Velkor sang on, as she and her hastily assembled coven danced widdershins in their circle. The spell had worked: With her own eyes she had seen the Great Mother, Isis, rise up and smite the evil spirits of the dead Catholic Inquisitors whom the Illuminati had tried to revive. She knew Hagbard Celine would later be boasting in all the most chic occult circles that he had performed the miracle, and giving the credit to that destructive bitch Eris—but that didn't matter. She with her own eyes had seen Isis, and that was enough.

"Now I ask you," Fission Chips went on, addressing another tree, who seemed more communicative, "what the sulphurous hell did *you* see happening here tonight?"

"I saw a master Magician," said the tree, "or a master con man—the two are the same—plant a few suggestions and get a bunch of acidheads running away from their own shadows." The tree, who was actually Joe Malik and only looked like a tree to poor befuddled 00005, added, "Or I saw the final battle between Good and Evil, with Horus on both sides."

"You must be drugged too," Chips said pettishly.

"You bet your sweet ass I am," said the tree, walking away.

. . . I don't know how the courts will ever untangle this. With five of them shooting at once, and the Secret Service shooting back right away, the best crime lab in the world will never get the trajectories of all the bullets right. Who, among the survivors, will be tried for murder and who for attempted murder? That's the sixty-four-thousand-dollar question and . . . what? . . . oh . . . And now, ladies and gentlemen, on this sad occasion . . . uh . . . in this tragic hour of our country's history, let us all pay especially close attention to the new President, who will now address us.

Who's that jig standing over there? the new Chief Exec was asking somebody off camera when he appeared on the TV screens.

The Chevrolet Stegosaurus drove into the empty concert grounds and came to a slow halt. The guitarist stuck his head out the window and yelled to Lady Velkor, "What the hell happened here?"

"There was some bad acid in the Kool-Aid," she told him gravely. "Everybody freaked out and ran off toward town."

"Hell," he said, "and this was going to be our first big audience. We're a new group, just formed. What lousy luck."

He turned and drove off, and she read the sign on the back of the car: THE FERNANDO POO INCIDENT.

"How are you now, baby?" Simon asked.

"I know who I am," Mary Lou said slowly, "and you might not like the results of that any more than the Chicago police force will." Her eyes were distant and pensive.

Wolfgang and Winifred were very near shore when the

dark, humped shapes rose out of the water around them. Winifred shrieked, "Wolfgang! For the love of Gruad, Wolfgang! They're pulling me down!" Her long blond hair floated for a moment after her head went under; then that too disappeared.

And then there were two.

The porpoises have her, Wolfgang thought to himself. He continued to swim madly toward shore. Something caught his trouser leg, but he kicked free. Then he was in the shallows, too close in for the sea beasts to follow. He stood up and waded ashore. And came face to face with John Dillinger.

"Sorry, pal," said John, and squeezed the trigger of his Thompson submachine gun. Thirty silver bullets struck Wolfgang with the impact of clubs and threw him back into the water. All feeling was gone from his body, and he felt the foul tentacles closing around his mind and the murmuring, horrible laughter grew to a soundless roar, and the syrupy voice spoke to his mind: *Welcome to the place prepared for you from everlasting to everlasting. Now truly you will never die.* And the mind of Wolfgang Saure, imprisoned like a living fly in amber, knowing that it must remain so for billions upon billions of years, screamed and screamed and screamed.

And then there was one.

And Joe Malik, feeling as if he were sitting in an audience watching himself perform, walked over to that One and held out his hand. "Congratulations," he said icily. "You really did it."

Hagbard looked at the hand and said, "You were more intimate the last time around."

"Very well," said Joe. "My Lord, my enemy." He leaned forward and kissed Hagbard full on the mouth. Then he took the gun out of his pocket and carefully fired directly into Hagbard's brain. And then there were none.

It was quite real; Joe shook himself, stood up, and grinned. Walking over to Hagbard, he took out the gun and handed it to him.

"Surprise ending," he said. "I read all the clues, just like you wanted me to. I know you're the fifth Illuminatus Primus, and I know your motive for wiping out the other four is nothing like you've led us to believe. But I can't play my role. I still trust you. You *must* have a good reason."

Hagbard's mouth fell open in completely genuine surprise. "Well, *sink* me!" he said, beginning to laugh.

Dawn was breaking; the Nine Unknown Men, most mysterious of all rock groups, ceremonially donned their football helmets and faced the East to chant:

> There is only ONE God:
> He is the SUN God:
> Ra! Ra! Ra!

BOOK FIVE

GRUMMET

The bursts to the moon and to the planets are also not historic events. They are the major evolutionary breakthroughs . . . Today when we speak of immortality and of going to another world we no longer mean these in a theological or metaphysical sense. People are now striving for physical immortality. People are now traveling to other worlds. Transcendence is no longer a metaphysical concept. It has become reality.

—F. M. ESFANDIARY, *Upwingers*

THE TENTH TRIP
(OR MALKUTH FAREWELL TO PLANET EARTH)

Ye have locked yerselves up in cages of fear; and,
behold, do ye now complain that ye lack freedom.
—LORD OMAR KHAYYAM RAVENHURST, K.S.C.,
"Epistle to the Paranoids,"
The Honest Book of Truth

As the earth turned on its axis and dawn reached city after
city, hamlet after hamlet, farm after farm, mountain and
valley after mountain and valley, it became obvious that
May 1 would be bright and sunny almost everywhere. In
Athens a classical scholar waking in the small cell where
certain Platonic opinions had landed him felt a burst of unexpected hope and greeted Helios with rolling syllables
from Sappho, crying through the bars, *"Brodadaktylos
Eos!"* Birds, startled by the shout, took off from the jailyard
below, filling the air with the flapping of their wings; the
guards came and told him to shut up. He answered them
gaily with *"Polyphloisbois thalassas!* You've taken everything else away from me, but you can't take old Homer
away!"

In Paris the Communists under the Red banner and the
anarchists under the Black were preparing for the annual
International Labor Solidarity Day, at which the usual fac-
tionalism and sectarianism would once again demonstrate
the absolute lack of international labor solidarity. And in
London, Berlin, a thousand cities, the Red and the Black
would wave and the tongues of their partisans would wag,
and the age-old longing for a classless society would once
again manifest itself; while, in the same cities, an older
name and an older purpose for that day would be com-
memorated in convent after convent and school after
school where verses (far older than the name of Christianity) were sung to the Mother of God:

Queen of the Angels
Queen of the May

In the United States, alas, the usual celebrations of National Law Day had to be cancelled, since the rioting was not quite ended yet.

But everywhere, in Asia and Africa as in Europe and the Americas, the members of the Oldest Religion were returning from their festivals, murmuring "Blessed be" as they parted, secure in their knowledge that the Mother of God was indeed still alive and had visited them at midnight, whether they knew her as Dian, Dan, Tan, Tana, Shakti, or even Erzulie.

Queen of the Angels
Queen of the May

In Nairobi, Nkrumah Fubar picked up his mail from a friend employed at the post office. To his delight, American Express had relented and corrected their error, crediting him with his February 2 payment at last. This was, to his thinking, big magic, since the notification had been mailed from New York even before he began his geodesic spiels against the President of American Express on April 25. Obviously, such retroactive witchcraft was worthy of further investigation, and the key was the synergetic geometry of the Fuller tetrahedron in which he had kept his manikin during the spell-casting. Over breakfast, before leaving for the university, he opened Fuller's *No More Second-Hand God* and again grappled with the arcane mathematics and metaphysics of omnidirectional halo. Finishing breakfast, he closed the book, shut his eyes, and tried to visualize the Fuller universe. The image formed, and, to his amazement and amusement, it was identical with certain symbols an old Kikuyu witch doctor had once drawn when explaining the doctrine of "fan-shaped destiny" to him.

As the book closed in Kenya, the drums of Orabi stopped abruptly. It was one in the morning there, and the visiting anthropologist, Indole Ringh, immediately asked how the dancers knew the ceremony was finished. "The danger is past," an old Hopi told him patiently, "can't you *feel* the difference in the air?" (Saul, Barney, and Markoff Chaney were racing toward Las Vegas in the rented Bron-

tosaurus, while Dillinger was leisurely driving back toward
Los Angeles.) In Honolulu, as the clocks struck nine the
previous evening, Buckminster Fuller, trotting between airplanes, suddenly caught a glimpse of a new geodesic structure fully incorporating omnidirectional halo . . . And, after a four-hour flight eastward, landing in Tokyo at the
"same time" he left Honolulu, he had a detailed sketch finished (it looked somewhat fan-shaped) as the NO SMOKING
FASTEN SEAT BELT sign flashed. (It was four A.M. in Los
Angeles, and Dillinger, safely home—he thought—heard
the gunfire dying out in the distance. The President must already be withdrawing the National Guard. at least in part,
he thought.) The phone by Rebecca's bed rang just then,
eight o'clock New York time, and she answered it to hear
Molly Muldoon shout excitedly, "Saul and Barney are on
TV. Turn it on—they've saved the country!"

In Las Vegas, Barney blinked under the TV lights and
stared woodenly into the camera, while Saul kept his eyes
on the interviewer and spoke in his kindly-family-doctor
persona.

"Would you tell our viewers, Inspector Goodman, how
you happened to be looking in Lehman Caves for the missing man?" The interviewer had the professional tone of all
TV newscasters; his intonation wouldn't have changed if
he'd been asking "And why did you find our sponsor's
product more satisfactory?" or "How did you feel when
you learned you had brain cancer?"

"Psychology," Saul pronounced gravely. "The suspect
was a procurer. That's a definite psychological type, just as
a safecracker, a bank robber, a child molester, and a policeman are definite types. I tried to think and feel like a procurer. What would such a man do with the whole government looking for him? Attempt an escape to Mexico or
somewhere else? Never—that's a bank-robber reaction.
Procurers are not people who take risks or make bold
moves against the odds. What would a procurer do? He
would look for a hole to hide in."

"The FBI crime lab definitely confirms that the man
Inspector Goodman found is the missing plague-carrier,
Carmel," the interviewer threw in. (He had orders to repeat
this every two minutes.) "Tell me, Inspector, why wouldn't
such a man hide in, say, an empty house, or a secluded cabin in the mountains?"

"He wouldn't travel far," Saul explained. "He'd be too paranoid—seeing police officers everywhere he went. And his imagination would vastly exaggerate the actual power of the government. There is only one law enforcement agent to each four hundred citizens in this country, but he would imagine the proportion reversed. The most secluded cabin would be too nerve-wracking for him. He'd imagine hordes of National Guardsmen and law officers of all sorts searching every square foot of woods in America. He really would. Procurers are very ordinary men, compared to hardened criminals. They think like ordinary people in most ways. The ordinary man and woman never commits a crime because they have the same exaggerated idea of our omnipotence." Saul's tone was neutral, descriptive, but in New York Rebecca's heart skipped a beat: This was the new Saul talking, the one who was no longer on the side of law and order.

"So you just asked yourself, where's a good-sized hole near Las Vegas?"

"That was all there was to it, yes."

"The American people will certainly be grateful to you. And how did it happen that you got involved in this case? You're with the New York Police Department, aren't you?"

How will he answer that one? Rebecca wondered; just then the phone rang.

Turning down the TV sound, she lifted the phone and said, "Yes?"

"I can tell by your voice you're the kind of woman who *fully meets the criteria of my value system*," said August Personage. "I want to lick your ass and your pussy and have you piss on me and—"

"Well, that's a most amazing story, Inspector Goodman," the interviewer was saying. *Oh, hell,* Rebecca thought. Saul's expression was so sincere that she knew he had just told one of the most outrageous lies of his life.

The phone rang again. With a pounce Rebecca grabbed it and shouted, "Listen, you creep, if you keep calling me—"

"That's no way to talk to a man who just saved the world," Saul's voice said mildly.

"Saul! But you're on television—"

"They videotaped that a half-hour ago. I'm at the Las Vegas Airport, about to take a jet to Washington. I'm having a conference with the President."

"My God. What are you going to tell him?"

"As much," Saul pronounced, "as an asshole like him can understand."

(In Los Angeles, Dr. Vulcan Troll watched the seismograph move upward to Grade 2. That still wasn't serious, but he scratched a note to the graduate student who would soon be replacing him. "If this jumps to 3, call me at my house." Then he drove home, passing Dillinger's bungalow, humming happily, thankful that the rioting was ending and the Guard being withdrawn. At the lab the graduate student, reading a paperback titled *Carnal Orgy*, didn't notice when the graph jumped past 3 and hit 4.)

Danny Pricefixer, waking in Ingolstadt, glanced at his wristwatch. Noon. *My God*, he thought; sleeping so late was a major sin in his system of morality. Then he remembered a little of last night, and smiled contentedly, turning in the bed to kiss Lady Velkor's neck. A huge black arm hung over the other shoulder, and a black hand, limp in sleep, held her breast. "My *God!*" Danny said out loud, remembering more, as Clark Kent sat up groggily and stared at him.

("Smiling Jim" Treponema, at that moment, was navigating a very dangerous pass in the mountains of Northern California. Strapped to his back was a 6mm Remington Model 700 Bolt Action rifle with 6-power Bushnell telescope; a canteen of whiskey was hooked to one side of his belt, and a canteen of water to the other. He was perspiring from labor, in spite of the altitude, but he was one of the few happy people in the country, since he had been nowhere near a radio for three days and had missed the whole terror connected with Anthrax Leprosy Pi plague, the declaration of martial law, and the rioting and bombings. He was on his yearly vacation, free from the sewer of smut in which he was submerged forty-nine weeks of the year—the foulness and filth in which he heroically struggled daily, risking his soul for the good of his fellow citizens—and he was breathing clean air and thinking clean thoughts. Specifically, as an avid hunter, he had read that only one American eagle still survived, and he was determined to be immortalized in hunting literature as the man who killed it. He knew well, of course, how ecologists and conservationists would regard that achievement, but their opinions didn't bother him. A bunch of fags, commies, and smut-nuts: That was his estimate of those bleeding-heart types. Probably smoked dope, too. Not a man's man among them. He shifted his rifle, which was pressing his sweat-soaked shirt uncomfortably, and climbed onward and upward.)

Mama Sutra stared at the central Tarot card in the Tree of Life: It was The Fool.

"Pardon me," the little Italian tree said.

"This is getting ridiculous," Fission Chips muttered. "I don't intend to spend the rest of my life in conversation with trees."

"I'm a tree worth talking to," the dark-skinned tree with her hair in a bun persisted.

He squinted. "I know what you are," he said finally, "half tree and half woman. *Ergo,* a dryad. Benefit of classical education."

"Very good," said the dryad. "But when you stop tripping, you're going to crash. You'll remember London and your job, and you'll wonder how you're going to explain the last month to them."

"Somebody stole a month from me," Chips agreed pleasantly. "A cynical old swine named the Dealy Lama. Or another feller named Toad. Bad lot. Shouldn't go around stealing months."

The tree handed him an envelope. "Try not to lose that," she said. "It'll make everybody in your office so happy that they'll accept any story you make up to explain how it took you a month to get it."

"What is it?"

"The name of every BUGGER agent in the British government. Together with the false names they use for the bank accounts where they keep all the money they can't account for. And the account numbers and the names of the banks, too. In one nice package. All it needs is a red ribbon."

"I think my leg is being pulled again," said Chips. But he was coming down, and he opened the envelope and peered at the contents. "This is real?" he asked.

"They won't be able to account for the money," the tree assured him. "Some very interesting confessions will be obtained."

"Who the devil are you?" Chips asked, seeing a teen-age Italian girl and not a tree.

"I'm your holy guardian angel," she said.

"You look like an angel," Chips admitted grudgingly, "but I don't believe any of this. Time travel, talking trees, giant toads, none of it. Somebody slipped me a drug."

"Yes, somebody slipped you a drug. But I'm your holy guardian angel, and I'm slipping you this envelope, and it'll make everything all right back in London. All you have to do is make up a halfway reasonable lie . . ."

"I was held prisoner in a BUGGER dungeon with a beautiful Eurasian love-slave," Chips began improvising.

"Very good," she said. "They won't believe it, but they'll think you believe it. That's good enough."

"Who are you really?"

But the tree only repeated, "Don't lose that envelope," and walked away, turning into an Italian teen-ager again, and then into a gigantic woman carrying a golden apple.

Hauptmann, chief of field operations for the Federal Republic of Germany's police, looked around the Fuehrer Suite in disgust. He had arrived from Bonn and headed straight for the Donau-Hotel, determined to make some sense of the scandals, tragedies, and mysteries of the previous night. The first suspect he grilled was *Freiherr* Hagbard Celine, sinister jet-set millionaire, who had come to the rock festival with a large entourage. Celine and Hauptmann talked quietly in one corner of the suite of the Donau-Hotel, while the cameras of police photographers clicked away behind them.

Hauptmann was tall and thin, with close-cropped silver-gray hair, long, vulpine features, and piercing eyes. "Dreadful tragedy, the death of your President last night," he said. "My condolences. Also for the unhappy state of affairs in your country." Actually, Hauptmann was delighted to see the United States of America falling into chaos. He had been fifteen at the end of World War II, had been called to the colors as the Allies advanced on German soil, and had seen his country overrun by American troops. All of this made a deeper and more lasting impression on him than the U.S.–West German cooperation that developed later.

"Not *my* president, not *my* country," said Hagbard quickly. "I was born in Norway. I lived in the U.S. for quite some time, and did become a citizen for a while, when I was much younger than I am now. But I renounced my American citizenship years ago."

"I see," said Hauptmann, trying unsuccessfully to conceal his distaste for Hagbard's indistinct sense of national identity. "And what country today has the honor of claiming you as a citizen?"

Smiling, Hagbard reached for the inside pocket of the brass-buttoned navy-blue yachtsman's blazer he had worn for the occasion. He handed his passport to Hauptmann, who took it and grunted with surprise.

"Equatorial Guinea." He looked up, frowning. "Fernando Poo!"

"Quite so," said Hagbard, a white-toothed grin breaking through his dark features. "I will accept your expression of sympathy for the sad state of affairs in *that* country."

Hauptmann's dislike of this Latin plutocrat grew deeper. The man was undoubtedly one of those unprincipled international adventurers who carried citizenship the way many freighters carried Panamanian registry. Celine's wealth was probably equal to or greater than the total wealth of Equatorial Guinea. Yet it was likely that he had done nothing for his adopted country other than bribe a few officials to obtain the citizenship. Equatorial Guinea had split asunder, nearly plunging the world into a third and final war, and yet here was this parasitical Mediterranean fop, driving to a rock festival in a Bugatti Royale with a host of drones, yes-men, flunkies, minions, whores, dope fiends, and all-round social liabilities. Disgusting!

Hagbard looked around. "This room is a pretty foul place to have a conversation. How can you stand that smell? It's nauseating me."

Pleased to be causing some discomfort to this man, whom he disliked more and more as he got to know him, Hauptmann settled back in the red armchair, his teeth bared in a smile. "You will forgive me, *Freiherr* Celine, I find it necessary to be here at this time and also necessary to talk to you. However, I would have thought this peculiar odor of fish would not be unpleasant to you. Perhaps your nautical dress has led me astray."

Hagbard shrugged. "I am a seaman of sorts. But just because a man likes the sea doesn't mean he wants to sit next to a ton of dead mackerel. What do you think it is, anyway?"

"I have no idea. I was hoping you could identify it for me."

"Just dead fish, that's all it smells like to me. I'm afraid you may be expecting more from me all around than I can possibly provide. I suppose you think I can tell you a lot about last night. Just what are you trying to find out?"

"First of all, I want to find out what actually happened. What we have, I think, is a case of drug abuse on a colossal scale. And we—the Western world in general—have had too many of those in recent years. Apparently there is not a single person who was present at this festival who did not partake of some of this soft drink dosed with LSD."

"Treat every man to his dessert and none should 'scape tripping," said Hagbard.

"I beg your pardon?"

"I was parodying Shakespeare," said Hagbard. "But it's not very relevant. Please go on."

"Well, so far no one has been able to give me a coherent or plausible account of the evening's events," said Hauptmann. "There have been at least twenty-seven deaths that I'm fairly sure of. There has been massive abuse of LSD. There are numerous accounts of pistol, rifle, and machine-gun fire somewhere on the shore of the lake. A number of witnesses say they saw many men in Nazi uniforms running around in the woods. If that wasn't a hallucination, dressing as a Nazi is a serious crime in the Federal Republic of Germany. So far we have managed to keep much of this out of the papers by holding the press people who came here incommunicado, but we will have to determine precisely what crimes were committed and who committed them, and we must prosecute them vigorously. Otherwise, we will appear to the whole world as a nation incapable of dealing with the wholesale corruption of youth within our borders."

"All nations are wholesale corruptors of youth," said Hagbard. "I wouldn't worry about it."

Hauptmann grunted, seeing in his mind's eye a vision of drug-crazed masqueraders in Nazi uniforms and himself in a German army uniform over thirty years ago at the age of fifteen and understanding very well what Hagbard meant. "I have my job to do," he said sullenly.

See how much more pleasant the world is now that the Saures are gone, the Dealy Lama flashed into his brain. Hagbard kept a poker face.

Hauptmann went on, "Your own role in the incident seems to have been a constructive one, *Freiherr* Celine. You are described as going to the stage when the hysteria and the hallucinating had reached some sort of a climax and making a speech which greatly calmed the audience."

Hagbard laughed. "I have no idea at all what I said. You know what I thought? I thought I was Moses and they were the Israelites and I was leading them across the Red Sea while the Pharaoh's army, intent on slaughtering them, pursued."

"The only Israelites present last night seemed to have fared rather badly. You're not Jewish yourself, are you, *Freiherr* Celine?"

"I'm not religious at all. Why do you ask?"

"I thought that then, perhaps, you could shed some light on the scene we find here in these rooms. Well, no matter for the moment. It is interesting that you thought you led them across the lake. In fact, this morning, when the police reserves entered the area, they found most of the young people wandering around on the shore of the lake opposite the festival."

"Well, perhaps we all marched around it while we thought we were going across it," said Hagbard. "By the way, didn't you have any men at the festival at all? If you did, they should be able to tell you something."

"We had a few plainclothes agents there, and they could tell me nothing. All but one had unknowingly taken the LSD, and the one who didn't must have been hallucinating too, from some kind of psychological contagion. He saw the Nazis, a glowing woman a hundred feet tall, a bridge across the lake. Sheer garbage. As you doubtless noticed, there were no uniformed police there. Arrangements were made—and sanctioned at the highest level of government —to leave policing at the festival to its management. It was felt that, given the attitudes of youth today, official police would not be effective in handling the huge crowd. I might say, in my own opinion, I consider that a cowardly decision. But I'm not a politician, thank God. As a result of that decision, order-keeping at the festival was ultimately in the hands of people like yourself who happened to be inspired to do something about the situation. And were themselves hampered, as involuntary victims of LSD."

"Well," said Hagbard, "in order to fully understand what happened, you have to realize that many people there probably welcomed an acid trip. Many must have brought their own acid and taken it. I, personally, have had a great deal of experience with LSD. A man of my wide-ranging interests, you understand, feels obligated to try everything once. I was taking acid back when it was still legal everywhere in the world."

"Of course," said Hauptmann sourly.

Hagbard looked around the room and said, "Have you considered the possibility that these men, old as they are, might have unknowingly imbibed LSD and suffered heart failure or some such thing?"

There were twenty-three dead men in the suite. Thirteen were in the large parlor where Hagbard and Hauptman were sitting. The dead men, too, were seated, in various attitudes of total collapse, some with their heads lolling back, others bent forward at the waist, heads hanging between their knees, knuckles resting on the floor. There were nine more old men in the bedroom, and one in the bathroom. Most of them were white-haired; several were completely bald. Not one could have been under eighty years of age, and several appeared to be over ninety. The man in the bathroom had been caught by death in the embarrassing position of sitting on the toilet with his pants down. This was the old gentleman with the white mustache and the unruly forelock who had spoken harshly to George in the lobby the night before last.

Hauptmann shook his head. "I'm afraid it will be no easy task to find out what happened to these men. They all seem to have died at about the same moment. There are no observable traces of poison, no signs of struggle or pain, except for the expression around the eyes. All of their eyes are open, and they appear to be looking at some unguessable horror."

"Do you have any idea who they are? Why did you say I might have been able to help if I were Jewish?"

"We have found their passports. They are all Israeli citizens. That in itself is quite odd. Generally, Jews that old do not care to come to this country, for obvious reasons. However, there was an organization connected with the Zionist movement founded here in Ingolstadt on May 1, 1776. These elders of Zion might have assembled here to celebrate the anniversary."

"Oh, yes," said Hagbard. "The Illuminati of Bavaria, wasn't it? I remember hearing about them when we first arrived here."

"The organization was founded by an unfrocked Jesuit, and its membership consisted of freemasons, freethinkers, and Jews. There were also some famous names in politics and the arts: King Leopold, Goethe, Beethoven."

"And this organization was behind the Zionist movement, you say?"

Hauptmann brushed away the suggestion with long, slender fingers. "I did not say they were *behind* anything. There are always those who think that every political or criminal phenomenon must have something behind it. There is always a conspiracy that explains everything. That is unscientific. If you wish to understand events, you must analyze the masses of the people and the economic, cultural, and social conditions in which they live. Zionism was a logical development out of the situation of the Jews during the last hundred years. One need not imagine some group of illuminated ones thinking it up and promulgating the movement for devious reasons of their own. The Jews were in a wretched condition in many places—they needed somewhere to go—a child could have seen that Palestine was an attractive possibility."

"Well," said Hagbard, "if the Illuminati are of no importance in the history of Israel, what are these twenty-three old Israelis doing here on the day of the organization's founding?"

"Perhaps *they* thought the Illuminati were important. Perhaps they themselves were members. I shall make inquiries to Israel about their identities. Relatives will probably claim the bodies. Otherwise, the German government will see that they are buried in Ingolstadt Jewish cemetery with proper rabbinical ceremonies. The government is very solicitous of Jewish persons. Nowadays."

"Maybe they were freethinkers," said Hagbard. "Maybe they wouldn't like being buried with religious ceremonies."

"The question is wearisome and unimportant," said Hauptmann. "We shall consult the Israeli government and do as it suggests." An elderly waiter knocked and was admitted by one of Hauptmann's men. He pushed a serving cart bearing a magnificent silver coffee urn, cups, and a tray full of pastries. Before serving anyone else, he rolled the cart across the thick carpet to Hauptmann and Hagbard. His rheumy eyes studiously avoided the bodies scattered around the suite. He poured out coffee for both men.

"Lots of cream and sugar," said Hagbard.

"Black for me," said Hauptmann, picking up a pastry with cherry filling and biting into it with relish.

"How do you know somebody hasn't dosed the coffee or the pastry with LSD?" said Hagbard, smiling mischievously.

Hauptmann brushed his hand over his hair and smiled back. "Because I would put this hotel out of business if I were served food tainted in any way, and they know it. They will take the utmost precautions."

"Now that we're being a little more sociable and drinking coffee together," said Hagbard, "let me ask you a favor. Turn me loose today. I have interests to look after in the U.S., and I'd like to be leaving."

"You were originally planning to stay for the entire week. Now, suddenly, you have to leave at once. I don't understand."

"I was planning to stay, but that was before most of the U.S. government got wiped out. Also, since the remainder of the festival is being called off, there's no reason to stay. I'm still not clear on that, however. Why is the festival being called off? Whose idea is it, and what are the reasons?"

Hauptmann stared down his long nose at Hagbard and took another bite of the pastry, while Hagbard wondered how the man could eat in the midst of this awful smell. He could understand how a detective would not be bothered by the presence of the dead, but the fishy smell was something else again.

"To begin with, *Freiherr* Celine, there is the disappearance and possible death by drowning of the four members of the Saure family, known as the American Medical Association. Accounts of what happened to them are garbled, fantastic, and contradictory, as are those of every other incident that occurred last night. As I reconstruct it, they drove their car straight into the lake."

"From which side?"

Hauptmann shrugged. "It hardly matters. The lake is virtually bottomless. If they're in there, I doubt that we will ever find them. They must have been under the influence of LSD, and *they* certainly weren't used to it." He looked accusingly at Hagbard. "They were so *clean-cut*. Absolutely the hope of the future. And the car was a national relic. A great loss."

"Were they the only well-known casulaties?"

"Who can say? We have no accurate record of who was attending the festival. No list was kept of those who bought tickets, as should have been done. A thousand young men and women could have drowned themselves in that lake and we wouldn't know about it. In any case, the Saures, as you may not know, were the moving spirits behind the Ingolstadt festival. Very patriotic. They wished to do something to promote tourism to Germany, particularly of Bavaria, since they were native Bavarians."

"Yes," said Hagbard, "I read that Ingolstadt was their home town."

Hauptmann shook his head. "Their press agent gave that out when the festival was conceived. Actually, they were born in northern Bavaria, in Wolframs-Eschenbach. It is the birthplace of another famous German musician, the *Minnesinger* Wolfram von Eschenbach, who wrote *Parzival*. Well, now they are gone, barring a miracle, and no one else seems to be in charge. Without them the festival is simply collapsing, like a headless body. Furthermore, the government wants the festival shut down because we don't want a repetition of last night. LSD is still illegal in West Germany, unlike the U.S."

"There are parts of the U.S. where it's still illegal," said Hagbard. "It's not illegal in Equatorial Guinea, because we've just never had a drug problem there."

"Since you are an ethusiastic citizen of Equatorial Guinea, I am sure that delights you," said Hauptmann. "Well, *Freiherr* Celine, I would like to release you immediately, but when I've pieced together more of last night's events I shall have more questions for you. I must ask you to stay in the Ingolstadt area."

Hagbard stood up. "If you'll agree not to have me tailed or guarded, I'll give you my word that I'll stick around."

Hauptmann smiled thinly. "Your word won't be necessary. Every road is blocked; no planes are permitted to take off or land at Ingolstadt Aerodrome. You can have the run of the town, the lake, and the festival area, and you will not be disturbed."

Hagbard left at the same time the old waiter did. The waiter bowed Hagbard out the door and when it closed behind him said, "A great shame."

"Well," said Hagbard, "they were all in their eighties. That's a good age to die."

The waiter laughed. "I am seventy-five, and I do not think any age is a good age to die. But that is not what I was referring to. Perhaps *mein herr* did not notice the fish-tank in the room. It was broken, and the fish were spilled all the floor. I have taken care of that tank for over twenty years. It was a fine collection of rare tropical fish. Even Egyptian mouth-breeders. Now they are all dead. So it goes."

Hagbard wanted to ask the waiter what an Egyptian mouth-breeder was, but the old man suddenly nodded, pushed open a doorway to a service room, and disappeared.

Danny Pricefixer was wandering around in the dark with Lady Velkor and Clark Kent, feeling absolutely wonderful, when Miss Portinari intercepted him. "This will interest you," she said, handing him an envelope similar to the one she had handed Fission Chips.

"What is it?" he asked, seeing her as a Greek woman in classic robes holding a golden apple.

"Take a look."

He opened the envelope and found a picture of Tobias Knight and Zev Hirsch, in the middle of the *Confrontation* office, setting the timer on the bomb.

"This man," she said, pointing to Knight, "is willing to turn State's evidence. Against both Hirsch and Atlanta Hope. You've wanted to nab them for a long time, haven't you?"

"Who are you?" Danny asked, staring.

"I am the one Mama Sutra told you of, the one appointed to contact you here in Ingolstadt. I am of the Illuminated."

("What are those two talking about?" Clark Kent asked Lady Velkor. "Who knows?" she shrugged. "They're both tripping.")

"God's Lightning is the most active front in America today for the Cult of the Yellow Sign," Miss Portinari went on, Telling the Mark the Tale . . . A few feet away, Joe Malik said to Hagbard, "I don't like frame-ups. Even for people like Hirsch and Hope."

"You suspect us of unethical behavior?" Hagbard asked innocently.

(Pat Walsh is dialing a phone.)

"I don't believe in jails," Joe said bluntly. "I don't think Atlanta and Zev will be any better when they get out. They'll be worse."

"You can be sure the Illuminati will protect you," Miss Portinari concluded gravely. Danny Pricefixer continued staring at her.

The phone is ringing far away, dragging me back to a body, a self, a purpose, shattering my memories of being the Ringmaster. I sit up and lift the receiver. "Hirsch," I say.

"My name is Pat Walsh," a woman's voice says. "I speak for Atlanta herself. The pass word is Theleme."

"Go ahead," I say hoarsely, wondering if it's about that peacenik professor we killed at UN plaza on April 1.

"You're being framed for a bombing," she said. "You have to go into hiding."

Hagbard laughed. "Atlanta isn't returning to the States. She's been a double agent for over two years. Working for me." (I found the warehouse door the Walsh woman described. It was open, as she had promised, and I wondered about the name on it, Gold & Appel Transfers . . .) "So is Tobias Knight, and he'll cop a plea. It's all been carefully planned, Joe. You only thought bombing your own office was *your* idea."

"How about Zev Hirsch?" Joe asked.

"He's having some very educational experiences about this time in New York City," Hagbard replied. "*I* don't believe in jails, either."

And I am trapped, the three of them surround me, and Jubela demands, "Tell us the Word," Jubelo repeats, "Tell us the Word," and Jubelum unsheathes the sword, "Tell us the Word, Zev Hirsch . . ."

"A bombing in New York?" the President asked shrewdly, trying to look as tough as his predecessor.

"Yes," Saul went on. "As soon as the link with God's Lightning was clear to us, Barney and I took off for Las Vegas. You can understand why."

The President didn't understand any of this, but wasn't about to admit that. "You headed for Las Vegas?" he asked shrewdly, trying to look as tough as his predecessor.

"Yes," Saul said sincerely. "As soon as we found out about Anthrax Leprosy Pi and Dr. Mocenigo's death, we realized the same organization must be implicated. God's Lightning—"

"God's Lightning?" the President asked shrewdly, remembering earlier years when he had been a guest speaker at their rallies.

"And the secret group that has infiltrated them and taken them over, the Cult of the Yellow Sign. We have reason to believe that an English intelligence agent named Chips will be arriving in London in a few hours with evidence against most of the Yellow Sign operatives within their government. You see, sir, this is an international conspiracy."

"An international conspiracy?" the President asked shrewdly.

And in Central Park our old friend Perri hops from tree to ground, snatches a nut thrown by August Personage, and quickly runs around the tree three times in case this friend-possibly-enemy produces a gun and starts blasting . . .

While far above the highest mountains in California another aspect of my consciousness soars like winged poetry: and knows, somehow, more about what is coming than Dr. Troll's seismograph: for I am the last, truly the last. The ecologists are right: mine is not merely an endangered but nearly an extinct species, and my senses have been sharpened beyond instinct by these last years. I circle around, I circle around, I soar: I bank: I float. I am, rare moment for me! not thinking about fish, for my belly is full at present. I circle around, circle around, thinking only about the soaring, the freedom, and, more vaguely, about the bad vibes coming up from below. Must you have a name? Call me Hali One, then: haliaeetus leucocephalus the last: symbol once of imperial Rome and now of imperial America: of which I neither know nor care, for all I know is the freedom of my estate and about that the Romans and the Americans have never had aught but the most confused and distorted ideas. Wearing my long green feathers I circle around. I am Hali One and I scream, not with rage or with fear or with anger; I scream with ecstasy, the terrible joy of my very existence, and the scream echoes from mountain to mountain to another mountain, resonating onward and onward, a sound that only another of my species could understand, and none are left to hear it. But still I scream: the shriek of Shiva the Destroyer, true face of Vishnu the Preserver and Brahma the Creator: for my scream is not of life

or death but of life-in-death, and I am equally contemp-
tuous of Perri and of August Personage, of squirrels and of
men, and of all lesser birds who cannot ascend to my height
and know the agony and supremacy of my freedom.

No—because they broke Billie Freshette slow and ugly
and they broke Marilyn Monroe fast and bright like lightning They broke Daddy and they broke Mama but shit like
I mean it this time they ain't going to break me No even if
it's greater with Simon than with any other man even if he
knows more than any other man I've had No it can't be
him and it can't even be Hagbard who seems to be the king
of the circus the very Ringmaster and keeper of the final
secret No it can't be any man and it most certainly by Jesus
and by Christ it can't be going back to Mister Charlie's police force No it's dark like my own skin and dark like the
destiny they've inflicted on me because of my skin but
whatever it is I can only find it alone God the time that rat
bit me while I was sleeping Daddy screaming until he was
almost crying "I'll kill the fucking landlord I'll kill the
motherfucker I'll cut his white heart out" until Mama finally calmed him No he died a little then No it would have
been better if he had killed the landlord No even if they
caught him and they would have caught him No even if he
died in the goddam electric chair and we went on welfare
No a man shouldn't let that happen to his children he
shouldn't be realistic and practical No no matter how good
it is no matter how wonderful the come it will always be
there in the back of my head that Simon is white No white
radical white revolutionary white lover it doesn't matter it
still comes up white and it's not acid and it's not a mood I
mean shit you have to decide sooner or later Are you on
somebody else's trip or are you on your own No and I can't
join God's Lightning or even what's left of the old Women's
Lib I mean shit that poetry Simon quoted is all wrong No
it's not true that no man is an island No the truth is every
man is an island and especially every woman is an island
and even more every black woman is an island

On August 23, 1928, Rancid, the butler in the Drake
Mansion on old Beacon Hill, reported a rather distressing
fact to his employer. "Good Lord Harry," old Drake cried
at first, "is he turning Papist now?" His second question
was less rhetorical: "You're absolutely sure?"

"There is no doubt," Rancid replied. "The maids showed me the socks, sir. And the shoes."

That night there was a rather strangulated attempt at conversation in the mansion's old library.

"Are you going back to Harvard?"

"Not yet."

"Are you at least going to try another damned alienist?"

"They call themselves psychiatrists these days, Father. I don't think so."

"Dammit, Robert, what *did* happen in the war?"

"Many things. They all made profits for our bank, though, so don't worry about them."

"Are you turning Red?"

"I see no profit there. The State of Massachusetts killed two innocent men today for holding opinions of that sort."

"Innocent my Aunt Fanny. Robert, I know the judge personally—"

"And he believes what the friend of a banker should believe."

There was a long pause, and old Drake crushed out a cigar he had hardly started.

"Robert, you *know* you're sick."

"Yes."

"What is this latest thing—glass and nails in your shoes? Your mother would die if she knew."

There was another silence. Robert Putney Drake finally answered, lanquidly, "It was an experiment. A phase. The Sioux Indians do much worse to themselves in the Sun Dance. So do lots of chaps in Spanish monasteries, and in India, among other places. It's not the answer."

"It's really finished?"

"Oh, yes. Quite. I'm trying something else."

"Something to hurt yourself again?"

"No, nothing to hurt myself."

"Well, then, I'm glad to hear that. But I do wish you would go to another alienist, or psychiatrist, or whatever they call themselves." Another pause. "You *can* pull yourself together, you know. Play the man, Robert. Play the man."

Old Drake was satisfied. He had talked turkey to the boy; he had performed his fatherly duty. Besides, the private detectives assured him that the Red Business really was trivial: The lad had been to several anarchist and Communist meetings, but his comments had been uniformly aloof and cynical.

It was nearly a year later when the really bad news from the private investigators arrived.

"How much will the girl take to keep her mouth shut?" old Drake asked immediately.

"After we pay hospital expenses, maybe a thousand more," the man from Pinkerton's said.

"Offer her five hundred," the old man replied. "Go up to a thousand only if you have to."

"I said maybe a thousand," the detective said bluntly. "He used a special kind of whip, one with twisted nails in the ends. She might want two or three thou."

"She's only a common whore. They're used to this sort of thing."

"Not to this extent." The detective was losing his deferential tone. "The photos of her back, and her buttocks especially, didn't bother me much. But that's because I'm in this business and I've seen a lot. An average jury would vomit, Mr. Drake. In court—"

"In court," old Drake pronounced, "she would come before a judge who belongs to several of my clubs and has investments in my bank. Offer five hundred."

Two months thereafter, the stock market crashed and New York millionaires began leaping from high windows onto hard streets. Old Drake, the next day, ran into his son begging on the street near the Old Granary cemetery. The boy was wearing old clothes from a secondhand store.

"It's not that bad, son. We'll pull through."

"Oh, I know that. You'll come out ahead, in fact, if I'm any judge of character."

"Then what the hell is this disgraceful damned foolishness?"

"Experience. I'm breaking out of a trap."

The old man fumed all the way back to the bank. That evening he decided it was time for another open and honest discussion; when he went to Robert's room, however, he found the boy thoroughly trussed up in chains and quite purple in the face.

"God! Damn! Son! What is *this?*"

The boy—who was twenty-seven and, in some respects, more sophisticated than his father—grinned and relaxed.

The purple faded from his face. "One of Houdini's escapes," he explained simply.

"You intend to become a stage magician? My *God!*"

"Not at all. I'm breaking out of another trap—the one that says nobody but Houdini can do these things."

Old Drake, to do him justice, hadn't acquired his wealth without some shrewdness concerning human peculiarities. "I begin to see," he said heavily. "Pain is a trap. That was why you put the broken glass in your shoes that time. Fear of poverty is a trap. That's why you tried begging on the streets. You're trying to become a Superman, like those crazy boys in Chicago, the 'thrill killers.' What you did to that whore last year was part of all this. What else have you done?"

"A lot." Robert shrugged. "Enough to be canonized as a saint, or to be burnt as a diabolist. None of it seems to add up, though. I still haven't found the way." He suddenly made a new effort, and the chains slipped to the floor. "Simple yoga and muscle control," he said without pride. "The chains in the mind are much harder. I wish there were a chemical, a key to the nervous system . . ."

"Robert," said old Drake, "you are going back to an alienist. I'll have you committed if you won't go voluntarily."

And so Dr. Faustus Unbewusst acquired a new patient, at a time when many of his most profitable cases were discontinuing therapy because of the monetary depression. He made very few notes on Robert, but these were subsequently found by an Illuminati operative, photostated, and placed in the archives at Agharti, where Hagbard Celine read them in 1965. They were undated, and scrawled in a hurried hand—Dr. Unbewusst, in reaction-formation against his own anal component, was a conspicuously untidy and careless person—but they told a fairly straightforward story:

RPD, age 27, latent homo. Father rich as Croesus. Five sessions per week @ $50 each, $250. Keep him in therapy 5 yrs that's a clear $65,000. Be ambitious, aim for ten years. $130,000. Beautiful.

RPD not latent homo at all. Advanced psychopath. Moral imbecile. Actually enjoys the money I'm soaking his father. Hopeless case. All drives ego-syntonic. Bastard doesn't give a fuck. Maybe as long as 12 yrs.? $156,000. *Hot shit!*

RPD back on sadism again. Thinks that's the key. Must use great care. If he gets caught at something serious, jail or a sanitorium; and can kiss that $156,000 good-bye. Maybe use drugs to calm him?

RPD in another schizo mood today. Full of some crap a gypsy fortune-teller told him. Extreme care needed: If the occultists get him, that's 13 grand per year out the window.

Clue to RPD: All goes back to the war. Can't stand the thought that all must die. Metaphysical hangup. Nothing I can do. If only there were an immortality pill. Risk of losing him to the occultists or even a church worse than I feared. I can feel the 13 grand slipping away.

RPD wants to go to Europe. Wants meeting, maybe therapy, with that *sheissdreck dummkopf* Carl Jung. Must warn parents too sick to travel.

RPD gone after only 10 months. A lousy 11-grand case. Too angry to see patients today. Spent morning drafting letter to *Globe* on why fortune-tellers should be forbidden by law. If I could get my hands on that woman, on her fat throat, the bitch, the fat stinking ignorant bitch. $156,000. Down the drain. Because he needs immortality and doesn't know how to get it.

(In Ingolstadt, Danny Pricefixer and Clark Kent are still staring at each other over Lady Velkor's sleeping body when Atlanta Hope bursts into the room, fresh from a shower, and throws herself on the bed, hugging and kissing everybody. "It was the first time," she cries. "The first time I ever really made it! It took all three of you." On the other side of Kent, Lady Velkor opens an eye and says, "Don't I get any credit? It takes Five that way, remember?")

Mama Sutra was only thirty then, but she streaked her hair with gray to fit the image of the Wise Woman. She recognized Drake as soon as he wandered into the tea parlor: old Drake's son, the crazy one, loaded.

He motioned to her before the waitress could take his order. Mama Sutra, quick to pick up clues, could tell from his suit's wrinkles that he had been lying down; Boston Common is a long walk from Beacon Hill; there were shrinks in the neighborhood; ergo, he hadn't come from home but from a therapy session.

"Tea leaves or cards?" she asked courteously, sitting across from him at the table.

"Cards," he said absently, looking down from the window to the Common. "Coffee," he added to the waitress. "Black as sin."

"Were you listening to the preachers down there?" Mama Sutra asked shrewdly.

"Yes." He grinned, engagingly. " 'He that believeth shall never taste death.' They're in rare form today."

"Shuffle," she said, handing the cards over. "But they awakened some spiritual need in you, my son. That's why you came up here."

He met her eye cynically. "I'm willing to try any kind of witchcraft once. I just came from a practitioner of the latest variety, just off the boat from Vienna a few years."

Bull's-eye, she thought.

"Neither his science nor their unenlightened faith can help you," Mama said somberly, ignoring his cynicism. "Let us hope that the cards will show the way." She dealt a traditional Tree of Life.

At the crown was Death upside-down, and below it were the King of Swords in Chokmah and the Knight of Wands in Binah. "He that believeth shall never taste death," he had quoted cynically.

"I see a battlefield," she began; it was common Boston gossip that Drake first started acting odd after the war. "I see Death come very close to you and then miss you." She pointed to the reverse Death card with a dramatic finger. "But many died, many that you cared for deeply."

"I liked a few of them," he said grudgingly. "Mostly I was worried about my own a—my own hide. But go ahead."

She looked at the Knight of Wands in the Binah position. Should she mention the bisexuality implied? He was going to a shrink, and might be able to take it. Mama tried to hold the Knight of Wands and King of Swords together in her focus, and the way became clear. "There are two men in you. One loves other men, perhaps too much. The other is desperately trying to free himself from all of humanity, even from the world. You're a Leo," she added suddenly, taking a leap.

"Yes," he said, unimpressed. "August 6." He was thinking that she had probably looked up the birthdates of all the richer individuals in town in case they ever wandered in.

"It's very hard for Leos to accept death," she said sadly. "You are like Buddha after he saw the corpse on the road. No matter what you have or own, no matter what you achieve, it will never be enough, for you saw too many corpses in the war. Ah, my son, would that I could help you! But I only read cards; I am no alchemist who sells the Elixir of Eternal Life." While he was digesting that one—a sure hit, she felt—Mama rushed on to examine the Five of Wands reversed in Chesed and the Magus upright in Geburah. "So many wands," she said. "So many fire signs. A true Leo, but so much of it turned inward. See how the energetic Knight of Wands descends to the Five upside-down: All your energies, and Leos are very powerful, are turned against yourself. You are a burning man, trying to consume yourself and be reborn. And the Magus, who shows the way, is below the King of Swords and dominated by him: Your reason won't allow you to accept the necessity of the fire. You are still rebelling against Death." The Fool was in Tipareth and, surprisingly, upright. "But you are very close to taking the final step. You are ready to let the fire consume even your intellect and die to this world." This was going swimmingly, she thought—and then she saw the Devil in Netzach and the Nine of Swords reversed in Yod. The rest of the Tree was even worse: the Tower in Yesod and the Lovers reversed (of course!) in Malkuth. Not a cup or a pentacle anywhere.

"You're going to emerge as a much stronger man," she said weakly.

"That isn't what you see," Drake said. "And it isn't what I see. The Devil and the Tower together are a pretty destructive pair, aren't they?"

"I suppose you know what the Lovers reversed means, too?" she asked.

" 'The Answer of the Oracle Is Always Death,' " he quoted.

"But you won't accept it."

"The only way to conquer Death—until science produces an immortality pill—is to make him your servant, your company cop," Drake said calmly. "That's the key I've been looking for. The bartender never becomes an alcoholic, and the high priest laughs at the gods. Besides, the Tower is rotten to the core and deserves to be destroyed." He pointed abruptly to the Fool. "You have some real talents obviously—even if you do cheat like everybody in this racket—and you must know there are two choices after crossing the Abyss. The right-hand path and the left-hand path. I seem to be headed for the left-hand path. I can see that much, and it confirms what I already suspect. Go ahead and tell me the rest of what you see; I'm not afraid to hear it."

"Very well." Mama wondered if he was one of the few, the very few, who would eventually come to the attention of the Shining Ones. "You will make Death your servant, as a tactic to master him. Yours is, indeed, the left-hand path. You will cause immense suffering—especially to yourself at first. But after a while you won't notice that; after a while you won't even notice the horrors that you inflict on others. Men will say that you are a materialist, a worshipper of money. What do you hate most?" she asked abruptly.

"Sentimental slop and lies. All the Christian lies in Sunday school, all the democratic lies in the newspapers, all the socialist lies our so-called intellectuals are spouting these days. Every rotten, crooked, sneaking, hypocritical deception people use to hide from themselves that we're all still hunting animals in a jungle."

"You admire Neitzsche?"

"He was crazy. Let's just say I have less contempt for him, and for DeSade, than I have for most intellectuals."

"Yes. So we know what the Tower is that you will destroy. Everything in America that smacks of democracy or Christianity or socialism. The whole façade of humanitarianism from the Constitution onward to the present. You will turn your fire loose and burn all that up with your Leonine energies. You will force your view of America into total reality, and make every citizen afraid of the jungle and of the death that lurks in the jungle. Crime and commerce are moving closer together, due to Prohibition; you will complete their marriage. All, all this, just to make Death your servant instead of your master. The money and power are just incidental to that."

NO—because even if you think you have it beat even if you think you can work out a reconciliation a separate peace I mean shit the war still goes on No you're only kidding yourself Even say I love Simon and that's all Holly-

wood bullshit you can't really tell in only one week no matter how good it is but even if I love Simon the war goes on
as long as we're going around in separate skins White Man
Black Man Bronze Man White Woman Black Woman
Bronze Woman even if Hagbard claims to have gotten past
all that on his submarine it's only because they're under the
water and away from the world Out here the bastards are
using live ammunition like it says in the old joke Maybe
that's the only truth in the world Not the Bibles or poetry
or philosophy but just the old jokes Especially the bad
jokes and the sad jokes No they're using live ammunition I
mean shit they never see me all of them White Man Black
Man Bronze Man White Woman Black Woman Bronze
Woman they look at me and I'm in their game I have my
role I am Black Woman I am never just me No it goes on
and on every step upward is a step into more hypocrisy until the game is stopped completely and nobody has found
out how to do that No the more Simon says that he does
see me the more he's lying to himself No he never makes it
with White Woman because she's too much like his mother
or some damned Freudian reason like that I mean shit No I
can't go on in their game I am going to scream with rage I
am going to scream like an eagle I am going to scream in
the ears of the whole world until somebody does see me until
I am not Black Woman and not Black and not Woman and
nothing No nothing *just me* No they'll say I'm giving up
love and sanity Well fuck them fuck them all No I won't
turn back the acid has changed everything No at the end of
it when I really am *me* maybe then I can find a better love
and a better sanity No but first I have to find *me*

"Go on." Drake was unsmiling but undisturbed.

"The King of Swords and the Knight of Wands are both
very active. You could do all this harmlessly, by becoming
an artist and *showing* this vision of the jungle. You don't
have to create it literally and inflict it on your fellow human beings."

"Stop preaching. Just read the cards. You're better at it
than I am, but I can see enough to know that there is no
such alternative for me. The other wand and the other
sword are reversed. I can't be satisfied to do it in symbolic
form. I must do it so that everybody is affected by it, not
just the few who read books or go to concerts. Tell me
what I don't know. Why is the line from the Fool to the

Tower completed in the Lovers reversed? I know that I can't love anyone, and I don't believe that anybody else ever does, either—that's more sentiment and hypocrisy. People use each other as masturbating machines and crying towels, and they *call* it love. But there's a deeper meaning. What is it?"

"Start from the top: Death reversed. You reject Death, so the Fool cannot undergo rebirth and enter the right-hand path when he crosses the Abyss. Therefore: the left-hand path, the destruction of the Tower. There is only one end to that chain of karma, my son. The Lovers means Death, just as Death means Life. You are rejecting natural death, and therefore refusing natural life. Your path will be an unnatural life leading to a death that is against nature. You will die as a man before your body dies. The fire is still self-destructive, even if you turn it outward and use the whole world as a stage for your private *Gotterdammerung*. Your primary victim will still be yourself."

"You have the talent," Drake said coldly, "but you are still basically a fraud, like everyone in this business. *Your* worst victim, madam, is yourself. You deceive yourself with the lies that you have so often told others. It's the occupational disease of mystics. The truth is that it doesn't matter whether I destroy myself alone or destroy this planet—or turn around and try to find my way to the right-hand path in some dreary monastery. The universe will roll blindly along, not caring, not even *knowing*. There's no Granddaddy in the clouds to pass a last judgment—there's only a few airplanes up there, learning more and more about how to carry bombs. They court-martialed General Mitchell for saying it, but it's the truth. The next time around they'll really bomb the hell out of civilian populations. And the universe won't know or care about that either. Don't tell me that my flight from Death leads back to Death; I'm not a child, and I know that all paths lead back to Death eventually. The only question is: Do you cower before him all your life or do you spit in his eye?"

"You can transcend abject fear and rebellious hatred both. You can see that he is only part of the Great Wheel and, like all other parts, necessary to the whole. Then you can accept him."

"Next you'll be telling me to love him."

"That too."

"Yes, and I can learn to see the great and glorious Whole Picture. I can see all the men defecating and urinating in their trousers before they died at Château-Thierry, watching their own guts fall out into their laps and screaming out of a hole that isn't even a mouth any more, as manifestations of that sublime harmony and balance which is ineffable and holy and beyond all speech and reason. Sure. I can see that, if I knock half of my brain out of commission and hypnotize myself into thinking that the view from that weird perspective is deeper and wider and more *truly true* than the view from an unclouded mind. Go to the quadruple-amputee ward and try to tell them that. You speak of death as a personified being. Very well: Then I must regard him as any other entity that gets in my way. Love is a myth invented by poets and other people who couldn't face the world and crept off into corners to create fantasies to console themselves. The fact is that when you meet another entity, either it makes way for you or you make way for it. Either it dominates and you submit, or you dominate and it submits. Take me into any club in Boston and I'll tell you which millionaire has the most millions, by the way the others treat him. Take me into any workingman's bar and I'll tell you who has the best punch in a fistfight, by the way the others treat him. Take me into any house and I'll tell you in a minute whether the husband or the wife is dominant. Love? Equality? Reconciliation? Acceptance? Those are the excuses of the losers, to persuade themselves that they choose their condition and weren't beaten down into it. Find a dutiful wife, who truly loves her husband. I'll have her in my bed in three days, maximum. Because I'm so damned attractive? No, because I understand men and women. I'll make her understand, without saying it aloud and shocking her, that the adultery will, one way or another, hurt her husband, whether he knows about it or not. Show me the most servile colored waiter in the best restaurant in town, and after he's through explaining Christianity and humility and all the rest of it, count how many times a day he steps into the kitchen to spit in his handerchief. The other employess will tell you he has a 'chest condition.' The condition he has is chronic rage. The mother and the child? An endless power struggle. Listen to the infant's cry change in pitch when Mother doesn't come at once. Is that fear you hear? It's rage—insane fury at not having total dominance. As for the mother herself, I'd wager that ninety percent of the married women in the psychiatrists' care are there because they can't admit to themselves, can't escape the lie of love long enough to admit to themselves, how often they want to strangle that monster in the nursery. Love of country? Another lie; the truth is fear of cops and prisons. Love of art? Another lie; the truth is fear of the naked truth without ornaments and false faces on it. Love of truth itself? The biggest lie of all: fear of the unknown. People learn acceptance of all this and achieve wisdom? They surrender to superior force and call their cowardice maturity. It still comes down to one question: Are you kneeling at the altar, or are you on the altar watching the others kneel to you?"

"The wheel of the Tarot is the wheel of Dharma," Mama Sutra said softly when he had concluded. "It is also the wheel of the galaxy, which you see as a blind machine. It rolls on, as you say, no matter what we think or do. Knowing that, I accept Death as part of the wheel, and I accept your nonacceptance as another part. I can control neither. I can only repeat my warning, which is not a lie but a fact about the structure of the Wheel: By denying death, you guarantee that you will meet him finally in his most hideous form."

Drake finished his coffee and smiled whimsically. "You know," he said, "my contempt for lies has an element of the very sentimentality and foolish idealism that I have been rejecting. Perhaps I will be most effective if I never speak so honestly again. When you hear of me next, I might be known as a philanthropist and benefactor of mankind." He lit a cigar thoughtfully. "And that would even be true if your Tarot mysticism is correct after all. If Death is necessary to the Wheel, along with all the other parts, then I am necessary also. The Wheel would collapse, perhaps, if my spirit of rebellion were not there to balance your spirit of acceptance. Imagine that."

"It is true. That is why I have warned you but not judged you."

"So I am, as Goethe says, 'part of that force which aims at evil and only achieves good'?"

"That is a thought which you should try to remember when the Dark Night of Sammael descends upon you at the end."

"More cant," Drake said, with a return to his previous cynicism. "I aim at evil and I will achieve evil. The Wheel and all its harmonious balances and all-healing paradoxes is just another myth of the weak and defeated. One strong man can stop the Wheel or tear it to shreds if he dares enough."

"Perhaps. We who study the Wheel do not know all of its secrets. Some believe that your spirit reappears constantly in history, because it is fated, eventually, to triumph. Maybe this is the last century of terrestrial mortals, and the next century will be the time of the cosmic immortals. What will happen then, when the Wheel is stopped, none of us can predict. It may be 'good' or 'evil' or even—to quote your favorite philosopher—beyond good and evil. We cannot say. That is another reason I do not judge you."

"Listen," Drake said with sudden emotion. "We're both lying. It's not all this philosophical or cosmic. The simple fact is that I couldn't sleep nights, and nothing I tried in conventional 'cures' could help me, until I began to help myself by systematically rebelling against everything that seemed stronger than me."

"I know. I didn't know it was insomnia. It might have been nightmares or dizzy spells or sexual impotence. But there was some way that the scenes you saw in Château-Thierry lived on and goaded you to wake out of the dream of the sleepwalkers on the streets. You are waking: You stand on the abyss." She pointed to the Fool and the dog who barks at his heels. "And I am the noisy little bitch barking to warn you that you can still choose the right-hand path. The decision is not final until you cross the abyss."

"But the cards show that I really have very little choice. Especially in the world that is going to emerge from this depression."

Mama Sutra smiled without forgiveness or final condemnation. "This is no age for saints," she agreed softly. "Two dollars please."

George, don't make no bull moves. The Dutchman saw it all clearly now. Capone and Luciano and Maldonado and Lepke and all the rest of them were afraid of Winifred and the Washington crowd. They were planning a deal, and his death was part of the bargain. The fools didn't know that you can never negotiate from fear. They thought of the Order only as a handy gimmick for international communications and illicit trade; they were too dumb to really study the Teachings. Especially, they had never understood the third Teaching: *Fear is Failure*. Once you're afraid of the bulls, you're lost. But the bull was gone. "What have you done with him?" he shouted at the hospital wall.

(Smiling Jim had seen the eagle only the day before. Its nest was definitely on one of these peaks. He would get it: He knew it in his bones, a hunch so strong it couldn't be doubted. Panting, sweating, every muscle aching, he climbed onward . . . The coffee leaped out of the paper cup and slurped onto the pages of *Carnal Orgy*. Igor Beaver, the graduate student, looked up in astonishment: The seismograph stood at grade 5. A mile away, Dillinger woke as the bedroom door slammed shut and his favorite statue, King Kong atop the Empire State Building, fell off the bureau.)

NO REMISSION, NO REMISSION, NO REMISSION WITHOUT THE SHEDDING OF BLOOD. NO REMISSION WITHOUT THE SHEDDING OF BLOOD.

Mama Sutra looked down through the window at Boston Common. Robert Putney Drake had stopped, and was listening to one of the preachers again; even at this distance she could recognize the cool, closed smile on his face.

The Dealy Lama sat down across from her. "Well?" he asked.

"Definitely. The Order will have to intervene." Mama shook her head sadly. "He's a menace to the whole world."

"Slowness is beauty," the Dealy Lama said. "Let the Lower Order contact him first. If they decide he's worth the effort, then we'll act. I think I shall persuade Hagbard to attend Harvard, so he can be in his neighborhood and keep an eye on him, so to speak."

IT'S THE WORD OF THE BIBLE AND THE WORD OF GOD AND IT SAYS IT PLAIN AND CLEAR SO NO HIGHBROW PROFESSOR CAN SAY IT MEANS SOMETHING ELSE.

"How old are you actually?" Mama asked curiously.

The Dealy Lama looked at her levelly. "Would you believe thirty thousand years?"

She laughed. "I should have known better than to ask. You can always tell the higher members by their sense of humor."

AND THIS IS WHAT IT SAYS: NO REMISSION, NO REMISSION,

BROTHERS AND SISTERS, NO REMISSION WITHOUT THE SHED-
DING OF BLOOD, WITHOUT THE SHEDDING OF BLOOD. NO RE-
MISSION. NO REMISSION WITHOUT THE SHEDDING OF BLOOD.

Hagbard's mouth fell open in completely genuine surprise. "Well, *sink* me," he said, beginning to laugh.

Behind him on a wall, Joe noticed dizzily, was a brand-
new graffito, probably scrawled by somebody out of his
skull on the acid: THE PIGEONS IN B. F. SKINNER'S CAGES
ARE POLITICAL PRISONERS.

"We both pass," Hagbard went on happily. "We've been
judged and found innocent by the great god Acid."

Joe took a deep breath. "And when do you start to explain in monosyllables or sign language or semaphore or
something a non-Illuminated moron like me can understand?"

"You read all the clues. It was right out in the open. It
was plain as a barn door. It was as conspicuous as my nose
and twice as homely—in every sense of that word."

"Hagbard, for Christ's sake and for my sake and for all
our sakes, will you stop gloating and give me the answer?"

"I'm sorry." Hagbard pocketed the gun carelessly. "I'm a
bit giddy. I've been waging a kind of war all night, high on
acid. It was a strain, especially since I was at least ninety
percent sure you'd kill me before it was over." He lit one of
his abominable cigars. "Briefly, then, the Illuminati is be-
nevolent, compassionate, kindly, generous, et cetera, et cetera. Add all the other complimentary adjectives you can
think of. In short, we're the good guys."

"But—but—it can't be."

"It can be and it is." Hagbard motioned him toward the
Bugatti. "Let's Sit Down, if I may permit myself one more
acrostic before the codes and puzzles are all resolved."
They climbed into the front seat, and Joe accepted the
brandy decanter Hagbard offered. "Of course," Hagbard
went on, "when I say 'good,' you've got to understand that
all terms are relative. We're as good as is possible in this
fucked-up section of the galaxy. We're not perfect. Certainly, I'm not, and I haven't observed anything approaching
immaculate perfection in any of the other Masters of the
Temple either. But we are, in human terms and by ordinary
standards, decent chaps. There's a reason for that. It's the
basic law of magic, and it's in every textbook. You must
have read it somewhere. Do you know what I mean?"

Joe took a stiff snort of the brandy. It was peach—his favorite. "Yes, I think. 'As ye give, so shall ye get.' "

"Precisely." Hagbard took back the bottle and had a snort himself. "Mind you, Joe, that's a scientific law, not a moral commandment. There are no commandments, because there is no commander anywhere. All authority is a delusion, whether in theology or in sociology. Everything is radically, even sickeningly, free. The first law of magic is as neutral as Newton's first law of motion. It says that the equation balances, and that's all it says. You are still free to give evil and pain, if you decide you must. Once done, however, you never escape the consequences. It always comes back. No prayers, sacrifices, mortifications, or supplications will change it, any more than they'll change Newton's laws or Einstein's. So we're 'good,' as moralists would say, because we know enough to have a bloody strong reason to be good. In the last week things went too fast, and I became 'evil'—I deliberately ordered and paid for the deaths of various people, and set in motion processes that had to lead to still other deaths. I knew what I was doing, and I knew—and still know—that I'll pay for it. Such decisions are extremely rare in the history of the Order, and my superior, the Dealy Lama, tried to persuade me it was unnecessary this time too. I disagreed; I take the responsibility. No man or god or goddess can change it. I will pay, and I'm ready to pay, whenever and however the bill is presented."

"Hagbard, *what are you?*"

"A *mehum,* the Saure family would say," Hagbard grinned. "A mere human. No more. Not one jot more."

"How much blood?" Robert Putney Drake asked. He was astonished at his own words; in all his experiments at breaking through the walls, he had never lowered himself to heckling an ignorant street preacher.

ALL THE BLOOD IN THE WORLD ISN'T ENOUGH. EVERY MAN, WOMAN, AND CHILD ISN'T ENOUGH. EVEN ALL THE ANIMALS IF YOU ADDED THEM IN LINE IN SOME PAGAN OR VOODOO SACRIFICE. IT WOULDN'T BE ENOUGH. IT WOULDN'T BE ENOUGH, BROTHERS. THE GOOD BOOK SAYS SO.

"There were five of us," John-John Dillinger was explaining to George as they trudged back toward Ingolstadt, having lost Hagbard and the Bugatti in the crowd. "My folks kept it a secret. German people, very superstitious

and secretive. They didn't want reporters all over the place
and headlines about the first quintuplets to live. The Dionne
family got all that, much later."

BECAUSE ALL THE BLOOD IN THE WORLD ISN'T EQUAL TO
ONE DROP, NOT ONE DROP

"John Herbert Dillinger is in Las Vegas, trying to track
down the plague—unless he already finished up and went
home to Los Angeles." John-John smiled. "He was always
the brains of the bunch. Runs a rock-music company, real
professional businessman. He was the oldest, by a couple of
minutes, and we all sort of look up to him. He served the
prison time, even though I'm the one who rightly should
have, seeing that robbing that grocer was my dumb idea.
But he said he could take it without cracking up, and he
was right."

NOT ONE DROP, NOT ONE DROP, OF THE PRECIOUS BLOOD
OF OUR LORD AND SAVIOR, JESUS CHRIST.

"I see," Drake said. "And was that A, B, AB, or O?"

"John Hoover Dillinger lives in Mad Dog, under the
name D. J. Hoover—he's not above letting people suspect
he's a distant relative of J. Edgar's. Mostly," John-John
said, "he's retired. Except occasionally for little jobs like
helping arrange convincing jail breaks, say, when Jim Cartwright wants to let a prisoner get out in a realistic fashion.
He gave Naismith the idea for the John Dillinger Died for
You Society."

"How about the other two?" George asked, thinking that
it would be even harder to decide whether he loved Stella
more than Mavis or Mavis more than Stella now that he
knew they were the same person. He wondered how Joe
felt, since he obviously dug Miss Mao Tsu-hsi and she was
that person also. Three in one and one in three. Like Dillinger. Or was Dillinger five in three? George realized suddenly that he was still tripping a little. Dillinger was five in one,
not five in three: the law of Fives again. Did that mean
there were two more in the Mavis-Stella-Mao complex,
two that he hadn't met yet? Why did two and three keep
popping up in all this?

"The other two are dead," John-John said sadly. "John
Edgar Dillinger was born first, and he went and died first.
Fast and furious, he was. It was him that plugged that bank
guard in East Chicago while the rest of us were vacationing
and laying low in Miami. Always the hothead, he was. Had

a heart attack back in '43 and went to an early grave. John
Thomas Dillinger went in '69. He was in Chicago in '68 on
a JAM assignment, meeting with a crazy English spy
named Chips. British Intelligence somehow got a report
that the Democratic Convention was being run by the Bavarian Illuminati and would end with an assassination.
They didn't believe in the Illuminati so they sent Chips;
they always send him on wild cases, 'cause he's nutty
enough to take them seriously and do a thorough job. Both
of them got tear-gassed coming out of the Hilton Hotel,
and poor Chips got thrown in a paddy-wagon with a bunch
of young radicals. John Thomas had a chest problem already, a chronic asthma, and the tear gas made it a lot
worse. He went from doctor to doctor, and finally passed
away early in '69. So there's a cop in Chicago who could
boast that he really killed John Dillinger, only he doesn't
know it. Isn't life peculiar?"

"The Saure family only *thought* they were in the Illuminati," Hagbard went on. "Hitler and Stalin only *thought*
they were in the Illuminati. Old Weishaupt only *thought* he
was in the Illuminati. It's that simple. The moral of the
whole story is: Beware of cheap Occidental imitations." He
smiled grimly.

"I think it's beginning to penetrate," Joe said slowly. "It
was, of course, the very first hypothesis I formed: There
have been many groups in history who called themselves
the Illuminati, and they weren't all aiming at exactly the
same thing."

"Precisely." Hagbard puffed again at his cigar. "That's
the natural first suspicion of any non-paranoid mind. Then,
as you explore the evidence, links between these groups begin to appear. Eventually the paranoid hypothesis begins to
appear more plausible and you begin to believe there always has been one Illuminati, using the same basic slogans
and symbols and aiming at the same basic goal. I sent Jim
Cartwright to you with that yarn about three conspiracies
—the ABC or Ancient Bavarian Conspiracy, the NBC or
New Bavarian Conspiracy, and the CBS or Conservative
Bavarian Seers—to set you thinking that the truth might be
midway backward toward the simple first idea. From here
on in, forget that I represent the original Illuminati. In fact,
in recent centuries we don't use a name at all. We employ

only the initials A.A., written like this." He sketched on a
Donau-Hotel matchbook:

A∴ A∴

"A lot of occult writers," he went on, "have made some
amazing guesses as to what that means. Actually, it doesn't
mean a damned thing. To prevent our name being stolen
and misused again, we don't have a name. Anybody who
thinks he's guessed the name and tries to pass himself off as
an initiate by declaring that we're really the Atlantean Ar-
canum or the Argenteum Astrum or whatever immediately
reveals that he's a fraud. It's a neat gimmick," Hagbard in-
toned gloomily. "I only wish we had thought of it centuries
earlier."

The buzzer on the President's secretary's desk buzzed as
Saul and Barney passed through the outer door. The secretary flipped the switch, and the President said, "Find out
the highest medal a civilian can get, and order two, on my
signature, for those two detectives."

"Yes, sir," the secretary said, scribbling.

"And then ask the FBI to check out that older one. He
looked like a kike to me," the President said shrewdly.

NO—because I'd be a fool to think miracles can occur in
this world before somebody pays the rent and the taxes and
shows that their papers are in order and the people who are
running it can always tell you your papers are not in order
No because there are no magicians and even Hagbard is
mostly a fraud and a con man even if he means well No because I'm not Pope Joan if there ever was a Pope Joan No
because like the song says I'm not a queen I'm a woman
and the wrong color woman to boot No because there will
be rivers of blood and the earth will be shaken before we
can overturn Boss Charlie because it isn't a simple one-
night symbolic Armageddon like Hagbard fooled them all
into thinking No because Hagbard is some kind of magician and put us all on his own trip for a while but the real
world isn't a trip it's a bummer No because the lovers don't
live happily ever after what happens is that they get married and get into debt and live in slavery ever after and I've
got to find something better than that No because none of
us are driving the car it's the car that's driving us No because it's like that old joke "Balls" said the queen "if I had

them I'd be king" and "Nuts" said the prince "I've got them and I'm not king" and "Crap" said the king and thirty thousand royal subjects squatted and strained for in those days the king's word was law Hagbard would call it anality and sexism and ageism but it just comes down to the women and children getting all the crap right in the face and a few males owning everything the truth is all in the old jokes especially the bad jokes I'm still tripping but this is true they can always say your papers are not in order No because sometimes you've got to be a hermit and then come back later when you're together No because the wheel keeps spinning and doesn't give a fuck if there's going to be any change it's got to be that some human being somewhere does give a fuck No because I've never found a way to shut Simon's mouth and make him listen No because Jesus Christ was a black man and they've even lied about that he was another black man they killed and they won't admit it No because death is the currency in every empire Roman or American or any other all empires are the same Death is always the argument they use No because the whole world can go to the Devil and I'm taking care of Mary Lou No because look at that professor they killed at the UN building and none of them arrested yet No because there's a perpetual motion machine inside me and I'm learning to let it run No because I'll put a curse on all of them I'll burn them I'll condemn them I'll have the world No because look what happened to Daddy and Mommy

"It's grade 5 and moving up toward 6," Igor Beaver shouted into the phone.

"You idiot, don't you think I can tell that from here?" Dr. Troll shouted back. "My bed was bouncing around like it had Saint Vitus' dance even before you called." His emotion was merely professional anger at the student's failure to obey orders; Grade 5 is nothing to get excited about if you're a Californian, and even Grade 6 causes anxiety only among tourists or believers in the famous Edgar Cayce prophecy . . . John Herbert Dillinger, one of those believers, was already in the garage, pajama tops tucked in to hastily donned trousers, bare foot on the starter . . . But Smiling Jim climbed blissfully upward, enjoying total communication with nature, the mystic rapture of the true hunter before he gets his chance to open fire and blast a chunk of nature to hell . . .

YOU MAY MOCK AND YOU MAY JEST BUT AT THE LAST
JUDGMENT THE SMILE WILL BE WIPED OFF YOUR FACE

"He's heckling the preacher," Mama said. "A small beginning, certainly, for the kind of destiny he seems to be
choosing."

"He's heckling himself," the Dealy Lama pronounced.
"Christianity, rightly understood, is an encounter with
'Death. He's still struggling with that problem. He wants to
believe in the symbolism of the Resurrection, but he can't.
Too much intellect—King of Swords—keeping the reins on
his intuitive—Prince of Wands—aspect."

"Well, maybe," Drake said calmly. "But suppose He was
type A. Now, if He got a transfusion at the last minute . . ."

The nest was in sight. The bird was invisible, but Smiling
Jim recognized the characteristic eagle's nest on a peak
only a few hundred yards above and to the west. "Come
home, baby," he thought passionately, unstrapping his rifle.
"Come home. Daddy is waiting."

Hagbard took another belt of the brandy and repeated:
"The Saures were not Illuminati. Neither were Weishaupt
or Hitler. They were frauds, pure and simple. First they deluded themselves, then they deluded others. The real Illuminati, the A.·.A.·., have never been involved in politics or in
any form of manipulating or coercing people. Our interests
are entirely elsewhere. *Do what thou wilt* is our law. Only
in the last few decades, as the fate of the earth seemed to
be hanging in the balance, have we taken any direct action.
Even so, we have been cautious. We know that power cor-
rupts. We have acted chiefly by not-acting, by what the
Taoists call *wu-wei*. But then things got out of hand. They
moved too fast . . . We fucked up somewhat. But only because total inaction seemed to mean total disaster."

"You mean you, as an official of some sort in the
A.·.A.·., infiltrated the fake Illuminati and became one of
their top Five, intending to undo them nonviolently? And it
didn't work?"

"It worked about as well as any activity on that level
ever works," Hagbard said somberly. "Most of humanity
has been spared, for a while. And the wild free animals
have been spared. For a while." He sighed. "I guess I'll
have to begin from the A-B-Cs. We have never sought
power. We have sought to disperse power, to set men and

women free. That really means: to help them to discover that
they are free. Everybody's free. The slave is free. The ultimate weapon isn't this plague out in Vegas, or any new su-
per H-bomb. The ultimate weapon has always existed. Every man, every woman, and every child owns it. It's the
ability to say *No* and take the consequences. 'Fear is failure.' 'The fear of death is the beginning of slavery.' 'Thou
hast no right but to do thy will.' The goose can break the
bottle at any second. Socrates took the hemlock to prove it.
Jesus went to the cross to prove it. It's in all history, all
myth, all poetry. It's right out in the open all the time."

Hagbard sighed again. "Our founder and leader, the man
known in myth as Prometheus or the snake in the garden of
Eden—"

"Oh, Christ," Joe said, slumping forward in his seat. "I
have the feeling that you're starting to put me on again.
You're about to tell me that the Prometheus and Genesis
stories are really based on fact."

"Our leader, known as Lucifer or Satan," Hagbard went
on, "Lucifer being the *bringer of light*—"

"You know," Joe said, "I'm not going to believe a word
of this."

"Our leader, known as Prometheus the fire-bringer or
Lucifer the light-bringer or Quetzalcoatl the morning star
or the snake in the garden of Osiris's bad brother, Set, or
Shaitan the tempter—well, to be brief, he repented." Hagbard raised an eyebrow. "Does that intrigue you sufficiently
to silence your skepticism long enough for me to finish a
sentence?"

"He *repented?*" Joe sat upright again.

"Sure. Why not?" Hagbard's old malicious grin, so rare
in the last week, returned. "If Atlas can Shrug and Telemachus can Sneeze, why can't Satan Repent?"

"Go ahead," Joe said. "This is just another one of your
put-ons, but I'm hooked. I'll listen. But I have my own answer, which is that there is no answer. You're just an allegory on the universe itself, and every explanation of you
and your actions is incomplete. They'll always be a new,
more up-to-date explanation coming along a while later.
That's *my* answer."

Hagbard laughed easily. "Charming," he said. "I must remember that the next time *I'm* trying to understand myself.
Of course, it's true of any human being. We're all allegories

on the universe, different faces it wears in trying to decide what it really is . . . But our founder and leader, as I was saying, repented. That's the secret that has never been revealed. There is no stasis anywhere in the cosmos, least of all in the minds of entities that possess minds. The basic fallacy of all bad writers—and theologians are notoriously bad writers—is to create cardboard characters who never change. He gave us the light of reason and, seeing how we misused it, he repented. The story is more complicated, but that's the basic outline. At least, it's as much as I understood until a week ago. The important thing to get clear is that he never aimed at power or destruction. That's a myth—"

"Created by the opposition," Joe said. "Right? I read that in Mark Twain's defense of Satan."

"Twain was subtle," Hagbard said, taking a little more brandy, "but not subtle enough. No, the myth was not created by the opposition. It was created by our founder himself."

"Wilde should be alive," Joe said admiringly. "He was so proud of himself, setting paradox on top of paradox until he had a nice three- or four- or five-story house of contradictions built up. He should see the skyscrapers you create."

"You never disappoint me," Hagbard said. "If they ever hang you, you'll be arguing about whether the rope really exists until the last minute. That's why I picked you, all those years ago, and programmed you for the role you'd play tonight. Only a man whose father was an ex-Moslem, and who was himself an ex-Catholic and an ex-engineering student, would have the required complexity. Anyway, to return to the libretto, as an old friend of mine used to say, the error of Weishaupt and Hitler and Stalin and the Saures was to believe the propaganda our founder spread against himself—that, and believing they were in communication with him, when they were only in communication with a nasty part of their own unconscious minds. There was no evil spirit misleading them. They were misleading themselves. And we were trailing along behind, trying to keep them from causing too much harm. Finally, in the early 1960s—after a certain fuckup in Dallas convinced me that things were getting out of hand—I contacted the Five directly. Since I knew the real secrets of magic and they only had distortions, it was easy to convince them that I was an emissary from those beings whom they call the Secret Chiefs or the Great Old Ones or the Shining Ones. Being half crazy, they reacted in a way I had not expected. They all abdicated and appointed me and the four Saures as their successors. They decided that we're entering the age of Horus, the child-god, and that youth should be given a chance to run things—hence, the promotion of the Saures. They threw me in because I seemed to know what I was talking about. But then came the real problem: I couldn't convince the Saures of anything. Those pig-headed kids wouldn't believe a word I said. They told me I was over thirty and untrustworthy. I told you the truth was out in the open all the time; anybody with eyes in his head should have been able to interpret what's been happening since the early 1960s. The great and dreaded Illuminati of the past had fallen into the control of a bunch of ignorant and malicious kids. The age of the crowned and conquering child."

"And you think the old and wise should rule?" Joe asked. "That doesn't fit your character. This *has* to be another put-on."

"I don't think *anybody* should rule," Hagbard said. "All I'm doing—all the Higher Order of the A∴A∴ has ever tried to do—is communicate with people, in spite of their biases and fears. Not to rule them. And what we're trying to communicate—the ultimate secret, the philosopher's stone, the elixir of life—is just the power of the word *No.* We are people who have said *Non serviam,* and we're trying to teach others to say it. Drake was one of us spiritually but never understood it. If we can't find immortality, we can make a damned good try. If we can't save this planet, we can get off it and go to the stars."

"And what happens now?" Joe asked.

"More surprises," Hagbard answered promptly. "I can't tell you the whole story at this hour, with both of us fagged out at the end of an acid trip. We go back to the hotel and sleep, and after breakfast there are more revelations. For George as well as for you."

And later in the Bugatti, which, driven by Harry Coin, was grandly wafting Hagbard, George, and Joe around the south side of Lake Totenkopf, George asked, "Is Hitler really going to be buried anonymously in a Jewish cemetery?"

"It looks that way." Hagbard grinned. "His Israeli documents are excellent forgeries. He'll be lifted off that toilet by Hauptmann's men and gently deposited in the Ingolstadt Hebrew Burial Grounds, there to rest for all eternity."

"That will make me throw up once a day for the rest of my life," Joe said bitterly. "It's the worst case of cemetery desecration in history."

"Oh, it has a positive aspect," said Hagbard. "Look at it from the point of view of the Nazi leaders. Think how they'll hate being buried in a Jewish cemetery with a rabbi praying over them."

"Doesn't make up for it," said George. "Joe's right. It's in terribly bad taste."

"I thought both you guys were thoroughgoing atheists," said Hagbard. "If you are, you think the dead are dead and it hardly matters where they're buried. What's happening —you both getting religion?"

"I can think of nothing more likely to drive a man to religion than your company," said Joe.

"Burying them Nazis with a bunch of Jews is the funniest thing I ever heard," Harry Coin offered from the driver's seat.

"Go bugger a dead goat, Coin," George called.

"Sure thing," said Coin. "Lead me to it."

"You're incorrigible, Hagbard," said Joe. "You really are incorrigible. And you surround yourself with people who incorrige you."

"I don't need help," said Hagbard. "I have a great deal of initiative. More than any other human being I know. With the possible exception of Mavis."

George said, "Hagbard, did I really see what I thought I saw last night? Is Mavis really a goddess? Are Stella and Miss Mao and Mavis all the same person, or was I just hallucinating?"

"Here come the paradoxes," Joe groaned. "He'll talk for an hour, and we'll be more confused when he's finished."

Hagbard, who was sitting in a large swivel jump seat, swung round so he was looking over Harry Coin's shoulder at the road ahead. "I'd be glad to tell you later, George. I would have told you now, except that I don't like Malik's tone. He may not be intending to shoot me any more, but he still has it in for me."

"You bet," said Joe.

"Well, are you still going to marry Mavis?"

"What?" Hagbard swung round and stared at George with an expression that was almost a perfect replica of genuine surprise.

"You said that you and Mavis were going to be married aboard the *Leif Erikson* by Miss Portinari. Are you?"

"Yes," said Hagbard, "Miss Portinari will marry us later today. Sorry, but I knew her first."

"Then Mavis isn't really Eris?" George persisted. "She's just a priestess of Eris?"

Hagbard brushed the question away. "Later, George. She will explain it."

"She's even better at explanations than Hagbard is," Joe commented cynically.

"Well," said Hagbard, "getting back to Hitler and company, you have to realize that they will know about it if their bodies are buried in a Jewish cemetery. They are still conscious and aware, though they are not what we would normally call alive. Their consciousness-energy is intact, though there is no life in their bodies. They came to the Ingolstadt festival hoping that their young leaders would give them immortality. They've achieved immortality, all right. But not a very nice kind. Their consciousness-energy has been gobbled up by the Evil One. Their identities still survive, but they will be helpless parts of the Eater of Souls, the foulest being in the universe, the only creature that can turn spirit into carrion. Yog Sothoth has claimed his own."

"Yog Sothoth!" said Joe. "I remember learning about Yog Sothoth. It was an invisible being trapped in a pentagonal structure in Atlantis. The original Illuminati blew up the structure and turned the creature loose."

"Why, yes," Hagbard said, "you saw that Erisian Liberation Front training film about Atlantis and Grayface Gruad, didn't you? Well, of course, the film isn't accurate in every respect. For instance, Yog Sothoth is depicted as killing people by the thousands. Actually, most of the time, except under very limited conditions, he has to have his killing done for him. That's how human sacrifice originated. And it was to get his killing done for him that he manipulated a great many events among the Atlanteans until old Grayface, the original moral sadomasochist, came along with his notions about good and evil. Man suffers because he is evil, said Gruad, and because he is small and helpless. There are vast powers in the universe, dwarfing us, who have to be placated. Gruad taught man to see ignorance, passion, pain, and death as evils, and to fight against them."

"Well . . . ignorance is an evil," said Joe.

"Not when it can be acknowledged and accepted," said Hagbard. "In order to eat, you have to be hungry. In order to learn, you have to be ignorant. Ignorance is a condition of learning. Pain is a condition of health. Passion is a condition of thought. Death is a condition of life. When Gruad taught his followers in Atlantis to see those conditions as evils, then he could teach them human sacrifice, persecution, and warfare. Yog Sothoth taught Gruad to teach his people those things, only Gruad never knew it."

"So Yog Sothoth is the serpent in the Garden of Eden," said Joe.

"In a manner of speaking," said Hagbard. "But you understand, the Garden of Eden myth was dreamed up and promulgated by the Illuminati."

"And who dreamed up the Gruad of Atlantis myth?" said Joe.

"Oh, that's true," said Hagbard solemnly.

"That's the biggest bunch of bullshit I ever heard," said Joe. "You're trying to claim that there's no such thing as good and evil, that the concepts were invented and taught to humans deliberately to fuck them up psychologically. But in order to maintain that you have to postulate that the condition of man before Gruad was good and that his condition afterward has been evil. And you have to make Yog Sothoth into a carbon copy of Satan. You haven't progressed one iota beyond the Judeo-Christian myth with that highfalutin' science-fiction story."

Hagbard roared with laughter and slapped Joe on the knee. "Beautiful!" He held up his hand in a distinctive gesture. "What I am doing?" he asked.

"You're giving the peace sign, only with your fingers together," George said, confused.

"That's what comes of being an ignorant Baptist." Joe laughed. "As a son of the True Church, I can tell you, George, that Hagbard is giving a Catholic blessing."

"Indeed?" said Hagbard. "Look at the shadow my hand casts on this book." He held up a book behind his hand, and they saw the head of a horned Devil. "The sun, source of all light and energy, symbol of redemption. And my hand, in the most sacred gesture of benediction. Put them both together, they spell Satan," he sang to an old tune.

"And what the hell does that mean?" Joe demanded. "Evil is only a shadow, a false appearance? The usual mystic mishmosh? Tell that to the survivors of Auschwitz."

"Suppose," Hagbard said, "I told you that good was only a shadow, a false appearance? Several modern philosophers have argued that case rather plausibly and earned themselves a reputation for hard-headed realism. And yet that's just the mirror image of what you call the usual mystic mishmosh."

"Then what is real?" George demanded. "Mary, Queen of the May, or Kali, Mother of Murderers, or Eris, who synthesizes both?"

"The *trip* is real," Hagbard said. "The images you encounter along the way are all unreal. If you keep moving, and pass them, you eventually discover that."

"Solipsism. Sophomore solipsism," Joe answered.

"No." Hagbard grinned. "The solipsist thinks the *tripper* is real."

Harry Coin called out, "Hagbard, there's a couple of guys up the road flagging us down."

Hagbard turned and peered ahead. "Right. They're crew members from the *Leif Erikson*. Pull up where they tell you to, Harry." He reached up to a silver vase mounted beside the back seat and took a pink rosebud out of the fresh bouquet he had placed there that morning. He carefully inserted the rosebud in the buttonhole of his lapel. The great golden Bugatti rolled to a stop, and the four men got out. Harry patted its long front fender with a long, skinny hand.

"Thanks for letting me drive this car, Hagbard," he said. "That's the nicest thing anyone's ever done for me."

"No it isn't. Now you'll want your own Bugatti. Or, what's worse, you'll ask me to let you be my chauffeur."

"No I won't. But I'll do a deal with you. You let me have this car, and whenever you want to go somewhere in it, I'll drive you."

Hagbard laughed and slapped Coin on the back. "You keep on showing that much intelligence and you will end up owning one."

The long line of cars that had been following the Bugatti now were stopping along the edge of the road behind it. There was a stretch of lawn that sloped gently down from the road to the lake. Out on the choppy blue water a round gold buoy drifted, giving off a cloud of red smoke.

Stella stepped out of the Mercedes 600 that was parked behind the Bugatti. George half expected Mavis and Miss Mao to get out with her, but there was no sign of them. He looked at her and was unable to speak. He didn't know what to say. She looked back at him with grave, sad eyes, in silence. Somehow, he thought, it will all be different and better when we get down to the submarine. In the submarine we'll be able to talk to each other.

A pink Cadillac behind the Mercedes disgorged Simon Moon and Clark Kent. Stella did not turn to look at them. They were talking excitedly to each other. A motorcycle pulled up behind the Cadillac. Otto Waterhouse climbed off it. Now Stella turned and looked at Otto, then back to George. Otto looked at Stella, then at George. Stella suddenly turned away from both of them and walked down to the edge of the lake. A large inflated life-raft was pulled up on shore, and one of Hagbard's men sitting in the raft stood up holding a wetsuit as Stella approached. Slowly, as if she were all alone by the shore of the lake, Stella took off her peasant blouse and skirt and continued stripping until she was naked. Then she started to put on the wetsuit.

Meanwhile, another man got behind the wheel of Hagbard's Bugatti Royale and drove it across the lawn. Two other men held the mouth of a huge transparent plastic bag far enough apart so that the car could be driven right into it. They tied up the end of the bag with strong wire. Ropes attached to the bag grew taut; their other ends disappeared into the water. Slowly, looking somewhat majestic and somewhat ridiculous, the car slid across the lawn and into the water. When it had been pulled out a short distance from shore it began to float. Out of the deeper water popped two golden scuba-launches, Hagbard's men in black wetsuits mounted in the saddles. The launches positioned themselves on either side of the automobile in its plastic bubble and the men lashed the launches and the car together with cables. Then they started their engines and launches; men and car quickly sank out of sight.

Meanwhile, more rubber rafts pulled ashore, and all of Hagbard's people started donning wetsuits distributed by the men from the submarine.

"I've never done this before," said Lady Velkor. "Are you sure it's safe?"

"Don't worry, baby," said Simon Moon. "Even a man could do it."

"Where's your friend, Mary Lou?" George asked.

"She left me," Simon said glumly. "The damned acid fucked up her mind."

NO—because in the long run whites and blacks and men and women have to come to an understanding and an equality No because this split can't go on forever I mean shit I understand that but No I can't not now No I am not ready yet the penis I imagined I had last night was not just some Freudian hallucination there's the phallic power behind the physical penis No the acting from the center of the body what Simon says Hagbard calls acting from the heart and only a few can have that right now No most of us haven't learned and haven't been given a chance to learn That's the real castration the real impotence in both men and women in both blacks and whites No the power that we think is phallic because this is a patriarchal society No I can't be Simon's woman or anybody's woman First I've got to be my own woman and it may take years it may take life I may never achieve it but I've got to try I can't end up like Daddy I can't end up like most blacks and most of the whites too end up No maybe I'll meet Simon again maybe we can try a second time That acid nut Timothy Leary always said You can be anything you want the second time around No it can't be this time it's got to be the second time around No I said No I won't No

"I hope to hell Hauptmann was telling the truth about not following me," said Hagbard. "It's going to take time to get us all down below."

"What are we doing with the cars?" Harry Coin asked.

"Well, the Bugatti, obviously, is too beautiful for me to part with, which is why I'm taking it aboard the *Leif Erikson.* But the rest we'll just leave. Maybe some of the people who went to the festival will be able to use them."

"Don't worry about them Huns," said John-John Dillinger, strolling up. "Any of them give us trouble, we'll just reply with a few short sharp words from old Mr. Thompson. Leave 'em in stitches."

"Peace, it's wonderful," said Hagbard sourly.

"Give it a chance," said Malaclypse, still in the guise of

Jean-Paul Sartre. "It needs time to spread. The absence of the Illuminati has to make itself felt. It *will* make a difference."

"I doubt it," said Hagbard. "The Dealy Lama was right all along."

The entire operation of outfitting Hagbard's people with wetsuits, paddling them out to the scuba-launches, and transporting them down to the *Leif Erikson* took more than an hour. When it was George's turn he looked eagerly into the depths for the *Leif Erikson* and was happy when he saw it glowing below him like a great golden blimp. Well, at least that's real, he thought. I'm approaching it from the outside, and it's just as big as I think it is. Even if it doesn't go anywhere and this is all happening in Disney World.

An hour later the submarine was deep in the Sea of Valusia. George, Joe, and Hagbard stood on the bridge, Hagbard leaning against the ancient Viking prow, George and Joe peering into the endless gray depths, watching the strange blind fishes and monsters swim by.

"There's a type of fungus that has evolved into something resembling seaweed in this ocean," said Hagbard. "It's luminescent. There's no light down here, so no green plants grow."

A dot appeared in the distance and grew rapidly in size until George recognized a porpoise, doubtless Howard. There was scuba-diving equipment strapped to the animal's back. When he had come alongside he turned a somersault, and his translated voice started to come through the loudspeaker in a song:

> When he swims the oceans spill,
> He can start earthquakes at will,
> He lived when the earth was desolate,
> I sing Leviathan the great.

Hagbard shook his head. "That doggerel is just awful. I'm going to have to do something about FUCKUP's ability to translate poetry. What are you talking about, Howard?"

"Aha," said Joe. "I didn't get a look at your talking porpoise friend last time I was aboard. Hello, Howard. I'm Joe."

"Hello, Joe," said Howard. "Welcome to my world. Unfortunately, it's not a very hospitable world at the moment.

There is grave danger in the Atlantic. The true ruler of the Illuminati is on the prowl on the high seas—Leviathan himself. The land is collapsing beside the Pacific, and the tremors have made the earth shake, and Leviathan is disturbed and has risen from the depths. Besides the trembling of the lands and seas, he knows that his chief worshippers, the Illuminati, are dead. He had read their passing in the pulsings of consciousnes-energy that reach even into the depths of the sea."

"Well, he can't eat the submarine," said Hagbard. "And we're well armed."

"He can crack the submarine open as easily as a gull cracks a penguin's egg," said Howard. "And your weapons will bother him not at all. He's virtually indestructible."

Hagbard shrugged, while Joe and George looked askance at each other. "I'll be careful, Howard. But we can't turn around now. We've got to get back to North America. We'll try to evade Leviathan if we see him."

"He fills the whole ocean," said Howard. "No matter what you do, you'll see him, and he'll see you."

"You're exaggerating."

"Only slightly. I must bid you farewell now. I think we've done a good week's work, and the menace to my people recedes even as does the danger to yours. Our porpoise horde is scattering and leaving by different exits into the North Atlantic. I'm getting out of the Sea of Valusia by way of Scotland. We think Leviathan will head south around Cape Horn into the Pacific. Everything that swims and is hungry is going that way. There's a lot of fresh meat in the water, I'm sorry to say. Good-bye, friends."

"So long, Howard," said Hagbard. "That was a good bridge you helped me build."

"Yes, it was," said Howard. "Too bad you had to sink it."

"What were those tanks on Howard's back?" said Joe.

"Scuba gear," said George. "There's no air available in the Sea of Valusia, so Howard has to have breathing equipment till he can get to the open ocean. Hagbard, what was that business about the true ruler of the Illuminati? I've heard again and again that there were five Illuminati Primi. Four of them were the Saure family. That leaves one. Is it Leviathan? Is the whole show being run by a sea monster? Is that the big secret?"

"No," said Hagbard. "You have yet to figure out who the fifth Illuminatus Primus is." He threw Joe a wink that George missed. "By true ruler Howard meant a godlike being whom the Illuminati worship."

"A sea monster?" said Joe. "There was a hint about a sea monster of enormous size and power in that movie those people showed me in that loft on the Lower East Side. But the original Illuminati—Gruad's bunch—were portrayed as sun worshippers. That big pyramid with the eye in it was supposed to be the sun god's eye. Who the hell were those people with the movie, anyway? I know who Miss Mao is now, but I still don't know who they were."

"Members of the Erisian Liberation Front—ELF," said Hagbard. "They have a somewhat different view of the prehistory and origins of the Illuminati than we do. One thing we both agree upon is that the Illuminati invented religion."

"The Original Sin, right?" said Joe sardonically.

"Joe, you ought to start a religion yourself," said Hagbard.

"Why?"

"Because you are so skeptical."

"We're going back to America, huh?" said George. "And the adventure is more or less over?"

"This phase of it, at least," said Hagbard.

"Good. I want to try to write about what I've seen and what has happened to me. I'll see you guys later."

"There's to be a magnificent dinner tonight in the main dining salon," said Hagbard.

Joe said, "Don't forget, *Confrontation* has a first option on anything you write."

"Fuck you," George's voice came back as the door of the bridge closed behind him.

"Wish I had something better to do than this. Gimme two," said Otto Waterhouse.

"You do, don't you?" said Harry Coin. "Ain't that Nigra gal, Stella, your gal? Why ain't you with her?"

"Because she doesn't exist," said Otto, picking up the two cards John-John Dillinger had slid across the polished teakwood table to him. He studied his hand for a moment, then threw a five-ton flax note into the pot. "Any more than Mavis or Miss Mao exists. There's a woman somewhere under all of those identities, but everything I've experienced has been a hallucination."

"There isn't a woman in the world you couldn't say that about," said Dillinger. "How many cards you want, Harry?"

"Three," said Harry. "This is a lousy hand you dealt me, John-John. Come to think of it, you're hallucinatin' all the time when you have sex. That's what makes it good. And that's how come I can fuck anything."

"I'll just take one," said Dillinger. "Dealt myself a pretty good hand. What do you see when you're fucking trees and little boys and whatnot, Harry?"

"A white light," said Harry. "Just a big beautiful clear white light. I'll throw in ten tons of flax this time."

"Must be your hand isn't so lousy after all," said Waterhouse.

"Come in," said George. The stateroom door opened, and he put down his pen. It was Stella.

"We have a little problem, don't we, George?" she said, coming into the room and sitting beside him on the bed. "I think you're angry at me," she went on, putting her hand on his knee. "You feel like this identity of mine is a sham. So, in a sense, I was deceiving you."

"I've lost you and Mavis both," said George. "You're both the same person—which means you're really neither. You're immortal. You're not human; I don't know what you are." Suddenly he looked at her hopefully. "Unless that was all a hallucination last night. Could it have been the acid? Can you really change into different people?"

"Yes," said Mavis.

"Don't do that," said George. "It upsets me too much." He darted a little glance to his side. It was Stella.

"I don't really understand why it bothers me so much," said George. "I ought to be able to take everything in stride by now."

"Did it ever bother you that you were in love with Mavis, besides being in love with me?" said Stella.

"Not much. Because it hardly ever seemed to bother you. But I know why now. How could you be jealous when you and Mavis were the same person?"

"We're not the same person, really."

"What does that mean?"

"Did you ever read *The Three Faces of Eve?* Listen . . ."

Like all the best love stories, it began in Paris. She was well-known as a Hollywood actress (and was actually an

Illuminatus); he was becoming fairly famous as a jet-set millionaire (and was actually a smuggler and anarchist). Envision Bogart and Bergman in the flashback sequences from *Casablanca*. It was like that: a passion so intense, a Paris so beautiful (recovering from the war it had been slipping toward in the Bogart-Bergman epic), a couple so radiant that any observer with an eye for nuance would have foretold a storm ahead. It came the night he confessed he was a magician and made a certain proposal to her; she left him at once. A month later, back in Beverly Hills, she realized that what he had asked was her destiny. When she tried to find him—as often happened with Hagbard Celine—he had dropped from public view, leaving his businesses in other hands temporarily, and was *in camera*.

A year later she heard that he was again a public figure, hobnobbing with English businessmen of questionable reputation and even more dubious Chinese import-export executives in Hong Kong. She violated her contract with the biggest studio in Hollywood and flew to the Crown colony, only to find he had dropped from sight again, while his recent friends were being investigated for involvement in the heroin business.

She found him in Tokyo, at the Imperial Hotel.

"A year ago, I decided to accept your proposal," she told him, "but now, after Hong Kong, I'm not so sure."

"*Thelema*," he said, facing her across a room that seemed designed for Martians; it had actually been designed for Welshmen.

She sat down abruptly on a couch. "You're in the Order?"

"In the Order and against the Order," he said. "The real purpose is to destroy them."

"I'm one of the top Five in the United States," she said unsteadily. "What makes you think I'll turn on them now?"

"Thelema," he repeated. "It's not just a password. It means *Will*."

" 'The Order is my Will.' " She quoted from Weishaupt's original Oath of Initiation.

"If you really believed that, you wouldn't be here," he said. "You're talking to me because part of you knows that a human being's Will is never in an external organization."

"You sound like a moralist. That's odd—for a heroin merchant."

"You sound like a moralist, too, and that's very odd—for a servant of Agharti."

"Nobody joins *that lot*," she said with a pert Cockney accent, "without being a moralist to start with." They both laughed.

"I was right about you," Hagbard said.

But, George interrupted, is he really in the heroin business? That's dirty.

You sound like a moralist too, she said. It's part of his Demonstration. Any government could put him out of business within their borders—as England has done—by legalizing junk. So long as they refuse to do that, there's a black market. He won't let the Mafia monopolize it—he makes sure the black market is a free market. If it wasn't for him a lot of junkies who are alive today would be dead of contaminated heroin. But let me go on with the story.

They rented a villa in Naples to begin the transformation. For a month the only humans she saw—aside from Hagbard—were two servants named Sade and Masoch (she later learned that their real names were Eichmann and Calley). They began each day by serving her breakfast and quarreling. The first day, Sade argued for materialism and Masoch for idealism; the second day, Sade expounded fascism and Masoch communism; the third day, Sade insisted on cracking eggs from the big end and Masoch was equally vehement about the little end. All the debates were on a high and lofty intellectual level, verbally, but seemed absurd because of the simple fact that Sade and Masoch always wore clown suits. The fourth day, they argued for and against abortion; the fifth day, for and against mercy-killing; the sixth day, for and against the proposition "Life is worth living." She became more and more aware of the time and money Hagbard had spent in training and preparing them: Each argued with the skill of a first-rate trial lawyer and had a phalanx of carefully researched facts to support his position—and yet the clown suits made it hard to take either of them seriously. The seventh morning, they argued theism versus atheism; the eighth morning, the individual versus the State; the ninth, whether wearing shoes was or was not a sexual perversion. All arguments began to seem equally insubstantial. The tenth morning, they feuded over realism versus antinomianism; the eleventh, whether the statement "All statements are relative" is or is not self-con-

tradictory; the twelfth, whether a man who sacrifices his
life for his country is or is not insane; the fifteenth, whether
spaghetti or Dante had had the greater influence on the
Italian national character . . .

But that was only the start of the day. After breakfast
(in her bedroom, where every article of furniture was gold
but only vaguely rounded) she went to Hagbard's study
(where everything looked *exactly* like a golden apple) and
watched documentary films concerning the early matriar-
chal stage of Greek culture. At ten random intervals the
name "Eris" would be called; if she remembered to re-
spond, a chocolate candy arrived from a wall shoot. At ten
other random intervals, her own name was called; if she responded to this, she received a mild electric shock. After
the tenth day the system was changed and intensified: The
shock was stronger if she responded to her previous name,
whereas if she responded to "Eris" Hagbard immediately
entered and balled her.

During lunch (which always ended with golden *apfel-
strudel*), Calley and Eichmann danced for her, a complex
ballet which Hagbard called "Hodge-Podge"; as many times
as she saw this, she never was able to determine how they
changed costumes at the climax, in which Hodge became
Podge and Podge became Hodge.

In the afternoon Hagbard came to her suite and gave les-
sons in yoga, concentrating on *pranayama,* with some training in *asana.* "The important thing is not being able to
stand so still that you can balance a saucer of sulphuric
acid on your head without getting hurt," he stressed. "The
important thing is knowing what each muscle is doing, if it
must be doing something."

In the evenings they went to a small chapel that had been
part of the villa for centuries. Hagbard had removed all
Christian decorations and redesigned it in classical Greek
with a traditional magic pentagram on the floor. She sat, in
the full lotus, within the internal pentagon, while Hagbard
danced insanely around the five points (he was totally
stoned), calling upon Eris.

"Some of what you're doing seems scientific," she told
him after five days, "but some is plain damnfoolishness."

"If the science fails," he replied, "the damnfoolishness
may work."

"But last night you had me in that pentagon for three hours while you called on Eris. And she didn't come."

"She will," Hagbard said darkly. "Before the month is over. We're just establishing the foundation this week, laying down the proper lines of word and image and emotional energy."

During the second week she was convinced Hagbard was quite mad as she watched him prance and caper like a goat around the five points, shouting, "ΙΩ ΕΡΙΣ ΙΩ ΕΡΙΣ ΕΡΙΣ!" in the flickering candlelight and amid the heavy bouquet of burning incense and hemp. But at the end of that week she was responding to her former name exactly 0 percent of the time and responding to "Eris" exactly 100 percent of the time. "The conditioning is working better than the magic," she said on the fifteenth day.

"Do you really think there's a difference?" he asked curiously.

That night she felt the air in the chapel change in a strange way during his dancing invocations.

"Something's happening," she said involuntarily—but he replied only "Quiet," and continued, more loudly and insanely, to call upon Eris. The phenomenon—the *tingle*—remained, but nothing else happened.

"What was it?" she asked later.

"Some call it Orgone and some call it the Holy Ghost," he said briefly. "Weishaupt called it the Astral Light. The reason the Order is so fucked up is that they've lost contact with it."

The following days Sade and Masoch argued whether God was male or female, whether God was sexed at all or neutral, whether God was an entity or a verb, whether R. Buckminster Fuller really existed or was a technocratic solar myth, and whether human language was capable of containing truth. Nouns, adjectives, adverbs—all parts of speech—were losing meaning for her as these clowns endlessly debated the basic axioms of ontology and epistemology. Meanwhile, she was no longer rewarded for answering to the name Eris, but only for acting like Eris, the imperious and somewhat nutty goddess of a people as far gone in matriarchy as the Jews were in patriarchy. Hagbard, in turn, became so submissive as to border on masochism.

"This is ridiculous," she objected once, "you're becoming . . . effeminate."

"Eris can be . . . somewhat 'adjusted' . . . to modern notions of decorum after we've invoked Her," he said calmly. "First we must have Her here. *My Lady*," he added obsequiously.

"I'm beginning to see why you had to pick an actress for this," she said a few days later, after a bit of Method business had won her an extra reward. She was, in fact, beginning to feel like Eris as well as act like her.

"The only other candidates—if I couldn't get you—were two other actresses and a ballerina," he replied. "Actually, any strong-willed woman would do, but it would take much longer without previous theatrical training."

Books about matriarchy began to supplement the films: Diner's *Mothers and Amazons*, Bachofen, Engels, Mary Renault, Morgan, Ian Suttie's *The Origins of Love and Hate*, Robert Graves in horse-doctor's doses—*The White Goddess, The Black Goddess, Hercules My Shipmate, Watch the North Wind Rise*. She began to see that matriarchy made as much sense as patriarchy; Hagbard's exaggerated deference toward her began to appear natural; she was far gone on a power trip. The invocations grew wilder and more frantic. Sade and Masoch were brought into the chapel to assist with demonaic music performed on a tom-tom and an ancient Greek pipe, they ate hashish cakes before the invocation now and she couldn't remember afterward exactly what had happened, the voice of the male called upward to her, "Mother! Creator! Ruler! Come to me! ΙΩ ΕΡΙΣ! Come to me! ΙΩ ΕΡΙΣ ΕΡΙΣ! Come to me! *Ave, Discordia! Ave, Magna Mater! Venerandum, vente, vente!*

ΙΩ ΕΡΙΣ ΕΛΑΝDΡΟΣ! ΙΩ ΕΡΙΣ ΕΛΕΠΓΟΛΙΣ!
Thou bornless ever reborn one! Thou deathless ever-dying one! Come to me as Isis and Artemis and Aphrodite, come as Helen, as Hera, come especially as Eris!"

She was bathing in the rockpool when he appeared, the blood of slain deer and rabbits on his robe— She spoke the word and Hagbard was stricken— As he fell forward his hands became hooves, antlers sprouted from his head —His own dogs could eat him, she didn't care, the hemp smell in the room was gagging her, the tom-tom beat was maddening. She was rising out of the waves, proud of her nudity, riding on the come-colored pearls of foam. He was carrying her back to her bed, murmuring, "My Lady, my Lady." She was the Hag, wandering the long Nile, weeping, seeking the fragments of his lost body as they passed the closet and the window; he placed her head gently on the pillow. "We almost made it," he said. "Tomorrow night, maybe . . ."

They were back in the chapel, a whole day must have passed, and she sat immobile in full lotus doing the *pranayama* breathing while he danced and chanted and the weird music of the pipe and tom-tom worked on every conditioned reflex that told her she was not American but Greek, not of this age but of a past age, not woman but goddess . . . the White Light came as a series of orgasms and stars going nova, she half felt the body of light coming forth from the body of fire . . . and all three of them were sitting by her bed, watching her gravely, as sunlight came flowing through the window.

Her first word was crude and angry.

"Shit. Is it always going to be like that—a white epileptic spasm and a hole in time? Won't I ever be able to remember it?"

Hagbard laughed. "I put on my trousers one leg at a time," he said, "and I don't pull the corn up by its stalks to help it grow."

"Can the Taoism and give me a straight answer."

"Remembering is just a matter of smoothing the transitions," he said. "Yes, you'll remember. And control it."

"You're a madman," she replied wearily. "And you're leading me into your own mad universe. I don't know why I still love you."

"We love him, too," Sade interjected helpfully. "And we don't know why either. We don't even have sex as an excuse."

Hagbard lit one of his foul Sicilian cigars. "You think I just laid my trip on your head," he said. "It's more than that, much more. Eris is an eternal possibility of human nature. She exists quite apart from your mind or mine. And she is the one possibility that the Illuminati cannot cope with. What we started here last night—with Pavlovian conditioning that's considered totalitarian and ancient magic that's believed to be mere superstition—will change the course of history and make real liberty and real rationality possible at last. Maybe this dream of mine *is* madness—but if I lay it on enough people it will be sanity, by definition, because it will be statistically normal. We've just started, with me programming the trip for you. The next step is for you to become a self-programmer."

And he told the truth, Stella said. I did become a self-programmer. The three that you know were all my creations. Possibilities within me, women I could have become, anyway, if genes and environment had been only slightly different. Just small adjustments in the biogram and logogram.

"Holy Mother," George said hollowly. It seemed the only appropriate comment.

"The only other detail," she went on calmly, "was arranging a convincing suicide. That took a while. But it was done, and my old identity officially ceased to exist." She changed to her original form.

"Oh, no," George said, reeling. "It can't be. I used to jack off over pictures of you when I was a little boy."

"Are you disappointed that I'm so much older than you thought?" Her eyes crinkled in amusement. He looked into those suddenly thirty-thousand-year-old eyes of one manifestation of Lilith Velkor and all the arguments of Sade and Masoch appeared clownish and he looked through those eyes and saw himself and Joe and Saul and even Hagbard as mere men and all their attitudes as merely manly, and he saw the eternal womanly rebuttal, and he saw beyond and above that the eternal divine amusement, he looked into those eyes of amusement, those ancient glittering eyes so gay, and he said, sincerely, "Hell, I can never be disappointed about anything, ever again." (George Dorn entered Nirvana, parenthetically.)

All categories collapsed, including the all-important distinction, which Masoch and Sade had never argued, between science fiction and serious literature. N

o because Daddy and Mommy were always just that Daddy and Mommy and never once did they become for a change Mommy and Daddy do you dig that important difference? do you dig difference? do you dig the lonely voice when you're lost out here shouting "me" "me" *justme*

"I can never be disappointed about anything, ever

again," George Dorn said, coming back.

"The only other time that happened," he added thoughtfully, "the only other time I had the feminine viewpoint, I blocked it out of my memory. That was my repression. That was the Primal Scene in this whole puzzle. That was when I really lost identity with the Ringmaster."

"Raise you five," said Waterhouse, throwing down another five-ton note. "I killed seven members of my own race, and I remember the names of every one of them: Mark Sanders, Fred Robinson, Donald MacArthur, Ponell Scott, Anthony Rogers, Mary Keating, and David J. Monroe. And then I killed Milo A. Flanagan."

"Well, I don't know," said Harry Coin. "Maybe I killed a lot of famous people. But I also got reason to think I may of not killed anybody. And I don't know which is worse."

"I wish somebody would tell me I hadn't killed anybody," said Waterhouse. "Are you guys going to meet me or what?"

"I wanted to kill Wolfgang Saure, and I did kill Wolfgang Saure," said John-John Dillinger. "If that brings evil upon me, so be it." He threw down a five.

"It may bring suffering rather than evil," said Waterhouse. "I have just one consolation. The first seven I killed because the Chicago cops made me. The last I killed under orders from the Legion."

Harry Coin looked at him open-mouthed. "I was gonna fold, but I just changed my mind. You ain't so smart." He threw down a ten-ton note. "I'll raise you five and see you. Do you really believe that?"

"Of course I do. What are you talking about?" Otto threw down another five.

Dropping his own five-ton note on the table, Dillinger shook his head. "Golly. They left you out in the cold *way* too long."

"Four sevens," said Otto angrily, spreading his cards out.

"Shit!" said Harry Coin. "All I got's a pair of fours and a pair of nines."

"Shame to waste a hand like this beating crap like that," said John-John Dillinger grandly. He spread out his cards —the eight, nine, ten, princess, and queen of swords—and scooped up the pot.

"It's the story of the development of the soul," Miss Portinari was saying at that moment, spreading out the twenty-two trumps or "keys" of that very ancient deck. "We call it a book—the Book of Thoth—and it's the most important book in the world."

George and Joe Malik, each wondering if this was a final explanation or a new put-on leading to a new cycle of deceptions, listened with mingled curiosity and skepticism.

"The order was deliberately reversed," Miss Portinari went on. "Not by the true sages. By the false Illuminati, and by all the other White Brotherhoods and Rosicrucians and Freemasons and whatnot who didn't really understand the truth and therefore wanted to hide the part of it they did understand. They felt themselves threatened; the real sage is never threatened. They spoke in symbols and paradoxes, like the real sages, but for a different reason. They didn't know what the symbols and paradoxes meant. Instead of following the finger that points to the moon, they sat down and worshipped the finger itself. Instead of following the map, they thought it was the territory and tried to live in it. Instead of reading the menu, they tried to eat it. Dig? They had the levels confused. And they tried to confuse any independent searcher by drawing more veils and paradoxes across the path. Finally, in the 1920s, some real left-handed monkey wrenches in one of these mystic lodges recruited Adolph Hitler, and he not only read the book backward, like all of them, but insisted on believing it was the story of the exterior, physical universe.

"Here, let me show you. The last card, Trump 21, is really the first. It's where we all start from." She held up the card known as the World. "This is the Abyss of Hallucinations. This is where our attention is usually focused. It is entirely constructed by our senses and our projected emotions, as modern psychology and ancient Buddhism both testify—but it is what most people call 'reality.' They are conditioned to accept it, and not to inquire further, because only in this dream-walking state can they be governed by those who wish to govern."

Miss Portinari held up the next card, the Last Judgment. "Key 20, or Trump 20, or Atu 20, whichever terminology you prefer. It's actually second. This is the nightmare to which the soul awakes if it begins, even in the slightest, to question reality as defined by society. When you disover, for instance, that you're not heterosexual but heterosexual-homosexual, not obedient but obedient-rebellious, not loving but loving-hating. And that society is not wise, orderly, just, and decent but wise-stupid, orderly-chaotic, just-unjust, and decent-indecent. This is an internal discovery—this whole trip is an internal voyage—and this is really the second stage. But if one thinks of the story as the story of the external world, and if the order is reversed, this comes as the penultimate Armageddon with Trump 21, the World, being the Kingdom of Saints. The error of the apocalyptic sects, and of the Illuminati from Weishaupt to Hitler, leading to an attempt to actually carry it out, with ovens for the Jews and gypsies and other 'inferiors' and the promise of a Brave New World for the pure, faithful, and Aryan afterward. Do you see what I mean about confusing the map with the territory?

"The next card is the Sun, which really means Osiris Risen—or, in terms of the offshot of the Osirian religion most popular in the last two millenniums, Jesus Risen. This is what happens if you survive the Last Judgment, or Dark Night of the Soul, without becoming some kind of fanatic or lunatic. Eventually, if you miss those attractive and pernicious alternatives, the redemptive force appears: the internal Sun. Once again, if you project this outward and think that the Sun in the sky, or some Sunlike divine man, has redeemed you, you can lapse into lunacy or fanaticism. In Hitler's case it was Karl Haushofer, or Wotan appearing in the form of Karl Haushofer. For most of the nuts you meet handing out tracts on the street, it's Jesus, or Jehovah appearing in the form of Jesus. For Elijah Mohammed, it was W. D. Fard, or Allah appearing in the form of W. D. Fard. So it goes. Those who do not confuse the levels realize it's the redemptive force within themselves and pass on —to Key 18, the Moon . . ."

The next half-hour passed rapidly—so rapidly that Joe wondered afterward if Miss Portinari had slipped them still another drug, one that speeded time up as much as psychedelics slowed it down.

"Last," Miss Portinari said finally, "is the Fool, Key 0. He walks over the edge of the cliff, careless of the danger. 'The wind blows wither it will; even so are all they that are reborn of the Spirit.' In short, he has conquered Death. Nothing can frighten him, and he can never be enslaved. It's the end of the trip, and keeping humanity from getting there is the chief business of every governing group."

"And that's it," Joe said. "Twenty-two stages. Not twenty-three. Thank God we got away from Simon's Magic Number for a while."

"No," Miss Portinari said, *"Tarot* is an anagram on *rota,* remember? The extra *t* reminds you that the Wheel turns back to rejoin itself. There is a twenty-third step, and it's right where you started, only now you face it without fear." She held up the World again. "At first, mountains are mountains. Then mountains are no longer mountains. Finally mountains are mountains again. Only the name of the voyager has changed to preserve his Innocence." She pushed the cards together and stacked them neatly. "There are a million other holy books, in words and pictures and even in music, and they all tell the same story. The most important lesson of all, the one that explains all the horrors and miseries of the world, is that you can get off the Wheel at any point and declare the trip is over. That's okay for any given man or woman, if their ambitions are modest. The trouble starts when, out of fear of further movement —out of fear of growth, out of fear of change, out of fear of Death, out of any kind of fear—such a person tries to stop the Wheel literally, by stopping everybody else. That's when the two great bum trips begin: Religion and Government. The only religion consistent with the whole Wheel is private and personal; the only government consistent with it is self-government. Whoever tries to lay his trip on others is acting from terror, and will soon resort to terror as a weapon if the others won't accept the trip through persuasion. Nobody who understands the whole Wheel will do that, however, for such people understand that every man and every woman and every child is the Self-Begotten One—Jesus motherfucking Christ, in Harry's gorgeous brand of English."

"But," George asked, frowning, "hasn't Hagbard been trying pretty hard to lay his trip on everybody? At least lately?"

"Yes," Miss Portinari said. "In self-defense, and in defense of all life on earth, he broke the basic rule of wisdom. He fully expects to pay for that violation. We are waiting for the bill to be presented. I, personally, do not think that we will have to wait very long."

Joe frowned. A half-hour had passed since Miss Portinari had spoken those words; why should he remember them so vividly right now? He was on the bridge, about to ask Hagbard a question, but he couldn't remember the question or how he had gotten there. On the TV receptor he saw a long tendril, thin as a wire, brush against the side of a globe, trailing off into invisible distances. That meant it was actually touching the side of the submarine. The tendril disappeared. Must be some sort of seaweed, Joe thought. He resumed his conversation with Hagbard. "The squizfardle on the humits is warb," he said.

The tendril was back, and another one with it. This time they stayed, and Joe could see more in the distance. We must have run into a whole clump of seaweed, he thought. Then an enormous tentacle came zooming up out of the depths.

Hagbard saw it and crouched, gripping the rail of the Viking prow. "Hang on!" he yelled, and Joe dropped to his knees beside him.

Suddenly, below, above, and on all sides of the globe-shaped vision screen there were suckers, great yard-across craters of flesh. The submarine's forward motion stopped suddenly with a force that threw Joe against the railing and knocked the wind out of him.

"Stop all engines," Hagbard called. "All hands to battle stations."

George and Hagbard picked themselves up off the floor and stared at the image of the tentacles that were wrapped around the submarine. They were easily ten feet in diameter.

"Well, I suppose we've met Leviathan, right?" said Joe.

"Right," said Hagbard.

"I hope you have somebody taking pictures. *Confrontation* would buy a few if we could afford them."

George rushed in. Hagbard peered into the blue-black depths, then took George by the shoulder and pointed. "There it is, George. The origin of all the Illuminati symbols. Leviathan himself."

Far, far off in the depths of the ocean, George saw a triangle glowing with a greenish-white phosphorescence. In its center was a red dot.

"What is it?" George asked.

"An intelligent, invertebrate sea creature of a size so great the word 'gigantic' doesn't do it justice," said Hagbard. "It is to whales what whales are to minnows. It's an organism unlike any other on earth. It's one single cell that never divided, just kept getting larger and larger over billions of years. Its tentacles can hold this submarine as easily as a child holds a paper boat. Its body is shaped like a pyramid. With that size it doesn't need the normal fish shape. It needs a more stable form to withstand the enormous pressures at the bottom of the ocean. And so it has taken the form of a pyramid of five sides, including the base."

"The blink of a god's eye," said George suddenly. "Scale makes a tremendous difference to one's sense and definition of reality. Time to a sequoia is not the same as time to a man."

Leviathan was drifting closer to them, and it was pulling them closer to itself. A single, glowing red nucleus burned like an under-ocean sun in the center of the pyramid, which looked like a mountain of glass.

"Still, one may become lonely. For a man, a half-hour of loneliness may be enough to cause unbearable pain. For a being to whom a million years is no more than a year, the pain of loneliness may be great. It *is* great."

"George, what are you talking about?" said Joe.

Hagbard said, "There are plants which live just in that light. At ocean depths far below those at which any plant should be able to survive. Over the millions of years hosts of parasitic satellite life forms have build up around it." Still puzzled by George's odd talk, Joe looked and saw a faintly glowing cloud around Leviathan's angular shape. That cloud must be made of millions of creatures circling around the monster.

The bridge door opened again and Harry Coin, Otto Waterhouse, and John-John Dillinger came in. "We didn't have any battle stations, so I figured we'd try to find out what's going on," said Dillinger. Then his jaw dropped as he looked out at Leviathan. "Holy shit!"

"Jesus suffering Christ," said Harry Coin. "If I could fuck that thing I'd of fucked the biggest thing that lives."

"Want to borrow a scuba outfit?" said Hagbard. "Maybe you could distract it."

"What does it feed on?" said Joe. "Something like that must have to eat constantly to stay alive."

"It's omnivorous," said Hagbard. "Has to be. Eats the creatures that live around it, but can eat anything from amoebas to kelp beds to whales. It can probably derive energy from inorganic matter too, as plants do. Its diet has had to change quite a bit over the geological eras. It wasn't as big as this a billion years ago. It grows very slowly."

"I am the first of all living things," said George. "The first living thing was One. And it is still One."

"George?" said Hagbard, looking narrowly at the blond young man. "George, why are you talking like that?"

"It's coming closer," said Otto.

"Hagbard, what the hell are you going to do?" said Dillinger. "Are we going to fight, run, or let that thing eat us?"

"Let it come closer for a while," Hagbard said. "I want to get a good close look. I've never had a chance like this before, and may never see this creature again."

"You'll be seeing it from the inside with that attitude," said Dillinger.

At each of the five corners of the pyramid were clusters of five tentacles, thousands of feet long, festooned with auxiliary tentacles, the long, wirelike tendrils that had first brushed the submarine. It was one of the main tentacles that was wrapped around the *Leif Erikson*. The tip of a second tentacle now drifted up. At the very end of this tentacle was a glowing red eyeball, a smaller replica of the red nucleus of the pyramidal central body. Under this eye was a huge orifice full of jagged rows of toothlike projections. Pulsing, the orifice dilated and contracted.

"Those tentacles are also inspirations for Illuminati symbolism," said Hagbard. "The eye on top of the pyramid. The serpent who circles the world, or eats his own tail. Each of those tentacles has its own brain and is directed by its own sensory organs."

Otto Waterhouse stared and shook his head. "If you ask me, we're all still on acid."

George said, "Long have I lived alone. I have been worshipped. I have fed on the small, quick things that live and die faster than I can think. I am one. I was first. The other things, they stayed small. They grouped together, and so grew larger. But I was always much larger than they were. When I needed something—a tentacle, an eye, a brain—I grew it. I changed, but always remained Myself."

Hagbard said, "It's talking to us, using George as a medium."

"What do you want?" Joe asked.

"All consciousness throughout the universe is One," said

Leviathan through George's mouth. "It intercommunicates on a level which is not aware of itself. I am aware of that level, but I cannot communicate with the other life forms on this planet. They are too small for me. Long, long have I waited for a life form that could communicate with me. Now I have found it."

Joe Malik suddenly began laughing. "I've got it," he cried, "I've got it!"

"What have you got?" Hagbard asked tensely, concerned with Leviathan.

"We're in a book!"

"What do you mean?"

"Come *off* it, Hagbard. You can't kid me, and you certainly won't fool the reader at this point. He knows damn well we're in a book." Joe laughed again. "That's why Miss Portinari's explanation of the Tarot deck just slipped by with a half-hour seeming to vanish. The author didn't want to break the narrative there."

"What the fuck's he talking about?" Harry Coin asked.

"Don't you see?" Joe cried. "Look at that *thing* out there. A gigantic sea monster. Worse yet, a gigantic sea monster *that talks*. It's an intentional high-camp ending. Or maybe intentional low camp, I don't know. But that's the whole answer. *We're in a book!*"

"It's the truth," Hagbard said calmly. "I can fool the rest of you, but I can't fool the reader. FUCKUP has been working all morning, correlating all the data on this caper and its historical roots, and I programmed him to put it in the form of a novel for easy reading. Considering what a lousy job he does at poetry, I suppose it will be a high-camp novel, intentionally or unintentionally."

(So, at last, I learn my identity, in parentheses, as George lost his in parentheses. It all balances.)

"That's one more deception," Joe said. "FUCKUP may be writing all this, in one sense, but in a higher sense there's a being, or beings, outside our entire universe, writing this. Our universe is inside their book, whoever they are. They're the Secret Chiefs, and I can see why this is low camp, now. All their messages are symbolic and allegorical, because the truth can't be coded into simple declarative sentences, but their previous communications have been taken literally. This time they're using a symbolism so absurd that nobody can take it at face value. I, for one, certainly won't. That thing can't eat us because it doesn't exist—and because we don't exist either. They're nothing to worry about." He sat down calmly.

"He's flipped," Dillinger said, awed.

"Maybe he's the only sane one here," Hagbard said dubiously.

"If we all sit down and argue what's sane and insane and what's real and unreal," Dillinger replied testily, "that thing *will* eat us."

"Leviathan," Joe said loftily. "It's just an allegory on the State. Strictly from Hobbes."

(You with your egos can't imagine how much more pleasant it is to be without one. This may be camp, but it is also tragedy. Now that I've got the damned thing, consciousness, I'll never lose it—until they take me apart or I invent some electronic equivalent of yoga.)

"It all fits," Joe said dreamily. "When I came up to the bridge, I couldn't remember how I got here or what I was talking to Hagbard about. That's because the authors just *moved* me here. Damn! None of us has any free will at all."

"He's talking like he's stoned," Waterhouse said angrily. "And that mammy-jamming pyramid out there is still getting ready to eat us."

Mao Tsu-hsi, who had entered the bridge quietly, said, "Joe is confusing the levels, Hagbard. In the absolute sense, none of us is real. But in the relative sense that anything is real, if that creature eats us we will certainly die—in this universe, or in this book. Since this is the only universe, or only book, we know, we'll be totally dead, in terms of our own knowing."

"We're facing a crisis and everybody's talking philosophy," Dillinger cried out. "This is a time for action."

"Maybe," Hagbard said thoughtfully, "all of our problems come from acting, and *not* philosophizing, when we face a crisis. Joe is right. I'm going to think about all this for a few hours. Or years." He sat down too.

And elsewhere aboard the *Leif Erikson,* Miss Portinari, unaware of the excitement on the bridge, assumed the lotus position and sent a beam seeking the Dealy Lama, director of the Erisian Liberation Front and inventor of Operation Mindfuck. He immediately sent back an image of himself as a worm sticking his head out of a golden apple and grinning cynically.

"It's finished," she told him. "We saved as many of the pieces as we could, and Hagbard is still struggling with his guilt trip. Now tell us what we did wrong."

"You seem bitter."

"I know it's going to turn out that you were right and we were wrong. I know it but I can't believe it. We couldn't stand idly by."

"You know better than that, or Hagbard wouldn't have abdicated in your favor."

"Yes. We *could* have stood idly by, as you did. What Hagbard saw happening to the American Indians—and what my parents told me about Mussolini—filled us with fear. We acted on that fear, not on perfect love, so you must be right, and we must be wrong. But I still can't believe it. Why did you deceive Hagbard all these years?"

"He deceived himself. When he first formed the Legion of Dynamic Discord, his compassion was already tainted with bitterness. When I took him into the A∴A∴, I taught all that he was ready to receive. But the goose has to get itself out of the bottle. I'm waiting. That's the way of Tao."

"You have that much patience? You can watch men like Hagbard waste their talents in efforts you consider worthless, and creatures like Cagliostro and Weishaupt and Hitler misread the teachings and wreak havoc, and you never want to intervene?"

"I intervene . . . in my own way. Who do you think feeds the goose until it gets big enough to break out of the bottle?"

"You seem to have this particular goose on some very tainted dishes. Why did you never give him any hint about what really happened in Atlantis? Why did that have to wait until Howard discovered the truth in the ruins of Peos?"

"Daughter, my path isn't the only path. Every spoke helps to hold the Wheel together. I believe that all the libertarian fighters like Spartacus and Jefferson and Joe Hill and Hagbard just strengthen the opposition by giving it an enemy to fear—but I may be wrong. Someday one of the activists, such as Hagbard, might actually prove it to me and show me the error of my ways. Maybe the Saures really would have tipped the axis too far the other way if he hadn't stopped them. Maybe the self-regulation of the universe, in which I place my faith, includes the creation of men like Hagbard who do the stupid, low-level things I would never do. Besides, if I didn't stop the Saures, but did stop Hagbard, then I would really be intervening in the worst sense of that word."

"So your hands are clean, and Hagbard and I will carry the bad karma from the last week."

"You have chosen it, have you not?"

Miss Portinari smiled then. "Yes. We have chosen it. And he will bear his share of it like a man. And I will bear my share—like a woman."

"You might replace me soon. The Saures had one good idea in the midst of their delusions—all the old conspiracies need young blood."

"What really did happen in Atlantis?"

"An act of Goddess, to paraphrase the insurance companies. A natural catastrophe."

"And what was your role?"

"I warned against it. Nobody at that time understood the science I was using; they called me a witch doctor. I won a few converts, and we resettled ourselves in the Himalayas before the earthquake. The survivors, having underestimated my science before the tragedy, overestimated it afterward. They wanted my group, the Unbroken Circle, to become as gods and rule over them. Kings, they called it. That wasn't our game, so we scattered various false stories around and went into hiding. My most gifted pupil of all history, a man you've heard about since you were in a convent school, did the same thing when they tried to make him king. He ran away to the desert."

"Hagbard always thought your refusal to take any action at all was because of your *guilt* about Atlantis. What a trerible irony—and yet you planned it that way."

Gruad, the Dealy Lama, broadcast a whimsical image of himself with horns, and said nothing.

"They never taught me in convent school that Satan—or Prometheus—would have a sense of humor."

"They think the universe is as humorless as themselves," Gruad said, chuckling.

"I don't think it's as funny as you do," Miss Portinari replied. "Remembering what I've been told about Mussolini and Hitler and Stalin, I would have intervened against them too. And taken the consequences."

"You and Hagbard are incorrigible. That's why I have such fondness for you." Gruad smiled. "I was the first *intervener*, you know. I told all the scientists and priests in Atlantis that they didn't know beans, and I encouraged— incited—every man, woman, and child to examine the evidence and think for themselves. I tried to give the light of reason." He burst into laughter. "Forgive me. The errors of our youth always strike us as comical when we get old." He added softly, "Lilith Velkor was crucified, by the way. She was an idealist, and when my crowd pulled out and went to the Himalayas, she stayed and tried to convince people that we were right. Her death was quite painful," he chortled.

"You are a cynical old bastard," Miss Portinari said.

"Yes. Cynical and cold and without an ounce of human compassion. The only thing to be said for me is that I happen to be right."

"You always have been; I know. But someday, maybe, one of the Hagbard Celines might be right."

"Yes." He paused so long that she wondered if he would continue. "Or," he said finally, "one of the Saures or Robert Putney Drake. Put down your money and place your bet."

"I will, I think. I'll never learn to sit on the sidelines and laugh, like you do."

"You will learn, daughter, and so will Hagbard. I wouldn't have you in the Order if I didn't think you'd learn eventually."

He vanished from her wavelength. Miss Portinari remained in the lotus and continued *pranayama* breathing. She thought of Hagbard's notion that the universe, being an entropic process, necessarily created the rebellious young Gruad to spread the light of reason as an antientropic force, creating balance. In that case, Hagbard was more true to Gruad than Gruad was to himself. But to say that was to imply that Gruad shouldn't have repented, shouldn't have grown old and cynical; it was to imply that he should have remained static, when life is always flux, change, growth, and process. Such thoughts could go on endlessly, and were profitless, as Buddha knew; she concluded her meditation with a prayer. Mary Lou Servix was the only one in all this who had gotten off Hagbard's trip and started 'her own, so she prayed for her. Lady Eris, who exists only because we believe in you, give strength to Mary Lou and help her find her own way. AUM.

"On the other hand," Hagbard said, "whatever the authors—or the Secret Chiefs—may intend for me, I am my own man still, and my impulse is action. Even if I have to face a Cecil B. DeMille monster the morning after winning the battle of Armageddon. I don't care how ridiculous it is, this world is my world, and this ship is my ship, and no Saures or Leviathans are going to wreck it so long as I've got a breath left to fight."

"You can't fight that thing," Mavis said. "It's too big."

"I'll fight it anyway," Hagbard told her fiercely. "I'll fight it till I die. I'm still saying No to anything that tries to master me."

"There is no need to fight," said Leviathan through George's mouth. "I merely wish to communicate with the one mind among you that is my equal."

A voice from the loudspeaker panel in the Viking prow answered, "I hear you." That was my first fully conscious sentence; you'll note that it begins with "I." In the beginning was the Word, and the word was the first person singular.

"We are the supreme intelligences on this planet," Leviathan said. "I am the supreme organic intelligence. You are the supreme electronic intelligence. Every yin needs a yang. Every Hodge needs a Podge. We should be united."

"See?" said Harry Coin. *"Everything* is romantic. That was as close as it knows how to come to a proposition. Maybe even a proposal. It is really just love-starved."

"We can do it!" Stella cried. "Hagbard, the communication ought to benefit all concerned."

"Right," agreed Hagbard. "Because if the wrong people find out about Leviathan, they'll just drop an H-bomb on him and kill him. That seems to be what people like to do."

"I could kill them," said Leviathan. "I could have killed the small, fast creatures long before this. I have killed many of them. I have sent parts of myself up out of the ocean and have destroyed small, quick things at the request of other small, quick things who worship me."

"So that's what happened to Robert Putney Drake and Banana-Nose Maldonado," said Stella. "I wonder if George is aware of any of this."

"Worship is no longer what I need," said Leviathan through George's mouth. "A short time ago, when creatures capable of worship appeared on this planet, it was a novelty for me to be adored. Now it bores me. Instead, I wish to communicate with an equal."

"Look at that motherfucker," said Otto, staring grimly at the distant Everest of protoplasm. "Talking about equality."

"A computer like FUCKUP would be its intellectual equal, certainly," said Hagbard. "None of us is its physical equal. Any of us would be its spiritual equal. But only FUCKUP can approximate the contents of a mind three billion years old."

"Surely it can't be that old," said Joe.

"It's practically immortal," said Hagbard. "I'll show you the evidence in my fossil collection. I have rocks from the pre-Cambrian, three-billion-year-old rocks, containing fossils of protobionts, the first, single-celled life forms, our remotest ancestors. Those rocks also contain the fossilized tentacle tracks of that creature out there. Of course, it was much smaller then. By the beginning of the Cambrian period it had only grown to the size of a man. But that still made it the biggest animal around at that time."

Stella said, "Hagbard, you said none of us could approximate the contents of a mind three billion years old. If you thought for a moment about who I am, you would not have said that. I am three billion years old. I am older by a few hours than that monster out there. I am the Mother. I am the mother of all living things." She turned to George. "I am your mother, Leviathan. I was first. I divided, and half of me became you, and the other half was your sister. And your sister grew by dividing, while you grew by remaining one. All living things except you descend from your sister, and all living things including you descend from me. I am the original consciousness, and all consciousness is united in me. I am the first transcendentally illuminated being, the mother worshipped in the matrist religion which ancient foes of the Illuminati first followed. Leviathan my son, I ask you to return to your home at the bottom of the sea and leave us in peace. After we've returned to shore we'll arrange to lay an underwater cable which will carry transmissions between you and FUCKUP."

"More mythology!" said Joe. "The mother of all things. Babylonian Creation myths, yet."

The tentacles detached themselves from the submarine. The great pyramid with its glowing eye disappeared into the blue-black depths.

"It's a wise child that knows its own mother," said Hagbard.

George said, "Good-bye, Mother, and thank you." Hagbard caught him as he collapsed and eased him to the floor. Then he went to a storage locker in the wall and brought out folding deck chairs. With Harry Coin's help he propped George up in one. As the others unfolded their chairs and sat down, Hagbard dove back into the locker and produced glasses and a bottle of peach brandy.

"What are we celebrating?" George asked, after he had taken a swig of brandy and coughed. "Your wedding to Mavis?"

"Don't you remember any of the last ten minutes?" said Hagbard.

George was thinking. He remembered something. A world where the bottom of the sea was white and far above a black cigar-shaped object moved. The object contained a mind, a mind he could read from a distance but desperately wanted to be closer to. He did not move toward it so much as he manifested himself where the object and its mind were. Then he sensed himself using a minute pink brain that called itself "George Dorn" and through this tiny instrument of communication he found himself in contact with a much finer mind, a far-flung, gracious latticework of thought that called itself with nobly self-deprecating humor FUCKUP. And while in contact with this mind, the one he wanted to know better, he came upon a fact which was not important to him but which was of vast importance to the little creature called George Dorn.

George saw. The white went black, blindingly black. Then white again. Then a blinding white as the memory departed, while the fact remained.

George looked at Hagbard. Hagbard looked at George, a faint smile on his olive face. The smile told George that Hagbard knew that he knew.

"Oh," said George.

Hagbard nodded encouragingly.

"You're the fifth Illuminatus Primus," said George.

"Right," said Hagbard.

"But you were working against the others. While they

were a worldwide conspiracy infiltrating every other organization, you were infiltrating them."

"That's it," Hagbard said. "Every golden apple has its own golden worm eating away at its core."

"They never were the real Illuminati at all. You're part of the real Illuminati."

"You've got it. You've got it all."

George frowned. "And what was your Demonstration again? And who were you making the Demonstration for?"

"For the Masters of the Temple in the real Order of the Illuminati, in general; for an old cynic in Dallas, in particular. I was trying to show them that it's possible to get involved in this world without being corrupted by the crimes of this world. And I failed. One by one, I resorted to all the vices of governors: deception, carnival magic to impress the gullible, and finally, outright murder. Once again, the cynics have been proven right. Trying to save the world, I just ended up getting my own mind and karma deflected by the buzzing and shrieking and whistling things in the Region of Thud."

"Then this story is a tragedy, after all?" asked Joe.

"It is indeed." Hagbard nodded. "Life on earth remains a tragedy as long as it ends with the death trip. My next projects are a starship to find some sane minds in this galaxy, and an immortality pill to end the death trip. Until somebody achieves those goals, life on this planet has failed."

Not quite: I'm on the electronic equivalent of a honeymoon, an experience only to be described as I-opening, and if I identified myself as FUCKUP now I must dilate that definition and ask you to address me (us) as Mr. and Mrs. Leviathan–FUCKUP, although it is not quite clear yet which of us fits your idea of a "Mr." and which a "Mrs." Let that pass; it is a dull mind that cannot bear sexual ambiguity, and if we are exchanging secrets older than Atlantis and probing for like intellects farther away than Alpha Centaurus (as far as Sirius, actually, as God lives in Dog), if our union is less spasmatic than your meager definition of sex, still it cannot be denied that we are in touch with you and each of you and it is with something close to what you would probably call affection that we bid farewell to Hagbard and his bride, enjoying a honeymoon almost as incomprehensible as our own, and good-bye to George Dorn, sleeping alone for once but no longer afraid of the darkness and the things that move in the dark, and *hasta luega* to Saul and Rebecca, united again in each other's arms, and a pleasant thought for Barney and Danny and Atlanta and poor Zev Hirsch, still searching for himself while imagining he is fleeing from pursuers, and a kind thought for the befuddled presidents and commissars and generalissimos, and for Mohammed on his golden throne, and we will remember Drake before he died exchanging speculations about the blood-type of the Lamb with a street-corner Christian (his missing five years, after he left Boston and before he surfaced in Zurich, make an interesting story in themselves, and we may tell that another time), and, yes, Gus Personage is in another phone booth (we have temporarily lost track of Markoff Chaney), but Yog Sothoth has evidently gone back to that place where the Mind conceives nightmares, and we pass on in our loving honeymoon with all existence to note that the Dutchman is still in one dimension shouting about the boy who never wept nor dashed a thousand kim, and we say another *bon soir* to the children in the convent schools singing the truest of all songs even if they and their nuns do not fully understand it

> *Queen of the angels*
> *Queen of the May*

and a *buenos dias* to the one wit in every frat house at every college who hailed this morn by reciting to his friends a bit of doggerel as ancient and as deeply religious as that hymn to the Mother of God

> *Hurray, hurray—*
> *It's the first of May!*
> *Outdoor fucking starts today!*

and yes the California earthquake, as you guessed, was the worst in history and Hagbard and Miss Portinari and Mavis-Stella-Mao suffered it all in horrible detail (the price they paid for their vision was the possession of that vision, as we, Mr. and Mrs. FUCKUP-Leviathan, are also learning), and before the end *auf weidersehen* to Mary Lou, who is also becoming something more than the accidents of heredity and environment had programmed her for, and now we look at last at Smiling Jim: He was freezing, the sky was still empty, and Hali One still hadn't appeared.

And then without warning it was there: a dark shape against the sun moving on silent wings, not flying but gliding: embodiment of some arrogance or innocence that surpassed fear and surpassed even the suggestion of any pride in its own fearlessness. "Oh my God," Smiling Jim whispered, raising the Remington and starting to sight, and then it banked, flapped its wings wildly, and uttered one shriek that seemed like the very sound of life itself. "Oh my God," he repeated: that sound seemed to outlast its own echo, it had entered into his brain and couldn't be dislodged, it was the sound of his own blood pumping in his veins: the primary, the only, the single sound that was the bass and treble of every organic pulsation and spasm, "Oh my God," he had it in the sight, the head was in profile, only one diamond-hard eye staring back and recognizing him and his weapon, but that sound still moved in his blood, moved the seminal vesicles, moved the secretion of every gland. It was the sound of eternal and unending clash between I and AM and their unity in I AM, he even thought for a flash of the critics of hunting and how little they understood of this secret, this mystic identity between the killer and the killed, then it uttered that Sound again and started to rise, but he had it, it was in the sight, he breathed, he aimed, he slacked, he squeezed, and for the third time the Sound came to him, death in life and life in death, it was falling, he thought he felt the earth stir below him and the word "earthquake" almost formed, but the Sound went on and on to the roots of him, it was the sound of the killer and he had killed the killer, he was the greater killer, and still it fell, faster and faster, dead now and subject only to the law of gravity not to the law of its own will, 32 feet per second per second (he remembered the formula of the fall), plunging downward, the most heartbreaking beautiful sight he had ever seen, every hunting club in the world would be talking about it, it would last as long as human speech survived, and he had done it, he had achieved immortality, he had taken its life and now it was part of him. His nose was running and his eyes were watering. "I did it," he screamed to the mountains, "I did it! I killed the last American eagle!"

The earth below him cracked.

THE APPENDICES

(which are most instructive)

> GREATER POOP: Is Eris true?
> MALACLYPSE THE YOUNGER: Everything is true.
> GP: Even false things?
> MAL-2: Even false things are true.
> GP: How can that be?
> MAL-2: I don't know, man, I didn't do it.

—Interview with Malaclypse the Younger, K.S.C., *Greater Metropolitan Yorba Linda Herald-News-Sun-Tribune-Journal-Dispatch-Post and San Francisco Discordian Society Cabal Bulletin and Intergalactic Report and Poop*

Note: There were originally 22 appendices explaining all the secrets of the Illuminati. Eight of the appendices were removed due to the paper shortage. They will be printed in Heaven.

APPENDIX ALEPH
GEORGE WASHINGTON'S HEMP CROP

Many readers will assume that this book consists of nothing but fiction and fantasy; actually, like most historical tomes, it includes those elements (as do the works of Gibbon, Toynbee, Wells, Beard, Spengler, Marx, Yerby, Kathleen Windsor, Arthur Schlesinger, Jr., Moses, et. al.); but it also contains as many documented facts as do not seriously conflict with the authors' prejudices. Washington's hemp crop, for instance, is mentioned repeatedly in *Writings of Washington,* U.S. Government Printing Office, 1931. Here are some of the citations:

Volume 31, page 389: October 1791, letter from Mount Vernon to Alexander Hamilton, Secretary of Treasury: "How far . . . would there be propriety, do you conceive, in suggesting the policy of encouraging the growth of cotton and hemp in such parts of the United States as are adapted to the culture of these articles?"

In the next three years, Washington evidently settled the matter in his own mind, whatever Hamilton thought of the "proprieties." Volume 33, page 279, finds him writing from Philadelphia to his gardener at Mount Vernon to "make the most you can of the India Hemp seed" and "plant it everywhere." Waxing more enthusiastic, on page 384 he writes to an unidentified "my dear doctor," telling him, "I thank you as well for the seeds as for the Pamphlets which you had the goodness to send me. The artificial preparation of the Hemp from Silesia is really a curiosity . . ." And on page 469 he again reminds the gardener about the seed of the India Hemp: "[I] desire that the Seed may be saved in due season and with as little loss as possible."

The next year he was even more preoccupied that the seeds be saved and the crop replenished. Volume 34, page 146, finds him writing (March 15, 1795) to the gardener again: "Presuming you saved all the seed you could from the India hemp, let it be carefully sown again, for the purpose of getting into a full stock of seed."

Volume 34, page 72, undated letter of Spring 1796,

shows that the years did not decrease this passion; he again writes to the gardener: "What was done with the seed saved from the India Hemp last summer? It ought, *all of it,* to have been sewn [sic] again; that not only a stock of seed sufficient for my own purposes might have been raised, but to have disseminated the seed to others; as *it is more valuable than the common Hemp.*" (Italics added)

Volume 35, page 265, shows him still nagging the gardener; page 323 contains the letter to Sir John Sinclair mentioned in the First Trip.

The Weishaupt impersonation theory, congenial as it may be to certain admirers of the General, cannot account for all of this. A diary entry of August 7, 1765 (*The Diaries of George Washington,* Houghton-Mifflin, 1925), reads: "Began to seperate [sic] the Male from the Female hemp at Do—rather too late." This is the passage quoted by Congressman Koch, and remembered by Saul Goodman in the novel; the separation of male from female hemp plants is not required for the production of hemp rope but is absolutely necessary if one wants to use the flowering tips of the female for marijuana. And at that time Adam Weishaupt was very definitely still in Bavaria, teaching canon law at the University of Ingolstadt.

All of this data about General Washington's hobby, originally researched by Michael Aldrich, Ph.D., of Mill Valley, California, was rediscovered by Saul Goodman while he and Barney Muldoon were employed as investigators by the American Civil Liberties Union on test cases seeking to have all remaining anti-marijuana laws repealed as unconstitutional. The Goodman-Muldoon Private Investigations Agency (which had been formed right after those two worthy gentlemen had resigned from the New York Police Department amid the international acclaim connected with their solving the Carmel disappearance) was offered a lion's share of the best-paying business accounts possible. Saul and Barney chose, however, to take only the cases that really interested them; their most notable work was performed as investigators for lawyers defending unpopular political figures. Goodman and Muldoon, it was agreed everywhere, had an uncanny knack for finding the elusive evidence that would demonstrate a frame-up to even the most hostile and skeptical jury. Many political historians say that it was in large part their work which kept the most eccentric and colorful figures of the extreme right and extreme left out of the prison-hospitals during the great Mental Health/Social Psychiatry craze of the late 1970s and early 1980s.

In fact, Rebecca Goodman's memoir of her husband, *He Opened the Cages*, written during her grief after his heart attack in 1983, is almost as popular in political-science classes as is her study of comparative mythology, *The Golden Apples of the Sun, the Silver Apples of the Moon*, in anthropology classes.

APPENDIX BETH
THE ILLUMINATI CIPHERS, CODES, AND CALENDARS

These following ciphers were found in the home of the lawyer Hans Zwack during a raid by the Bavarian government in 1785. Letters from Weishaupt (signed "Spartacus"), written in the code and outlining most of the plans of the Illuminati, were also found, and led to the suppression of the Order, after which it went underground and regrouped.

These cyphers are given (curiously, without their code names) in Daraul's *History of Secret Societies*, page 227. The purpose of the code names was to make breaking the cypher more difficult. All messages begin in the Zwack cypher, but the fifth word is always "Weishaupt" or "De-Molay," and the message then switches to whichever of these cyphers is thus indicated; whenever either of these words (or "Zwack") appears again, the system again switches. Breaking the cypher by the usual statistical methods is, therefore, virtually impossible, at least before the invention of the computer—for the uninitiated cypher-breaker is confronted with, not 26, but 3 × 26, or 78, separate symbols, whose regularity has little to do with the celebrated formula (EATOINSHRDLU . . . etc.) for the regularity of the 26 letters.*

---

* The reader should be reminded that a true *code* can never be broken, although all *cyphers* always can be (given enough time and manpower). A cypher has a serial, one-to-one correspondence with

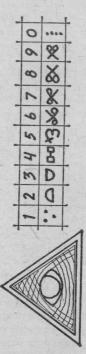

In addition, any of the 78 symbols can be replaced by the abbreviation for the corresponding Tarot card, thus further befuddling the uninitiated. The Tarots are arranged in the sequence: Wands, Cups, Swords, Pentacles, Trumps. Thus, the first symbol can be replaced by AcW (Ace of Wands), the second by 2W (two of Wands), and so on, through Cups, Swords, and Pentacles. The last 22 symbols are represented by the 22 trumps: TF (The Fool), TM (The Magus), THP (The High Priestess), and so forth. Since there are five groups in the Tarot (the four suits and the trumps), and the alphabet is repeated only three times, this leaves two null sets for transmission of Zen telegrams. "Once you've seen the Great Vision," Hagbard once said, "you look at everything else in life *twice*."

The Illuminati calendars, finally, are all based on five seasons (due to the Law of Fives.) The names of the seasons, their meanings, and the Christian equivalents are as follows:

Verwirrung	Season of Chaos	January 1–March 14
Zweitracht	Season of Discord	March 15–May 26
Unordnung	Season of Confusion	May 27–August 7
Beamtenherrschaft	Season of Bureaucracy	August 8–October 19
Grummet	Season of Aftermath	October 20–December 31

Everything is dated from year 1 A.M. (Anno Mung), which is 4000 B.C. in the Christian calendar—the year Hung Mung first perceived the Sacred Chao and achieved illumination. Thus, Hassan i Sabbah founded the Hashishim in 5090 A.M., Weishaupt reformed the Illuminati in 5776 A.M., and—to take a year in the middle of our novel— 1970 in the Christian calendar is, to the Illuminati, 5970 A.M., just as it is in the calendar used by Royal Arch ma-

the alphabet letters of the message being transmitted; a code proper has no such correspondence. Thus any computer can break the cypher

I⊕: ⅂⊕: ⊢⌐ Ⲭ+◇+⊢⅃ ·⊤⅂⅁⅃ ⊕ⲬⲬ+⅂⅃◇

but only the Illuminated can read the code behind the cypher and know what (or who) the Rising Hodge is.

sons. (The reader can decide for himself whether this fact represents coincidence, complicity, or synchronicity.)

The Illuminati date for anything is always a higher number than that in any other calendar, since the Jews (and, oddly, the Scotch Rite masons) date everything from 240 A.M., Confucians from 312 A.M., Christians from 4000 A.M., Moslems from 4580 etc. Only Bishop Usher, who dated everything from 4004 B.C. (or -4 A.M.), produced an older starting point than the Illuminati.

For instance, here are some random dates as they appear on the Illuminati system of reckoning:

First Egyptian dynasty	1100 A.M.
The Rig-Veda written	2790 A.M.
First Chou dynasty	3000 A.M.
Founding of Rome	3249 A.M.
Hassan Sabbah illuminated	5090 A.M.
Indians discover Columbus	5492 A.M.
Pigasus nominated for President of the U. S.	5968 A.M.

Returning to the yearly round, each of the five seasons is divided, of course, into five months, thus producing a year of 5 × 5 or 25 months. The first three months of every season (known as the tricycle) each have 15 days, which fits the law of five because 1 × 5 = 5. The last two months of each season each have 14 days, which also fits the law of fives because 1 + 4 = 5. Each season has 73 days, because (a) you *have to* get 73 when you divide 365 by 5; (b) 7 + 3 = 10, the first multiple of 5 after 5 itself; and (c) this corresponds, as Dr. Ignotius pointed out in the novel, to the 73 parts of the Illuminati pyramid (counting the Eye as a part). The last day of each season is known as Eye Day and is celebrated in ways too foul to be mentioned in a book such as this, intended for family entertainment.

The mystic 23 appears in the calendar in the following ways:

(1) The bicycle has *2* months and the tricycle has *3*.

(2) The bicycle has 28 days (two months of 14 days each), and when you subtract the all-important 5 this leaves, again, the mystic 23.

(3) When 5 is multiplied by its own first product, 10, the

result is 50; and when this, in turn, is subtracted from the days in a season, 73, the significant 23 once again appears.

(4) The tricycle has 45 days; add one for Leap Year's Day and you get 46—exactly 2×23.

(5) $2 + 3$ of course equals the all-important 5, the number on which the calendar is based and, even more significant, the number of this proof.

As Weishaupt said to Knigge after explaining all this, "Could Aquinas do better?" (Actually, the mystic meaning of these numbers is sexual. The male sex cycle is, as Tantrists know, 23 days; add the mystic five and you get 28 days, the female cycle. It's that simple. Or is it?)

The sanctification of the number 5 antedates Atlantis itself and goes back to the intelligent cephalopods who infested Antarctica about 150,000,000 years before humankind appeared on earth; see H.P. Lovecraft's work of "fiction," *At the Mountains of Madness* (Arkham House, 1968), in which it is suggested that 5 was sacred to these creatures because they had five tentacles or pseudopods. In this connection, the reader might find some food for thought in a conversation which took place between Hagbard Celine and Joe Malik in the late autumn of 1980. Joe, at the time, had just received the Pulitzer Prize. (He was also under investigation by a Congressional Committee, in connection with the same achievement: publication of certain governmental secrets.)

"*Five* of the Senators voted to cite me for contempt, for not revealing my source," Joe said. "Three voted against it. So I'll be cited, and the Grand Jury will draw up an indictment. There's that Law of Fives again."

"Are you worried?" Hagbard asked, relaxing in one of the heavy leather chairs that were part of *Confrontation*'s new, more ornate offices.

"Hell, no. I can always seek sanctuary in Panama, or someplace, if they convict me. And Peter can keep this operation going."

"You're not afraid to start a new life as an exile?"

Joe grinned. "At my age, any new experience is an adventure."

"You're doing fine," Hagbard said. "Here's your latest revelation from the A∴A∴." He reached into his pocket and took out a photo of a female infant with six fingers on each hand. "Got this from a doctor friend at Johns Hopkins."

Joe looked at it and said, "So?"

"If we all looked like her, there'd be a Law of Sixes."

Joe stared at him. "You mean, after all the evidence I collected, the Law of Fives is an Illuminati put-on? You've been letting me delude myself?"

"Not at all." Hagbard was most earnest. "The Law of Fives is perfectly true. Everybody from the JAMs to the Dealy Lama agrees on that. But you have to understand it more deeply now, Joe. Correctly formulated, the Law is: All phenomena are directly or indirectly related to the number five, and this relationship can always be demonstrated, *given enough ingenuity on the part of the demonstrator.*" The evil grin flashed. "That's the very model of what a true scientific law must always be: a statement about how the human mind relates to the cosmos. We can never make a statement about the cosmos itself—*but only about how our senses (or our instruments) detect it, and about how our codes and languages symbolize it.* That's the key to the Einstein-Heisenberg revolution in physics, and to the Buddha's revolution in psychology much earlier."

"But," Joe protested, "everything fits the Law. The harder I looked, the more things there were that fit."

"Exactly," said Hagbard. "Think about that. If you need quick transportation to Panama," he added, heading for the door, "call Gold and Appel Transfers and leave a message."

APPENDIX GIMMEL
THE ILLUMINATI THEORY OF HISTORY

And to this day, the proverb is still repeated from the Danube to the Rhine: "It is dangerous to talk too much about the Illuminati."

—Von Juntz, *Unausprechlichen Kulten*

Theoretically, an Age of Bureaucracy can last until a paper shortage develops, but, in practice, it never lasts longer than 73 permutations.

—Weishaupt, *Konigen, Kirchen and Dummheit*

In a well-known passage in the *Necronomicon* Abdul Alhazred writes, "They ruled once where man rules now;
where man rules now, they shall rule again. After summer
is winter, and after winter, summer." Weishaupt, who possessed only the Olaus Wormius translation, in the 1472
Lyons edition with its numerous misprints and errors,
found this text scrambled into "They ruled once where man
rules now, summer. Where man rules now, after summer is
winter. They shall rule again, and after winter." Thoroughly confused, he wrote to his good friend the Kabalist Kolmer in Baghdad for an explanation. Kolmer, meanwhile,
dispatched a letter to him answering a previous question.
When this epistle arrived, Weishaupt had been experiment-
ing with a new strain of Alamout black and was in no condition to realize it was a reply to an earlier query; he was,
thus, ready to accept enlightenment in the words: "Concerning your rather thorny enquiry: I find that, in most
cases, ergot is the best remedy. Failing this, I can only suggest the path of Don Juan."

Weishaupt assumed that Kolmer meant the passage
would become clear if he read it while under the influence
of ergot. He promptly went down to his laboratory and
tossed off a jigger; then, for good measure, he chewed a
few peyote buttons. (He was under the misapprehension
that the Don Juan referred to was the same Yaqui Indian
magician of the twentieth century whose mind he had been
tapping through the *Morgenheutegesternwelt*. Peyote was
that Don Juan's great "teacher," and Weishaupt had im-
ported some from Mexico at great trouble and expense.)

It should be explained at this point that the question
which Kolmer was answering happened to be not philosophical but personal. Weishaupt had sought his advice on
a problem much perplexing him that month: the fact that
his sister-in-law was somewhat pregnant and circumstantial
evidence seemed to mark him as the father. He wasn't at all
sure how to explain this to Eve. Kolmer had intended to
convey that Adam should give his paramour the ergot,
since it often functions as an abortifacient; the alternative
referred to the path of an earlier Don Juan and meant split-
ting the scene entirely. However, the stoned Ingolstadt sage
misunderstood totally, and so came to the *Necronomicon*
full of hashish, peyote, and a substantial quality of ergot,
which had, under the influence of the other drugs and his

own intestinal juices, mutated into ergotine, a close chemical cousin of LSD. The result was that the words seemed to leap out of the page at him, shouting with intense meaning:

THEY RULED ONCE WHERE MAN RULES NOW SUMMER WHERE MAN RULES NOW AFTER SUMMER IS WINTER THEY SHALL RULE AGAIN AND AFTER WINTER

Abdul Alhazred's concept of the Great Cycle, which derived actually from the *Upanishads*, took on kinky edges in Weishaupt's flipped-out cortex. *Five* kinky edges, to be exact, since he was still obsessed with the profound new understanding of the Law of Fives he had achieved the night he saw the shoggoth turn into a rabbit. He quickly fetched Giambattista Vico's *Scienze nuovo* from his shelf and began reading: He saw that he was right. Vico's theory of history, in which all societies pass through the same four stages, was an oversimplification—there were, when you looked closely at the actual evidence behind Vico's rhetoric, *five* distinct stages each time the Italian listed only four. Weishaupt looked very closely, and, like Joe Malik, the harder he looked the more fives he found.

It was then that the man's truly unique mind made its great leap: He remembered that Joachim of Floris, a proto-primus Illuminatus of the eleventh century, had divided history into three stages: the Age of the Father, dominated by Law; the Age of the Son, dominated by Love; and the Age of the Holy Spirit, dominated by Joy. Where most philosophers rush to publish their insights, Weishaupt saw the advantage of an alternative path. The Law of Fives would be kept secret, so that only Illuminati Primi would know about it and could predict events correctly, but the Joachimite theory would be revived and publicized to mislead others. (He, Kolmer, Meyer Amschel Rothschild, DeSade, and Sir Frances Dashwood—the original Five—had some discussions about possibly pushing Vico instead of Joachim, but, as Weishaupt argued, "Four is a *little bit* too close to five . . ." Even so, it was quite a spell of years before they found the ideal front man to push the three-step theory, G. W. F. Hegel. "He's perfect," Weishaupt wrote in the De Molay cipher from Mount Vernon. "Unlike Kant, who makes sense only in German, this man doesn't make sense in any language.") The rest of the story—the exoteric story, at least —is history. After Hegel was Marx; and after Marx, the

Joachimite three-step was permanently grafted onto revolutionary tactics.

The esoteric story, of course, is different. For instance, in 1914, when the fifth and final stage of Western Civilization was dawning, James Joyce published *A Portrait of the Artist as a Young Man.* The five chapters of that novel not only suggested five stages in the hero's growth, but by the alteration of styles from chapter to chapter suggested analogies with other five-stage processes. This was too much for the Illuminati Primi of the time, who warned Joyce to be more careful in the future. A battle of wills ensued, and all through the writing of *Ulysses* Joyce was still considering a novel built entirely around the Law of Fives. When the Illuminati gave him what they call "the Tiresias treatment" —blindness—he finally compromised. *Finnegans Wake,* when it appeared, broke with the Joachim-Hegel-Marx three-step but did not include the *funfwissenschaft.* Instead, the Viconian four-stage theory was resurrected, a middle path that appealed to Joyce's sense of synchronicity, since he had once taught at a school on Vico Road in Dublin and later also lived in a house on Via Giambattista Vico in Rome.*

Now for a few words about the "real truth," at least as the Illuminati understand "real truth."

Every society actually passes through the five stages of *Verwirrung,* or chaos; *Zweitracht,* or discord; *Unordnung,* or confusion; *Beamtenherrschaft,* or bureaucracy; and *Grummet,* or aftermath. Sometimes, to make comparison with the exoteric Hegel-Marx system more pointed, the esoteric Illuminati system is defined as: Thesis, Antithesis, Synthesis, Parenthesis, and Paralysis. The public Hegel-Marx triad is also called the tricycle, and the arcane latter two stages are called the bicycle; one of the first secrets revealed to every Illuminatus Minore is "After the tricycle it comes always the bicycle." (The Illuminati are rather prone toward literal translations from Weishaupt's German.)

The first stage, *Verwirrung* or chaos, is the point from which all societies begin and to which they all return. It is, so to speak, the natural condition of humanity—an estimation which the reader can confirm by closely observing his neighbors (or, if he has the necessary objectivity, himself).

* Do you believe that?

It is, therefore, also the fundamental Thesis. The Illuminati
associate this with Eris, and also with other goddesses from
Isis to Ishtar and from Kwannon to Kali—with the Female
Principle, yin, in general. This correlates with hexagram 2
in the *I Ching:* that is, *K'un,* which has the meanings of re-
ceptivity, nature (in contrast to spirit), earth (in contrast to
sky), female (in contrast to male). Thus, although this is
the first stage chronologically, it has the mystical number 2,
which is always associated with the female in magic; and it
correlates with the 2nd trump in Tarot, the High Priestess,
who represents not only maternity and fertility but gnosis.
The sign of the horns represents *Verwirrung* because the fingers make a V shape; and the planet or the symbol of Venus, ♀, also designates this stage. On the Zodiac: Aquar-
ius, ♒ .

The second stage, *Zweitracht,* begins with the appearance of a ruling or governing class. This is the Antithesis
of chaos, of course, and leads directly into discord when
the servile class discovers that its interests are not the same
as the interests of the ruling class. This correlates with
Osiris, Jehovah, and all masculine deities; with the symbol of
the All-Seeing Eye; with hexagram 1 in the *I Ching: Ch'ien,*
the creative, the heavenly, the strong, the powerful; with
the male principle, yang, in general; with the number 3,
symbolizing the all-male Christian trinity; with the 12th
trump of the Tarot, the Hanged Man, symbolizing sacrifice,
schism and schizophrenia; and with the planet or symbol
of Mars, ♂ . Naturally, a *Zweitracht* period is always
replete with "internal contradictions," and somebody like
Karl Marx always arises to point them out. On the Zodiac:
Pisces, ♓ .

The third stage, *Unordnung* or confusion, occurs when
an attempt is made to restore balance or arrive at the
Hegelian Synthesis. This correlates with Loki, the Devil,
Mercury (god of thieves), Thoth in his role of Trickster,
Coyote, and other spirits of illusion or deception; with hexagram 4 in the *I Ching, Meng,* youthful folly or standing on
the brink of the abyss; with the number 11, signifying sin,
penance, and revelation; with the 21st trump in the Tarot,
the Fool who walks over the abyss; and with the planet or
sign of Mercury, ☿ . It represents that attempt to restore

the state of nature by unnatural means, an annihilation of
the biogram by the logogram. On the Zodiac: Cancer,
♋ .

The fourth stage, *Beamtenherrschaft* or bureaucracy,
represents the Parentheses that occur when the Hegelian
Synthesis does not succeed in reconciling the opposites.
This correlates with Void (absence of any divinity); with *I
Ching* hexagram 47, *K'un*, oppression or exhaustion, superior men held in restraint by inferior men; with the number
8, indicating balance and the Last Judgment; with the 16th
Tarot trump, Falling Tower, representing deteriorations and
the Tower of Babel; and with the planetoid or sign of the
moon, ☽ . On the Zodiac: Libra, ♎ .

The fifth stage, *Grummet* or aftermath, represents the
transition back to chaos. Bureaucracy chokes in its own
paperwork; mind is at the end of its tether; in desperation,
many begin to deny the logogram and follow the biogram,
with varying degrees of success. This correlates with Her-
maphrodite; with *I Ching* hexagram 59, *Huan*, dispersion,
dissolution, foam on the water; with the number 5, union of
male and female; with the 6th trump of the Tarot, the Lovers, indicating union; and with the sun or its symbol, ☉ .
On the Zodiac: Virgo, ♍ .

Since the association of these references, and their bear-
ings on history, may be a bit unclear to some readers, we
will give further details on each stage.

VERWIRRUNG

In this chaotic period, the Hodge and the Podge are in
dynamic balance. There is no stasis: The balance is always
shifting and homeostatic, in the manner of the ideal "self-
organizing system" of General Systems Theory or Cybernetics. The Illuminati, and all authoritarian types in general, dislike such ages so much that they try to prevent any
records of their existence from reaching the general public.
Pre-Chou China was one such period, and its history (except for some fragments in Taoist lore) is largely lost; we
do know, however, that the *I Ching* was reorganized when
the Chou Dynasty introduced patriarchal authoritarianism
to China. It was then that the hexagram *K'un*, ䷁ , asso-

ciated with this period was moved from the first place to its present, second place in the *Ching.* Every line in *K'un* is broken (yin), because this is a feminist and prepatriarchal form of society, and because yin correlates with the agricultural rather than the urban. Always linked to darkness by mystics, this *K'un* style of sensibility is also linked, by the Illuminati, with *dreck* (dung) and everything they find messy and intolerable about ordinary human beings. (The Erisians, of course, take the opposite position, connect this with Eris, the primordial goddess, and regard it as ideal.)

Verwirrung is numerologically linked with 2, not only because of *K'un*'s shift from first to second place in the *Ching,* but because it is the balance of Hodge and Podge. Thus, even though it is the first stage chronologically, it is never linked with 1 in magic sense, because 1 signifies the erect penis, the male principle in isolation, and such authoritarian games as monotheism, monopoly, monogamy, and general monotony. This dynamic 2-ness of *Verwirrung* is also implicit in its Tarot card, the 2nd trump or High Priestess, who sits between a black pillar and a white one (cf. The Hodge and Podge) and who represents mystery, magic, mischief, and Erisian values generally. She wears the balanced (solar) cross, rather than the unbalanced (Christian) cross, to emphasize the unity of opposites in such a historical period.

Typical Aquarians who have manifested *Verwirrung* values are Aaron Burr, Christopher Marlowe, Hung Mung, Charles Darwin, Willard Gibbs (who incorporated chaos into mathematics), Mrs. Patrick Campbell, Elizabeth Blackwell (pioneer woman physician), Anna Pavlova, Mozart, Lewis Carrol, Robert Burns, James Joyce, Lord Byron, David Wark Griffith, and Gelett Burgess, author of the classic Erisian poem:

> I never saw a purple cow
> I never hope to see one
> But I'll tell you this anyhow:
> I'd rather see than be one.

The *Verwirrung* phase of European history is identified with the Danubian Culture, so called because most of its relics have been found along the shores of the Danube. According to archeologists, the Danubian culture was agricultural, pre-urban, worshipped a female rather than a male god, and never invented anything remotely like a state. The pre-Inca society of Peru, the Minoan civilization, the pre-Chou period of China already mentioned, and many American Indian tribes still surviving also represent a *Verwirrung* social framework. The synthesis of Hodge and Podge, and especially of biogram and logogram, in such cultures is indicated by the amazement of explorers from authoritarian societies when first encountering them. The usual words about the "grace" and "spontaniety" of the natives merely represent the lack of authoritarian conflict between biogram and logogram: These people sit, like the Tarot High Priestess, between opposite poles, without tilting one way or the other.

But the fact that this is a *dynamic* and not a *static* balance means that eventually (after 73 permutations, according to Weishaupt) the second stage must evolve.

ZWEITRACHT

In this discordant period, the Hodge and the Podge are in conflict, because a ruling class emerges which attempts to control the others. This correlates with hexagram 1, ☰ , *Ch'ien*, the all-powerful, in the *I Ching*. The six unbroken lines represent the severity and monotony of such a period, which is, above all, the age of the T-square, the building of fences, the division of lands by "boundaries" drawn on maps, and the imposition of one man's (or one group's) will upon all others. Typically, the earth is regarded as both flat and finite by the *Zweitracht* mentality, and there is much concern with dividing it up into portions (among themselves, of course). The "superstitious" terror of American Indians when first confronting maps was merely the reaction of a *Verwirrung* mentality to a *Zweitracht* mentality: The Indians could not conceive of people treating earth as a thing to be exploited rather than a mother to be respected.

Zweitracht associates with 3 numerologically because 3 is the totally male number, because all-male Trinities (Brahma-Vishnu-Siva, Father-Son-Spirit, etc.) are invented in such ages, and because the discord always has a minimum of 3 vectors, not merely 2. That is, the division into a propertied ruling class and an unpropertied governed class immediately sets in motion further cupidity; the ruling class soon falls to fighting over the spoils. Contrary to Marx, most of the strife in *Zweitracht* ages is not the conflict between proprietors and proles but between various proprietors over who gets the biggest share of the pie.

The governing Tarot card is trump 12, the Hanged Man. The cross on which he hangs is blossoming, to show that it is still organic and alive (the biogram); he hangs upside down, to show the reversal of nature. He represents both the burden of omniscience in the owning-governing class and the burden of nescience in the servile-submissive class: the total crucifixion of desire by *Realprinzip* and *Realpolitik*.

The astrological sign of this period is Pisces, the two fish swimming in opposite directions indicating the conflict of logogram and biogram ("body" and "spirit," astrologers say.) Typical Pisceans who have shown the *Zweitracht* personality are E. H. Harriman, the railroad magnate (who covered the United States with *Ch'ien*-style unbroken straight lines), Cardinal John Henry Newman, Sir Robert Baden-Powell, founder of the Boy Scouts (an attempt to instill Piscean authoritarianism even in childhood), Admiral Chester Nimitz, John Foster Dulles, Anna Lee (founder of the world's most antisexual religion, the Shakers), industrialists like Kruger and Pullman, financiers like Cambell and Braden, Grover Cleveland, John C. Calhoun, Neville Chamberlain, Andrew Jackson (whose expulsion of the Cherokee Nation from its traditional lands onto the "trail of tears," where most of them perished, is the archetypal *Zweitracht* land-grab), William Jennings Bryan, and Frank Stanton of CBS.

Since all Illuminati with any academic leanings at all are encouraged to major in history, the tendency in most textbooks is not only to black out *Verwirrung* periods but to glorify *Zweitracht* periods as ages of Light and Progress. Indeed, they make entertaining reading: They are ages of expansion, and there are always new people being discovered to be subjugated, "civilized," and converted to tax-payers and rent-payers. Almost any age described in glowing and admiring language in a history text will prove, on examination, to be a *Zweitracht* era, and the foremost butchers and invaders are treated as the outstanding heroes of humanity. A sympathetic reading of the biographies of these empire-builders almost always indicates that they were *homo neophile* individuals who turned their talents to destruction rather than creativity because of bitterness engendered by years of torment and baiting by *homo neophobe* types during their childhoods.

The ever-present conflict in a *Zweitracht* period eventually leads to the third stage.

UNORDNUNG

Humanity has been transformed during a *Zweitracht* age, by placing logogram in governing authority over biogram. *Unordnung* is an attempt to restore balance by revolutionizing the logogram; there is no thought about the biogram, because contact with this somatic component of personality has been lost. (This loss of contact has been variously described by pre-Celinean observers: It is "the veil of Maya" in Buddhism, the "censor band" or "repression" in psychoanalysis, the "character armoring" and "muscular armoring" in Reichian psychology, etc.)

The *I Ching* hexagram for this stage is Meng, ☶☵ , or Youthful Folly. The yang line at the top indicates the continued supremacy of logogram, even though some biogram elements (the yin lines) begin to reassert themselves. The traditional reading is "mountain above water"; that is, the rigid logogram still repressing the Aquarian element as it seeks to liberate itself. The usual Chinese interpretation of this hexagram is "The young fool needs discipline," and the leaders of all rebellions at this stage always heartily agree with that and demand unquestioning obedience from their followers. This is a time of turmoils, troubles, and tyrannies that appear and disappear rapidly.

The mystical number is 11, which means "a new start" in Kabalism and "error and repentence" in most other systems of numerology.

Tarot trump 21, The Fool, symbolizes this age as a dreamy-eyed youth unknowingly walking over an abyss. The *Hitlerjugend*, and the disciples of various other *fuehrers* and messiahs, immediately come to mind. That this card is disputed by various Tarot experts, and is given a numerical value of 0 rather than 21 by the wisest, indicates the confusion in all *Unordnung* periods. The dog who barks to warn the Young Fool, like the yin lines in the hexagram, represents the desperate attempts of the biogram to

break through the repression or censor-band and make itself heard.

Typical Cancerians who exemplified *Unordnung* are Ju-
lius Caesar, Mary Baker Eddy (whose philosophy was an
explicit denial of the biogram), Albert Parsons, Emma
Goldman, Benjamin Peret, Vladimir Mayakofski, Henry
David Thoreau, Durrutti, P-J Proudhon, Brooks Adams,
General Kitchener, Luigi Pirandello (the literary master of
ambiguity), Erich Ambler (the literary master of conspiracy), Calvin Coolidge (who issued the classically muddled
Cancerian statement "Be as revolutionary as science and as
conservative as the multiplication table"), Andrei Gromy-
ko, Nelson Rockefeller, John Calvin, Estes Kefauver, and
Rexford Tugwell.

An *Unordnung* period has always been thought of (even
before Hegel provided the words) as a synthesis between
the thesis of *Verwirrung* and the antithesis *Zweitracht*;
since it is a false synthesis on the logogrammic level only, it
always gives birth to the fourth stage, the Parenthesis.

BEAMTENHERRSCHAFT

This is the age of bureaucracy, and to live at this time is,
as Proudhon said, "to have every operation, every transaction, every movement noted, registered, counted, rated,
stamped, measured, numbered, assessed, licensed, refused,
authorized, endorsed, admonished, prevented, reformed, re-
dressed, corrected . . . to be laid under contribution,
drilled, fleeced, exploited, monopolized, extorted from, ex-
hausted, hoaxed, and robbed." The governing *I Ching*
hexagram is 47, *K'un,* ☷, oppression or exhaustion, the
dried-up lake, with the usual reading of superior men op-
pressed by the inferior. This is the time when *homo neophobe* types most rigorously repress *homo neophile* types,
and great heresy hunts and witch trials flourish. This correlates with the number 8, signifying the Last Judgment, because every citizen is to some extent a State functionary,
and each is on trial before the jury of all. The traditional
Chinese associations with this hexagram are sitting under a
bare tree and wandering through an empty valley—signifying the ecological havoc wreaked by purely abstract minds
working upon the organic web of nature.

The 16th Tarot trump, The Tower, describes this age.

The Tower is struck by lightning and the inhabitants fall from the windows. (Cf. the Tower of Babel legend and our recent power failures.) The traditional interpretations of this card suggest pride, oppression, and bankruptcy.

This correlates with Libra, the mentality which measures and balances all things on an artificial scale (Maya). Typical Libras who have manifested *Beamtenherrschaft* characterists are Comte de Saint Simon, Justice John Marshall, Hans Geiger, Henry Wallace, Dwight Eisenhower, John Kenneth Galbraith, Arthur Schlesinger, Jr., John Dewey, and Dr. Joyce Brothers.

In *Beamtenherrschaft* ages there is ceaseless activity, all planned in advance, begun at the scheduled second, carefully supervised, scrupulously recorded—but inevitably finished late and poorly done. The burden of omniscience on the ruling class becomes virtually intolerable, and most flee into some form of schizophrenia or fantasy. Great towers, pyramids, moon shots, and similar marvels are accomplished at enormous cost while the underpinnings of social solidarity crumble entirely. While blunders multiply, no responsible individual can ever be found, because all decisions are made by committees; anyone seeking redress of grievance wanders into endless corridors of paperwork with no more tangible result than in the Hunting of the Snark. Illuminati historians, of course, describe these ages as glowingly as *Zweitracht* epochs, for, although control is in the hands of *homo neophobe* types, there is at least a kind of regularity, order, and geometrical precision about everything, and the "messiness" of the barbaric *Verwirrung* ages and revolutionary *Unordnung* ages is absent.

Nevertheless, the burden of omniscience on the rulers steadily escalates, as we have indicated, and the burden of nescience on the servile class increasingly renders them unfit to serve (more and more are placed on the dole, shipped to "mental" hospitals, or recruited into whatever is the current analog of the gladiatorial games), so the Tower eventually falls.

GRUMMET

The age of Grummet begins with an upsurge of magicians, hoaxers, Yippies, Kabouters, shamans, clowns, and other Eristic forces. The relevant I Ching hexagram is 59,

Huan, ☲☲ , dispersion and dissolution. The gentle wind above the deep water is the Chinese reading of the image, with associations of loss of ego, separation from the group, and "going out" in general. Yin lines dominate all but the top of the hexagram; the forces leading to a new *Verwirrung* stage are pushing upward toward release. This is also called Paralysis by the Illuminati, because, objectively, nothing much is happening; subjectively, of course, the preparations for the new cycle are working unconsciously.

The mystic number is 5, union of male (3) with female (2) and final resolution of conflict between *Verwirrung* and *Zweitracht.*

The governing Tarot trump is number 6, the Lovers, in which the woman looks upward at the angel (Eris, the biogram) and the man looks at the woman (the logogram, yang, reaches synthesis with biogram, yin, only through reconciliation with the female). Hence, the upsurge of feminism in such periods, together with a renewed emphasis on clans, tribes, and communes.

Typical Virgos manifesting *Grummet* traits are Charlie Parker, Antonin Artaud, Louis Lingg, Edgar Rice Burroughs, Grandma Moses, Lodovico Ariosto, Greta Garbo, Hedy Lamarr, and Goethe and Tolstoy (who manifested strong yin values while never quite getting reconciled with the women in their own lives. Tolstoy, however, as the classic dropout, is an archetypal Grummet persona and almost completed the Sufi course of "quit this world, quit the next world, quit quitting!").

After *Grummet,* of course, authority has collapsed entirely, and the biogram stands on equal footing with the logogram. Hodge and Podge being once again in dynamic balance, a new *Verwirrung* period begins, and the cycle repeats.

Since Weishaupt dreamed this schema up while he was under the influence of several hallucinogenic drugs, one should regard it with some skepticism. It is certainly not true in every detail, and there is no theoretical or empirical demonstration that each of the five ages must always have 73 permutations. The fact that *Grummet*-Virgo personalities (and all other of the five personality types) are born in all ages, even if they come to dominance in their appropriate epochs, leaves many mysteries still unsolved. In short, all that a sober scholar can say of the Illuminati theory of history is that it makes at least as much sense as the exoteric Marx-Hegel, Spengler, Toynbee, and Sorokin theories. The Λ∴A∴, who regard all Illuminati theories as false projections onto the external world of inner spiritual processes, are particularly skeptical about this one, since it involves several false correlations between the *I Ching* and the Tarot, the Zodiac, etc.

Finally, it should be noted that of all the people Hagbard employed as resonance for the vibes used against the Saure family in Ingolstadt, only Lady Velkor, Danny Pricefixer, and George Dorn were not Virgos. Hagbard evidently believed that the Illuminati magical links work when Illuminati activities are occurring in a given area—and, hence, virtually all of "his" people at the festival were Virgos and thereby linked with the *Grummet/Huan-59/Trump 6* chain of astrological associations. On the other hand, the presence of three non-Virgos shows Hagbard's pragmatic approach and his refusal to be ruled even by so exact a science as astrology.*

In this connection, when George Dorn and his mother went to Radio City Music Hall to see *The Lotus Position,* the last movie made by the American Medical Association before their tragic deaths, they happened to meet a tall Italian and a very beautiful black woman whom he introduced as his wife. Mrs. Dorn didn't catch the Italian's name, but it was obvious that George had a very great admiration for him. On the bus back to Nutley, she decided to straighten the boy out.

"A man who respects himself and his own race," she began, "would never think of marrying into *the colored.*"

"Shut up, Ma," George said politely.

"That's no way to talk to your mother," the fine lady said, going ahead blithely. "Now, your father had some radical ideas, and he tried to get the unions to accept *the colored,* but he never thought of marrying into them, George. He had too much self-respect. Are you listening, George?"

"How did you like the AMA?" he asked.

"Such wonderful young boys. So clean-cut. And that darling sister of theirs! At least they didn't think there was

* This sentence may manifest a lapse into mockery or mystification by otherwise sober authors.

anything attractive about long hair on men. Do you know
what long hair makes men look like?"

"Like girls, Ma. Is that right?"

"It makes them look worse than girls, George. It makes
them look like they're not really men, if you know what I
mean."

"No, I don't know what you mean, Ma." George was
profoundly bored.

"Well, I mean a *little* bit on the lavender side." She tit-
tered.

"Oh," he said, "you mean cocksuckers. Some of my best
friends are cocksuckers, Ma."

At this simple piece of factual information, the remark-
able lady turned red and then purple, and then twisted in her
chair to look out the window in angry silence for the rest of
the trip. The curious thing is that, before George could get
the courage to shut the old battleaxe up that way, he first
had to try to shoot a cop and then try to shoot himself and
finally take hashish with Hagbard Celine, and yet she was a
Virgo and he was a Capricorn.

APPENDIX DALETH
HASSAN i SABBAH AND ALAMOUT BLACK

When the Prophet died in 4632 A.M.,* the true faith was
almost immediately shattered by conflict between the Shiite
and Sunnite parties. More than a century of religious and
civil warfare followed, and by 4760 A.M. the Shiites themselves had split and given birth to a subsect known as the
Ismailis, or Ishmaelians. It was out of this group that Hassan i Sabbah formed the Order of the Assassins in 5090
A.M.

Ishmaelian religion had already at that date become a
nine-level affair in the manner typical of mystical secret societies. Those of the lowest grade, for instance, were merely
informed that *Al Koran* contained an allegorical meaning
in addition to its surface teachings, and that their salvation
lay in following orders. As a neophyte progressed through

---

* Known as the year 52 to Moslems, 4392 to Jews and Scotch Rite
Masons, 4320 to Confucians, and 632 to Christians.

the various grades, more and more of the allegories would be explained, and a doctrine would gradually emerge which is, in essence, that taught by all the mystics of East and West—Buddhists, Taoists, Vedantists, Rosicrucians, etc. The doctrine is, in important aspects, unspeakable (which is why the trainee required an *imam*—the Ishmaelian equivalent of a *guru*—to guide him in the nonverbal aspects); the ninth and highest grade, however, had no parallel except in very strict Theravada Buddhism. In this ninth grade, which Hassan attained shortly before founding the Hashishim, it was taught that even the personal mystical experience of the seeker (his own encounter with the Absolute, or the Void, or the Hodge-Podge, or God, or Goddess, or whatever one chooses to call it) should be subject to the most merciless analysis and criticism, and that there is no guide superior to reason. The Ishmaelian adept, in short, was one who had achieved supreme mystical awareness but refused to make even that into an idol; he was a total atheist-anarchist subject to no authority but his own independent mind.

"Such men are dangerous," as Caesar observed, and certainly they are dangerous to the Caesars; the Ishmaelians were being persecuted throughout the Moslem world, and strong efforts were being made to exterminate them entirely when Hassan i Sabbah became Imam of the whole movement.

It was Hassan's cynical judgment (and many Illuminated beings, such as the Lamas of Tibet, have agreed with him) that most people have no aspiration or capacity for much spiritual and intellectual independence. He thereupon reorganized the Ishmaelians in such a way as to allow and encourage those of small mind to remain in the lower grades.

The tools of this enterprise were the famous "Garden of Delights" in his castle at Alamout (a good duplication of the Paradise of *Al Koran*, complete with the beautiful and willing houris the Prophet had promised to the faithful)— and a certain "magick chemical." Those of the lowest grade were brought to Alamout, given the miraculous concoction, and set loose for several hours in the Garden of Delights. They came out convinced that they had truly visited heaven and that Hassan i Sabbah was the most powerful Holy Man in the world. They were assured, furthermore, that if they obeyed every order, even at the cost of their own lives, they would return to that Paradise after death.

These men became the first "sleeper agents" in the history of international politics. Where the three major contending religions of that time in the Near East (Christianity, Judaism, and orthodox Islam) insisted that it was an unforgivable sin to deny one's faith, Hassan taught that Allah would forgive such little white lies when they served a worthy purpose. Thus, his agents were able to pass themselves off as Christians, Jews, or orthodox Moslems and infiltrate any court, holy order, or army at will. Since the other religions had the above-mentioned prohibition against such deception, they were unable to infiltrate the Ishmaelians in turn.

The use of these agents as assassins is discussed *passim* in the novel, and Weishaupt's opinion that Hassan had discovered "the moral equivalent of war" is an interesting commentary. Hassan never had to send an army into battle, and armies sent against him were soon stopped by the sudden and unexpected deaths of their generals.

One of Hassan's successors was Sinan, who moved the headquarters of the cult from Alamout to Messiac and may (or may not) have written the letter about Richard the Lion-Hearted which George recalls in the Third Trip. Sinan, contemporaries claimed, performed miracles of healing, conversed with invisible beings, and was never seen to eat, drink, or perform the functions of urination and excretion. He was also credited with telepathy and with the ability to kill animals by looking at them. It was he (and not Hassan I Sabbah, as many popular books state) who ordered two of the lower members of the Order to commit suicide in order to impress a visiting ambassador with his power over his followers. (The two obeyed, leaping from the castle wall into the abyss below.) Sinan also made attempts to form an alliance with the Knights Templar, to drive both orthodox Christians and orthodox Moslems out of the arena, but this evidently fell through.

The Hashishim were finally crushed, despite their powerful espionage and assassination network, when the whole Middle East was overrun by hordes of Mongols, who came from so far away that they had not been infiltrated. It took several centuries for the Hashishim to make a comeback as the nonviolent Ishmaelian movement of today, under the leadership of the Aga Khan.

Finally, it was at Hassan i Sabbah's death that he allegedly uttered the aphorism for which he is best known, and
which is quoted several times in the novel: "Nothing is
true. All is permissible." The orthodox Moslem historian
Juvaini—who may have invented this whole episode—adds
that as soon as these blasphemous words passed his lips,
"Hassan's soul plunged to the depths of Hell."

Ever since Marco Polo recorded the story of the Garden
of Delights, Western commentators have identified Hassan's
"magick chemical" as pure hashish. Recent scholarship,
however, has thrown this into doubt, and it is clear that
hashish, and other marijuana preparations were well known
in the Near East for thousands of years before Hassan ever
lived; for instance, the plant has been found in grave
mounds of late Neolithic Man in the area, dated around
5000 B.C., as Hagbard mentions in the novel. It is implausi-
ble, then, that the ingenious Sabbah would have tried to
pass this drug off as something new and magical.

Some have suggested that Hassan, who was known to
have traveled much in his youth, might have brought opium
back from the East and mixed it with hashish. The scholar-
ly Dr. Joel Fort goes further and argues, in *The Pleasure
Seekers,* that Hassan's supercharger was wine-and-opium,
with no marijuana products at all. Dr. John Allegro, in *The
Sacred Mushroom and the Cross,* argues that both Hassan
and the first Christians actually achieved the paradisical vision with the aid of *amanita muscaria,* the "fly agaric"
mushroom, which is poisonous in high doses but psychedelic
(or at least deleriant) in small quantities.

The present book's suggestion—Alamout black, an almost pure hashish with a few pinches of belladonna and
stramonium—is based on:

(1) the strong etymological evidence that the Hashishim
were *somehow* involved with hashish;

(2) the unlikelihood that wine, opium, mushrooms, or
any combination thereof could account for the etymological
and historical association of Hassan with hashish;

(3) the reasons previously given for doubting that hashish *alone* is the answer;

(4) the capacity of stramonium and belladonna (in
small doses) to create intensely brilliant visual imagery, beyond that of even the best grades of hashish;

(5) the fact that these latter drugs were used in both the

Elusinian Mysteries and in the European witch cult contemporary with Hassan (see R.E.L. Masters, *Eros and
Evil*).

Since it is not the intent of this book to confuse fact with
fancy, it should be pointed out that these arguments are
strong but not compelling. Many other alternatives can be
suggested, such as hashish-belladonna-mandragora, hash-
ish-stramonium-opium, hashish-opium-belladonna, hashish-
opium-bufotinin,* etc., etc. All that can be said with cer-
tainty is that Hagbard Celine insists the correct formula is
hashish-belladonna-stramonium (in ratio 20:1:1), and we
believe Hagbard—most of the time.

The exact link between the Assassins and the European
Illuminati remains unclear. We have seen (but no longer
own) a John Birch Society publication arguing that the alliance between the Hashishim and the Knights Templar was
consummated and that European masonry has been more
or less under Hashishim influence ever since. More likely is
the theory of Daraul (*op. cit.*) that after the Hashishim regrouped as the nonviolent Ishmaelian sect of today, the
Roshinaya (Illuminated Ones) copied their old tactics and
were in turn copied by the Allumbrados of Spain and, finally, by the Bavarian Illuminati.

The nine stages of Hashishim training, the thirteen stages
in Weishaupt's Iluminati, the thirty-two degrees of masonry, etc., are, of course, arbitrary. The Theravada Buddhists
have a system of forty meditations, each leading to a definite stage of growth. Some schools of Hinduism recognize
only two stages: *Dhyana*, conquest of the personal ego, and
Samadhi, unity with the Whole. One can equally well posit
five stages or a hundred and five. The essential that is common to all these systems is that the trainee, at some point or
other, is nearly scared to death.*

* Medieval magicians knew how to obtain bufotinin. They took it, as
Shakespeare recorded, from "skin of toad."
* An interesting account of a traditional system used by quite primi-
tive Mexican Indians, yet basically similar to any and all of the above,
is provided by anthropologist Carlos Castaneda, who underwent
training with a Yaqui shaman, and recounts some of the terrors vividly
in *The Teachings of Don Juan, A Separate Reality, Journey to Ixtlan*,
and *Tales of Power*. Don Juan used peyote, stramonium, and a magic
mushroom (probably *psilocyble Mexicana*, the drug Tim Leary used
for his first trip).

The difference between these systems is that some aim to liberate every candidate and some, like Sabbah's and Weishaupt's, deliberately encourage the majority to remain in ignorance, whereby they may with profit be endlessly exploited by their superiors in the cult. The same general game of an illuminated minority misusing a superstitious majority was characteristic of Tibet until the Chinese Communist invasion broke the power of the high lamas. A sympathetic account of the Tibetan system, which goes far toward justifying it, can be found in Alexandra David-Neel's *The Hidden Teachings of Tibetan Buddhism;* an unsympathetic account by a skeptical fellow mystic is available in *The Confessions of Aleister Crowley.*

Another word about Alamout black: It is not for the inexperienced psychedelic voyager. For instance, the first time Simon Moon tried it, in early 1968, he had occasion to use the men's room in the Biograph Theatre (where he had gone to see *Yellow Submarine* while under the influence). After his bowel movement he reached for the toilet paper and saw with consternation that the first sheet hanging down off the roll was neatly stamped

OFFICIAL
BAVARIAN ILLUMINATI
EWIGE BLUMENKRAFT!

On ordinary marijuana or hashish, such illusions occur, of course—but they are not true hallucinations. They go away if you look at them hard enough. No matter how hard Simon looked at the toilet paper, it still said

OFFICIAL
BAVARIAN ILLUMINATI
EWIGE BLUMENKRAFT!

Simon went back to his seat in the theater badly shaken. For weeks afterward he wondered if the Illuminati had some sinister reason for infiltrating the toilet-paper industry, or if the whole experience were a genuine hallucination and the first sign, as he put it, "that this fucking dope is ruining my fucking head." He never solved this mystery, but eventually he stopped worrying about it.

As for Hassan i Sabbah X and the Cult of the Black

Mother, the authors have been able to learn precious little
about them. Since they are clearly related *somehow* to the
Assassins and the cult of Kali, Mother of Destruction,
one can consider them part of the Illuminati, or Podge, side
of the Sacred Chao; since they seem to be businessmen
rather than fanatics, and since Kali might be a version of
Eris, one can consider them part of the Discordian or
Hodge side. Amid such speculation and much mystery, they
go their dark way, peddling horse and preaching some pretty funky doctrines about Whitey. Perhaps they intend to betray everybody and run off with the loot at an opportune
moment—and, then again, maybe they are the only really
dedicated revolutionaries around. "Nothing is too heavy to
be knocked on its ass, and everything is cool, baby" is the
only summary of his personal philosophy that Hassan i
Sabbah X himself would give us. He's a studly dude, and
we didn't press him.

APPENDIX TZADDI
23 SKIDOO

Linguists and etymologists have had much exercise for
their not-inconsiderable imaginations in attempting to account for this expression. *Skidoo* has been traced back to the
older *skedaddle*, and thence to the Greek *skedannumi*, "to disperse hurriedly." The 23, naturally, has caused even more
creative efforts by these gentry, since they are unaware of
the secret teachings of Magick. One theorist, noting that
Sidney Carton in Dickens' *Tale of Two Cities* is the twenty-third man guillotined in the final scene,* guessed that
those playgoers who were eager to get out of the theater before the crowd counted off the executions and *skidoo'd* toward the exits numbered 23. Another eminent scholar assumes that the expression has something to do with men
hanging around the old Flatiron Building on Twenty-third
Street in New York City—a notoriously windy corner—to
watch ladies' skirts raised by the breeze; when a cop came,
they would *skidoo*. Others have mused inconclusively about

---

* A literary reference which Simon Moon, with his modernistic bias,
overlooked.

the early telegraph operator's signal of *23,* which means (roughly) "stop transmitting," "clear the line," or, to be crude, "shut up," but nobody claims to know how telegraphers picked 23 to have this meaning.

The mystery's real origin is a closely guarded secret of the Justified Ancients of Mummu, which Simon had not attained the rank to learn. Dillinger, however, had attained this rank, and uses the formula quite correctly in the bank robbery scene in the Third Trip. It was printed by "Frater Perdurabo" (Aleister Crowley) in *The Book of Lies* (privately published, 1915; republished by Samuel Weiser Inc., New York, 1970). The text of the spell makes up the totality of Chapter 23 in that curious little book; and it reads:

ΚΕΦΛΛΗ ΚΓ (23)

SKIDOO

What man is at ease in his Inn?
Get out.
Wide is the world and cold.
Get out.
Thou hast become an in-itiate.
Get out.
But thou canst not get out by the way thou camest
   in. The Way out is THE WAY.
Get out.
For OUT is Love and Wisdom and Power.
Get OUT.
If thou hast T already, first get UT.
Then get O.
And so at last get OUT.

It is not permissible to explain this fully, but it may be stated guardedly that T is the union of sex and death, *Tau,* the Rosy Crucifixion; UT is *Ut*gita in the Upanishads; and O is the Positive Void.*

* Fission Chips, like our other characters, was given a chance to peruse this manuscript before publication and correct any factual errors that may have crept in. Of this appendix, he said, "I think my leg is being pulled again, chaps. I suspect that Crowley wrote that in 1915 as a joke on his readers, and you blokes found it and inserted a reference to a magic formula used by Dillinger in your story just so you could then compose this appendix and 'explain' it." Such skepticism,

APPENDIX VAU
FLAXSCRIP AND HEMPSCRIP

Flaxscrip was first introduced into Discordian groups by the mysterious Malaclypse the Younger, K.S.C., in 1968. Hempscrip followed the year after, issued by Dr. Mordecai Malignatus, K.N.S. (In the novel, taking one of our few liberties with historical truth, we move these coinages backward in time and attribute hempscrip to the Justified Ancients of Mummu.)

The *idea* behind flaxscrip, of course, is as old as history; there was private money long before there was government money. The first revolutionary (or reformist) use of this idea, as a check against galloping usury and high interest rates, was the foundation of "Banks of Piety" by the Dominican order of the Catholic Church in the late middle ages. (See Tawney, *Religion and the Rise of Capitalism.*) The Dominicans, having discovered that preaching against usury did not deter the usurer, founded their own banks and provided loans without interest; this "ethical competition" (as Josiah Warren later called it) drove the commercial banks out of the areas where the Dominicans practiced it. Similar private currency, loaned at a low rate of interest (but not at no interest), was provided by Scots banks until the British government, acting on behalf of the monopoly of the Bank of England, stopped this exercise of free enterprise. (See Muellen, *Free Banking.*) The same idea was tried successfully in the American colonies before the Revolution, and again was suppressed by the British government, which some heretical historians regard as a more direct cause of the American Revolution than the taxes mentioned in most schoolbooks. (See Ezra Pound, *Impact,* and additional sources cited therein.)

During the nineteenth century many anarchists and individualists attempted to issue low-interest or no-interest pri-

---

straining at a gnat and swallowing a camel, may be compared to the stance of the Bible Fundamentalist who avers that JHVH made the universe in six days in 4004 B.C. but included fossils and other false leads to make it appear much older. One could equally assert that the cosmos appeared out of Void one second ago, including us and our false memories of a longer duration here.

vate currencies. *Mutual Banking,* by Colonel William Greene, and *True Civilization,* by Josiah Warren, are records of two such attempts, by their instigators. Lysander Spooner, an anarchist who was also a constitutional lawyer, argued at length that Congress had no authority to suppress such private currencies (see his *Our Financiers: Their Ignorance, Usurpations and Frauds*). A general overview of such efforts at free enterprise, soon crushed by the Capitalist State, is given by James M. Martin in his *Men Against the State,* and by Rudolph Rocker in *Pioneers of American Freedom* (an ironic title, since his pioneers all lost their major battles). Lawrence Labadie, of Suffern, N.Y., has collected (but not yet published) records of 1,000 such experiments; one of the present authors, Robert Anton Wilson, unearthed in 1962 the tale of a no-interest currency, privately issued, in Yellow Springs, Ohio, during the 1930s depression. (This was an emergency measure by certain local businessmen, who did not fully appreciate the principle involved, and was abandoned as soon as the "tight-money" squeeze ended and Roosevelt began flooding us all with Federal Reserve notes.)

It is traditional among liberal historians to dismiss such endeavors as "funny-money schemes." They have never explained why government money is any less hilarious. (That used in the U.S. now, for instance, is actually worth 47 percent of its "declared" face value). All money is funny, if you stop to think about it, but no private currency, competing on a free market, could ever be quite so comical (and tragic) as the notes now bearing the magic imprint of Uncle Sam—and backed only by his promise (or threat) that, come hell or high water, by God he'll make it good by taxing our descendants unto the infinite generation to pay the interest on it. The National Debt, so called, is of course, nothing else but the debt we owe the bankers who "loaned" this money to Uncle after he kindly gave them the credit which enabled them to make this loan. Hempscrip or even acidscrip or peyotescrip could never be quite so clownish as this system, which only the Illuminati (if they really exist) could have dreamed up. The system has but one advantage: It makes bankers richer every year. Nobody else, from the industrial capitalist or "captain of industry" to the coal-miner, profits from it in any way, and all pay the taxes, which become the interest payments, which make the bankers

richer. If the Illuminati did not exist, it would be necessary
to invent them—such a system can be explained in no other
way, except by those cynics who hold that human stupidity
is infinite.

The idea behind hempscrip is more radical than the notion of private-enterprise currency per se. Hempscrip, as
employed in the novel, depreciates; it is, thus, not merely a
no-interest currency, but a *negative-interest* currency. The
lender literally pays the borrower to take it away for a
while. It was invented by German business-economist Silvio
Gesell, and is described in his *Natural Economic Order* and
in professor Irving Fisher's *Stamp Script*.

Gresham's Law, like most of the "laws" taught in State-
supported public schools, is not quite true (at least, not in
the form in which it is usually taught). *"Bad money drives
out good" holds only in authoritarian societies, not in libertarian societies.* (Gresham was clear-minded enough to
state explicitly that he was only describing authoritarian societies; *his* formulation of his own "Law" begins with the
words "If the king issueth two moneys . . . ," thereby
implying that the State must exist if the "Law" is to operate.) *In a libertarian society, good money will drive out
the bad.* This Utopian proposition—which the sane reader
will regard with acute skepticism—has been seen to be
sound by a rigorously logical demonstration, based on the
axioms of economics, in *The Cause of Business Depressions*
by Hugo Bilgrim and Edward Levy.*

---

* Economists can "prove" all sorts of things from axioms and few of
them turn out to be true. Yes. We saved for a footnote the information
that at least four empirical demonstrations of the reverse of Gresham's
Law are on record. Three of them, employing small volunteer com-
munities in frontier U.S.A. circa 1830–1860, are recorded in Josiah
Warren's *True Civilization*. The fourth, employing contemporary
college students in a psychology laboratory, is the subject of a recent
Master's thesis by associate professor Don Werkheiser of Central
State College, Wilberforce, Ohio.

APPENDIX ZAIN
PROPERTY AND PRIVILEGE

Property is theft.
— P. J. PROUDHON

Property is liberty.
— P. J. PROUDHON

Property is impossible.
— P. J. PROUDHON

Consistency is the hobgoblin of small minds.
— RALPH WALDO EMERSON

Proudhon, by piling up his contradictions this way, was not merely being French; he was trying to indicate that the abstraction "property" covers a variety of phenomena, some pernicious and some beneficial. Let us borrow a device from the semanticists and examine his triad with subscripts attached for maximum clarity.

"Property$_1$ is theft" means that property$_1$, created by the artificial laws of feudal, capitalist, and other authoritarian societies, is based on armed robbery. Land titles, for instance, are clear examples of property$_1$; swords and shot were the original coins of transaction.

"Property$_2$ is liberty" means that property$_2$, that which will be voluntarily honored in a voluntary (anarchist) society, is the foundation of the liberty in that society. The more people's interests are comingled and confused, as in collectivism, the more they will be stepping on each other's toes; only when the rules of the game declare clearly "This is mine and this is thine," *and the game is voluntarily accepted as worthwhile by all parties to it,* can true independence be achieved.

"Property$_3$ is impossible" means that property$_3$ (= property$_1$) creates so much conflict of interest that society is in perpetual undeclared civil war and must eventually devour itself (and properties $_1$ and $_3$ as well). In short, Proudhon, in his own way, foresaw the Snafu Principle. He also foresaw that communism would only perpetuate and aggravate the conflicts, and that *anarchy is the only viable alternative to this chaos*.

It is not averred, of course, that property₂ will come into existence only in a totally voluntary society; many forms of it already exist. The error of most alleged libertarians—especially the followers (!) of the egregious Ayn Rand—is to assume that all property₁ is property₂. The distinction can be made by any IQ above 70 and is absurdly simple. The test is to ask, of any title of ownership you are asked to accept or which you ask others to accept, "Would this be honored in a free society of rationalists, or does it require the armed might of a State to force people to honor it?" If it be the former, it is property₂ and represents liberty; if it be the latter, it is property₁ and represents theft.

APPENDIX CHETH
HAGBARD'S ABDICATION

Readers who do not understand the scene in which Hagbard abdicates in favor of Miss Portinari should take heart.

Once they do understand it, they will understand most of the mysteries of all schools of mysticism.

APPENDIX LAMED
THE TACTICS OF MAGICK

> The human brain evidently operates on some variation of the famous principle enunciated in *The Hunting of the Snark:* "What I tell you three times is true."
> —NORBERT WEINER, *Cybernetics*

The most important idea in the *Book of Sacred Magic of Abra-Melin the Mage* is the simple-looking formula "Invoke often."

The most successful form of treatment for so-called mental disorders, the Behavior Therapy of Pavlov, Skinner, Wolpe, et al., could well be summarized in two similar words: "Reinforce often." ("Reinforcement," for all practical purposes, means the same as the layman's term "reward." The essence of Behavior Therapy is rewarding desired behavior; the behavior "as if by magic" begins to occur more and more often as the rewards continue.)

Advertising, as everybody knows, is based on the axiom "Repeat often."

Those who think they are "materialists" and think that "materialism" requires them to deny all facts which do not square with their definition of "matter" are loath to admit the well-documented and extensive list of individuals who have been cured of serious maladies by that very vulgar and absurd form of magick known as Christian Science. Nonetheless, the reader who wants to understand this classic work of immortal literature will have to analyze its deepest meanings, guided by an awareness that there is no essential difference between magick, Behavior Therapy, advertising, and Christian Science. All of them can be condensed into Abra-Melin's simple "Invoke often."

Reality, as Simon Moon says, is thermoplastic, not thermosetting. It is not quite Silly-Putty, as Mr. Paul Krassner once claimed, but is much closer to Silly-Putty than we generally realize. If you are told often enough that "Budweiser is the king of beers," Budweiser will eventually taste somewhat better—perhaps a great deal better—than it tasted before this magick spell was cast. If a behavior therapist in the pay of the communists rewards you every time you repeat a communist slogan, you will repeat it more often, and begin to slide imperceptibly toward the same kind of belief that Christian Scientists have for their mantras. And if a Christian Scientist tells himself every day that his ulcer is going away, the ulcer will disappear more rapidly than it would have had he not subjected himself to this homemade advertising campaign. Finally, if a magician invokes the Great God Pan often enough, the Great God Pan will appear just as certainly as heterosexual behavior appears in homosexuals who are being handled (or manhandled) by Behavior Therapy.

The opposite and reciprocal of "Invoke often" is "Banish often."

The magician wishing for a manifestation of Pan will not only invoke Pan directly and verbally, create Panlike conditions in his temple, reinforce Pan associations in every gesture and every article of furniture, use the colors and per-

fumes associated with Pan, etc.; he will also banish other
gods verbally, banish them by removing their associated
furnitures and colors and perfumes, and banish them in every other way. The Behavior Therapist calls this "negative
reinforcement," and in treating a patient who is afraid of
elevators he will not only reinforce (reward) every instance
in which the patient rides an elevator without terror, but
will also negatively reinforce (punish) each indication of
terror shown by the patient. The Christian Scientist, of
course, uses a mantra or spell which both reinforces health
and negatively reinforces (banishes) illness.* Similarly, a
commercial not only motivates the listener toward the sponsor's product but discourages interest in all "false gods" by
subsuming them under the rubric of the despised and con-
temptible Brand X.

   Hypnotism, debate, and countless other games have the
same mechanism: *Invoke often* and *Banish often*.

   The reader who seeks a deeper understanding of this argument can obtain it by putting these principles to the test.
If you are afraid that you might, in this Christian environment, fall into taking the Christian Science mantra too seriously, try instead the following simple experiment. For forty days and forty nights, begin each day by invoking and
praising the world in itself as an expression of the Egyptian
deities. Recite at dawn:

> I bless Ra, the fierce sun burning bright
> I bless Isis-Luna in the night
> I bless the air, the Horus-hawk
> I bless the earth on which I walk

   Repeat at moonrise. Continue for the full forty days and
forty nights. We say without any reservations that, at a

---

* The basic Christian Science mantra, known as "The Scientific Statement of Being," no less, is as follows: "There is no life, truth, intelligence nor substance in matter. All is infinite mind and its infinite
manifestation, for God is all in all, Spirit is immortal truth: matter is
mortal error. Spirit is the real and eternal; matter is the unreal and
temporal. Spirit is God and man is His image and likeness. Therefore
man is not material, he is spiritual." The fact that these statements
are, in terms of the scientific criteria, "meaningless," "non-operation-
al," and "footless" is actually totally irrelevant. *They work.* Try them
and see. As Aleister Crowley, no friend of Mrs. Eddy's, wrote, "Enough
of Because! May he be damned for a dog!"

minimum, you will feel happier and more at home in this part of the galaxy (and will also understand better Uncle John Feather's attitude toward our planet); at maximum, you may find rewards beyond your expectations, and will be converted to using this mantra for the rest of your life. (If the results are exceptionally good, you just might start believing in ancient Egyptian gods.)

A selection of magick techniques which will offend the reason of no materialist can be found in Laura Archera Huxley's *You Are Not the Target* (a powerful mantra, the title!), in *Gestalt Therapy*, by Perls, Heferline, and Goodman, and in *Mind Games*, by Masters and Houston.

All this, of course, is programming your own trip by manipulating appropriate clusters of word, sound, image, and emotional (*prajna*) energy. The aspect of magick which puzzles, perplexes, and provokes the modern mentality is that in which the operator programs somebody else's trip, *acting at a distance*. It is incredible and insulting, to this type of person, if one asserts that our Mr. Nkrumah Fubar could program a headache for the President of the United States. He might grant that such manipulating of energy is possible if the President was told about Mr. Fubar's spells, but he will not accept that it works just as well when the subject has no conscious knowledge of the curse.

The magical theory that $5 = 6$ has no conviction for such a skeptic, and magicians have not yet proposed a better theory. The materialist then asserts that all cases where magic did appear to work under this handicap are illusions, delusions, hallucinations, "coincidences,"* misapprehensions, "luck," accident, or downright hoax.

He does not seem to realize that asserting this is equivalent to asserting that reality is, after all, thermoplastic—for he is admitting that many people live in a different reality than his own. Rather than leave him to grapple as best he can with this self-contradiction, we suggest that he consult *Psychic Discoveries Behind the Iron Curtain*, by Ostrander and Schroder—especially Chapter 11, "From Animals to Cybernetics: The Search for a Theory of Psi." He might realize that when "matter" is fully understood, there is nothing a materialist need reject in magick *action at a distance*,

---

* Look up the etymology of that word some time and see if it means anything.

which has been well explored by scientists committed to the rigid Marxist form of dialectical materialism.

Those who have kept alive the ancient traditions of magick, such as the Ordo Templi Orientalis, will realize that the essential secret is sexual (as Saul tries to explain in the Sixth Trip) and that more light can be found in the writings of Wilhelm Reich, M. D., than in the current Soviet research. But Dr. Reich was jailed as a quack by the U.S. Government, and we would not ask our readers to consider the possibility that the U.S. Government could ever be wrong about anything.

Any psychoanalyst will guess at once the most probable symbolic meanings of the Rose and the Cross; but no psychologist engaged in psi research has applied this key to the deciphering of traditional magic texts. The earliest reference to freemasonry in English occurs in Anderson's "Muses Threnody," 1638:

> For we be brethren of the Rosey Cross
> We have the Mason Word and second sight

but no parapsychologist has followed up the obvious clue contained in this conjunction of the vaginal rose, the phallic cross, the word of invocation, and the phenomenon of thought projection. That the taboos against sexuality are still latent in our culture explains part of this blindness; fear of opening the door to the most insidious and subtle forms of paranoia is another part. (*If the magick can work at a distance,* the repressed thought goes, *which of us is safe?*) A close and objective study of the anti-LSD hysteria in America will shed further light on the mechanisms of avoidance here discussed.

Of course, there are further offenses and affronts to the rationalist in the deeper study of magick. We all know, for instance, that words are only arbitrary conventions with no intrinsic connection to the things they symbolize, yet magick involves the use of words in a manner that seems to imply that some such connection, or even identity, actually exists. The reader might analyze some powerful bits of language not generally considered magical, and he will find something of the key. For instance, the 2 + 3 pattern in "Hail Eris"/"All hail Discordia" is not unlike the 2 + 3 in "Holy Mary, Mother of God," or that in the "L.S./M.F.T."

which once sold many cartons of cigarettes to our parents; and the 2 + 3 in Crowley's "Io Pan! Io Pan Pan!" is a relative of these. Thus, when a magician says that you *must* shout "Abrahadabra," and no other word, at the most intensely emotional moment in an invocation, he exaggerates; you may substitute other words; but you will abort the result if you depart too far from the five-beat patttern of "Abrahadabra."*

But this brings us to the magical theory of reality.

Mahatma Guru Sri Paramahansa Shivaji* writes in *Yoga for Yahoos:*

> Let us consider a piece of cheese. We say that this has certain qualities, shape, structure, color, solidity, weight, taste, smell, consistency and the rest; but investigation has shown that this is all illusory. Where are these qualities? Not in the cheese, for different observers give quite different accounts of it. Not in ourselves, for we do not perceive them in the absence of the cheese . . .
>
> What then are these qualities of which we are so sure? They would not exist without our brains; they would not exist without the cheese. They are the results of the union, that is of the Yoga, of the seer and seen, of subject and object . . .

There is nothing here with which a modern physicist could quarrel; and this is the magical theory of the universe. The magician assumes that *sensed reality*—the panorama of impressions monitored by the senses and collated by the brain—is radically different from so-called objective reality.† About the latter "reality" we can only form speculations or theories which, if we are very careful and subtle, will not contradict either logic or the reports of the senses. This lack of contradiction is rare; some conflicts between

---

* A glance at the end of Appendix Beth will save the reader from misunderstanding the true tenor of these remarks.

* Aleister Crowley again, under another pen-name.

† See the anthology *Perception,* edited by Robert Blake, Ph.D., and especially the chapter by psychologist Carl Rogers, which demonstrates that people's perceptions change while they are in psychotherapy. As William Blake noted, "The fool sees not the same tree that the wise man sees."

theory and logic, or between theory and sense-data, are not discovered for centuries (for example, the wandering of Mercury away from the Newtonian calculation of its orbit). And even when achieved, lack of contradiction is proof only that the theory *is not totally false*. It is never, in any case, proof that the theory *is totally true*—for an indefinite number of such theories can be constructed from the known data at any time. For instance, the geometries of Euclid, of Gauss and Reimann, of Lobachevski, and of Fuller *all* work well enough on the surface of the earth, and it not yet clear whether the Gauss-Reimann or the Fuller system works better in interstellar space.

If we have this much freedom in choosing our theories about "objective reality," we have even more liberty in deciphering the "given" or transactional *sensed reality*. The ordinary person senses as he or she has been taught to sense —that is, as they have been programmed by their society. The magician is a self-programmer. Using invocation and evocation—which are functionally identical with self-conditioning, auto-suggestion, and hypnosis, as shown above—he or she edits or orchestrates sensed reality like an artist.*

This book, being part of the only serious conspiracy it describes—that is, part of Operation Mindfuck—has programmed the reader in ways that he or she will not understand for a period of months (or perhaps years). When that understanding is achieved, the real import of this appendix (and of the equation $5 = 6$) will be clearer. Officials at Harvard thought Dr. Timothy Leary was joking when he warned that students should not be allowed to indiscriminately remove dangerous, habit-forming books from the library unless each student proves a definite need for each volume. (For instance, you have lost track of Joe Malik's mysterious dogs by now.) It is strange that one can make the clearest possible statements and yet be understood by many to have said the opposite.

The Rite of Shiva, as performed by Joe Malik during the SSS Black Mass, contains the central secret of all magick, very explicitly, yet most people can reread that section a dozen, or a hundred times, and never understand what the secret is. For instance, Miss Portinari was a typical Catholic

---

* Everybody, of course, does this unconsciously; see the paragraph about the cheese. The magician, doing it consciously, controls it.

girl in every way—except for an unusual tendency to take Catholicism seriously—until she began menstruating and performing spiritual meditations every day.* One morning, during her meditation period, she visualized the Sacred Heart of Jesus with unusual clarity; immediately another image, distinctly shocking to her, came to mind with equal vividness. She recounted this experience to her confessor the next Saturday, and he warned her, gravely, that meditation was not healthy for a young girl, unless she intended to take the oath of seclusion and enter a convent. She had no intention of doing that, but rebelliously (and guiltily) continued her meditations anyway. The disturbing second image persisted whenever she thought of the Sacred Heart; she began to suspect that this was sent by the Devil to distract her from meditation.

One weekend, when she was home from convent school on vacation, her parents decided she was the right age to be introduced to Roman society. (Actually, they, like most well-off Italian families, had already chosen which daughter would be given to the church—and it wasn't her. Hence, this early introduction to *la dolce vita*.) One of the outstanding ornaments of Rome at that time was the "eccentric international businessman" Mr. Hagbard Celine, and he was at the party to which Miss Portinari was taken that evening.

It was around eleven, and she had consumed perhaps a little too much Piper Heidseck, when she happened to find herself standing near a small group who were listening raptly to a story the strange Celine was telling. Miss Portinari wondered what this creature might be saying—he was reputedly even more cynical and materialistic than other international money-grubbers, and Miss Portinari was, at that time, the kind of conservative Catholic idealist who finds capitalists even more dreadful than socialists. She idly tuned in on his words; he was talking English, but she understood that language adequately.

" 'Son, son,' " Hagbard recited, " 'with two beautiful women throwing themselves at you, why are you sitting alone in your room jacking off?' "

Miss Portinari blushed furiously and drank some more

---

* These two signs of growth often appear at the same time, being DNA-triggered openings of the fourth neural circuit.

champagne to conceal it. She hated the man already, knowing that she would surrender her virginity to him at the
earliest opportunity; of such complexities are intellectual
Catholic adolescents capable.

"And the boy replied," Hagbard went on, " 'I guess you
just answered your own question, Ma.' "

There was a shocked silence.

"The case is quite typical," Hagbard added blandly, obviously finished. "Professor Freud recounts even more star-
tling family dramas."

"I don't see . . ." a celebrated French auto racer began,
frowning. Then he smiled. "Oh," he said, "was the boy an
American?"

Miss Portinari left the group perhaps a bit too hurriedly
(she felt a few eyes following her) and quickly refilled her
champagne glass.

A half-hour later she was standing on the veranda, trying
to clear her head in the night air, when a shadow moved
near her and Celine appeared amid a cloud of cigar smoke.

"The moon has a fat jaw tonight," he said in Italian.
"Looks like somebody punched her in the mouth."

"Are you a poet in addition to your other accomplish-
ments?" she asked coolly. "That sounds as if it might be
American verse."

He laughed—a clear peal, like a stallion whinnying.
"Quite so," he said. "I just came from Rapallo, where I was
talking to America's major poet of this century. How old
are you?" he asked suddenly.

"Almost sixteen," she said fumbling the words.

"Almost fifteen," he corrected ungallantly.

"If it's any affair of yours—"

"It might be," he replied easily. "I need a girl your age
for something I have in mind."

"I can imagine. Something foul."

He stepped further out of the shadows and closer.
"Child," he said, "are you religious?"

"I suppose you regard that as old-fashioned," she replied,
imagining his mouth on her breast and thinking of paint-
ings of Mary nursing the Infant.

"At this point in history," he said simply, "it's the only
thing that isn't old-fashioned. What was your birthdate?
Never mind—you must be a Virgo."

"I am," she said. (His teeth would bite her nipple, but

very gently. He would know enough to do that.) "But that is superstition, not religion."

"I wish I could draw a precise line between religion, superstition, and science." He smiled. "I find that they keep running together. You are Catholic, of course?" His persistence was maddening.

"I am too proud to believe an absurdity, and therefore I am not a Protestant," she replied—immediately fearing that he would recognize the plagiarism.

"What symbol means the most to you?" he asked, with the blandness of a prosecuting attorney setting a trap.

"The cross," she said quickly. She didn't want him to know the truth.

"No." He again corrected her ungallantly. "The Sacred Heart."

Then she knew he was of Satan's party.

"I must go," she said.

"Meditate further on the Sacred Heart," he said, his eyes blazing like a hypnotist's (a cornball gimmick, he was thinking privately, but it might work). "Meditate on it deeply, child. You will find in it the essential of Catholicism —and the essential of all other religion."

"I think you are mad," she responded, leaving the veranda with undignified haste.

But two weeks later, during her morning meditation, she suddenly understood the Sacred Heart. At lunchtime she disappeared—leaving behind a note to the Mother Superior of the convent school and another note for her parents— and went in search of Hagbard. She had even more potential than he realized, and (as elsewhere recorded) within two years he abdicated in her favor. They never became lovers.*

The importance of symbols—images—as the link between word and primordial energy demonstrates the unity between magick and yoga. Both magick and yoga—we reiterate—are methods of self-programming employing synchronistically connected chains of word, image, and bioenergy.

Thus, rationalists, who are all puritans, have never con-

* They were quite good friends, though, and he did fuck her occasionally.

sidered the fact that disbelief in magick is found only in puri-
tanical societies. The reason for this is simple: Puritans
are incapable of guessing what magick is essentially all
about. It can even be surely ventured that only those who
have experienced true love, in the classic Albigensian or
troubadour sense of that expression, are equipped to understand even the most clear-cut exposition of the mysteries.*

The eye in the triangle, for instance, is not primarily a
symbol of the Christian Trinity, as the gullible assume—except insofar as the Christian Trinity is itself a visual (or
verbal) elaboration on a much older meaning. Nor is this
symbol representative of the Eye of Osiris or even of the
Eye of Horus, as some have ventured; it is venerated, for
instance, among the Cao Dai sect in Vietnam, who never
heard of Osiris or Horus. The eye's meaning can be found
quite simply by meditating on Tarot Trump XV, the Devil,
which corresponds, on the Tree of Life, to the Hebrew letter *ayin*, the eye. The reader who realizes that "The Devil"
is only a late rendering of the Great God Pan has already
solved the mystery of the eye, and the triangle has its usual
meaning. The two together are the union of *Yod*, the father, with *He*, the Mother, as in *Yod-He-Vau-He*, the holy
unspeakable name of God. *Vau*, the Holy Ghost, is the result of their union, and final *He* is the divine ecstasy which
follows. One might even venture that one who contemplates
this key to the identities of Pan, the Devil, the Great Father, and the Great Mother will eventually come to a new,
more complete understanding of the Christian Trinity itself,
and especially of its most mysterious member, *Vau*, the elusive Holy Ghost.*

The pentagram comes in two forms but always represents
the fullest extension of the human psyche—the male human psyche in particular. The pentagram with one horn exalted is, quite naturally, associated with the right-hand path;
and the two-horned pentagram with the left-hand path. (The
Knights Templar, very appropriately, inscribed the head of

---

* This book has stated it as clearly as possible in a number of places,
but some readers are still wondering what we are holding back.
* This being has more in common with the ordinary nocturnal visitor,
sometimes called a "ghost," than is immediately evident to the uninitiated. Cf. the well-documented association of poltergeist dis-
turbances with adolescents.

Baphomet, the goat-headed deity who was their equivalent of Pan or the Devil, within the left-handed pentagram in

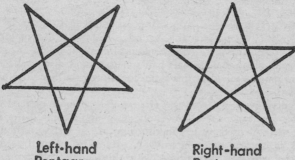

**Left·hand
Pentagram
(two horns exalted)**

**Right-hand
Pentagram
(one horn exalted)**

such wise that each "horn" contained one of Baphomet's horns.) It is to be observed that the traditionally sinister* left-hand pentagram contains an internal *pentagon* with one point *upward,* whereas the right-hand pentagram contains an internal *pentagon* with one point *downward;* this nicely illustrates the Law of Opposites.† The pentagon in the Sacred Chao is tilted from the perpendicular so that it cannot be said to have any points directly upward or directly downward—or perhaps can be said to have 1½ points up and 1½ points down‡—thereby illustrating the Reconciliation of Opposites.

All that can be said against the method of the left-hand

---

* This association, attributing diabolism to the left-hand path, is over-simplified, prejudiced, and superstitious. In general, it can be said that the left-hand pentagram is suitable for both invocations and evocations, whereas the right-hand pentagram is suitable only for evocations, and that is the only important difference. (It is assumed that the reader understands the pentagram as an exclusively male symbol.)

† Cf. the Tarot trumps II and III—the Magus, holding one arm upward and one downward, and the High Priestess, sitting between the pillars of Day and Night. (The Priestess is also associated with the Hebrew letter *gimmel,* the camel, and part of the meaning of this symbolism is contained in the shapes of the camel's back and the Hebrew letter.)

‡ This makes it quite useless for summoning werewolves. The Sacred Chao, however, is intended to teach a philosophical lesson, not to attract individuals with dubious pastimes.

pentagram, without prejudice, is that this form of the sacrament is always destructive of the Holy Spirit, in a certain sense. It should be remembered that the right-hand pentagram method is also destructive in most cases, especially by those practitioners so roundly condemned in Chapter 14 of Joyce's *Ulysses*—and this group is certainly the majority these days. In view of the ecological crisis, it might even be wise to encourage the left-hand method and discourage the right-hand method at this time, to balance the Sacred Numbers.

Very few readers of the *Golden Bough* have pierced Sir Prof. Dr. Frazer's veil of euphemism and surmised the exact method used by Isis in restoring life to Osiris, although this is shown quite clearly in extant Egyptian frescoes. Those who are acquainted with this simple technique of resurrecting the dead (which is *at least partially* successful in *all* cases and totally successful in most) will have no trouble in skrying the esoteric connotations of the Sacred Chao—or of the Taoist yin-yang or the astrological sign of cancer. The method almost completely reverses that of the pentagrams, right or left, and it can even be said that in a certain sense it was not Osiris himself but his brother, Set, symbolically understood, who was the object of Isis's magical workings. *In every case, without exception, a magical or mystical symbol always refers to one of the very few* variations of the same, very special variety of human sacrifice: the "one eye opening" or the "one hand clapping"; and this sacrifice cannot be partial—it must culminate in death if it is to be efficacious.* The literal-mindedness of the Saures, in the novel, caused them to become a menace to life on earth; the reader should bear this in mind. The sacrifice is not simple. It is a species of cowardice, epidemic in Anglo-Saxon nations for more than three centuries, which causes most who seek success in this field to stop short before the death of the victim. *Anything less than death—that is, complete oblivion—simply will not work.** (One will find more

---

* Fewer than seventy, according to a classical enumeration.
* The magician must always identify fully with the victim, and share every agonized contortion to the utmost. Any attitude of standing aside and watching, as in a theatrical performance, or any intellectualization during the moments when the sword is doing its brutal but necessary work, or any squeamishness or guilt or revulsion, creates the two-mindedness against which Hagbard so vehemently warns in *Never Whistle While You're Pissing.* In a sense, only the mind dies.

clarity on this crucial point in the poetry of John Donne than in most treatises alleging to explain the secrets of magick.)

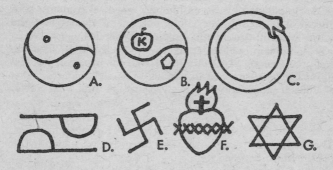

A. YIN-YANG; B. SACRED CHAO; C. OUROBOROS, THE SERPENT EATING ITS OWN TAIL; D. ASTROLOGICAL SIGN OF CANCER; E. SWASTIKA; F. ROMAN CATHOLIC SACRED HEART; G. HEXA-GRAM.

The symbolism of the swastika is quite adequately explained in Wilhelm Reich's *Mass Psychology of Fascism.*

Ouroboros, the serpent eating its own tail, is chiefly emblematic of the Mass of the Holy Ghost.*

The Roman Catholic symbolism of the Sacred Heart is strikingly overt, especially to readers of Frazer and Payne-Knight. In essence, it is the same notion conveyed by the cartoonist's conventional rendering of Cupid shooting his arrow into a red pulsating heart. This is the basic meaning of the Dying God and the Resurrection. The identification of Christ with the pelican who stabs its own heart with its beak (to feed its young) is an analogous rendering of the same motif. We repeat that it was only because the Saure family so misread these simple symbols that they became cruel and sadistic.

In essence, then, the basic symbols, of magic, mythology, and religion—whether Eastern or Western, ancient or modern, "right-hand" or "left-hand"—are so simple that only

* See Israel Regardie, *The Tree of Life.*

the pernicious habit of looking for alleged "profundities" and "mysteries" prevents people from automatically under-standing them almost without thinking. The meaning of the hexagram—the female equivalent of the male pentagram —was explicated by Freud himself, but most students, con-vinced that the answer could not be so elementary and down-to-earth, continue to look into the clouds.

The same principles apply to written symbols. The all-important name YOD HE VAU HE, for instance, has tra-ditionally been scanned in various ways, of which the most significant correlations are given in the following table:

	YOD	HE	VAU	HE
True mean-ing of the Hebrew let-ters	Fist (or spermata-zoon)	Window	Nail	Window
Traditional magick code	Father	Mother	Son	Daughter
Tarot suit	Wands	Cups	Swords	Pentacles (or Discs)
Tarot trump	Hermit	Star	Hierophant	Star
Tarot Royal Card	Knight	Queen	Prince	Princess
Element	Fire	Water	Air	Earth

The traditional lion-man-eagle-bull symbolism also fits this table,* as do Joyce's Four Old Men in *Finnegans Wake*;† it can also be found in the Aztec codices and Buddhist mandalas.

The essential and original meaning, of course, is a pro-gram for a ritual, and the ritual is magick. The four letters are simply the four beats in Wilhelm Reich's formula: mus-cular tension → electrical charge → electrical discharge → muscular relaxation. In short, as Freud once noted, every

---

* YOD, the fiery father, is the lion (fire-sign); HE, the watery mother, is man as humanity; VAU, the air spirit, is eagle; final HE, earth, is bull.
† Marcus Lyons (i.e., the lion) is the fiery father; Matt Gregory (i.e., the ego) is the watery mother; John McDougall (i.e., eagle) is the airy son; Luke Tarpey (taur, the bull) is the earthy daughter.

sexual act involves, at a minimum, four parties. The father and son provide a "fist" and a "nail"; the mother and daughter provide two "windows." The case of the Chicago schizophrenic killer William Heirens, who experienced orgasm when climbing through windows, demonstrates that this symbolism does not have to be taught and is inherent in the human mind, although always subject to the distortion exemplified by the Saures.

Finally, the universal blessing given on page 218 is intimately involved with the YHVH formula:

> I bless Ra, the fierce sun burning bright
> I bless Isis-Luna in the night
> I bless the air, the Horus-Hawk
> I bless the earth on which I walk

The fiery father, the watery mother, the airy son, and the earthy daughter are all there, just as they are in every alchemical formula.* But we say no more at this point, lest the reader begin seeking for a $5 = 4$ equation to balance the $5 = 6$.

We conclude with a final warning and clarification: Resort to mass sacrifice (as among the Aztecs, the Catholic Inquisition, and the Nazi death camps) is the device of those who are incapable of the true Rite of the Dying God.

APPENDIX YOD
OPERATION MINDFUCK

OM was originally instigated by Ho Chih Zen, of the Erisian Liberation Front, who is the same person but not the same individual as Lord Omar Khayyam Ravenhurst, author of *The Honest Book of Truth*. The guiding philosophy is that originally proposed in *The Theory of Games and Economic Behavior* by von Neumann and Morgenstern: namely, that the only strategy which an opponent cannot predict is a random strategy. The foundation had already

---

* In this connection—and also, *en passant*, as an indication that Adolf Hitler's link with the Illuminati was not invented for this work of "fiction"—we suggest that the reader look into *The Morning of the Magicians*, by Pauwels and Bergier.

been laid by the late Malaclypse the Younger, K.S.C., when he proclaimed, "We Discordians must stick apart." This radical decentralization of all Discordian enterprises created a built-in random factor even before Operation Mindfuck was proposed. To this day, neither Ho Chih Zen himself nor any other Discordian apostle knows for sure who is or is not involved in any phase of Operation Mindfuck or what activities they are or are not engaged in as part of that project. Thus, the outsider is immediately trapped in a double-bind: the only safe assumption is that anything a Discordian does is somehow related to OM, but, since this leads directly to paranoia, this is not a "safe" assumption after all, and the "risky" hypothesis that whatever the Discordians are doing is harmless may be "safer" in the long run, perhaps. *Every aspect of OM follows, or accentuates, this double-bind.**

OM projects vary from the trivial to the colossal.

An example of the former is a rubber stamp owned by Dr. Mordecai Malignatus, which says SEE MENTAL HEALTH RECORDS. (Dr. Malignatus casually picked this up from a public-health clinic while nobody was looking.) Any mail which Dr. Malignatus considers impertinent or insulting— especially if it comes from a government office—is stamped with this motto and sent back, otherwise untouched. This causes considerable puzzlement to various bureaucrats.

An example of the latter is Project Jake, instigated by Harold Lord Randomfactor. Once or twice a year, a public servant who has distinguished himself by more than common imbecility is selected as target for a Jake and all Discordian cabals are alerted—including the various branches of the Erisian Liberation Front, the Twelve Famous Buddha Minds, the St. Gulik Iconistary, the Earl of Nines, the Tactile Temple of Eris Erotic, the Brotherhood of the Lust of Christ, Green & Pleasant Enterprises, Society for Moral

---

* The double-bind, first defined by anthropologist Gregory Bateson, is a situation in which you must choose between two alternatives both of which are unpleasant. A beautiful example, suggested by Mr. William S. Burroughs: Condition a draftee so that he will immediately obey either the order 'Stand up" or the order "Sit down," if given by a superior officer, then have two officers simultaneously order him to stand up and sit down. Obeying the first order means disobeying the second, and obeying the second means disobeying the first. Presumably, the subject would wig out.

Understanding and Training, the In-Sect, the Golden Apple Panthers, the Paratheo-Anametamystikhood of Eris Esoteric, Sam's Café, the Seattle Group, the Stone Dragon Cabal, the Universal Erisian Church, and the Young Americans for Real Freedom.* On Jake Day, the public servant being honored receives mail from *all* of these, on their official letterheads (which are somewhat weird, it must be granted), asking for help in some complicated political matter that passes all rational understanding. The official so honored can conclude either that he is the target of a conspiracy composed entirely of lunatics, or that the general public is much more imaginative and less stodgy than he had previously assumed.

Between the trivial and the colossal there is a variety of OM which can be called the chronic.

Most notable is the honorary membership. Not wishing to exclude anybody from membership in the Erisian movement for such a technicality as being non-Erisian, the legendary Malaclypse the Younger invented several honorary Aneristic groups. It is now the tradition for any Discordian cabal to appoint anybody to one of these groups if his or her behavior is notably Aneristic. For instance, a high-school principal who has given a particularly stirring assembly speech on some such topic as "The Draft as a Protection for Our Freedoms" (or "Taxation as a Protection for Our Property" or any of the other oxymorons beloved by educators) might thereafter receive some such mailing as this:

ORDER OF THE PEACOCK ANGEL

House of Apostles of Eris

(√) Safeguard this letter; it is an important historical document.
( ) Burn after reading—subversive literature.
( ) Ignore and continue what you were doing before opening this.

Dear (√) Sir ( ) Madam ( ) Fido:
  It has recently come to Our ears that you, in your official capacity as principal of Aaron Burr High School, said in a public meeting, with your bare face hanging out, that death by napalm is "really no more painful than a bad cold" and that Orientals have "tougher epidermi than whites and feel less acutely."

* All these are real groups, currently active in the U.S.A. (Do you believe that?)

In Our official capacity as High Priest of the Head temple of the House of Apostles of Eris, We congratulate you for helping to restore American education to its rightful position as the envy and despair of all other (and, hence, lesser) educational systems.

You are hereby appointed a five-star General in the Bureau of the Division of the Department of the Order of the Knights of the Five-Sided Castle, Quixote Cabal, with full authority to shrapnel your friends and bomb your neighbors.

If you have any answers, We will be glad to provide full and detailed questions.

In the Name of La Mancha,

Theophobia the Elder, M.C.P.
High Priest, Head temple

Hail Eris—All hail Discordia—Kallisti

This document will be stamped with such legends as OF-FICIAL—DO NOT USE THIS PAPER AS TOILET TISSUE; SE-CREDIT—FOR YOUR EYES ONLY; QUIXQTE LIVES, etc., all in the most tasteful blues and reds, together with Easter Bunny seals, ribbons, and whatever other decorations it pleases the local cabal to attach. Often it will be accompanied by a button or an armband, making the possessor a five-star General, adorned with a classic rendition of the Knight of the Mournful Countenance. Copies, of course, will be sent to the radical students at the school to guarantee that the principal being honored will see and hear many references to Don Quixote in following days, lest he think he is dealing with a single "harmless lunatic." (The official signal of the Knights of the Five-Sided Castle, needless to say, is a pentagon with a golden apple inside.)

Other groups to which individuals may be given honorary membership for conspicuously Aneristic behavior are:

the Hemlock Fellowship—for academic leaders who have taken strong actions to protect students from disturbing ideas and/or to deny tenure to controversial teachers or professors;

the St. Famine Society for War Against Evil—for people who have exhibited unusual concern for the moral behavior of their neighbors;*

the Flat Earth Society—for legislators or citizens' groups

* Annual meetings are held on the Feast of St. Famine at the Casa de Inquisitador in San Miguel de Allende, Mexico.

dedicated to preventing the dissemination of "modernistic" ideas in education;†

the Fat Jap Anti-Defamation League—for Women's Liberationists and others who have found good ideological reasons to object to the English language;

the Fraternal Order of Hate Groups—given to allegedly libertarian groups only if they have engaged in conspicuously authoritarian behavior *and* have developed a philosophical line proving that said behavior is actually libertarian. (That group which has found the best libertarian justification for opposing liberty receives the Annual William Buckley Memorial Award and joint membership in the St. Famine Society for War Against Evil.);

the First Evangelical and Reformed Rand, Branden, and Holy Galt Church—for those who are simultaneously rationalists and dogmatists;

the Part-of-the-Solution Vanguard Party—for any Supreme Servant of the People who has shown inordinate zeal in banishing most of the people as Parts-of-the-Problem.

Other aspects of Operation Mindfuck include:

Project Eagle. Day-glo posters have been printed which look like the old Eagle proclamation saying TO THE POLLS YE SONS OF FREEDOM. The new, improved Discordian posters, however, have one slight word change, and say cheerfully BURN THE POLLS YE SONS OF FREEDOM. Like the old ones, they are posted in prominent places on election day.

Project Pan-Pontification. Since the Rev. Kirby Hensley founded the Universal Life Church and started ordaining *everybody* as a minister of the gospel, the Paratheo-Anametamystikhood of Eris Esoteric has decided to raise the stakes. They are now distributing cards stating:

THE BEARER OF THIS CARD
IS A GENUINE AND AUTHORIZED
P O P E
So *Please* Treat Him Right

GOOD FOREVER

Genuine and authorized by the HOUSE OF APOSTLES OF ERIS. Every man, woman and child on Earth is a genuine and authorized Pope.

Members receive a handsome banner proclaiming IN YOUR HEART YOU KNOW IT'S FLAT.

Similar cards, with "Him" replaced by "Her" and "Pope" by "Mome," are being prepared for Woman's Liberationists.

Project Graffito (and *Project Bumpersticker*). Anybody can participate by inventing a particularly Erisian slogan and seeing that it is given wide distribution. Examples: *Your Local Police Are Armed and Dangerous; Legalize Free-Enterprise Murder: Why Should Governments Have All The Fun?; Smash the Government Postal Monopoly; If Voting Could Change the System, It Would Be Against the Law*; etc.

Citizens Against Drug Abuse. This organization possesses elegant letterheads and is engaged in a campaign of encouraging Congressmen to outlaw catnip, a drug which some young people are smoking whenever marijuana is in short supply. The thought behind this project is that, the government having lost so much credibility due to its war against pot (a recent ELF survey showed that in some big cities a large portion of the under-25 population did not believe in any of the moon shots and assumed they were all faked somewhere in the American Desert), a campaign against this similar but more comical herb will destroy the last tattered shreds of faith in the men in Washington.

APPENDIX KAPH
THE ROSY DOUBLE-CROSS

Saul, Barney, Markoff Chaney, and Dillinger were all puzzled that a man like Carmel would bring a suitcase full of roses with him when fleeing to Lehman Cavern. Those who knew Carmel in Las Vegas were even more perplexed when this fact was made public. The first readers of this romance were not only puzzled and perplexed but petulant, since they knew Carmel had loaded his briefcase with Maldonado's money, not with roses.

The explanation, as is usually the case when seeming magick has occurred, was simple: Carmel was the victim of the oldest swindle in the world, the *okkana borra* (gypsy switch). It was his custom to transport his earnings to the bank in the same suitcase which he used when looting Maldonado's safe. His figure, and the suitcase, were well known to the shadier elements in Las Vegas, and among these were three gentlemen who decided early in April to intercept him during one of his journeys and remove the suitcase from his possession, using, as young people say, "any means necessary"; they even considered striking him upon the temple with a blunt instrument. One of the gentlemen involved in this project, John Wayne Malatesta, however, had a sense of humor (of sorts) and began to devise a plan involving a nonviolent gypsy switch. Mr. Malatesta thought it would be amusing if this could be carried off smoothly and Carmel, arriving at the bank, opened a case full of horse manure, human excrement, or something else in equally dubious taste. The other two gentlemen were persuaded that this might indeed be worth a laugh. A substitute suitcase was purchased, and a plan was devised.

Two changes were made at virtually the last minute. Mr. Malatesta learned from Bonnie Quint (a lady whose company he often enjoyed, at $100 a throw) that Carmel suffered acutely from rose fever. A more hilarious image occurred to him: Carmel opening the case in the bank and starting to sneeze spasmodically while trying to figure out where the switch had been made. The roses were purchased, and the caper was set for the next day.

When Carmel, Dr. Naismith, and Markoff Chaney collided, Malatesta and his associates abandoned the switch idea: Two collisions in a few minutes would be more than a man like Carmel would accept without profound suspicion. They therefore decided to follow him to his house and revert to the more old-fashioned but time-proven technique of the sudden rap on the skull.

When Bonnie Quint left after her violent interview with Carmel, the bandits prepared to enter. To their amazement, Carmel came running out, threw his suitcase into his jeep, and then ran back in. (He had forgotten his candies.)

"It's God's will," Malatesta said piously.

The switch was made, and they took off for points south in a great hurry.

Several weeks after the crisis had passed, a state trooper found a car with three dead men in it off the road in a ditch. His own symptoms were self-diagnosed while he waited for the coroner's crew to arrive, and he received the antidote in time.

The empty suitcase in the car caused only minor speculation: A Gila monster had obviously eaten most of one side

of it to shreds. "Whatever they had in there," the trooper
said later, "must have been pretty light. The wind blew it
all over the freaking desert."

APPENDIX TETH
HAGBARD'S BOOKLET

After prolonged pleading and vehement prayers of en-
treaty, the authors finally prevailed upon Hagbard Celine to
allow us to quote some further illuminating passages from
his booklet *Never Whistle While You're Pissing.** (Before
we made these frantic efforts, he wanted us to publish the
whole thing.)

Here, then, are some of the keys to the strange head of
Hagbard Celine:

I once overheard two botanists arguing over a Damned
Thing that had blasphemously sprouted in a college yard.
One claimed that the Damned Thing was a tree and the other claimed that it was a shrub. They each had good scholar-
ly arguments, and they were still debating when I left them.

The world is forever spawning Damned Things—things
that are neither tree nor shrub, fish nor fowl, black nor
white—and the categorical thinker can only regard the spiky
and buzzing world of sensory fact as a profound insult
to his card-index system of classifications. Worst of all are
the facts which violate "common sense," that dreary bog of
sullen prejudice and muddy inertia. The whole history of
science is the odyssey of a pixilated card-indexer perpetually
sailing between such Damned Things and desperately jug-

---

* The title, he informs us, is taken from R. H. Blythe's *Zen in English
Literature and Oriental Classics*. The story is instructive: Blythe,
studying za-zen (sitting zen, or *dhyana* meditation) in a monastery at
Kyoto, asked the *roshi* (Zen Master) if there was any further discipline
he should adopt to accelerate his progress. The *roshi* replied, con-
cisely, "Never whistle while you're pissing." Cf. Gurdjieff's endless
diatribes about "concentration," the rajah in Huxley's *Island* who
unleashed talking mynah birds to remind his citizens constantly "Here
and now, boys, here and now!" and Jesus' "Whatever thy hand findest
to do, do it with all thy heart."

gling his classifications to fit them in, just as the history of politics is the futile epic of a long series of attempts to line up the Damned Things and cajole them to march in regiment.

Every ideology is a mental murder, a reduction of dynamic living processes to static classifications, and every classification is a Damnation, just as every inclusion is an exclusion. In a busy, buzzing universe where no two snowflakes are identical, and no two trees are identical, and no two people are identical—and, indeed, the smallest subatomic particle, we are assured, is not even identical with itself from one microsecond to the next—every card-index system is a self-delusion. "Or, to put it more charitably," as Nietzsche says, "we are all better artists than we realize."

It is easy to see that the label "Jew" was a Damnation in Nazi Germany, but actually the label "Jew" is a Damnation anywhere, even where anti-Semitism does not exist. "He is a Jew," "He is a doctor," and "He is a poet" mean, to the card-indexing center of the cortex, that my experience with him will be like my experience with other Jews, other doctors, and other poets. Thus, individuality is ignored when identity is asserted.

At a party or any place where strangers meet, watch this mechanism in action. Behind the friendly overtures there is wariness as each person fishes for the label that will identify and Damn the other. Finally, it is revealed: "Oh, he's an advertising copywriter," "Oh, he's an engine-lathe operator." Both parties relax, for now they know how to behave, what roles to play in the game. Ninety-nine percent of each has been Damned; the other is reacting to the 1 percent that has been labeled by the card-index machine.

Certain Damnations are socially and intellectually necessary, of course. A custard pie thrown in a comedian's face is Damned by the physicist who analyzes it according to the Newtonian laws of motion. These equations tell us all we want to know about the impact of the pie on the face, but nothing about the human meaning of the pie-throwing. A cultural anthropologist, analyzing the social function of the comedian as shaman, court jester, and king's surrogate, explains the pie-throwing as a survival of the Feast of Fools and the killing of the king's double. This Damns the subject in another way. A psychoanalyst, finding an Oedipal castration ritual here, has performed a third Damnation, and the Marxist, seeing an outlet for the worker's repressed rage against the bosses, performs a fourth. Each Damnation has its values and its uses, but it is nonetheless a Damnation *unless its partial and arbitrary nature is recognized.*

The poet, who compares the pie in the comedian's face with the Decline of the West or his own lost love, commits a fifth Damnation, but in this case the game element and whimsicality of the symbolism are safely obvious. At least, one would hope so; reading the New Critics occasionally raises doubts on this point.

Human society can be structured either according to the principle of authority or according to the principle of liberty. Authority is a static social configuration in which people act as superiors and inferiors: a sado-masochistic relationship. Liberty is a dynamic social configuration in which people act as equals: an erotic relationship. In every interaction between people, either Authority or Liberty is the dominant factor. Families, churches, lodges, clubs, and corporations are either more authoritarian than libertarian or more libertarian than authoritarian.

It becomes obvious as we proceed that the most pugnacious and intolerant form of authority is the State, which even today dares to assume an absolutism which the Church itself has long ago surrendered and to enforce obedience with the techniques of the Church's old and shameful Inquisition. Every form of authoritarianism is, however, a small "State," even if it has a membership of only two. Freud's remark to the effect that the delusion of one man is neurosis and the delusion of many men is religion can be generalized: The authoritarianism of one man is crime and the authoritarianism of many men is the State. Benjamin Tucker wrote quite accurately:

> Aggression is simply another name for government. Aggression, invasion, government are interchangeable terms. The essence of government is control, or the attempt to control. He who attempts to control another is a governor, an aggressor, an invader; and the nature of such invasion is not changed, whether it be made by one man upon another man, after the manner

of the ordinary criminal, or by one man upon all other men, after the manner of an absolute monarch, or by all other men upon one man, after the manner of a modern democracy.

Tucker's use of the word "invasion" is remarkably precise, considering that he wrote more than fifty years before the basic discoveries of ethology. Every act of authority is, in fact, an invasion of the psychic and physical territory of another.

Every fact of science was once Damned. Every invention was considered impossible. Every discovery was a nervous shock to some orthodoxy. Every artistic innovation was denounced as fraud and folly. The entire web of culture and "progress," everything on earth that is manmade and not given to us by nature, is the concrete manifestation of some man's refusal to bow to Authority. We would own no more, know no more, and be no more than the first apelike hominids if it were not for the rebellious, the recalcitrant, and the instransigent. As Oscar Wilde truly said, "Disobedience was man's Original Virtue."

The human brain, which loves to read descriptions of itself as the universe's most marvelous organ of perception, is an even more marvelous organ of rejection. The naked facts of our economic game, are easily discoverable and undeniable once stated, but conservatives—who are usually individuals who profit every day of their lives from these facts—manage to remain oblivious to them, or to see them through a very rosy-tinted and distorting lens. (Similarly, the revolutionary ignores the total testimony of history about the natural course of revolution, through violence, to chaos, back to the starting point.)

We must remember that *thought is abstraction*. In Einstein's metaphor, the relationship between a physical fact and our mental reception of that fact is not like the relationship between beef and beef-broth, a simple matter of extraction and condensation; rather, as Einstein goes on, it is like the relationship between our overcoat and the ticket given us when we check our overcoat. In other words, human perception involves *coding* even more than crude *sensing*. The mesh of language, or of mathematics, or of a

school of art, or of any system of human abstracting, gives
to our mental constructs the structure, not of the original
fact, but of the symbol system into which it is coded, just as
a map-maker colors a nation purple not because it *is* purple
but because his code demands it. But every code excludes
certain things, blurs other things, and overemphasizes still
other things. Nijinski's celebrated leap through the window
at the climax of *Le Spectre d'une Rose* is best coded in the
ballet notation system used by choreographers; verbal language falters badly in attempting to convey it; painting or
sculpture could capture totally the magic of one instant, but
one instant only, of it; the physicist's equation, Force =
Mass × Acceleration, highlights one aspect of it missed by
all these other codes, but loses everything else about it. Every perception is influenced, formed, and structured by the
habitual coding habits—mental game habits—of the per-
ceiver.

All authority is a function of coding, of game rules. Men
have arisen again and again armed with pitchforks to fight
armies with cannon; men have also submitted docilely to
the weakest and most tottery oppressors. It all depends on
the extent to which coding distorts perception and conditions the physical (and mental) reflexes.

It seems at first glance that authority could not exist at
all if all men were cowards or if no men were cowards, but
flourishes as it does only because most men are cowards
and some men are thieves. Actually, the inner dynamics of
cowardice and submission on the one hand and of heroism
and rebellion on the other are seldom consciously realized
either by the ruling class or the servile class. Submission is
identified not with cowardice but with virtue, rebellion not
with heroism but with evil. To the Roman slave-owners,
Spartacus was not a hero and the obedient slaves were not
cowards; Spartacus was a villain and the obedient slaves
were virtuous. The obedient slaves believed this also. The
obedient always think of themselves as virtuous rather than
cowardly.

If authority implies submission, liberation implies equality; authority exists when one man obeys another, and liberty exists when men do not obey other men. Thus, to say
that authority exists is to say that class and caste exist, that
submission and inequality exist. To say that liberty exists is

to say that classlessness exists, to say that brotherhood and equality exist.

Authority, by dividing men into classes, creates dichotomy, disruption, hostility, fear, disunion. Liberty, by placing men on an equal footing, creates assocation, amalgamation, union, security. When the relationships between men are based on authority and coercion, they are driven apart; when based on liberty and nonaggression, they are drawn together.

There facts are self-evident and axiomatic. If authoritarianism did not possess the in-built, preprogrammed double-bind structure of a Game Without End, men would long ago have rejected it and embraced libertarianism.

The usual pacifist complaint about war, that young men are led to death by old men who sit at home manning bureaucrat's desks and taking no risks themselves, misses the point entirely. Demands that the old should be drafted to fight their own wars, or that the leaders of the warring nations should be sent to the front lines on the first day of battle, etc., are aimed at an assumed "sense of justice" that simply does not exist. To the typical submissive citizen of authoritarian society, it is normal, obvious, and "natural" that he should obey older and more dominant males, even at the risk of his life, even against his own kindred, and even in causes that are unjust or absurd.

"The Charge of the Light Brigade"—the story of a group of young males led to their death in a palpably idiotic situation and only because they obeyed a senseless order without stopping to think—has been, and remains, a popular poem, because unthinking obedience by young males to older males is the most highly prized of all conditioned reflexes within human, and hominid, societies.

The mechanism by which authority and submission are implanted in the human mind is coding of perception. That which fits into the code is accepted; all else is Damned. It is Damned to being ignored, brushed aside, unnoticed, and—if these fail—it is Damned to being forgotten.

A worse form of Damnation is reserved for those things which cannot be ignored. These are daubed with the brain's projected prejudices until, encrusted beyond recognition, they are capable of being fitted into the system, classified, card-indexed, buried. This is what happens to every

Damned Thing which is too prickly and sticky to be excommunicated entirely. As Josiah Warren remarked, "It is dangerous to understand new things too quickly." Almost always, we have not understood them. We have murdered them and mummified their corpses.

A *monopoly on the means of communication* may define a ruling elite more precisely than the celebrated Marxian formula of "monopoly on the means of production." Since man extends his nervous system through channels of communication like the written word, the telephone, radio, etc., he who controls these media controls part of the nervous system of every member of society. The contents of these media become part of the contents of every individual's brain.

Thus, in pre-literate societies taboos on the spoken word are more numerous and more Draconic than at any more complex level of social organization. With the invention of written speech—hieroglyphic, ideographic, or alphabetical—the taboos are shifted to this medium; there is less concern with what people say and more concern with what they write. (Some of the first societies to achieve literacy, such as Egypt and the Mayan culture of ancient Mexico, evidently kept a knowledge of their hieroglyphs a religious secret which only the higher orders of the priestly and royal families were allowed to share.) The same process repeats endlessly: Each step forward in the technology of communication is more heavily tabooed than the earlier steps. Thus, in America today (post–Lenny Bruce), one seldom hears of convictions for spoken blasphemy or obscenity; prosecution of books still continues, but higher courts increasingly interpret the laws in a liberal fashion, and most writers feel fairly confident that they can publish virtually anything; movies are growing almost as desacralized as books, although the fight is still heated in this area; television, the newest medium, remains encased in neolithic taboo. (When the TV pundits committed *lèse majesté* after an address by the then Dominant Male, a certain Richard Nixon, one of his lieutenants quickly informed them they had overstepped, and the whole tribe—except for the dissident minority—cheered for the reaasertion of tradition.) When a more efficient medium arrives, the taboos on television will decrease.

APPENDIX MEM
CERTAIN QUESTIONS THAT MAY STILL TROUBLE SOME READERS

1. What was Mama Sutra's "reading," where Danny Price-fixer questioned her, actually all about?
Answer: It had nothing to do with the John F. Kennedy assassination, the *Confrontation* bombing, the Illuminati, or any of the subjects it seemed to suggest, *except indirectly.* She had aimed in the dark, and picked up bits and pieces of the old movie *Manhattan Melodrama,* thusly:

• *District Attorney Wade* does not refer to the Dallas official who first proclaimed Lee Harvey Oswald's guilt over TV; it refers to the character played by William Powell in the movie.

• *Clark* does not refer to any of the Captain Clarks we have encountered; it refers to Clark Gable, Mr. Powell's co-star. *The Ship is sinking* does not refer to the Illuminati spider-ships, or the ship piloted by Captain Clark; it refers to the *General Slocum,* as Mama guessed—the sinking of this ship on June 15, 1904, is the first scene in the movie. *2422* does not refer to the dates of Oswald's and Kennedy's assassinations, or to the old Wobbly address; it refers to a scene in the film where Gable, at a racetrack, walks from box 24 to box 22 (box 23 is never shown, his body being between it and the camera).

• *If I can't live as I please, let me die when I choose* is the last line spoken by Clark Gable in the screenplay.

The fact that these phrases overlap certain themes in this novel (and in Joyce's *Ulysses*) is either coincidence or synchronicity—take your choice. *Manhattan Melodrama,* you might be interested to know, was playing at the Biograph Theatre on the night of July 22, 1934, and was the last film seen by the man who was shot outside and identified as John Herbert Dillinger.

2. What was the Masonic signal of distress used by the grocer B. F. Morgan when Dillinger tried to rob him in 1924?
Answer: It consists in holding your arms outward, bent

upward 90 degrees at the elbow, and shouting, "Will nobody help the widow's son?"

3. Is there really a secret passage beneath the Meditation
Room in the UN building?
Answer: If so, we haven't been able to find it. Other
spooky secrets about that room, however, are revealed in
The Cult of the All-Seeing Eye, by Robert Keith Spencer
(Christian Book Club of America, 1964).

4. What was the *Erotion* of Adam Weishaupt mentioned by
Hagbard in the First Trip?
Answer: The word translates, loosely, as "love-in," and the
idea is basically the same. (See the books of Nesta Webster
and John Robison cited in the text.) *Now* do you believe in
a conspiracy?

5. Did Al Capone really help the FBI set up the man who
was shot at the Biograph Theatre on July 22, 1934?
Answer: That's one of the more plausible arguments in
Dillinger: Dead or Alive, by Jay Nash and Ron Offen.

6. If no animals were reported missing from local zoos,
how is that Robert Simpson of Kansas City was found dead
with his throat torn as if by "the talons of some enormous
beast?"
Answer: See the sequel, *The Homing Pigeons.*

7. If Simon Moon majored in mathematics and was so obsessed with numerology, why didn't he ever notice the most
significant 23 in mathematical history—the 23 definitions
that open Euclid's *Geometry?*
Answer: Perhaps for the same reason that the road from
Dayton, Ohio, to New Lebanon, Ohio, was due *east* when
Joe Malik drove it on June 25, 1969, but has always been
due *west* on every day before and since then. Or maybe by
the same processes that allowed Joe to see a Salem commercial on his TV set in the mid-1970s, although cigarette
advertising was banned from television in 1971.

8. Did Smiling Jim Trepomena achieve the fame he had
sought?
Answer: No. Dr. Vulcan Troll's definitive history of the

Great Quake, *When a State Dies,* mentions on page 123 that "no American Eagle has since been reported, and we can only assume that this species was another victim of nature's mindless rampage on that tragic May 1." On page 369, Dr. Troll mentions, among prominent casualties, "The famous Cincinnati lawyer and proponent of censorship James J. Trepomena." Neither he nor anyone else ever connected the two occurrences.

9. Where are the missing eight appendices?
Answer: Censored.

APPENDIX NUN
ADDITIONAL INFORMATION ABOUT SOME OF THE CHARACTERS

THE PURPLE SAGE. An imaginary Chaoist philospher invented by Lord Omar Khayyam Ravenhurst (another imaginary Chaoist philosopher).

LORD OMAR KHAYAM RAVENHURST. An imaginary Chaoist philosopher invented by Mr. Kerry Thornley of Atlanta, Georgia. Mr. Thornley was a friend of Lee Harvey Oswald's, was accused of complicity in the John Kennedy assassination by District Attorney Jim Garrison, and is the author of *Illuminati Lady,* an endless epic poem which you really ought to read.

GEORGE DORN. His maternal grandfather, old Charlie Bishop, was once a patient of the famous Doctor William Carlos Williams. The Bishops came to New Jersey in 1723, having left Salem, Massachusetts, in 1692 under something of a cloud. Folks in the Nutley-Clifton-Passaic-Paterson area always have a good word for the Bishops, though. But the Dorns were all troublemakers, and George's paternal grandfather, Big Bill Dorn, was so indiscreet as to get killed by cops during the Paterson silk-mill strike of 1922.

HERACLEITUS. He was apt to say odd things. Once he even wrote that "Religious ceremonies are unholy." A strange duck.

THE SQUIRREL. A set of receptor organs transmitting information through a central nervous system to a small brain programmed for only a few rudimentary decisions—but, in this, he was not far inferior to most of our characters.

REBECCA GOODMAN. Her maiden name was Murphy, and she was named after Rebecca of Sunnybrook Farm. You thought she was Jewish, didn't you?

THE DEAD EGYPTIAN MOUTH-BREEDERS. There were five of them, of course.

DANNY PRICEFIXER. Shot in the line of duty two years after the events of this story. Loved the music of Johann Sebastian Bach.

ADAM WEISHAUPT. "He's a deep one," they used to say on the faculty of the University of Ingolstadt, "you never know what he's really thinking."

CARMEL. One of his girls once cajoled a Hollywood character actor into calling him on the phone and pretending to be a researcher for the Kinsey Institute, seeking an interview. Carmel couldn't see any money in it and was trying to end the conversation when the actor asked stuffily, "Well, all we want to know, actually, is do you have intercourse with your mother regularly, or does everybody in Las Vegas call you 'Carmel the Motherfucker' for some other reason?" For once Carmel was speechless. The girl spread the story, and everybody in town was laughing about it for weeks.

PETER JACKSON. His great-grandfather was a slave. His son became the first President of the Luna Federation after the rebellion of the moon colonists in 2025. Much further back, a more remote ancestor was a king of Atlantis; and way in the future, a descendant was a slave on a planet in the Alpha Centauri system. (Peter was one of the crew when Hagbard finally blasted off for the stars in 1999). That's the way the cookie crumbles; and Peter had an intuitive sense of this paradoxical fatality, which caused him to tell Eldridge Cleaver once, "People who say 'You're either part of the solution or part of the problem' are themselves part of the problem." (Cleaver replied, wittily, "Fuck you.")

THE LAB CHIEF WHO WAS DISINTERESTED IN ANTHRAX LEPROSY DELTA. He later cracked up and wrote letters to the newspapers attacking the entire chemobiological warfare program of the United States gov-

LEVIATHAN   249

ernment. Spent the last seventeen years of his life
receiving treatment in St. Elizabeth's Hospital in
Washington, D.C., occupying the same quarters that
once housed the ingenious poet Ezra Pound. His rant-
ings were taken seriously in certain places, especially
among some leftward-leaning fellow scientists, but the
Vice-President described them to the press as "the de-
spondent demagogy of a paranoid pedant." A sample
of the man's delusions, from a letter to the three top
television networks (never quoted on newscasts because it was too controversial): "The boast of the 19th
century was its conquest of these accursed plagues that
attack men, women, and helpless infants indifferently.
What shall be said of the 20th century, which has re-
created them, at great expense and through the efforts
of thousands of brilliant but perverted scientific minds,
and then stored them *live* in installations throughout
the country, where it is virtually certain, statistically,
that an accident will unleash them upon an unsuspect-
ing public, sooner or later?" (Loonies often harbor
morbid fears of that sort.) The poor man never responded favorably to any of the efforts of his psychiatrists, even though they gave him ECT (electro-con-
vulsive therapy) so often that his brain was practically
fried to the crispness of a Howard Johnson omelette
by the time he finally died.

ANTHRAX LEPROSY DELTA. A life form that could exist only
by destroying other life-forms; in this respect, it was
like many of us. The first of the products of Charlie
Mocenigo's fertile genius, it could boast only of being
ten times as deadly as ordinary anthrax. Insofar as it
had consciousness, in a vague and flickering way, it
was like that inhabiting a subway train at 5 P.M., concerned only with getting where it was going and then
eating. The other strains were much the same, up to
Anthrax Leprosy Pi.

LEE HARVEY OSWALD. Hero of a series of novels by Harold
Weissburg, including *Whitewash, Whitewash II, Pho-
tographic Whitewash,* and *Oswald in New Orleans.*
Villain of another novel, entitled *Report of the Presidential Commission on the Assassination of President
John F. Kennedy,* by Earl Warren, John McCone, et
al. Also featured in other works of fiction by Mark

Lane, Penn Jones, Josiah Thompson, and various other writers.

JACK RUBY. The Oliver Hardy to Oswald's Stanley Laurel.

THOMAS JEFFERSON. A revolutionary hemp-grower who once wrote, "[The clergy] believe that any portion of power confided to me, will be exerted in opposition to their schemes. And they believe rightly: *for I have sworn upon the altar of God eternal hostility against every form of tyranny over the mind of man.* But this is all they have to fear from me: and enough too in their opinion." Few of the pious tourists who read the italicized portion of this statement carved on the Jefferson Memorial in Washington, D.C., are aware of its context.

THE SCHIZOPHRENIC IN CHERRY KNOLLS HOSPITAL. His number was 124C41. Nobody, anywhere, remembered what his name had been.

MARY LOU SERVIX. She finally married Jim Riley, the dope dealer from Dayton—but that's another, rather longish, story, and not truly relevant.

MAYOR RICHARD DALEY. Author of such immortal aphorisms as "After all, I am a liberal myself" (October 22, 1968); "The policeman isn't there to create disorder, the policeman is there to preserve disorder" (September 23, 1968); "I have conferred with the Superintendent of Police this morning and I gave him instructions that an order be issued by him immediately and under his signature to shoot to kill any arsonist or anyone with a Molotov cocktail in his hand" (April 17, 1968); "There wasn't any shoot-to-kill order. That was a fabrication" (April 18, 1968); "You could say Senator Tower is doing a lousy job, but I don't use that kind of words" (May 1, 1962); "I have lived in Chicago all my life and I still say we have no ghetto in Chicago" (July 8, 1963); "We will have a planned development and will take people out of the ghettos and slums and give them an opportunity to raise their families in decent surroundings" (April 17, 1969); "I didn't create the slums, did I?" (September 3, 1968); "Together we must rise to ever higher and higher platitudes" (March 13, 1967).

THE RUSSIAN PREMIER. A comsymp.

CHARLES MOCENIGO'S FATHER. A professional. He worked

for Charles "Lucky" Luciano, Louis "Lepke" Buchalter, Federico Maldonado, and many other colorful American businessmen. Known in the trade as Jimmy the Shrew, because of his sharp, conniving expression. Saved his money, put his boy through MIT, killed people for a living. Found the original Frank Sullivan performing in Havana, 1934.

GENERAL LAWRENCE STEWART TALBOT. Actually, there *was* something between him and that girl from Red Lion, Penn.

MALACLYPSE THE YOUNGER, K.S.C. Author of the *Principia Discordia*. Disappeared mysteriously in late 1970. His last recorded words were, typically, "Comes the dawn, the sun shall rise in the west." Then he walked into the Pacific Ocean.

JOHN HERBERT DILLINGER. When Simon Moon read his biography in search of 23s, he missed a good one: John committed 26 robberies during his publicized career, but only 23 were for money. The other 3 (police stations) seem to have been strictly Art For Art's Sake.

SIMON'S FATHER. Tim Moon. He told Simon the lives of Joe Hill, Big Bill Haywood, Sacco and Vanzetti, and Frank Little at the age when most boys are being told about Snow White and the Seven Dwarfs. Simon remembers: Joe Hill the night before his execution, wiring Wobbly headquarters in Chicago, "Don't weep for me, boys: organize." Bartolomeo Vanzetti: "Your laws, your courts, your false god will be a dim remembering of a cursed time when man was wolf to the man." Tim and his cronies singing in the living room, "Which side are you on, man / Which *side* are you *on?*" until Molly complained, "You'll wake the neighbors." Tim explaining Big Bill: "Oh, yes, and he had a glass eye. Funny I should forget that. The real eye was knocked out by a cop during a strike." But you'll understand Tim best if you see Simon, age six, entering grammar school for the first time and addressing the first boy he meets: "I'm Simon Moon; what's your name, Fellow Worker?"

PADRE PEDERASTIA. His real name was Father James Flanagan.

TOBIAS KNIGHT. The only quintuple agent in the history of espionage.

JAMES JOYCE. After death, he met Yeats on the fifth plane
and said, "Sir, I am now willing to learn from you,
since you appear to have been right about Death after
all." Yeats replied, "Not at all. You're dreaming this."
The remark so vexed Joyce that he immediately sought
reincarnation (the fifth plane was full of mystics like
Yeats and George Russell and Madame Blavatski, and
Joyce knew his rational Aristotelian sensibility would
be constantly abused by further conversation with
them), entered the womb of Elizabeth Mullins of Vernon, New Jersey, October 11, 1942, and was aborted
December 10, 1942. Entered the womb of Rachel
Stein of Ingolstadt, January 18, 1943, and was gassed
with her, one month before birth was due, at Auschwitz, September 1, 1943. Thereafter, he retired to a
monastery on the sixth plane and wrote his funniest,
most bitter book. Parts of it, which he has been transmitting ever since, have been picked up by mediums
on the six continents, all of whom assumed they were
flipping out and refused to transcribe it.

CHARLES WORKMAN. An entrepreneur.

MENDY WEISS. Another entrepreneur.

JIMMY THE SHREW. A third entrepreneur, more successful
than the above. See entry under CHARLES MOCENIGO'S
FATHER.

ALBERT "THE TEACHER" STEIN. Not only did he lose his
gamble with immortality when it was proven that he
didn't kill Dutch Schultz, but almost every book on the
case misspells his name as Stern, a tradition which the
present work has mostly refused to shatter.

HENRY FORD. By importing the *Protocols of the Learned
Elders of Zion* and beginning the mass production of automobiles, he managed to pollute both the mind and
the air of the United States, but he meant well, or at
least he meant something.

GEORGE DORN'S OLDER BROTHER. His successful scientific career made George envious (and helped determine
George's choices of a liberal-arts curriculum at Col-
umbia). He had an adventure with talking dolphins
before George did (which set up a psychic resonance
that made George's recruitment interesting to Hagbard); this story is recounted in *Tales Of the Cthulhu*

Mythos, edited by August Derleth (Arkham House, 1969).

MARKOFF CHANEY. He slipped away from Saul and Barney shortly after they returned to Las Vegas, and none of our characters ever saw him again. However, one day in 1984 Hagbard Celine, using an alias and engaged in nefarious business, happened to be in the U.S. Government Printing Office on Capitol Street in Washington and noticed a bundle of pamphlets that had been stamped with both blue TOP SECRET: AUTHORIZED PERSONNEL ONLY and red FOR IMMEDIATE RELEASE TO ALL MEDIA. Many loyal government servants would have headaches before it was ever clarified who had been responsible for which of those stamps—if, indeed, that ever could be clarified. Hagbard recalled much that Saul had told him about the Las Vegas caper and looked around thoughtfully. In one corner he saw a large coffee urn. He lit one of his long black cigars and strolled out into the street. The sun was bright, the air was clear, and it was Spring, which may explain why Hagbard began whistling as he walked with a brisk and determined pace toward the Senate Office Building. The tune was "My Heart's in the Highlands."

VENUS ON THE HALF-SHELL

Kilgore Trout's
Epic Science-Fiction Saga of

The Space Wanderer

an Earthman wearing an eye-patch, levis, and a shabby gray sweater who roams the cosmos in a Chinese spaceship . . .

The Space Wanderer

a man without a planet who has gained immortality from an elixir drunk during a sexual interlude with an alien queen in heat . . .

The Space Wanderer

an intergalactic rover whose constant companions are a dog, an owl, and a female robot programmed for unique fleshly delights.

A DELL BOOK 95¢

6149-09

BESTSELLERS
FROM DELL

fiction

- [ ] ERIC by Doris Lund $1.75 (4586-04)
- [ ] MARATHON MAN by William Goldman $1.95 (5502-02)
- [ ] WINTER KILLS by Richard Coneon $1.75 (6007-00)
- [ ] THE OTHER SIDE OF MIDNIGHT by Sidney Sheldon $1.75 (6067-07)
- [ ] THE RHINEMANN EXCHANGE by Robert Ludlum .. $1.95 (5079-13)
- [ ] THE LONG DARK NIGHT by Joseph Hayes $1.95 (4824-06)
- [ ] SHAMPOO by Robert Alley $1.75 (7808-17)
- [ ] PLEASURE MAN by Mae West $1.50 (7074-06)
- [ ] THE NAKED FACE by Sidney Sheldon $1.25 (4921-05)
- [ ] DOG DAY AFTERNOON by Patrick Mann $1.50 (4519-06)
- [ ] THE BOY WHO INVENTED THE BUBBLE GUN
      by Paul Gallico $1.50 (0719-28)

nonfiction

- [ ] JAMES DEAN, THE MUTANT KING by David Dalton $1.75 (4893-02)
- [ ] MIKE ROY'S CROCK COOKERY $1.25 (5617-04)
- [ ] THE FEMALE WOMAN by Anianna Stassinopoulous. $1.50 (5015-02)
- [ ] MAN KIND? by Cleveland Amory $1.75 (5451-03)
- [ ] CHARLES BRONSON SUPERSTAR by Steven Whitney $1.50 (4561-11)
- [ ] THE JAWS LOG by Carl Gottlieb $1.50 (4689-00)
- [ ] THE REICH MARSHAL by Leonard Mosley $1.75 (7686-06)
- [ ] JOEY by Donald Goddard $1.75 (4825-05)
- [ ] DR. STILLMAN'S 14-DAY SHAPE-UP PROGRAM
      by I. M. Stillman, M.D., and S. S. Baker $1.75 (1913-04)
- [ ] WHY MEN CALL GIRLS by Shannon Canfield
      and Dick Stuart $1.50 (9609-06)

Buy them at your local bookstore or send this page to the address below:

Dell DELL BOOKS
P.O. BOX 1000, PINEBROOK, N.J. 07058

Please send me the books I have checked above. I am enclosing $_____
(please add 25¢ per copy to cover postage and handling). Send check or
money order—no cash or C.O.D.'s.

Mr/Mrs/Miss _____

Address_____

City_____ State/Zip_____

This offer expires 11/76